Damned Yankee

The Story of a Marriage

Carolyn P. Schriber

Published by Katzenhaus Books
P. O. Box 1629
Cordova, TN 38088-1629
Cover Design by Avalon Graphics

ISBN-10: 0984592873
ISBN-13: 9780984592876
Library of Congress Control Number: 2014935759
Katzenhaus Books, Cordova, TN

Table of Contents

1

Black Eyes, Real and Symbolic
March 1860

Susan frequently urged him to have Hector bring the surrey around and drive him to work, but Jonathan preferred to walk. Even though the sight of a white man being driven by a slave was the norm in Charleston, Jonathan found it disturbing. He understood the need for slave labor on the plantations and around the large households of the city, but he refused to ask another man to do those things he could do for himself. Besides, he felt energized after a brisk morning stroll, and that energy kept him alert and enthusiastic in his classroom.

Charleston was beautiful in the mornings. The cobblestone streets sparkled after their overnight cleansing, and the sidewalks were still empty of loiterers. The white steeple of St. Michael's Church made a sharp contrast with the deep blue of the sky. Breezes barely ruffled the palm fronds, and newly opened roses and azaleas pushed their way through iron fence posts to share their fragrance with the city. The morning stillness was interrupted only by the occasional clatter of a milk wagon or the sleepy calls of awakening birds. The graveyard of the Circular Church offered deep shadows softened by the green-gray sheen of swaths of Spanish moss. Then came the market area, enlivened by the musical sounds of slave voices chattering in Gullah and the shouts of purveyors unloading their merchandise. Jonathan breathed deeply, relishing the sights and sounds that inspired him.

His steps quickened as he approached Charleston's new Apprentices' Library Society building on Meeting Street. He took great pride in the theory behind the society's establishment of classes for young working-class whites. The founders had acted on the belief that even common laborers could benefit from a broad education. The founders' goal was to provide an education that not only taught the boys their mechanical skills but also gave them a heightened cultural awareness resulting from the study of literature and history. The Apprentices' Library Society drew its support from civic-minded businessmen in the city. The students attended for free, needing only a recommendation and released time from their family or employer. Jonathan loved teaching the young men who came into his classroom, still fresh-faced and eager. They challenged him to offer the kinds of knowledge that would help them become better citizens as well as better workers.

This morning, however, Jonathan's usually springy steps slowed as he caught sight of a small figure crouched on the steps of the school. "Declan?" he asked. "Declan McDermitt? Whatever is wrong? Have you been crying?"

The boy scrubbed his eyes furiously with his fists, refusing to look up at his favorite teacher.

Jonathan dropped his book satchel and sat down on the step next to him. Gently, he caught the boy's chin with two fingers and turned his head to face him. Declan's red hair usually complemented his creamy complexion, but, on this morning, his cheeks were flushed with an angry, clashing red, and a deep blue and purple bruise surrounded one eye.

"What happened to you?"

"Just had a fight. Doesn't matter." The words were soft and quivering, betraying the boy's seeming indifference.

"Declan, you are definitely not the fighting sort!" Jonathan said. "Who hit you?"

The boy jerked his head away, his lips pressed tight in an effort to control their trembling. Jonathan waited, understanding the boy's distress.

"Mr. Grenville, why are you a damyankee?" The words came out in a rush, although the boy kept his head turned.

Jonathan caught his breath at those words coming from a fourteen-year-old child. For a few moments he could not find his own voice. His heart hammered as he realized the implications behind the simple question.

"What makes you say that?" he asked, once he could trust his own composure. "Where did you hear it?"

"My Da says that's what you are. He says you're a damyankee for telling us things in class that aren't true." Declan was angry now and ready to confront the man he had idolized for so long.

"What did I ever tell you that was untrue?"

"You said that congressman from South Carolina was wrong to attack Senator Sumner. You said states don't have the right to defy the federal government. You said slavery is wrong and needs to be abolished. You said . . ." As his anger sputtered to an end, so, too, did his words.

"I did say all those things, Declan," Jonathan admitted. "I said them because I believe them. But—"

"And I guess that's why you're a damyankee . . . whatever that is. You said them, and I believed you, and I went home and told my Da that I believed them, too, because you said they were true, and he hit me. That's the whole story. And now my Da's inside talking to the headmaster and telling him that I can't go to school here anymore because you're a damnyankee." Declan's lower lip trembled, and tears welled in his eyes.

"Oh, Declan. I am so sorry to have been the cause of your pain." Jonathan felt as if a giant hand had clutched at his chest and was squeezing the blood right out of his heart. "Perhaps I can make it better."

"There's nothing you can do. When my Da makes up his mind, there ain't . . . uh, isn't . . . any way of making him think different. I just want to know what a damnyankee is, so's the next time I run into one, I'll know better than to believe what he says."

Jonathan let out his breath in a rush. "Fair enough. But let's break the words down, shall we? Just like we do in class. It's not all one word. The term your father used was 'Damned Yankee.' Might as well get shunt of the 'damned' part first: I've seen you at church, so I know that you have been told about damnation. It means that a person is such a sinner that he will spend the rest of eternity in hell. And you should understand that only God can make a decision to damn someone. People sometimes get angry at one another and threaten damnation, but it's an empty threat. I hope I'm not one of the damned, but I leave that decision to God.

"Now, what is a Yankee? Well, a Yankee is just someone who was born in New England, and I'm certainly guilty of that. I was born and raised in rural Massachusetts, and I went to college in Boston. I graduated from Harvard, and, in many people's minds, that does indeed make me a Yankee. Do you remember when we studied the Revolutionary War? The song we sang? 'He's a Yankee Doodle Dandy'?"

"Yeah . . ."

"Well, back then, Americans were proud of being called Yankees. The word meant more than just being born in New England. It meant they were standing up for life, liberty, and freedom from tyranny. But now, some folks use it to mean being against the South, and I guess that's what your father meant."

"He says you want to destroy everything the South stands for."

"Oh, no . . . no, Declan. That's not what I want at all. I've lived in the South for over twenty years because I love it here. I'm a transplanted Yankee. I married a wonderful Southern girl, and, since my own parents died, her family has become my own. The Dubois family owns cotton and rice plantations outside of Charleston, and, yes, we are slave owners, too. Someday, Mrs. Grenville and I will inherit all those plantations, and I'm doing my best to learn what is involved in raising cotton in the South. I understand the need for slave labor. But, at the same time, I recognize that slavery can be brutal and dehumanizing, and I long for a day when we find a way to do without it." Jonathan stopped and scanned the boy's face, looking for signs that Declan understood what he was trying to say.

The boy's expression hardened. "Da says you can't have it both ways. You're either for the South or agin' it. And you sound like you're agin' it. Now, get away from me. My Da catches me talking to you, he'll blacken my other eye for me."

Jonathan's shoulders slumped as he watched the boy stomp off to lean against a palm tree further down the block. Despite his best efforts, the discussion had gone badly. A student lost was a teacher's failure, in Jonathan's mind. He was still sitting there when Mr. McDermitt came out of the building, caught his son roughly by the arm, and marched him up the street.

"Mr. Grenville!" The voice coming from behind him was harsh and commanding. He stood and turned to face the school's headmaster, Dr. Adamson.

"In my office, if you please."

The ensuing discussion felt like a replay of the conversation with young Declan. Once again, Jonathan had to try to explain his Northern origins, his marriage into a Southern family, his understanding of slavery, and his moral reservations against it. He was no more successful than he had been with the boy.

Dr. Adamson glared at him, twirling his white mustache and shaking his head to indicate that he was not accepting these explanations. "You can't have it both ways, Grenville. Our country is headed toward a showdown with those who want to destroy our entire way of life. You're either a Southerner, a supporter of slavery, and a believer in states' rights, or you're an evil interloper from the nefarious North."

"Oh, come now, Dr. Adamson. There's nothing evil about me or my personal ethical stance. I understand the arguments for states' rights, but I believe that human rights take precedence. I refuse to accept the conclusion that these issues must end by tearing our great nation apart."

"And that attitude has cost us a valuable student—several students, I'm afraid, since Mr. MeDermitt is now threatening to talk to all his neighbors and have them pull their boys out of our classes, too."

"Surely not."

"Surely so! We can't afford to have a teacher like you in our midst. We're trying to prepare these boys for what lies ahead of them, trying to move them up the social ladder so they don't have to compete against slave labor. Our efforts are designed to strengthen the boundaries that separate white and black. Your views, I'm afraid, contradict everything the South stands for."

"That's a terrible exaggeration!" Jonathan realized that he was not helping his case, but he could not meekly accept such an unfair reprimand. "I have never spoken out against the South. I only speak in support of what I believe to be fair and just and right in the eyes of God."

"Eh! You have an unusual and unpopular idea of what is right and just! You're either for the South or against it. You can't be both, and it's quite clear that your attempts to fence-sit have landed you on the wrong side."

"I believe that we all need to compromise at some point. As intelligent people, we must allow our reason to control our emotional responses. That's all I have ever tried to teach my young students."

"Well, you won't be teaching them to compromise for long. You may finish out this term, since we have only a few weeks to go. But then you'll need to clear out your desk and think about moving into another line of work. We can't have an abolitionist working here. If you have a final bit of pay coming to you, I'll send a slave to bring it to your house—that is, if you'll accept it from a slave!"

And just that quickly, a twenty-year career crumbled under the weight of public opinion in 1860.

2

The End of a Career
March 1860

"Sarah, the silver service in the dining room is starting to look quite dingy. Please have one of the girls polish it before dinner tonight."

"Yesm, Miss Susan. I be sho fuh do dat. Dere be anyting else need doin dis mornin?"

"Only the usual chores, I think. Oh, and ask Hector to clean the dry leaves off the piazza. I love our live oaks, but I hate the way they shed in the spring. It makes the yard look as if it has its seasons mixed up."

Sarah nodded and ducked her head, trying unsuccessfully to hide her grin. "He do dat ebry mornin, but he caint keep de leafs fro fallin."

"I know. But still . . ."

Their conversation was interrupted by the oldest Grenville son, who came bouncing into the room as he always did in the mornings. "Mother, Charley and I are leaving now. Charley says to tell you she won't be home for lunch because she's meeting one of her friends after her French lesson. And I have tutoring sessions all day long. I'll be so glad when we get my college plans settled so

I can quit trying to fill the holes in my application letters." Johnny grinned at Susan and gave her a quick hug before bounding out the door and catching up with his more decorous sister.

Susan watched them go, marveling at how adult they both looked and wondering where the years had gone. Then she hurried off to round up the younger children. "Eddie! Mary Sue! Becca! Robbie! Hurry up, now. Finish washing your hands and get ready for school. Mr. Wilson is already downstairs waiting for you."

"Me, too, Momma." Little Jamey toddled down the hall, headed for the back stairs.

"No, you don't, young man!" Susan caught him up with a practiced scoop and kissed him in the soft spot on his neck behind his ear. "You're spending your morning in the nursery with Rosie, just as soon as I find her. Sarah, where is that girl?"

"She be comin, Miss Susan. She be comin soons she roun up de chikkun what scaped fro der coop."

"And how did the chickens get out of the coop?" Susan cringed even as she asked the question, sure she didn't want to know the answer. To her relief, she didn't get one.

"Don know, Miss Susan, but dey be back now, an dey dint eat all de new onion in de veggable garden, neider! Here—you go on wit you. I gwine take Massa Jamey back to de nursery."

"Thank you, Sarah." She let out a huge sigh as she realized that everyone in the family was at last taken care of. From the lower-level classroom came a reassuring murmur of reciting voices. Hector was whistling in the yard, the other slave girls were chattering in Gullah as they piled the silver serving dishes on the table, and she could hear Jamey giggling as Sarah carried him upstairs.

This was her time at last. She shut the parlor door firmly and let her hand trail over the soft rosewood of her new melodeon.

10

Much as she had enjoyed pounding out familiar tunes on her old upright piano, this new instrument called her to take her musical talents further. The piano tinkled, but the melodeon sang, and its music penetrated deep into her soul.

Not wanting to rush the experience, she sat for a few moments on the little round stool, testing its swivel and balance. Her fingers traced phantom notes above the ivory keys. Next, she began to work the pedals, building up the pressure in the bellows. Only then did she allow her fingers to touch the keyboard. The études she had learned as a girl translated themselves into new exercises on this fascinating instrument. As the chords and runs filled the room, her whole body stretched to meet them. Forward and back she leaned; then she swayed from side to side as her feet found a new rhythm on the pedals.

At last she segued into her current favorite melody, Bach's "Jesu, Joy of Man's Desiring." Until she tried the piece on the melodeon, she had never realized that it could be played in many different styles. Easter services at the Circular Church had reminded her of the triumphant nature of the music when it was played with fully open stops and a stately, regular tempo. But she also heard a celebration of spring when she added a slight syncopation, making it playful as well as joyous. That more accurately caught her mood this morning, and she tossed her head as she reveled in that dotted quarter note followed by its jaunty eighth note.

"Bravo!"

Startled, she looked up to find her husband leaning against the doorway. "Jonathan! What are you doing home? Are you all right?" Her surprise gave way to a different kind of fear. He never came home in the middle of the day unless something dreadful had occurred.

"I'm sorry to have frightened you. I'm fine, really."

"The children?"

"Hush. Nothing is wrong. Well, hardly anything. I just needed some time to think and talk to you. I gave my students a research assignment in the library stacks and escaped out the back door." He tried to chuckle but ended up sounding a little defensive.

Susan closed the keyboard and moved toward him. Cradling his cheeks in her palms, she stared into his eyes. "What is it, my dear? You look . . . I don't know . . . haunted, maybe?"

"Hunted, more likely. I've been fired."

"Fired? Nonsense! You're the best teacher the Apprentices' Library Society has ever hired, and no one is more aware of that than the headmaster. He tells me so at every faculty gathering. He's quite proud of you."

"Not any more, he isn't." He led her to the settee and sat, leaning forward, hands clasped between his knees, trying to describe the morning's horrible confrontations in a way that would not sound self-serving.

Susan listened with her heart as well as her ears. She could feel the pain behind his words, even though she could not fully understand his attitudes toward slavery and the current tensions in the South.

"Do you really think Mr. McDermitt will go around convincing the other families to pull their children out of the school? I'm sure he's angry, but that kind of anger usually turns into bravado and then fades away with the next crisis."

"You're always the optimist, my dear! I don't know, honestly, whether the issue will go further. Maybe it will prove to be the proverbial tempest in a teapot. But given the current nature of public opinion, the war talk, the inflammatory newspaper articles about the evils of abolition—I don't think the headmaster is ever going to pat me on my head and tell me all is forgiven."

"You defended your personal moral standards. That's not reason for dismissal."

"I challenged the *raison d'être* behind the Apprentices' Library Society. That is certainly cause for dismissal."

"I don't understand. Are you saying that the Apprentices' Library Society exists for the sole purpose of perpetuating the peculiar institution of slavery—by making sure that white workers are better educated than the slaves with whom they compete?"

"Yes, I'm afraid so."

"I can't accept that view of my fellow Southerners. My family has owned slaves for as long as we can remember, both here and on the island of Martinique. We try to be responsible slave owners. We're certainly not the cruel ogres that Northern newspapers delight in portraying. We own slaves because our very livelihoods depend on them. We don't hate them or fear them or think they are less than human. We need them, and so we try to take care of them. I love our household slave family. Sarah and I grew up together, and we have always been as close as sisters. I knew her mother better than I knew my own . . ." Susan's voice trailed off as she struggled to reconcile her husband's view of the world with her own.

"I'm not denying any of that. Unfortunately, not everyone is as kind and compassionate as you are. And, actually, Dr. Adamson's points are well-taken. I have been trying to teach my students that the Southern point of view is not the only way to look at things. I've tried to teach them about compromise and understanding in a world where everyone else is busy choosing up sides and preparing for mayhem. I've encouraged them to think about abstracts such as equality and justice for all. I'm an idealist, and there's not much room for me or my ideas in our current society."

"So you're giving up?"

"I don't know what I'm doing yet. But I think I'm finished at the Apprentices' Library Society. Where I go from here, I just don't know."

"But you've always been a teacher. That's your calling. How can you turn your back on it?"

Jonathan shook his head. He had no answers for her.

Susan plunged ahead, determined to find a wonderful answer to this perplexing problem. "There's got to be a way," she insisted. "Let's see. You could start your own school. You could use the basement room where Mr. Wilson teaches our little ones. Maybe your students from the Apprentices' Library Society would follow you. You could—"

"Not here, Susan. Not even in Charleston. That would simply engender more hard feelings."

"Not in Charleston? Where else is there?"

"This is a big, wide world, my dear, and it is filled with opportunities. You've been in one spot too long!"

"It's my home!"

"Yes, of course, but if this war talk continues, it's going to turn into a very inhospitable place, at least for me." Jonathan hesitated, knowing that what he was about to suggest would bring his wife's life crashing around her feet. "Actually, I've been thinking that we might be well-advised to . . . to return to Massachusetts. Johnny will be headed there for college in the fall anyway, and the move would keep us closer to him."

"And farther from my mother, from my land, from my friends, from everything I value most."

"Really? I would have thought our family held a higher place on the list of what you value most." Even as he said the words he realized that they had opened a dangerous topic—one that could threaten the very basis of their marriage.

"You can't do this to me!" Susan's eyes brimmed with tears.

"I'm not trying to do anything to you. It's my problem. I'm the Yankee. Everything about me is rooted in my Northern upbringing. I learned my values early, in church, in school, and at my parents' knees. And they all taught me the same basic principles—love of God and the Bible, love for my country, and hatred of anything that threatened the loss of life, liberty, and equality among all men."

"You can't practice those principles here?"

"How can I do so and at the same time support the practice of slavery, or join in the talk of breaking up the United States, or encourage the idea of going to war against my own origins? No, I can't, Susan."

Susan's face suddenly twisted, turning her half-smile into a sneer. "Of course you can do it. You've been doing it for twenty years!"

Jonathan's head snapped backward as if he had been slapped. He stared at her, speechless.

But she wasn't through. "Look at you—all moral righteousness now, when you need to justify the fact that you've lost your job. But when we married, when you were young and naive and clueless about the world, you were willing to make any sacrifice. I tried to warn you that Charleston society was not about to fall at your feet just because you married one of their own. And you replied that you intended to work very hard to be worthy of Southern acceptance. You didn't hesitate over the knowledge that I might one day inherit cotton plantations. It didn't bother you that I brought slaves with me into our home. It never occurred to you to suggest that we might live out our married life in Boston. You wanted to be a wealthy Southern gentleman, and you displayed no moral scruples about what that lifestyle might require of you. But now—"

"You're being terribly unfair. I didn't marry you for your money, and I chose to live here because I knew it would make you happy."

"Strangely enough, Jonathan, if you had asked me at age seventeen to move to Boston with you, I would have jumped at the chance. It would have been a grand adventure. My sister, Annaliese, did it. She married her Northern beau, and she's up there in New York, happy as a clam. No, you didn't choose Charleston for me—you chose it for you, and now you've got it, with all its partisan warts."

"I didn't know . . ."

"No, you probably didn't. You didn't know, for example, that while the South appears to be genteel and cultured and carefree, it actually has a deeply embedded fear of its own inferiority. And when you talk about your moral reservations about any Southern practice, you come across as arrogant and condescending. It doesn't have to be politics. You could criticize our Southern cooking and get the same reaction."

"I had no idea twenty years ago that we would find ourselves in this kind of political turmoil."

"Of course you didn't. How could you? But it's too late now to choose Boston over Charleston. We've changed. I've changed. I'm the heiress to all my late father's lands. I'm responsible for the lives of hundreds of slaves. I cannot and will not give that up to serve your latest whim. There's an old saw about making your bed and having to lie in it. You made yours twenty years ago, and by now it's getting old and wrinkled. You might be happier with an entirely new bed. But if you want to me to continue to occupy your bed, you're going to have to settle for the old one and accept all the conditions that come with it."

3

To Become a Southerner
May 1860

A day or so later, Susan broached the topic again. "We can't go on not talking to one another about this, Jonathan. We have a huge problem, and we need to settle it together, one way or the other. There are other choices open to you, you know. Maybe it's time you think about a second career."

"And what would that be? What would make me an acceptable citizen of South Carolina? A cotton planter?"

"Why not! There's already some truth in that description. You've always known that since Father and my brother died, I am the heiress to all the Dubois lands. And since you are my husband, you are considered the legal heir as well. Mother is still trying to keep the family holdings together, but she's not going to be able to do it on her own for much longer. Maybe this is the time when we need to step in and assume our rightful place as plantation owners."

"I don't know the first thing about raising cotton, or growing rice, for that matter."

"You could learn. That Harvard education of yours must have given you some understanding of business and finance. A planter doesn't have to do the digging, you know. He just has to be able to manage the diggers."

"You would turn me into a typical slave owner, complete with whip and chains!"

"No! I would see you as a forward-looking planter, treating his black workers as equals and proving that the institution can grow into a mutually profitable venture for both owner and slave."

Jonathan looked out the window, trying to picture the change his wife was suggesting. His eyes closed and his mouth drew inward. He shook his head.

"Or even better," Susan persisted, "you could follow both careers! Mother has already told me that she does not think she can spend another winter living all alone out in the house at Harbor View Plantation. Edisto Island is a lovely location, but she misses the social outlets she has here in Charleston. She'd be more than happy to have us all move out there for the planting season. And, while you may have forgotten, there's already a schoolhouse on the property. Father had it built when Robert and Annaliese and I were children. I'm sure it could be refurbished quickly, and you could set up a school for the children on neighboring plantations. Mr. Wilson could go with us to teach the younger children, and you could handle the teenagers. You could continue teaching and be learning about cotton cultivation at the same time. What do you think?"

"You're seriously proposing that we share a house with the Dragon Lady?"

"Jonathan! I hate it when you call my mother that!"

"Sorry, but you know she has never thought of me as good enough for you. This situation will only help to convince her that she's been right about me all along, and she's not likely to turn over any part of the family business to my incompetent hands. The living arrangements would be intolerable."

"Well, then. We'll just have to encourage her to stay in Charleston all winter and let us have the plantation to ourselves. The children would love it, I know. It could work well, Jonathan. I know it could."

"I'll think about it. That's the most I can promise you right now. I'd rather we keep the children out of the discussion until we're sure of what we're going to do. I have several more weeks of instruction to finish up under my contract with the Apprentices' Library Society. Let me get through those obligations, and then we'll have the summer to decide where we go from here."

For the next several weeks, Jonathan Grenville became a new and intensely private person. Instead of walking to work and enjoying his neighborhood, he did as his wife had been suggesting. Every morning, just before school was scheduled to start, Hector hitched the surrey and drove his master to the front door of the Charleston Apprentices' Library Society. Jonathan got down, slapped the horse on its hindquarters in a kind of offhand farewell, and entered the building without exchanging a word with his driver. To a casual observer, it would have been a normal scene—a master and his slave. To those who knew Jonathan best, it would have seemed completely out of character.

In the afternoons, Jonathan emerged from the building, looked around, and gave a shrill between-the-teeth whistle. He expected that whistle to summon his driver once again, and so it did. Silently, he climbed into the surrey, spoke a couple of sharp words to Hector, and settled back into the seat with his eyes closed until they reached his own backyard. Dismounting, he strode into his house without a backward glance or a thank-you. On these occasions, Hector watched him until the door closed behind him; then the slave turned with a sigh, admitting that his former friend had become a stranger to him.

Jonathan's demeanor in the classroom changed as well. He abruptly dropped his series of lectures on the hope and promise of the young United States. Instead, he began a new unit on the relationship of history and science. Each day, he and his students explored a discovery or invention that had somehow changed the world. They examined Greek architecture and its dependence on the theorems of geometry. They studied the stars and the astrolabe as the precursors to ocean navigation. They studied the designs of buildings and marveled at the forces that had been necessary to build the Seven Wonders of the World. They built model levers and pulleys and fulcrums. They used mirrors to study the reflections of light. The lessons were valuable and particularly suited to a class of young apprentices who expected to spend their lives engaging in the mechanical arts.

If the students recognized that their classes had taken a sharp turn from their former direction, none of them questioned the reasons for the change. But an observer might have noticed that several words seemed to have been banished from their classroom vocabulary. They discussed foreign countries but did not address the nature of their governments. They measured the slopes and shadows of the pyramids but never mentioned the slave labor that had built them. Their history lessons skipped over wars as if they had never occurred. Freedom, equality, and justice played no role in the developments they studied. Politics had become the classroom's dirty word.

At home, Jonathan closed himself into the gentlemen's parlor, which he had turned into his personal library and study. He read until the last light faded, immersing himself in philosophy and classical literature. Only then would he come out, seeking a late dinner. Susan learned to feed the children early so she would not have to send them to bed too late. On the occasional evening when Jonathan dined with the family, he addressed each child with a formal question—"What did you learn at school today?"—but he didn't seem to listen to the answers. If the children missed sharing their lives with their father, they kept their feelings to themselves.

On the last day of classes at the Apprentices' Library Society, Jonathan packed a small valise and summoned Hector's son Eli to drive him to Edisto Island. He spent three days on the Harbor View Plantation, talking to the slave drivers, prowling through the house, inspecting the fields and outbuildings. For some periods of hours, he simply sat under the trees, staring off across the water. The slaves watched, mystified. Then, as suddenly as he had appeared, he was gone again.

Jonathan's steps were springier as he entered his house on Logan Street. He had a friendly nod for Hector and a quick question: "Everything going all right?"

"Yes, Massa. I dun takes care uh de house whiles you bin gone."

"Thanks, Hector."

He encountered Sarah in the central hallway and smiled at her. "Is your mistress in the parlor?"

"Yassuh! She be playin dat newfangle melody ting." Sarah watched as he slid open the pocket door to interrupt his wife's practice session. Sarah shook her head. "I neber gwine unnerstan dese white mens."

But Jonathan did not realize that both house slaves were registering surprise at his new behavior. He had eyes only for the swaying back of his wife as she ran through her childhood études at the melodeon. He bent over her and kissed her neck.

Susan's head came up with a jerk, clipping Jonathan sharply on the chin. "Ow!" Two voices, the same reaction, then a laugh as Susan whirled on her stool and threw herself into her husband's arms. "Sorry, but you did startle me! When did you get home? How was . . . uh, did you . . . Oh, talk to me. I've been alone for so long." Her eyes filled with tears.

"I'm back, my dear, and in every sense of that word. Come. Sit with me and tell me what has been happening here. No crises?"

"Everyone's fine. But you! Where have you been and what has changed? You're like your old self."

"I hope I am. I feel renewed, thanks to your Harbor View Plantation."

"Hector told me that was where you were headed, but he wasn't sure why. What did you discover?"

"Well, first, the plantation is in excellent condition. Your sainted mother has outdone herself in keeping the place running after your father's death."

Susan was grinning. "My sainted mother? What happened to the Dragon Lady?"

"She's both, of course. I'm just impressed with her efforts at the moment."

"Good. I hope that attitude lasts for a few days. Did your visit make you feel like a cotton planter?"

"I'm not sure of that, but I did feel at home. The house could use some whitewash, thanks to the sea spray, but it's spotless on the inside and roomier than I remembered. The schoolhouse will need a bit more work, but it, too, is functional and well-furnished. The animals are healthy, and the cotton plants are growing faster than the weeds in the fields.

"The visit also taught me a couple of things I wasn't expecting. For one, I had forgotten how quiet and peaceful the plantation is. Charleston, in contrast, seemed like a bustling metropolis when we returned this morning. I felt positively jangled by the clatter of wheels and the chatter of voices. Not a seagull to be heard, and I missed their soft calls. I think my nerves needed the soothing quiet of the island.

"Second, I was a bit overwhelmed by the number of slaves living on the property. In the past, I had avoided the slave village because I did not want to be associated with it. This time, I walked the slave street and talked with the people. I really had no idea that it takes close to 300 workers to raise our cotton crop there. Intellectually, I always understood that slave labor was necessary for cotton production, but I had no idea of the magnitude of the task.

"I was also pleased to see that our slaves are generally healthy and cheerful. They didn't cringe when I approached. They welcomed me and were eager to show me what they were doing. The women have wonderful vegetable plots around their cabins. Inside, the floors are swept, and there are little homey touches—baskets and throws—that told me they were proud of their homes. The children were giggly but polite, and the workers in the fields seemed to be enjoying their tasks. I expected to be shocked and ashamed of being treated like a slave owner. Instead, I felt almost proud."

"So . . .?"

"So I think you had a good plan. I'm excited about starting my own school at last, and it feels much more doable than it did when you first suggested it. I sat in that schoolhouse and remembered how impressed, but intimidated, it once made me feel. Your father showed it to me when I first arrived twenty years ago, and the idea of teaching there scared me to death. I have the experience now—I can do this!"

"And you're willing to live at Harbor View during the winter season? As a cotton planter?"

"I'll have a lot to learn, but there's no better place to do so. Roger Withers, the overseer, was pleasant and welcoming. He's willing to stay on and share his knowledge for as long as I need him. Now all we need is the approval of your 'sainted mother'."

"Yes. We'll need to discuss all this with her before we alert the children to an impending move. I think Mother will be pleased, although she may temporarily revert to being the Dragon Lady before she realizes that you are sincere in your intentions."

"Why wouldn't she be pleased? I'll be taking all that responsibility off her shoulders, so she can get back to playing whist with her lady friends."

"Oh, Jonathan, you are a wonderful father and husband, but you're a typical man when it comes to your attitude about women. You mustn't imply that she is unable to run the plantation on her own or that she has no business doing so—even if that is what you really believe. You just acknowledged to me that she has done an excellent job of stepping into Father's footsteps. You need to let her know that. And what you just said about Mr. Withers? That's true of her as well. You need to ask her to share her knowledge with you."

"I'm getting a mental picture of me groveling at her feet."

"If that's what it takes, then grovel. You mustn't offer to send her toddling off to her whist club. You need to offer her a new and important role in your life—as a teacher and exemplar. That's what will keep her from breathing fire at you."

4

Facing Down the Dragon
May 1860

Susan squeezed Jonathan's arm reassuringly as they waited for someone to answer their knock. "Remember, you need to take the lead in this discussion. Mother can be a bully when she senses weakness, but she's also used to knuckling under to a strong man. So make her feel important, but don't give her an opportunity to dominate the conversation."

"Easier for you to give that advice than for me to follow it, but I'll try. Good morning, Elsie. Would you tell Mrs. Dubois that Jonathan Grenville and his wife are here to see her?"

Elsie looked at Susan, puzzled, and then protested, "But, Massa, aint she . . ."

"She's Mrs. Jonathan Grenville," he repeated. "Please tell your mistress that Jonathan Grenville would like to see her." The young slave looked at him wide-eyed and then scurried away. Since they had not been invited beyond the doorway, they stood uncomfortably in the hall until Elizabeth Dubois appeared to escort them into the parlor. "For heaven's sake, come in. What did you say to my maid? She was so frightened she couldn't tell me who was at the door."

"I simply gave her my name. She must be new."

"No, but never mind. To what do I owe the honor of a formal visit from the two of you this afternoon?"

"I have some news for you, Mother Dubois. There have been some changes in our circumstances, and I could use your advice on our next steps."

"You're not getting a divorce, are you?"

"Oh, certainly not! You may have already heard, however, that I'm giving up my teaching position with the Charleston Apprentices' Library Society. The headmaster and I reached an impasse over what sort of political history lessons I should be offering in the face of the current talk going on about war between the North and South. He felt that I would be thought an abolitionist unless I came out overtly in favor of slavery and states' rights, and I was unwilling to alter my interpretation of the Constitution in order to suit the more inflammatory rhetoric of the secessionists. So we reached an amicable parting, and I am now looking at the possibility of starting a school of my own—not one to support any particular point of view, but rather one totally independent of political extremists."

"I don't know that I approve of your throwing over a perfectly good job when you have a family of seven children to support. Surely—"

"Excuse me, Mrs. Dubois, but that isn't the issue. I have already left the position. What I want to talk with you about is the possibility of using the schoolhouse on the grounds of Harbor View Plantation. Susan and I feel that our whole family would benefit from a seasonal move to Edisto Island. It's time I learned more about the operation of a cotton plantation, and Susan would like the younger children to have more chances to run free in natural surroundings rather than in the increasingly crowded streets of Charleston.

"Our plan—with your approval, of course—would be to move the whole family to Harbor View for the winter season. Mr. Wilson, the children's tutor, would travel with us and continue to teach them, along with any other island children who might be interested. And I would split my time between learning about the plantation and offering some classes for the older children on the island."

"And what do you plan to do with me? Am I to be booted out of my own home to gratify your family's desires?"

Jonathan saw a flash of the Dragon Lady but chose to ignore it. "Certainly not, Mother Dubois. Your knowledge of and familiarity with the plantation are an integral part of the plan. Some day—and we hope that day will not come for a very long time—Susan will inherit her father's estates, and I will need to be there to help her with them. But I can't be prepared to do that without your guidance, and I hope you'll be willing to share with me the knowledge of South Carolina agriculture that Mr. Dubois left as his legacy to you."

"That's all in his books in the library. I still don't understand what it is you want from me. Is it your intention that I should live at Harbor View with you?"

"If you would like that, certainly. It is your house and will remain so for the rest of your life. We would be staying there only on your sufferance, not the other way around."

"I'm not sure I can imagine that. I love all of you, of course, but you do have seven children, and four or five of them are still at the squirmy, whiny, get-under-foot stage. I raised my own children and have no desire to raise yours. I prefer to be able to spoil them for a few hours and then send them home."

"That choice is yours. If you would prefer to spend the winter here in your comfortable Charleston home, only visiting the plantation for short periods and giving advice where needed, we would be happy with that solution, too."

Mrs. Dubois stared at Jonathan for a long moment, then arose and walked to the window. The Grenvilles matched her silence. At last she turned to face them down. "Why? Why are you really willing to do this?"

Jonathan met her gaze steadily. "I'm willing to do this because I love my wife, and this is what we have decided will best serve our family."

"And you?" Mrs. Dubois turned to her daughter. "I haven't heard you say a word."

"Mother, you have always drummed into my head the fact that I am only a woman," Susan began. "You taught me I have no right to vote or speak in public or gain more than a basic education. That I cannot own property so long as there is a male member of my family—father, brother, husband, or adult son—to whom I must defer. That women have no head for business. That my place is in the home. I am trying hard to remember those restrictions. Now that both my father and my only brother are dead, I must rely on my husband to manage any business or property to which I may fall heir. This plan is designed to put Jonathan in a position from which he can best handle my affairs."

Mrs. Dubois cocked a skeptical eyebrow at them but then shrugged. "All right, then. I'll go along. Feel free to take over Harbor View. I would like nothing more than to spend the winter in Charleston rather than on that isolated island. But there will be restrictions. I will visit whenever I please, and I will always have access to the plantation accounts. All profits beyond your actual family expenses will accrue to me for my lifetime. In other words, you will manage Harbor View for me, Jonathan, but it will not be yours until your wife legally inherits it."

"That's all we ask, Mother Dubois, and I promise you that I will do my best to act in your best interests in all plantation matters."

As the Grenvilles walked home, Jonathan peered down at his wife. "Did you mean all those things you said about your status as a woman? Do you really feel as if you have no rights because of your womanhood?"

"That's the Southern view of the world, and I really have heard it all my life. Do I believe it? Yes, sometimes I do. It was easy for me to recite it today because it was what my mother wanted to hear."

"But you are a strong, capable woman."

"Yes, and don't you forget it!" Susan was grinning at him. "At the same time, you need to understand that all the women in the South, including your wife and daughters, are raised to be useful ornaments, not productive human beings."

"That's preposterous!"

"Of course it is, but it's also the truth. You know it. You've seen it. How many Southern girls have you known who have gone off to get a college education?"

"Well, uh, none that I can remember. But surely there are women's colleges. Back home, almost all intelligent girls have a chance to graduate from high school and go on to Teacher's College if they choose. Why, in Philadelphia, there's even a Women's Medical School. Are there really no such institutions in the South?"

"There's no demand for them. Women are not meant to be gainfully employed. They may be cultured, conversant in the arts, even aware of the world around them, but only because that makes them better conversationalists over a dinner table. Look at me."

Jonathan smiled down at her. "I love looking at you."

"No, I mean, really look at me. I speak French and a few passable phrases of Italian. I play several musical instruments but do so only for my own enjoyment and for the entertainment of my family. I have been well-schooled in the family histories of all the upper crust of Charleston society. I am creative enough to be able to decorate a fine house and set a beautiful table—so long as I have slaves to do the actual work for me. I understand fashion, and I can embroider a fine edge on a handkerchief. But don't ask me to make a whole dress for myself or a shirt for you. We have slaves for that sort of thing. When we give a party, I plan the menu and send it off for the cook to prepare. I teach our children to mind their manners and charm their elders. But the hard work of raising them—blowing their noses and changing their diapers and cleaning up their messes? That's the point at which I call the nanny to come take over. I am a creation—a character in a well-orchestrated play. I know my role and perform it well. But what you see is simply that—play-acting. That's the definition of Southern womanhood.

"We women have been taught from the cradle to accept our societal role, which also implies, by the way, inferior status. We accept the fiction that we are delicate creatures who need to be coddled and protected. We learn not to ask why we can't vote or have a career outside the home. And sometimes, actually more often than not, we come to believe that we really are weak and helpless. But that doesn't mean we like it."

"Why is it, then, that I—and most men I know—turn to you women when we need to make hard choices, such as the one we've just made?"

"Yes, you do, but only in private. In public, no Southern man I know ever asks his wife for an opinion. You accept the fiction that we're just sweet and innocent. If we want to accomplish something, we have to be quite clever about convincing our menfolk to do as we wish."

"That being the case, what is your plan for convincing the children that this move is in their best interests?"

"They don't get a choice, of course, especially the girls. But now that the decision is made, we can try to put a good face upon it."

"Should we call them all together and make a grand pronouncement?"

"Better to do it casually over dinner, I think. You'll just need to be prepared to answer their questions with blandishments designed to turn their fears into promises of joys to come."

"You know, I'm beginning to think there are two Dragon Ladies in this family. You talk about weakness, but you bend all of us to your will with no apparent effort."

Susan squeezed his arm and looked up at him with an impish grin. "And you love every minute of it! Say what you will about the Southern style of life, but Southern women keep their men happy, even when those men don't quite understand what has happened to them."

5

Growing Pains
May 1860

Jonathan waited until dessert appeared before he broached the evening's touchy subject. "Your mother and I have some news that we're excited about. We're stepping in to take over the management of your grandparents' Harbor View Plantation, starting in the fall."

"What does that mean: 'take over the management'? How do you do that? The land's miles and miles from here." Charlotte, as the eldest of the children, had taken the lead, while the others alternated watching her and watching their parents. All were aware that something momentous was going on, since dinnertime conversations lately had been limited to those polite inquiries about what each child was learning in school.

"Yes, Father. I don't mean to question your ability, but how can you teach classes here in Charleston and oversee things on Edisto Island at the same time?" young Jonathan asked.

"That's the point, actually. I've given up my teaching post here at the Apprentices' Library Society."

"What? Why?"

"I'd rather not get into the specifics of it, and I'm not sure that you children need to know. I simply found that the headmaster and I have such different opinions that it was becoming impossible for us to work together."

"Political opinions?"

"Well, yes, but, uh . . ."

Susan stepped in to rescue her husband, who, she could tell, was becoming a bit flustered. "Johnny, I'm sure that you and Charley are both aware of the current controversies between the North and the South. And you know that your father is widely known as a Yankee. No one has ever hidden the fact that he comes from Massachusetts. Right now, there are some parents who don't want a Yankee influence in their schools, so . . ."

"That's enough, Susan. You needn't apologize for me. I told my students some hard truths about the state of their country, and one of the parents objected. So to save embarrassment and further trouble in case this nonsense continues to escalate, I decided to remove myself from an awkward situation. That's all there is to it."

"But, Father, you've lived in the South for over twenty years. You must understand the Southern viewpoint. Surely you don't side with the abolitionists who are doing nothing but stirring up trouble."

"I'm not going to discuss the issue of slavery with you tonight, Johnny. The fact remains that I am no longer employed in Charleston, so the family is free to move to Edisto come cooler weather, and that's what we will be doing."

Susan could have guessed the reactions of most of her children. Johnny looked puzzled and concerned; she could almost see him doing calculations in his head. Charley, always a rather petulant young woman, pressed her lips tightly together, as if forcefully restraining herself from an outburst. She settled for glaring at her parents and then refusing to look at them at all. Eddie was confused. "What?" he kept muttering. "How? When?" Mary Sue bubbled with enthusiasm: "We can maybe get ponies! What fun!" Becca's eyes widened in fear of the unknown, Robbie watched his sisters for clues about how to react, and little Jamey squirmed to get down from the table.

"We know this is sudden and surprising, but you'll have a long time to make plans. We won't move to Edisto Island until after the first frost—probably around the first of November." Jonathan hoped to soothe them by postponing the inevitable.

"But I have to decide about college before then!" Johnny protested. "If you've quit your job, will there be money for me to go at all, or should I plan on joining you in learning to be a farmer?"

"Nothing will change for you, Johnny. College is a necessity, not an option. All Grenville men have attended Harvard, and so shall you. You have a family legacy there, and we'll handle the bills somehow. You just worry about keeping your studies up to snuff so that you are not behind when you arrive in Massachusetts. Must uphold the family dignity and all that."

But Johnny was not about to be bought off by humor. "Wait a minute, Father. I'm not going to Harvard, not with war coming on. I don't want to be caught in enemy territory."

"Massachusetts is not, and will never be, enemy territory, son. It's our ancestral home."

"You may see it that way, but I'm a Southerner, born and bred. If South Carolina follows through on her threat to secede, I'll be on the side of the Rebels. And if war comes in a year or so, I'll be a soldier. So I've been thinking about going to the Citadel instead. That way, I'll be in place and ready to fight."

"No!" His mother looked at him in horror. "I have raised you to be a scholar. I've visualized you as a professor like your father, or maybe a doctor, or a lawyer, or a minister—but never a soldier. I won't hear of it."

"Besides," his father broke in, "all your friends are headed north to school. Reverend Croft told me just recently that his son Alex is going to Princeton."

"No, he's not. They've changed their minds about sending him up there. He's enrolling at South Carolina College in Columbia."

"John Calhoun is following his family tradition at Yale," Jonathan persisted, "and I hear several of the Middleton cousins will be enrolled at Brown. You're Charleston's Harvard representative."

"That's where you are wrong, Father. None of my friends are willing to go north for school anymore. Some are staying right here at the College of Charleston, John Calhoun will be going to Columbia with Alex, and I hear several Middletons are signing on at the Citadel. We all intend to be home on the ground when trouble arises."

"All admirable young men with strongly held viewpoints, I'm sure. But since you, like all of them, are also under the age of eighteen and totally dependent on your parents for your support, I'm afraid this is not your decision to make. I will take your desires under advisement, but we're not making a choice tonight, so let's let it rest."

"And what about me?" Charlotte jumped in before the family could make a move to leave the table. "This move affects me as well."

Jonathan looked at his daughter in surprise. "How so? You're still deeply engaged in your studies of language and music, I understand—nothing that cannot be continued wherever we happen to be living."

"You haven't been around much lately," she answered with a bit of impertinence that made Jonathan clench his jaw. "Grandmother Dubois told me just this week that she wants me to start my debutante year this fall season. I can hardly do that in the middle of a swampy island!"

"My mother told you that?" Susan had been trying to stay out of these confrontations, but this revelation shocked her. "She had no right to be doing that. The choice is not hers. Your father and I will decide when you make your debut. You're only seventeen, and barely that. You have several more years before—"

"Not if our country goes to war!" Charlotte was close to tears. "Where will all our beaus come from if they're off shooting at Yankees?"

"I don't believe this conversation," Jonathan said, shaking his head in dismay. "Not another word from any of you. And no, Mary Sue, you can't have a pony!" His two youngest daughters dissolved into sobs as their parents and older siblings left the table. The pudding, untouched at each place, began to weep and sag.

Jonathan left the house early the next morning without seeing any member of his family. He intended only to take a brisk walk that would work off his anger, but his footsteps eventually led him toward Meeting Street. His destination turned out to be not his former school building but the Battery end of Meeting and the imposing three-story red-brick home of his longtime friend and minister, the Reverend David Croft. He knocked at the street door hesitantly, hoping it was not too early. When a slave opened the door to peer out, Jonathan asked only if he could leave a message for Reverend Croft. Instead, a booming voice came from over the slave's shoulder.

"Jonathan Grenville! What a pleasant surprise. I've been sitting here on the piazza with a cup of coffee and wishing I had someone to chat with. Come in and join me, won't you? Samuel, bring another service and a fresh pot of coffee, if you please."

"Are you sure I'm not disturbing you?"

"Not at all. In fact, I've been thinking about you, ever since I heard the report of your resignation from the Apprentices' Library Society. Oh, don't look so surprised. Word like that travels fast in Charleston. Is that what brings you here this morning? Or is it something else? You look distressed. Everything all right at home?"

"Yes . . . no . . . I don't know! I need someone to tell me if what I'm doing is the right course, and since you have sometimes acted as my spiritual advisor, I thought . . ."

Over fresh coffee, the whole story came spilling out—the "Damned Yankee" episode, the fight with Susan, Jonathan's struggle to find a new purpose for his life, the decision to take over the plantation, and the abysmal mess he had made of telling his children of his decisions. Reverend Croft listened sympathetically. When Jonathan's tale finally ran out, the reverend simply nodded.

"You know, Jonathan, you and I are quite a bit alike. We are both 'Damned Yankees,' and, if I'm not mistaken, we arrived in Charleston about the same time twenty years ago. We both married wealthy Southern girls and raised large families. And we both made a conscious choice to become residents of this wonderful city—to become slave-owning Southerners, with all that implies."

"Yes, I guess so."

"On the other hand, hard as we may try, we can't get over that Northern training that tells us that a society based on slavery is wrong."

Jonathan winced. "I try to be a benevolent master."

"Of course you do. As do I. But it's still there, isn't it? And our born-and-bred Southern friends will never understand us. I've learned to accept that as a given. You may remember the brouhaha I got into with our congregation a year or so ago when I helped organize the Zion Presbyterian Church for slaves. People accused me of being an abolitionist and told me to go back where I came from. But I chose not to leave."

"I remember. At the time, some of the attacks were quite vicious. Why didn't you leave?"

"Well, I came to realize that I could not help the cause of the slaves by turning my back on them. Instead, I chose to stay and continue to be what you just described as a benevolent master. Social change takes a long time, but perhaps someday others will learn from my example. I think you follow the same goal, whether or not you have yet realized it."

"But when I look at my children, I have to wonder, David. Are they learning anything from me? I don't see any evidence of it so far. Young Jonathan is ready to secede and go to war. Charlotte is only concerned that a war will disrupt her social life. And the younger children? They only ask what I can give them."

"They're children, Jonathan. God's not through with them yet, and neither are you. Give them the time to grow up—and to grow into their full heritage, both North and South."

"Johnny tells me that you have decided not to send Alex to Princeton after all. Is that what you mean?"

"Partially, yes. It was always my fondest wish to send a son back to my *alma mater*. Our oldest son, Harris, was not much of a scholar, and he's wanted to be a soldier as long as I can remember. That's what we are letting him do. But Alex? Oh, he has such a bright mind. I've always imagined him wearing a Princeton school tie. But I've had to accept the realities of the current political atmosphere. If I insisted he study in the North, there's every chance that the other students would make his life miserable for being a Southerner, and his friends back here would reject him for going to school in New Jersey. A couple of months ago, I sent a letter to Princeton withdrawing his application. As I explained to Reverend Thornwell at South Carolina College as well, I changed my mind 'by a deference to present public feeling and to the just claims of the South'."

"And you don't regret the decision?"

"No. He'll get a good education in Columbia. The school has a great library and a first-rate faculty. And it has the advantage of being an easy train ride away from home, a fact my wife, Margaret, appreciates even more than I do."

"But wasn't there trouble there a few years back? I don't quite remember the whole story but . . ."

"You're probably thinking of the Guardhouse Riot, which turned out to be nothing more than a small drunken prank. The college used to have military training as a central part of its curriculum, and all the students had assigned weapons with which to drill. One night, when a cadet came back to campus inebriated, he got into a scuffle with the chief marshal. The marshal locked him in the guardhouse to sober up, but the other students demanded his release and surrounded the guardhouse while displaying their weapons as a threat. At that point, the mayor of Columbia panicked and called out the militia to deal with an insurrection. No shots were fired, but the Cadet Corps was disbanded, the military component removed from the curriculum, and all the weaponry locked away in a storage room under the library."

"My Susan will be happy to hear that. She is dead set against Johnny becoming a soldier."

"Well, no one can make any promises once war breaks out, but, until then, you can feel safe sending young Jonathan to Columbia along with his friends. I'll give you a letter of introduction to Reverend Thornwell to ease your way. Take Johnny up there—a trip for just the two of you. You can look over the campus and find his lodgings in one of the nearby boarding houses. I'll point you to the one we've chosen for Alex. They would make good housemates, I think."

"And you think that will solve the issues between us?"

"I think it will go a long way in showing your son that you accept his Southern affiliation. And that's all a son really wants—just evidence that his father accepts him for who he is."

6

Girl Talk
June 1860

Susan Grenville sat at the melodeon, her feet pumping the pedals slowly and her fingers trailing absent-mindedly over the keys. Try as she might this morning, she could not concentrate on her music—the one factor in her life that usually soothed her. Her fingers tense, she struck a discordant group of notes, slowing working them to a harmonic resolution. As the tones echoed through the room, she shook her head at her own discomfiture. She felt responsible for the tension within her family, all the more because Jonathan and his son were gone on a bonding adventure to Columbia.

Why couldn't she reach out to her daughter in the same way? She and Charlotte had barely exchanged a dozen words since that night when Charlotte had demanded her right to make her debut. The subject had not come up again, but it hovered between them as an impenetrable barrier. Susan brought both hands crashing down on the keyboard and stood up in frustration.

Susan found her daughter on the piazza reading a book. "Come!" she said. "We're going to see your grandmother and try to work out a solution to the debutante problem."

"Really?" Charley looked hopeful for a moment and then reverted to suspicion. "Is this one of your clever little schemes to have all the adults gang up against me?"

"No. Your grandmother does not know we're coming. Perhaps we won't even find her at home, but I'm ready to try anything."

The two women walked silently for a few minutes. Then Charley ventured a petulant question. "Is there some reason you think I shouldn't become a debutante? Do you think I will embarrass you? Or is it that you are unwilling to spend the money?"

"No, certainly not. Neither of those is true. I guess the real reason is that . . . I don't know anything about how a young woman makes her debut. I'm a little afraid to let you embark on a process I don't understand, for fear I'll fail you badly. That's why we're going to discuss it with my mother. I'm hoping she can guide both of us."

"Wait—are you saying you were never a debutante? Why ever not? You were the oldest daughter of one of the wealthiest families in Charleston. How could you not . . .?"

"Because I married at seventeen."

"I didn't realize you were that young," Charley said. "Wasn't Father willing to wait until you had your few weeks in the spotlight?"

"We were in somewhat of a hurry," Susan said, her jaw tight.

"But surely you . . . uh . . . oh! That kind of a hurry?" She looked at her mother as if seeing her for the first time. Then a further thought occurred. "That means it was actually my fault that you couldn't . . .?"

"Not your fault, my darling daughter. But, yes, if I had made my debut, you would have been right there with me." Susan could feel her face starting to flush, but she forced herself to look directly at Charlotte. "And, furthermore, I have never regretted that particular lack in my life, so don't you go reading more into this than just what it is."

Charlotte was shocked into speechlessness, perhaps for the first time in her life.

The slave girl Elsie opened the door as she had earlier in the week. "Yes'm?" She gave a slight smile as she recognized Susan and then looked beyond her fearfully, as if she expected Jonathan to leap out at her from the shrubbery.

"Good morning, Elsie. Would you see if my mother has time for a short visit, please?"

But Elizabeth Dubois was once again right at her maid's heels. "Run along, Elsie. Good morning, Susan. And Charlotte! How are you, dear? What brings you both here this time?"

"May we come in, Mother?"

"Of course, of course. You know this is always your house. You don't need to ask permission. But this must be some sort of special occasion."

"It's time for some girl talk. Charlotte tells me that she would like to make her debut this fall, and, as you can imagine, I'm going to need some advice on whether or not we can manage it."

"Humph! I should think so! You certainly have no experi . . ." Mrs. Dubois stumbled to a halt. Even she was reluctant to let family skeletons out of their closets.

"It's all right, Mother. Charlotte knows why I was unable to be a debutante. The question is, how much time, effort, and money does it take? Can Jonathan and I manage to present her to society while we are spending most of our time on Edisto Island?"

"No, you probably can't," Mrs. Dubois said, "but I can. Don't look so stricken, Charlotte. If this is what you want, we'll try to make it happen."

"But, Grandmother, don't fathers usually present their daughters at their coming out? I mean—not that I'm not grateful for your offer—but won't Father have to be there?"

"Of course, and so he shall, or I'll know the reason why! However, men are useless during the debutante season except for their formal functions. A father presents his daughter at the final Grand Ball and dances with her one time. Then he is expected to disappear, and most fathers are delighted to do exactly that. He's not needed again except to pay the bills. The debutante also needs a beau to escort her during the formal dances. Other than that, the season is a women's affair, and, if a mother is uncomfortable in her role or unavailable, it is not unusual for a grandmother or aunt to fill in now and then. We'll be able to handle it all quite nicely."

"How many events are there, Grandmother?"

"There will be an introductory ladies' tea in the summer, an evening garden party or two once fall starts, and however many balls the local social mavens choose to present. The only one that really counts, however, is the Grand Ball, which will be held at the New Year. That one is always scheduled during the holidays to be sure that enough presentable young men are home from college and available for escort duty.

"You'll need a frilly tea dress and a formal white ball gown, but my seamstresses will be able to handle those. Other than that, you'll need to be prepared to smile prettily, make pleasant chitchat with lecherous old men who come out to ogle the young ones, and be able to nibble at your food without spilling anything on your gown. I presume you can do all that. Except for the beau, of course. Do you have anyone in mind, Susan? Does young Johnny have a suitably presentable friend?"

"I have someone in mind, Grandmother."

"You do?" Mother and grandmother alike looked startled.

"I haven't been living in a convent, you know, and my friends have brothers. I'd really like to pick my own beau if he's going to play that big a role in my social life."

"And who, exactly, are we talking about?"

"Peter Rogers. Peter Middleton Rogers, to be exact. He's a Middleton cousin. His sister Grace takes French lessons with me, and Peter often comes by to walk her home. We've had several lovely talks, and he has asked if I am allowed to entertain gentlemen callers. So far, I've told him no, but if I'm a debutante . . ."

"What about his family? Have we met his parents?"

"No, Mother, I don't think so. His father is a lawyer, and for years they lived in Columbia where Mr. Rogers did something with the state government. They've just moved back to Charleston to be nearer Mrs. Rogers's family, who, as I've said, are a branch of the Middletons. They're quite respectable—I've even seen them at the Circular Church recently. You'll like Peter, too, I hope. He's very tall and handsome, with perfect manners, an infectious grin, a great conversationalist, a—"

"Enough. We get the idea! He does indeed sound wonderful, but we will have to meet the family before the debutante season gets underway."

"Of course. I'll try to introduce you at church for starters. So that's as good as settled. But I'm still not sure how we can do all this. If the family is living on Edisto Island . . ."

"You'll live with me during the season," Mrs. Dubois said with a smile. "I will be happy for your company, provided you behave yourself. The early events will all take place before your parents move to Harbor View, so your mother will be here for the tea and opening suppers. I will insist that the family come back to Charleston for Christmas and the New Year anyway, so that will take care of the Grand Ball."

"Oh, Grandmother, how can I thank you?"

"Well, you can start by making life easier for your mother while she's making all these new arrangements. And you must promise that you won't be too disappointed if the season gets cancelled all together."

"What?"

"It's a possibility, darling. With all the war talk, it's hard to know when some radical politician is going to make a foolish statement and set off a conflagration."

"You don't really think there is going to be a war, do you? That would spoil everything!"

"It would do a great deal more than that," Susan warned. "I can't even bring myself to imagine what it would be like."

"I'm afraid we are headed toward war, and time is running out to put a stop to it. However, I don't think it will break out until after we know the results of the presidential election in November. I'm counting on nothing happening until after the first of the year. That's why I wanted to encourage Charlotte to make her debut this season. There may not be another chance."

7

A Fly in the Ointment
November 6, 1860

It was Election Day, but the question of who might become the next president of the United States was not troubling Susan on this afternoon. She was, of course, interested in a non-involved sort of way, but she figured she had enough to do without worrying about a decision in which she had no voice. At the moment, she was relaxing on the front porch of the house at Harbor View, enjoying a breeze that was still warm and listening to the sound of small waves lapping at the shore. She had not realized how happy she would be to revisit her childhood home again. This was the house in which she had grown up for half of every year, and it was full of pleasant memories. Her greatest concern at this juncture was to be sure that her family enjoyed their stay here as much as she was going to. Mentally she reviewed the family, checking to make sure each member was pleased with the change.

Jonathan had been caught in a whirlwind ever since they arrived. So far, he had not started to hold classes for any of the older neighborhood children. He had all he could handle as he tried to learn what was involved in a cotton harvest. As their carriage passed the first cotton field on their arrival, Jonathan had leaned forward in alarm. "Look," he said. "The slaves are already out picking cotton. We must be very late. I had hoped to be here in time to see to the picking from the start."

"Then you would have had to come a month or more ago," Susan had answered. "Sea Island cotton is different in that it doesn't all ripen at once. It's usual to see blossoms, developing bolls, and fully open cotton all on the same stem. And this fine cotton has to be picked as soon as it opens, to keep the long fibers from being damaged by the weather. The picking probably started in September and will continue until Christmas or beyond. The pickers move through the fields and then start all over again, making maybe ten or twelve passes over the same ground. You'll have plenty of chances to observe the process."

Jonathan was equally fascinated with the slave women's task as they spread the picked cotton on the drying floor and then painstakingly picked over it to remove leaves, debris, and yellowed fibers. He watched, enthralled, as they passed the cleaned bolls through a barrel-like object called a whipper that gently shook the remaining dirt and broken fibers out. Then came the ginning, which used rollers and comb-like teeth to separate seeds from fiber, followed by a final sorting, or moting. The process ended with trained slaves packing the cotton into bales by hand so as not to damage the fibers. Jonathan followed the process step by step, asking questions at every stage and taking careful notes.

The teacher has become a student, Susan thought to herself as she listened to her husband recite his lessons to her every night. He was learning volumes, and Susan knew not to display her own understanding of the cotton grower's art. She simply smiled, nodded, and took a quiet delight in Jonathan's enthusiasm. If he was enjoying his new career, Susan could relax in her own contentment.

From her mother's frequent letters, Susan was also comforted by the assurance that Charlotte was blossoming as a Charleston debutante. The sulky teenager had turned into a self-assured young woman, according to Elizabeth Dubois. She handled herself with poise during the many social occasions in which she was on display. She could charm the mavens of social propriety with questions about their own lives, flirt with their husbands without raising an eyebrow, compliment her peers with complete sincerity, and cling to her escort's arm with the perfect appearance of innocence.

When Charlotte herself wrote to her mother, she enthusiastically described how kind and helpful Peter and his parents were. Mr. and Mrs. Rogers had attended every one of the debutante events, and Peter had escorted her faithfully. "I'm not sure I could have done all this without him," Charley had written. "When I get scared or start to worry, Peter always knows just what to say to calm me down. And when he offers me his arm, and I take it, I feel as if I could conquer the world."

She's officially in love, Susan thought, *even if she hasn't said so. She's awfully young, but then, so was I when I met Jonathan. I wish we knew the boy better, but I'll have to trust the judgment of those who are seeing them together. We'll work on getting to know him over Christmas. That will be soon enough. For now*, Susan breathed a sigh, relieved that her sometimes-wayward daughter was maturing so effortlessly.

At college, young Johnny was developing into a full-fledged scholar, if his letters home were to be accepted at face value. He had always loved books, Susan remembered, but never before had she seen him taking such delight in the concepts behind the words. He and his classmates at the boarding house stayed up late most nights, discussing and debating the ideas they had encountered in their lecture halls. They were charmed by the wisdom of ancient philosophers and excited by the new discoveries of modern science. Could they reconcile the two? They seemed determined to try.

Both Susan and Jonathan realized, of course, that Johnny was not telling his parents about all the high jinks that he and his mates indulged in, but he seemed to be spending a satisfactory amount of time in the college library, and some of the papers he sent home were surprisingly eloquent. Jonathan took responsibility for Johnny's education as his duty and wrote his son long letters encouraging him to concentrate on matters of history and constitutional law. By some unspoken agreement, discussions of slavery itself did not enter into their correspondence, for which Susan was grateful.

She was also pleased with the college's stance on the military training of its students. Ever since the Guardhouse Riot in 1856, the Cadet Corps had been banned, and the board of directors was determined to keep it that way. War talk on campus echoed the threats students heard at home, but professors refused to encourage it. Every fall the subject of reconstituting the Cadet Corps came up and, just as quickly, was buried under a discussion of curriculum or plans for a spring debate season. *I'm so glad we convinced Johnny to go to Columbia*, Susan decided. *His removal from Charleston has dropped him into a world where controversy misses him, where he does not have to think about fighting his fellow citizens—or his father. We're very lucky!*

Then there's Eddie, Susan thought. *And what a wonderful change in him this move has wrought!* Eddie had always been a loner—too young to keep up with his older siblings, too old to be amused by the childish interests of his little sisters and brothers. He wasn't much interested in books or music. He didn't make friends easily. He became tongue-tied when an adult tried to make casual conversation. At home on Logan Street, he could most often be found in the stable yard, stroking a horse on the nose or following the stable hands around wistfully as they went about their tasks.

Ah, but here, Susan reflected, here he is the oldest for a change, and he has found a new interest in the whole process of cotton production. At first, Jonathan had worried about how to continue Eddie's education while he himself was busy with plantation matters. He had solved the problem by taking Eddie with him and presenting him with science lessons and mathematics problems as they arose around agricultural matters. Now the two of them were busy from dawn to dusk. Eddie happily trailed his father, keeping copious notes in a small moleskin-bound notebook and puzzling over new solutions to age-old problems. Most recently, Eddie had been speculating about the feasibility of using the cows' milk from the barnyard to begin a cheese-making operation. Susan did not understand most of the details of these discussions, but she listened in as often as she could for the sheer pleasure of hearing her second son talk like a grown-up.

As for the smaller children, the move to the plantation had been painless. Jamey, of course, was still in the nursery, and as long as his meals came regularly and he received a lot of attention from his caregivers, he didn't much mind where he was. The three other children had settled happily into their new schoolroom as soon as they realized that their teacher was still there. Mary Sue had pouted for a couple of days over the fact that she was not to have her own pony. But once the family arrived at Harbor View, she discovered a litter of piglets and some baby ducklings just waiting for her attention. She soon had named them all and visited them regularly with table scraps and lots of loving.

Becca had always been her mother's daughter, Susan realized. Quiet, shy, eager to please, she moved like a small shadow among the more turbulent comings and goings of her siblings. Give her a book, and she would read it until someone took it out of her hands. If she came to the end before that happened, she simply started over, always finding pleasure and escape in the written word. She had music in her soul as well. She loved to listen to her mother play the melodeon and could barely wait until her legs were long enough to reach the pedals. Susan had found a tall stool for her to use and had started to teach her the scales. As she did with a book, Becca happily ran her chubby fingers up and down the keys for as long as her mother could keep pumping the bellows.

Robbie was still something of a mystery. At the age of five, he was old enough to start his lessons, but in many ways he was still a baby. Quiet by nature, he was an observer of those around him, and his behavior reflected that of his sisters. Eddie was too much older to serve as a role model, and Jamey was still in the nursery. Robbie must feel rather alone in this large family, Susan realized. Because he was quiet, everyone seemed to overlook him. We need to start paying more attention to him, Susan decided, but all in all he seems happy enough.

All was well in the Grenville household, Susan assured herself. The children were happy and healthy. Jonathan was engrossed in his new career. The weather was good for the cotton crop, and the old plantation house had absorbed her family without discomfort. She stretched her arms above her head and gulped in the soft, briny sea air. The move had been right for every member of their family. This is as close to heaven as it gets, she thought. I could stay here forever.

But it was November 6, 1860. Election Day. And the lanky Kentuckian who had campaigned on a presidential platform of no new slave states was about to deliver his country a potentially fatal blow.

8

The Earth Shifts
December 20, 1860

"Jonathan, does it seem to you that there are more people in the streets of Charleston than usual?" Susan sat erect, looking to one side and then the other as their carriage made its way through the narrow streets of their old neighborhood.

"Yes, there certainly are, and it worries me."

"It could just be Christmas excitement, I suppose."

"No, there are almost no women and children out and about. These are young and old men, business leaders and laborers. Something is afoot, something that is drawing the attention of all the city's varied inhabitants."

"I don see no black in dat mix, Massa." Hector spoke up from his driver's seat. "Dis be a white man crowd, sho nuf."

"They're all moving up toward the Market. Let's avoid Meeting Street and cut over Rutledge to Tradd," Jonathan suggested. "I'm glad we're not trying to open the Logan Street house for Christmas. We should find Mrs. Dubois's neighborhood more peaceful."

"Yes, please, Hector," Susan added. "I just want to get to my mother's house and see our two long-lost children. It's been a hard day's journey, and we don't need crowds of people, whatever they are celebrating."

The welcome awaiting them at the Dubois house was as understated as the atmosphere in the center of town had been raucous. Elizabeth Dubois met her daughter and son-in-law with embraces but few words. She hugged each of the children and sent them tumbling into the parlor to see the Christmas tree the housemaids were decorating. Then she turned to Susan with a cautionary finger to her lips.

"Mother, what's going on? People are rushing every which way outside, and you look as if you are expecting the roof to fall in at any minute."

"It's a difficult day. I'm very relieved that you are here now and safely out of that crowd."

"Safe? Is there danger?" Susan had caught the whiff of fear that permeated her mother's words. "Where are Johnny and Charley? Are they all right? Are they here?"

"They're fine, as far as I know."

"As far as you know!" Susan's voice was taking on a touch of hysteria. "Where are they?"

"Charlotte and Peter are at a meeting called for all the debutantes. I don't know what's afoot, but I suspect they are being told that the Grand Ball has been cancelled."

"Oh, no! Charley will be devastated!"

"Susan, your daughter has grown up a great deal in the last few weeks. One of the changes you'll find in her is that she no longer answers to that tomboy nickname. If you want to get off on the right foot with her, you'll start calling her Charlotte. And, for that matter, your little Johnny is about to become a man. They are both trying very hard to be adults in a world that is crumbling all around them. Don't treat them like children. They have enough on their minds." Elizabeth was more in control of herself when she found something about which to chide her daughter, but Susan was not about to be distracted.

"And just where is Johnny?"

"He left here some time ago with Alex Croft and young John Calhoun. The Calhoun boy said he knew a back way into St. Andrew's Hall so that they could witness the vote."

Now Jonathan was alarmed. "A vote? About what?"

"The Secession Convention is meeting there this afternoon."

"But I thought it had been decided that any decision about secession was to be made in the state legislature."

"Yes, but that was before smallpox broke out in Columbia. That's how Johnny got home from school early, too, by the way. The college sent the students home, and the delegates decided to move their convention here to Charleston, just to be safe."

Jonathan and Susan looked at one another, silently agreeing that their idyllic fall on Edisto Island had isolated them from what was really going on in the rest of South Carolina.

"Is the vote really in question?" Jonathan asked.

"No, of course not! It's been a foregone conclusion ever since that Lincoln fellow got himself elected. But the delegates, to give them credit, are all bending over backward to appear impartial. They represent the finest families in the state, and they are taking their responsibilities seriously. They understand, from what the newspapers tell us, that this vote to secede from the United States is an epoch-making one."

"It is that, and one that may affect every one of us badly. I fear the outcome of this day."

"I'm sure you do, Jonathan." Elizabeth's voice was suddenly harsh. "But it really is a Southern decision—a matter for Southerners alone."

"Mother!"

"Never mind. Here come Charlotte and Peter. Maybe they can tell us more about what's happening."

But as the three adults watched from the doorway, Charlotte and Peter stopped in the street, their whole attention riveted on each other. Peter was gesturing emphatically while Charlotte kept shaking her head, her defiant chin thrust out as she stared up at him. Without warning, she slapped him across the cheek and ran toward the house. She burst through the door, sobbing, and headed for the stairs.

"Charlotte? Darling?" Susan's concerned voice finally caught her attention. The young woman turned, saw her mother, and threw herself into her arms. "Momma! Oh, Momma! Whatever am I to do?"

Susan was in tears as well, though for another reason. It had been years since her rebellious daughter had called her "Momma." All she wanted to do for the moment was to cradle her daughter and protect her from whatever threatened her happiness.

Eventually, of course, the emotional turmoil settled itself, and the whole story came tumbling out.

"Yes, Grandmother, the Debutante Grand Ball has been cancelled. According to Mrs. Wentworth, who was in charge of it, the feeling was that Charleston will need to expend all its energy and money on the coming war effort, not waste it on a night of frivolity. And that's all right with me. I've about had my fill of prancing around in that frilly dress, simpering and being sweet to grumpy old men and crotchety old ladies. Oh, not you,

Gran. You know the ones I mean. And it's been fun. But I've had enough, particularly now that I know . . ." The tears started to flow again.

"Know what, darling?"

"Know . . . know that Peter cares more for his mates and their silly posturing than he does for me."

"And you know that because . . .?"

"Because he's leaving school and joining the militia! He says that some of the professors at the College of Charleston have already signed on with the Charleston Battalion, and his whole senior class is going to petition to be given a leave of absence so that they can join the war effort. He's going to go off and fight and get himself killed, and I'll be left here alone to live out my life as an old maid!"

"Whoa! Whoa!" Jonathan jumped into this unfamiliar territory. "Aren't you getting ahead of yourself, young lady? First of all, there's no war—not yet, at any rate. Second, just because the students ask for leave doesn't mean they'll get it. Third, there's no guarantee that any of the local militias will accept a bunch of fresh-faced children, and there's certainly nothing to make you think Peter will be getting himself killed. And, finally, any talk of becoming an old maid assumes questions of marriage that you are far too young to be contemplating."

"I'm not too young!" Charlotte was sobbing again.

"Jonathan, be quiet." Susan and Elizabeth spoke with a single voice. "This is girl talk," Susan added.

"It's war talk, and I hate what it's doing to Peter! Why do people have to go around stirring up trouble?"

"My dear child," Mrs. Dubois said, "there is much you still have to learn about men, and particularly about men and their relationship with guns. You cannot offer a man a chance to fight and expect him to turn his back on it. That would label him a coward, both in his own mind and in the minds of everyone around him. Poor Peter. It sounds to me as if you offered him a choice—be a soldier or be your beau. What did you expect him to say? Of course he has to stand with his mates. Believe me, you wouldn't want him if he didn't."

"That's not fair. I don't count at all? You're saying I just have to accept it? And I'm supposed to be happy about it?"

"Hallo!" A familiar voice echoed from the back hall. "Mother? Father? Are you here yet?" Johnny came bounding into the parlor, flushed with excitement and seeming to fill the room with his energy.

"Father." He stretched out his hand, leaving Jonathan befuddled for a moment at the idea of shaking his son's hand rather than kissing him on the cheek. Awkwardly he took the boy's hand, and then, shaking his head, pulled him into a hug that his son gratefully accepted.

"And Mother—beautiful as always."

Susan wasted no time in embracing her son. "I've missed you so much," she murmured, "but you look wonderful. College agrees with you."

"That it does, but give full credit to this amazing day. I have never been more proud of my birthplace. I wish you could have been there for the reading of the Ordinance of Secession!"

"I'm sure we'll want to hear all about it. Has the decision been made, then?" Jonathan's stern face belied the enthusiasm he was trying to convey in his voice.

"Well, it's not completely done. The president of the convention read out the ordinance and called for a voice vote. After 169 delegates voted in favor, he made the formal announcement: 'The union now subsisting between South Carolina and other States, under the name of The United States of America, is hereby dissolved.' I'll never forget those words. The hall at St. Andrews proved too small for the witnessing crowds, so everyone is moving to Independence Hall for the official signing, which won't happen until 6:30 this evening. That delay gave me time to come by the house and check on your safe arrival."

"You're going back?"

"Of course. I must see the signing for myself. This is a historic moment. You can all come with me, if you like."

"I don't think that's a good idea—for any number of reasons. You forget that a Yankee might not be welcome in such a crowd. Besides, we're tired, and we seem to have a minor crisis going on right here."

"Crisis? What?" Johnny looked around for his younger siblings and then caught sight of his sister, curled up with grief on the settee. "So what have we here? This wouldn't have anything to do with what's going on outside, would it?"

"You mean your celebration? Hardly!" Charlotte sniffled and glared at her brother just because he seemed so happy.

"No, actually, I was referring to the young man who is sitting cross-legged at the foot of our front steps with his head in his hands."

"What? Peter's still outside?"

"Apparently. At least I assume that's who he is. He never noticed me. He can't seem to take his eyes off the front door."

"Oh!" Charlotte slowly uncurled herself and walked to the window, carefully pulling the curtain aside just far enough to see out. "Oh, my. He didn't leave me after all." Dashing the last of the tears from her cheeks, she walked to the door, hesitated, and then stepped out onto the porch.

Jonathan started to move after her, but Susan put out her hand in restraint. "Let them be. It's not a moment for anyone but the two people involved. You'll know the outcome soon enough, just as I'm sure we'll hear when the Ordinance of Secession becomes final."

As if on cue, two cannons boomed and church bells began to peal. In the distance, the first of several brass bands struck up their music, and lanterns flickered on throughout the neighborhood as celebrants poured into the streets.

"We should be feeling the earth shift beneath our feet any moment now," Jonathan remarked.

Elizabeth Dubois looked at him in surprise and then remarked, "No, that was yesterday. We really did have a small earthquake yesterday afternoon. Perhaps it was warning us of the momentous changes that were coming."

9

Christmas Sidelined
December 1860

Eighteen-sixty was the year Charleston forgot to celebrate Christmas. It wasn't intentional. The city was just so full of secession frenzy that every normal holiday celebration turned itself into another occasion for patriotic music, brass bands, fancy dress, and pealing church bells—all in honor of the grand occasion of independence from the hated United States of America.

Even the Grenvilles, who were doing their best to ignore the political rhetoric, found it hard to be festive about anything else. Casual greetings on the street turned into reports of the latest developments. Seamstresses were overloaded with orders for military dress uniforms. Church services emphasized God's approval of South Carolina's decision. Bands forgot to play Christmas music and turned to marching tunes instead. Impromptu parties popped up all over town and turned into raucous displays of military prowess.

Susan encouraged her family to stay off the streets, preferring to hold them all as close as possible for a little while longer. While others seemed to view secession as an open doorway to the future, Susan saw it as the end of life as she had known it.

She missed having access to a melodeon during their visit to her mother's house. Perhaps pumping away at the pedals might have worked off some of her tension. Instead, she plunked away at the old piano in the parlor, but the tunes she played from memory were mournful ones.

On Christmas Day, Mrs. Dubois put on her usual holiday dinner, and the children pitched into it with enthusiasm, while Susan and Jonathan picked at their food and envied the young their ability to live in the moment. Surrounded by platters of ham and roast turkey, oysters, corn pudding, sweet potatoes, green beans and field peas, and rice with gravy, along with the promise of blackberry pie, gingerbread men, and fruitcake to come, the children vied with one another to see how much they could eat. Susan looked at the laden table and wondered if she would ever see another such holiday meal.

Once dessert had been served, young Johnny leaned back in his chair and patted his waistline. "Grandmother Dubois, your cook has outdone herself again, but I fear I will have to change the measurements I sent in for my cadet uniform. I'm sure I have gained several inches." He meant it only as a joke, but his words terrified his mother.

"What uniform?" Susan demanded.

"The South Carolina College Cadets have been reinstated. I told Father, so I assumed you knew."

Susan glared at her husband, all the while realizing that he had only shielded her from more bad news. "I'm afraid I didn't. What exactly does reinstatement imply?"

"I don't know all the details myself. John Calhoun's maternal grandfather is on the board of directors, so what I've heard has come through the Calhouns. Apparently, the board met on the day after the secession vote, because nearly all the college officials were here in town for the occasion. They decided that the college needed to start up military training again as part of the curriculum. All the Cadet Corps paraphernalia is still stored in the basement of the library and will be brought out when we get back. We'll be getting brand new uniforms, however, and all returning students have been told to send in their measurements so the tailors can get busy."

"Uniforms for what purpose?"

"We'll be getting parade dress so that we can make a grand impression when we march. From what Calhoun tells me, our uniforms will be closely modeled after the ones used at West Point—trousers with a side stripe, long gray coats with tails, three rows of brass buttons, and braided chevrons."

"And that's all you think you are going to be doing—marching?"

"Yes, Mother. Please don't look so worried. I saw a partial list of our new rules. They say that we cannot be called to active service except by the president."

"Meaning the president of the college? Or the president of our new country—who, I might remind you, has not even been elected yet." Jonathan's worried frown now matched his wife's expression.

"Not the college president," Johnny guessed. "I think they mean something like a general draft in the case of actual warfare."

"What else do these new rules have to say?"

"The ones I read said that we will not be allowed access to actual weapons without proven need, and that we will not be allowed to hold company suppers or other festivities. We'll simply be learning about military discipline, close-order drilling, and the conventions of righteous warfare."

"Righteous warfare? Is there such a thing?" Susan's question hung in the air, unanswered.

At last Charlotte broke the silence. "Since we seem to be dropping bombshells, I have one to add."

"An unfortunate figure of speech, Charlotte. Bombshells are not proper dinner table topics, particularly at this moment. May we presume that you have an announcement?"

"An announcement, then," Charlotte said, more than a little amused. "Or perhaps I ought to form it as a request. May I invite Peter to join us tomorrow evening for supper? From past Christmases, I remember that we usually gather to pick at the dinner leftovers, which always taste better the second time around, anyway. Peter and I have a little something we'd like to discuss with you, and that kind of informal setting would be perfect."

"Of course, dear. Your friends are always welcome here."

Charlotte beamed at her grandmother, but Susan watched her expression with growing unease. Her two oldest children seemed to have a talent for creating crises in tandem.

The next evening, Peter Rogers announced himself at the front door. Despite her worry, Susan smiled to see that he looked freshly washed, his hair still a bit damp and his cheeks reddened from a recent shave. He was also dressed rather formally in a stiff white shirt and cravat.

Charlotte glowed as she greeted him, but the two were careful not to touch. They had little to say to each other as they settled in at the dining room table. Since everyone else seemed to be waiting to hear what Charlotte wanted to talk about, conversation faltered except for requests to pass the potatoes.

Jonathan, always uncomfortable with silence, cleared his throat. "Peter, Charlotte tells us that you are considering leaving school to join a militia."

"Uh, well, I was . . . I was thinking about it, yes, but not any more. We seniors approached the College of Charleston a couple of days ago, and they provided a reasonable solution. We are not going to be allowed to take a leave of absence to go off to war—"

"Because there is no war!" Jonathan could not resist jumping into the convoluted explanation.

"Yes, sir—I mean, no, sir. Since the war hasn't started, we're to go back to school and finish our studies as quickly as possible. We can join a militia group, if we can find someone who is willing to take us on, but we can only participate in their drills and other functions after school hours. The provisions may change if war is actually declared and our units get called up to fight, but for now this is the best way we can serve."

"Sounds to me much like the path that South Carolina College is following," Johnny remarked. "I've heard it said that the best way we can serve our state right now is by getting our education so that we are prepared to build our state after any war is over."

"That's right, Johnny. That's a great way to look at it." Jonathan looked at his son with pride. "Any nation will need its teachers and doctors and lawyers in order to rebuild after the war."

"I still don't like all this war talk," Susan said. "Sometimes people make something happen just by expecting it to do so. I wish everyone would just relax and think well of our neighbors to the north instead of expecting to be attacked at any moment. Maybe that will never happen."

"There's a fine line between being optimistic and being oblivious to real danger, my love." Jonathan reached over to pat his wife's hand, but she jerked it away in irritation.

"Uh, excuse me, but Peter and I said we had something to discuss with you all, and this isn't exactly it. I hate the way war talk dominates every conversation!" Charlotte was half standing to get the attention of her parents.

Peter grinned at her and spoke under his breath. "But it is all connected. You might as well admit it."

She sank back into her chair. "All right. Do you want to tell them, or shall I?"

"I think it's my job." Peter took a deep breath before he started. "Mr. and Mrs. Grenville, I have the great honor to . . . to ask if you . . . will allow me to marry your daughter." The final words came out in a rush.

"What!"

"Surely this is not the time to . . ."

"It's exactly the time, Mother." Charlotte sounded very grown-up. "We don't know what the future will hold for any of us. We may not have a future. Now, more than ever, we have only the present moment, and I don't intend to let it get away."

"But—"

"I know I'm still in school, sir, but I have a small trust fund on which to live." Peter addressed his remarks now to Jonathan. "I can support Charlotte, and, whatever I am called upon to do in the future, I'll be better at it if I know that she is by my side."

"How romantic!" Johnny commented and received a kick in the shin from his sister in retaliation.

"But you're both too young to make a decision like this," Mrs. Dubois chimed into the discussion.

"Gran! You let Mother marry when she was younger than I am."

"Well, yes, but . . ."

Now it was Susan's turn to nudge her mother under the table. "I don't think we need to go into all that right now."

Mrs. Dubois was not to be dissuaded. "That's not why you two need to get married, is it?"

"No!" Charlotte flushed a deep red, while Peter looked puzzled. "There is a great deal of difference between our circumstances and those of my parents twenty years ago. But the most important difference is that—like it or not—there is a war coming. If we do not marry now, we may never get another chance."

"But a wedding takes time and preparation. When you say 'now,' what exactly do you mean?"

"I've already studied the calendar, Mother. I don't want this to interfere with Peter's finishing up his college work, so we're not planning to run off tomorrow. And I do want a lovely wedding, just as I've always dreamed of having. After all, I have a beautiful white gown just waiting to be used." She laughed. "I didn't mind seeing the Grand Ball cancelled, but I'm determined to wear that dress!"

"The two of you seem to have this all planned out, but you're going to have to take into consideration the fact that the family will be living out on Edisto for the rest of the winter," Jonathan remarked.

"Of course we've considered that, Father. You've always taught me to be logical, haven't you? So how about April 6?"

"What about Lent? When's Easter? You can't marry during a liturgical period." Susan was busy counting on her fingers.

"Easter occurs early—on March 31. So Lent begins in mid-February, and we couldn't be ready by then, anyhow. But April 6 is clear of other holidays, and the cotton crop should be well along by then. Most Edisto families come back to Charleston in early April. Peter will be finished with classwork by then, too."

"We seem to have been outvoted by logic, my dear. Shall we give the happy couple our formal approval?" Jonathan stood and reached out to take his wife's hand, squeezing it to warn her to control her motherly instincts. He then shook Peter's hand while Susan embraced her daughter.

"I think we need a toast," announced Mrs. Dubois. "Tillie, send Marcus to the wine cellar for a bottle of champagne. And bring out six—no, seven of our best champagne flutes. Then you can take the little ones up to the nursery, if you please."

"Seven flutes?" Susan looked around in puzzlement. "For . . .?"

"Quit acting like a mother hen, Susan. Young Eddie has been sitting here quiet as a mouse through this whole discussion. He deserves to celebrate his sister's engagement with a small taste of champagne."

Eddie looked flustered but pleased, and his older brother gave him a grin of approval. For the rest of this one evening, the Grenvilles allowed themselves to shut away the outside world and enjoy their newly expanding family.

10

A Wedding and a Call to Duty
April 1861

"I'm so glad we could come back to Charleston a little early in the summer season, so that Charlotte could have the wedding she dreamed of." Susan sighed, sounding a bit melancholic as she lay in bed in the dark. "It was a lovely wedding, wasn't it? I can still close my eyes and see Charlotte in that wonderful white gown, with eyes for no one but her Peter. And he, so handsome, even if he was wearing his new military uniform. That bothered me, I admit. Jonathan, do you think he wore the uniform just to let us know that he intends to be a Confederate soldier?"

"I think you're overthinking it, my dear. That uniform was undoubtedly the fanciest suit of clothing he owned, and he was honoring his bride by wearing it. From the looks of those two, they had nothing at all on their minds but each other."

"I suppose you're right, but still . . . one doesn't wear a military uniform unless the plan is to go off to war."

"Go off and fight? In that getup? Really, Susan! These militia units are just playacting at the moment. When it comes time to fight, you'll see them setting out in the drabbest, loosest, most comfortable clothing they can find. You don't wear patent leather boots with spats to go tromping off through the swamps of South Carolina. You wear heavy brogues and pants that can withstand a good dunking in pluff mud."

They lay quietly for a few more minutes, but Susan was too keyed up from the emotions of the day to sleep. "You still think we're going to war, don't you?"

"I don't see how it can be avoided."

"I've been hopeful. I was frightened when that fool Major Anderson slipped his troops into Fort Sumter right after Christmas. That could have given all our secessionist friends an excuse to start hostilities, but they didn't. Then there was that horrible day back in January when a Citadel cadet fired a cannon ball across the bow of a ship headed for Fort Sumter. I thought surely that was the shot that would start the war, but it didn't. So I've been trying to believe that all the war talk is just rhetoric. That's possible, isn't it?"

"No, I can't agree. You have to look at those events in perspective. Back in the days right after the vote for secession, it was indeed all talk. South Carolina didn't have a country or a constitution or a government or an army or any support from her neighbors. But conditions are different now. Six other states have joined the rebellion. They've formed a government and inaugurated a president and vice president of the Confederate States of America. They've written a constitution and sent out the initial call for 100,000 volunteer soldiers. This is a new country now, and a fully-fledged country is a much bigger threat to the United States than South Carolina was when she stood all alone."

"But we haven't made any moves against the United States, other than declaring our independence from them."

"That's not quite so, either. The United States has a military arsenal right here in town, and the Charleston Battalion has been keeping pickets around it ever since December 20, making sure that those weapons cannot be extracted and turned against the Confederates. When Anderson led his men out of Fort Moultrie, Charleston militiamen moved right in to strengthen the fortifications both there and at Fort Johnson. Seizing federal property and arming it against the federal government could be taken as an act of war any time President Lincoln chooses to do so. And now that he has been officially inaugurated, I suspect that he will feel the need to make a decisive move. He'll have to do that soon if his presidency is to have any credibility."

"Sometimes, Jonathan, you really do sound like a Yankee. I can't tell which side you're on. You keep living here and behaving like a cotton planter, but when you talk about the South, I never hear you say 'we.' It's always 'they.' Are you loyal to the Confederacy or not?"

"Sometimes I'm not sure myself. I wish . . ."

"Wish what?"

"Wish that the vote of secession had never happened. Wish that adults on both sides could accept an honorable compromise. Wish that I was not torn between the land and family that nurtured me and the new land and family I have found here. Wish that I could say that I am now a true Southerner and not feel guilty about it."

"You're frightening me. Do you really feel guilty about marrying into a Southern family? Are you thinking of leaving us?"

"Oh, no, no, of course not, my love. My tightest bonds are right here at your side. I could never leave you. I just feel a pang of regret now and then for a time when loyalties were simpler."

"I, for one, would refuse to consider making a choice between family and country. But I do understand regrets, and I'm trying to understand how you must feel."

"And what do you have to regret? Not your decision to marry a Yankee, I hope."

"Never! Don't be silly. But I do regret that young Johnny was not here for his sister's big day. I know he wrote that the South Carolina cadets were all taking their exams early and that he couldn't be excused from classes, but it seems such a pity to miss a family occasion."

"Your motherly instincts make a hash of your priorities sometimes, my love." For a brief moment Jonathan felt anger swell in him. This woman, whom he loved so deeply, had a shallow side that disturbed him. He had been about to confess his deepest concerns about being a Yankee in a Southern family. Then, suddenly, she had turned the conversation back to trivial matters. Swallowing his impatience, he said, "Johnny would have been here if he could, but he knows how important his education is right now."

"I know. See? We all must have regrets, mustn't we? And all we can do is try to choose the course of action that seems right at the time. So I forgive my son for missing his sister's wedding. But I don't regret that he is safely at the college, buried in books and intellectual pursuits, for as long as the rest of this crazy world keeps up its insistence on making trouble."

Susan's idealistic wishes were not to be realized. Just three days later, a small black child delivered a note to the back door of the house on Logan Street. He handed it to Sarah, saying, "De young massa, he gib me dis note fuh carry tuh he fambly."

Sarah took it formally, gave the child a pat on the head, and said, "Tankee," before she brought it to Susan.

> *Dear Mother and Father,*
>
> *I hope this letter finds you well. I am scribbling a few words while riding a train, which is making my writing a bit shaky. I want you to know that my fellow cadets and I are on our way to Charleston to answer President Davis's call to action. It turns out that was the reason the college scheduled our exams early. They have released us. Most of our professors have also left. We were scrambling around to find a way to get to Charleston, but one of the professors lent our cadet corps $100.00 to purchase train tickets for all of us.*
>
> *We are to report to Hibernian Hall for assignments once we arrive. I will try to let you know where I will be stationed, but I do not think I will be allowed to come home. I will not need any clothes because we are all wearing our uniforms. Such is the military life.*
>
> *Fondly, your son Johnny*

Susan sat paralyzed. Her little Johnny was leading a "military life." He was waiting for orders and going to war. "No," she whispered to herself. "Not my baby with a rifle in his hands. Not my baby facing cannon fire." She tried to swallow and couldn't. Fear coursed through her veins.

Desperate to stop Johnny from following his set path, she ran downstairs to where Jonathan was tutoring several teenagers. She thrust the letter at him, saying, "Do something! You've got to stop him!"

Jonathan clenched his jaw as he apologized to his students. "Work on these problems among yourselves for a few moments. I seem to have a family crisis."

Then he grasped Susan's elbow and turned her back through the door into the hallway. "Don't you ever do that when I'm in the middle of teaching!"

"Let go. Your precious students can rot, for all I care. This is your son!"

Only then did Jonathan open the letter. He read it slowly. "I see. What is it you think I can do about this?"

"Go down there. Find him. Bring him home!"

"No. Johnny's an adult, according to the law, and he is eligible for military service. I couldn't stop him even if I wanted to—which I don't."

"You want to see him killed?" Susan was still shouting at him.

"Of course not. I want to see him making his own decisions, as a man must."

"He's not a man. He's still a boy."

"Susan, you're wrong. He's over sixteen now. I've been trying to prepare you for this day, but your refusal to believe anything you don't like has clouded your judgment."

"How dare you!"

"I dare because I love you. I want you to face reality, because that's all we have. When you hide from the truth, the truth jumps up and slaps you. When you accept the truth of a situation, you can deal with it. And you must deal with the fact that we are at war—North and South."

"So we seem to be." Susan's eyes flashed in anger as she stared at her husband. "We're still North and South, too, aren't we? And here we are, at war with each other. This is what I really fear when I think about this whole secession business—that it will end up tearing our family apart."

"Then we must work to keep that from happening, and it appears it's up to me. I'm the outsider here—the 'Damned Yankee,' to quote young Declan McDermitt. But I love you, and I love this land. Our children have been raised in the South, and I've chosen to live my life here. So I'm more of a Southerner than I have cared to admit.

"You want to know how I feel about young Johnny going to war? Besides the normal fear of any parent? I'm proud of him. I want him to stand up for what he believes, and if that means he joins the Confederate Army to fight against the federal government, then so be it. He is my son, and I will support him in whatever he chooses to do. And to do so, I will support the Confederacy with every ounce of my being, and I will swallow any moral scruples that raise their annoying little heads. This damned conflict may tear apart the borders of America, but I will not let it tear apart my family!"

11

Firing the First Shots
April 12, 1861

The Grenvilles were shaken out of sleep in the early dawn of April 12. Susan clutched at her husband's shoulder as he tried to burrow under a pillow. "Jonathan, what was that boom? Is this the beginning of the war? Are we in danger?"

"It's cannon fire, I think, but it's fairly far away. No one is trying to blow us out of bed."

"But who's shooting? And at whom?"

"I have no idea, but we'll know as soon as it gets light." He walked to the window and peered through the curtains. "I see tracer shells off toward the harbor. Perhaps we can see more from our widow's walk. Want to come with me?"

"No! I've vowed never to go up there!"

"Why ever not?"

"Call me superstitious. I have no desire to be a widow, and I won't tempt fate by walking on a spot designed for a grieving widow."

"That is definitely superstition, but since I have no desire to make you a widow, either, I'll indulge you for the moment. Back in a jiffy."

In a few moments he returned. "It appears that the South Carolina forces are attacking Fort Sumter from several different vantage points. Guns are firing from Fort Moultrie and other batteries on Sullivan's Island, from Fort Johnson, and from Cummings Point. So far I have seen no return fire from Major Anderson's men."

"Fort Sumter is a federal fort, armed and manned by federal troops. Shooting at it is an act of war, then, isn't it?"

Jonathan sat down on the side of the bed and took his wife's hand, hoping to quiet the note of panic he heard in her voice. "Yes. I have heard talk that General Beauregard has been negotiating with Major Anderson for a peaceful evacuation of the fort. Those talks must have fallen apart. I don't think Beauregard would start shooting unless all hope of peace had been lost. We might as well dress and go outside. From what I can see, the streets are filling with spectators heading toward the harbor. We'll get a better idea of what is going on from there."

It was a gloomy morning, intermittent rain mixing with fog and the smoke from dozens of guns that surrounded the harbor. Even after sunrise, the light from tracer shells lit up the gloom of the low-hanging clouds. Susan hesitated at the steps of the piazza.

"No," she said, turning back toward the door. "These people look like they are headed off to a celebration or a show. I won't join them. I support my son's decision and the Confederate cause in general, but I'll be damned if I will enjoy it!"

"Susan! I don't think I've ever heard you use profanity before."

"I've never had so harsh a cause."

"Then I won't go, either. You have a valid objection. Let's have some coffee and hope to hear from our Johnny soon."

"Do you think he's among the troops who are attacking?"

"I doubt it. I've been stressing the fact that he is an adult, but the fact remains that he and his friends are very young adults, and a few days of college drilling will not make a soldier out of any of them."

"Well, if they are not to be allowed to fight, what is to become of them?"

"I don't know, but General Beauregard is not fool enough to turn a bunch of untrained recruits loose at the very beginning of the war. I'll see what I can find out. Later this morning, I'll walk over to Reverend Croft's house and see if he has heard anything from the boys."

David Croft had indeed talked to some of the college cadets. "They're all fine, as far as I know. I ran into a group of Alex's friends while walking to the church yesterday morning. They were hanging out on Meeting Street, hoping their fancy uniforms would catch the attention of some of Charleston's young ladies—without much success, I gathered."

"Are they being assigned anywhere?"

"They were about to be sent over to Sullivan's Island and put up in one of the inns near Fort Moultrie. They have been given guns to drill with but with strict orders not to fire them. I suspect they're over there now, marching up and down and watching the attack on Fort Sumter. I wouldn't worry about them, Jonathan," David said, slapping him on the back. "The boys have had a chance to offer their services to Governor Pickens, and they seem to be having a fine time playing at being soldiers. Give them a couple of more weeks in those long wool coats while the weather heats up, and they will be more than happy to return to the college."

Jonathan was relieved to know that the college cadets were safely beyond the reach of enemy guns, but Susan had found something more to worry about. Shortly after Jonathan returned from his walk, Charlotte arrived for a visit.

"Have you heard from Johnny, Mother?"

"Not since his initial note, but your father has learned that he is safe on Sullivan's Island. He's not involved in the fighting, and it appears that he and his friends will not be assigned to units yet. They will probably be headed back to school soon."

"I'm glad. It's bad enough that I have to worry about my husband. I don't want somebody shooting at my brother, too."

"Where is Peter?"

"You knew that he joined one of the local militias, didn't you? Right now, they just drill, but Peter thinks they are going to be getting artillery training soon. Major Huger is organizing an artillery battalion to strengthen the defenses on Hilton Head Island, and Peter expects to be picked to join that unit."

"What makes him think so?"

"It's all family connections. General Thomas Drayton is in line to take over the Third Military District, Department of the South, and the Draytons are good friends and neighbors of the Middletons. They're putting together an artillery battalion for Hampton's Legion, and Charleston is going to organize two companies for that battalion. Oh, I sound like I know what I'm talking about, but it's all so confusing. All I really know is that by next month, Peter may be headed south to Hilton Head and I'll be left behind."

"That's usually the case in times of war, Charlotte. You didn't expect to go off fighting with Peter just because you're married to him, did you?"

"No, but . . . I didn't expect this to happen so soon. We've only been married a week! If he does go, can I come back here to live, Mother? Mr. and Mrs. Rogers are very nice to me, but I don't really know them well enough to be comfortable on my own."

"What does Peter think? He's your husband now. You have to consult him."

"He thinks I should follow him as far as Beaufort and find a little room to rent, but I don't know anyone there. Peter doesn't understand why I would not be willing to sit there day after day waiting for him to visit occasionally. I can't imagine doing that."

"This will always be your home, and you are always welcome. Heaven knows I've gone home to my mother any number of times. But give yourself time. Things tend to change quickly in this new war. Maybe it will all come to nothing."

"Perhaps. I'm trying not to get ahead of myself, but it's hard not to worry. I wanted to be sure you and Father were still planning to be here if I need you."

"Where else would we be?"

"I don't know. I was afraid Father would be talking about getting out of Charleston again, now that the war is really happening. I know in the past people have made life uncomfortable for him because he's from Boston. Under conditions of war, won't he be considered the enemy?"

"There was a time not long ago that that was true, but he is now determined to rise above such talk. Your father is firmly committed to the Confederacy. He's become a plantation holder, he admits he is a slave owner, and his interest is in our cotton and rice crops. He is firmly tied to South Carolina, I promise you."

Susan watched her daughter until she rounded the corner on her way back to her husband's home. Facing the troubles within her own marriage had made her more sensitive to Charlotte's concerns about Peter. Being a woman is hard, she thought to herself. On the one hand, we are expected to be dainty and helpless and sweet. Men treat us as if we are made of glass. They open the doors and hold our chairs. They do the heavy lifting and serve as our protectors. But when they have real work of their own to do, we become nuisances. We're not to interrupt them or mention matters that they don't want to be bothered with. And we're certainly not expected to put our own desires above theirs.

Poor Charlotte. Peter's going to leave her for a chance to go to war, there's no doubt. And he'll never understand why she would not be willing to traipse after him, sitting all alone in a room and waiting for him to get done fighting. It's as if a man doesn't realize that a woman has a life of her own apart from his. I wish I knew what to tell her to do, but this is a problem the two of them will have to work out on their own. I'd love to have her back home, of course, but I can't tell her that. And I can't talk to Jonathan about it, either. He would only see Peter's side.

Susan gave her head a decisive shake, as if to dislodge these thoughts. It wasn't going to help, she knew, to dwell on the differences between men and women. That was a chasm too deep, too dark at the bottom, too dangerous to be crossed. As she usually did when she was upset, she turned to the melodeon. A friend had given her a sweet but rather maudlin piece of sheet music in honor of the war. The Stephen Foster tune was simple and the words soothingly repetitive.

> *Bring my brother back to me,*
> *From the battle strife.*
> *Thou who watchest o'er the good*
> *Shield his precious life.*

When this war has passed away,
Safe from all alarms
Bring my brother home again,
To my longing arms.
Bring him back! Bring him back!
With his smiling healthful glee.
Bring him back! Bring him back!
Bring my brother back to me.

Such a useful sentiment, Susan thought. All the singer has to do is change the single word *brother* to *husband*, *lover*, *father*, *dear son*, *fiancé*, *loved one*, or *grandson*. The longing is all the same. The men choose to leave and the women can only wait for their return. Perhaps the song will be of some comfort to Charlotte one day, she thought. But it certainly wasn't cheering her mother up on this fateful day.

Susan straightened her spine and jutted her chin into the air. I will be strong. Strong enough for me and for Charlotte, too. If our menfolk can welcome this war, then I must do the same. Her feet pumped at the pedals, and her hands flew over the keys, hitting them emphatically with each note of her new theme song: *Oh, I wish I was in the land of cotton.*

12

The Hazards of War
Summer 1861

From the moment the guns manned by the German Artillery of Charleston fired on Fort Sumter, Peter Rogers had longed to shoot one of those cannons. Once the initial fervor of the attack died down, he applied to join that same German militia group and was accepted with a certain amount of tolerance for his youth. The old hands taught him the basic operation of their guns and then put him to work as a cleaning detail. He swabbed away at the barrels and oiled the mechanisms, happy to have any part in a brotherhood with such firing power at their command. Peter's wife, Charlotte, tried to look impressed, but she hated every moment of it.

In the early part of 1861, Senator Wade Hampton—now Colonel Wade Hampton—accepted an appointment to create a Legion of Honor from his home state of South Carolina. Hampton had not supported the original push for secession and held a healthy respect for the federal government. His decision to play a role in the Confederate Army influenced many other Southerners to support the cause. When Hampton put an ad in the *Charleston Courier* on May 3, 1861, calling for 10,000 volunteers for his legion, the response was instantaneous. Among the militia units answering the call was the German Artillery of Charleston, and, on May 24, they became Company B of the First Battalion, South Carolina Artillery. Charlotte cried as Peter proudly donned his Confederate uniform.

The company's first assignment was to Hilton Head Island, where they were to man the guns at Fort Walker. The fort, however, was still under construction. Work had progressed slowly because it was being carried out by local slaves whose owners lent them out when the cotton crops did not need tending. Despite the fact that the walls were not yet built, orders came in early July for Company B to travel via the Charleston and Savannah Railroad to Pocataligo, from which depot they were to march and haul their artillery to the tip of Hilton Head. Peter packed his duffle cheerfully, while Charlotte pleaded to be allowed to return to her parents' home.

Peter accompanied her to the Logan Street house, carrying her trunk and cases. Already in uniform, he saluted his father-in-law, kissed his wife, and patted his mother-in-law on the shoulder. "Take good care of my little wife," he told them as he strode down the front steps and headed for the railroad station.

"All he can think about is war," Charlotte sobbed. "He doesn't care about me at all."

"He may just be trying to hide his emotions, dear. Men do that." Susan tried to smooth over the moment, but Charlotte was having none of it. In tears, she dashed up the stairs to her old room, slamming the door behind her.

Susan took out her distress on her husband. Whirling on him, she shook her finger under his nose. "Don't you ever . . ."

"I'm not going anywhere. You'll never see me in a uniform, so don't compare me to Peter."

When Charlotte failed to appear for dinner, Susan sent a slave girl up to her room with a tray. "Just leave it in the hall," a muffled voice instructed through the closed and locked door.

"You hasta eat, missus. You be wastin way to nuttin."

"I'm fine, Lily. I've actually gotten fatter since I got married. I'll have something to eat when I get hungry. Go away now, please." But the tray was still untouched in the morning.

Susan was getting worried. She knocked on the door and shouted at the crack. "Charlotte? Open this door at once!"

"Go away!"

"I will do no such thing. This is my house, and you are still my daughter. You need to come down and have some breakfast."

"I'll be there in a few moments. Give me time to dress." But she did not appear.

Frustrated, Susan turned to Sarah. "Would you try? Charlotte has always loved you because you were her nanny. At least, see if she's all right."

In a few minutes, Sarah reappeared, carrying a covered chamber pot. "Dat girl sick. She be trowing up in de pot. She need she mama."

Susan dashed up the stairs to find her daughter lying across her bed. She was pale, covered in sweat, and trembling, but a hand to her forehead revealed no fever. "How long have you been ill, Charlotte?"

"I don't know. Weeks, it seems. I wake up feeling good, but, as soon as I rise, the room swirls and I have to lie back down. I'll be better this afternoon, I promise. Just don't make me eat anything."

Susan looked at her daughter with a combination of sympathy and pity. "You're pregnant, my love."

"No! I can't be! Not in wartime!"

"Babies seldom ask if it's convenient for them to arrive."

"But I can't. Whatever will I do with a baby?"

"You'll love it, of course. As will we all, Peter included. Now, you need to try to get up. That child needs food to grow on. Sarah can make you some dry toast and ginger tea, and I'll send a message to Dr. Eastman asking him to stop by later this afternoon, just to have him confirm it. I've had seven children, remember? I recognize the symptoms."

For the rest of the Grenville family, the summer of 1861 provided a quiet interlude. Johnny was home from college, doing a lot of reading in his chosen fields of study and spending long hours with his classmates from Charleston as they debated the eventual course of the war and their roles in it.

They had all been disappointed to be sent back to Columbia after their brief stay on Sullivan's Island in January. News of the firing on Fort Sumter had not even reached them before the federal forces had surrendered peacefully. To make matters even more irritating, the College Cadets had returned to Columbia to discover that over half of their classmates had left school to join regular units. So had the majority of the faculty—so many, in fact, that only six professors remained on campus.

Alex Croft complained that his mother had no understanding of the war at all. She kept writing him encouraging letters, telling him that it was his duty to remain safe because the country would need educated men like him once the war was over. Safety, however, was not his goal. He longed for action and resented his older brother, who was already on active duty with the Twenty-Fourth South Carolina Infantry, another branch of Hampton's Legion.

Similarly, Johnny Grenville had little sympathy for his parents' complaints about Peter Rogers, who had so carelessly abandoned Charlotte to go off to build cannon batteries at Hilton Head. In Johnny's mind, Peter had made the right choice, while he, dutifully following his parents' plans for him, was stuck in a useless cadet corps that functioned only as a social club.

In July, the cadet conversations focused on the Battle of Manassas, where the Confederate forces had won, but at a high cost. It had been the first real land battle of the war, and, as such, it showed up the weaknesses in both armies. The Rebels had suffered 387 killed and 1,582 wounded, but only thirteen men remained missing. In the end, they had set the Federals running for cover and had scooped up over 1,300 prisoners who might be useful later as bargaining chips. The United States had also had 460 men killed and 1,124 wounded. Manassas made clear to observers that the war was destined to be a long and bloody one.

"Our troops suffered from their inexperience," suggested one cadet.

"True enough, but the Federals are just as inexperienced as we are. I blame the generals for our losses. There were bungled orders and poor communications all over the battlefield."

"At least our South Carolina troops did themselves proud," Alex insisted. "My brother Harris was there, and he says that Wade Hampton's legion did well, along with General Jackson's men."

"Speaking of Jackson, what are we to make of his new nickname—Stonewall Jackson? Is that a compliment or an insult?"

"Evidently, General Bee used the term first, describing Jackson as standing like a stone wall. I take that to mean standing firm and unmovable."

"It could also be taken as being stupid as a stone wall, not knowing what to do next."

"Maybe so, but in my mind, I like it. I'd prefer to think we'll be able to stonewall the Federals whenever they try to drive us from the field."

"If we ever get to the field," said Johnny. "What do you think? Do we go back to college in the fall and wait to be called up again, or do we jump in now?"

"I think I'll stonewall it and wait to be called up," Alex said. "Now that North Carolina, Tennessee, Arkansas, and Virginia have joined us, we should have more than enough men willing to fight. If President Davis sends out another call, though, or if there's a threat of imminent invasion of South Carolina, I'll wait no longer."

If the college cadets were impatient to see military action, the Grenvilles were even more anxious to avoid all the discussions of war that dominated conversations in Charleston. Jonathan and Eddie were particularly eager to get back to Harbor View and check on their first real cotton crop. By September, Jonathan had convinced himself, if not Susan, that it would be safe to return to Edisto Island.

"I've lived here all my life, Jonathan. Will you listen to me, please?" Susan begged. "Cases of swamp fever always peak in September, just as the bug population does. Is there a connection? Some people think yes and some think no, but what I know is that if you wait until first frost, the bugs are gone and so is the swamp fever."

"We have mosquitoes here in Charleston, too, but people don't get swamp fever from them."

"That you know of!"

"Well, I've never heard of one. And this year, our mosquitoes were the worst in July. Since then it's been dry, and I haven't had a single bite. I think it's worth checking to see if the same is true of Edisto."

"Yes, Mother," Eddie said. "Father's been asking people, and everyone says the same thing: no mosquitoes this year. And we really need to see how early the first cotton bolls ripen in this kind of weather."

"You sound like a little old farmer! Can we compromise? The two of you go out to the island for a couple of days and check on things. If the mosquitoes are really gone, we might plan on moving back in October, but no earlier."

"We can do that, can't we, son?"

"Sure, and we'll be good about avoiding the really swampy areas."

"Go ahead, then, but promise me that you'll come right back if there is fever on the island. Remember that I lost my only brother to the fever just a few years ago. I won't risk the health of anyone else in this family for the sake of a few cotton plants."

"Everything will be fine, I promise. It's important that we get the crop harvested before the Union decides to blockade the Atlantic coast. It won't do us any good to harvest a bumper crop if we can't get it to market."

"Everything comes down to the war, doesn't it?" Susan felt a little shiver run down her spine as she spoke.

13

The Inconveniences of Family
October 1861

B y September Charlotte had felt fat, and by October she was waddling. "Are you sure this baby's not due until January?" her mother asked.

"Believe me, Mother, if I thought there was a chance of it coming sooner, I'd be the first one to announce it. But no, I was not pregnant before April, so January it is."

"I'm still concerned. You don't appear to have gained a lot of weight in your face, and your feet and ankles aren't swelling, but . . ."

"But I look like a barrel, don't I?" Charlotte's eyes filled as she look downward. "I'll have to take your word about my feet not swelling. I can't see them at all."

Two days later, Dr. Eastman dropped by the Logan Street house, responding to a note from Mrs. Grenville. "Is Charlotte at home? I'm glad you suggested that I stop by and check on her and the baby."

"She's in her room. She's already finding it hard to climb the stairs, so she stays there most of the day."

"She'd be better off getting some fresh air," the doctor said.

"I agree, but she really is miserable. I'll take you up to see her."

After the usual chitchat, Dr. Eastman asked Charlotte to lie on the bed, and he pulled a small ear trumpet out of his black bag. Pressing the large end against her abdomen, he listened and frowned. "May I do a bit of prodding?" he asked. "Let me know if I'm hurting you." Gently but firmly, he pressed her stomach from both sides. Then he listened again.

At last he stepped back and motioned Susan to approach the bed. "How would you like to hear your grandchild's heartbeat?" he asked. He handed her the ear trumpet and pointed to Charlotte's left side. "Place the large end right there and listen."

Susan did as instructed. Absolute quiet reigned for a few seconds. Then she gasped. "I do hear it. It's strong and steady, isn't it?"

"Yes, indeed! Now try it over here on the other side."

Again, she listened for a moment and then looked up, puzzled. "But it's just as loud way over here. How can that be?"

Dr. Eastman smiled as he took the instrument from her. "They have good, healthy hearts. Both of them."

"What!" Charlotte struggled to sit up. "My baby has two hearts?"

"No. You have two babies."

"Twins? Oh, my Lord!" Susan sat down suddenly, as if her legs would no longer support her.

Charlotte remained speechless, looking in near panic from the doctor to her mother and back again. She shook her head. "No," she said at last. "No, I can't possibly have twins. I don't know what to do with one baby, let alone two of them. And there have never been twins in our family. I won't hear of it!"

"I'm afraid it's not a choice you get to make. From what I can tell, you have two healthy babies in there, and they are already getting restless. You'll be taking quite a kicking for the next month, what with four legs going at it rather than the usual two. Never fear, though. They'll be here quite soon."

"No," Charlotte said, but then she curled her arms around her belly protectively. "Twins," she said.

The doctor smiled. "She'll be fine," he said, turning to Susan. "I'd like to schedule regular weekly checks from here on, however, just to make sure everything is progressing normally."

"But we're getting ready to move the whole family to Harbor View next week. We won't be back in Charleston until Christmas."

"Christmas!" The doctor shook his head. "I don't think so."

"Yes, that's the plan. My husband is managing the Dubois plantation on Edisto Island now."

"I'm sorry to disrupt your plans, but it won't be possible to have Charlotte living out there for the last month of her pregnancy. At the latest, she'll be ready to deliver by the end of November."

"November?" Susan and Charlotte spoke at the same moment. Susan looked closely at Charlotte, her eyes narrowed. Charlotte blushed.

"You didn't realize that you're within a month of your delivery?" The doctor merely sounded curious.

"No, I . . . I thought . . . I got married in April, and I . . ."

"You told me the baby wouldn't be here until January! Can you not count, Charlotte, or did you deliberately lie to me?" Susan was having trouble controlling her anger.

"All right! So we may have anticipated the event by a few weeks, but at least we waited until we had your permission to get married, unlike you and . . ."

"Excuse me, but I don't think this is the time to continue with a family argument," the doctor said. "Whatever the circumstances of their beginnings, babies come when they are ready. Then, too, twins have a tendency to arrive early, in which case the mother may need extra medical assistance with the delivery. And there are other medical complications that can arise. I simply cannot advise a move to Edisto at this stage. Is there someone else with whom she can stay while you are gone?"

"I'll have to see what I can arrange."

"Please quit talking about me as if I am not here. Mother, I will not stay with the Rogers family, so don't even suggest it. And Grandmother Dubois tends to panic in moments of crisis, as you well know. Maybe they will let Peter come home."

"They?" The doctor looked curious.

"They. The army. He's in Hilton Head building a fort or something. If they knew he was soon going to be the father of twins, don't you think they'd let him come home?"

"Not likely, I'm afraid. Not until something disastrous happens, and by that time it would be too late for him to be of help."

"All right, Doctor. We'll work something out. My husband and I will discuss it this evening, and we will let you know what we decide."

Susan sounded firm and optimistic when she dismissed the doctor, but she was less so when it was time to confront Jonathan.

"Twins!" Jonathan shouted. "And they are going to keep us from going to Harbor View?" He was not happy. "I don't understand you, Susan. You were the one who wanted me to be a Southerner. You wanted me to take over the plantation. You wanted to move out to the land where you spent your happy childhood. So I did all you asked. And now you're throwing every possible roadblock in the way of my doing a good job of running the plantation! First mosquitoes, and now twins?"

"This isn't just my opinion, Jonathan. And it's not the same thing as worrying about mosquitoes. The doctor says the babies will be coming within the next few weeks, and there may be complications."

"The next few weeks? I thought you said she was due in January."

"That's what I thought, until she admitted today that . . ."

"Oh, no. I don't want to hear the sordid details."

"Fine, but your hiding from the details doesn't change the fact that Charlotte's eight months pregnant, and we can't take her out to Edisto Island and expose her to those risks."

"Then she can stay here. She has a set of in-laws who will also be grandparents to these babies. Why can't they oversee the last part of her pregnancy?"

"Because she doesn't feel at home there without Peter."

"Damn that boy, then! He was the one who got her pregnant. He can bloody well come home and take care of her!"

"It took both of them, dear, as you well know. And he did formally enlist in the Confederate Army. He can't just walk away."

"Then Charlotte can go and live with your mother. She's done it before when she wanted something."

"Yes, and she's swearing she will never do it again."

"And since when does our daughter dictate to all the rest of this family? We didn't raise her that way. She's never gotten away with imposing her will on us. Why should she be allowed to do so when she's an adult?"

"She's still our child."

"You have to admit that giving birth to twins is a pretty adult thing to do!"

"Maybe so, but it's also a terrifying thing to do. Please, Jonathan. Help me find a solution instead of fighting me over the problem."

"I don't see a solution. Do you?"

"Yes, although I don't like it." When he glared back at her, she added, "Really, I don't like it one bit!"

"And that is?"

"I stay here with Charlotte and the younger children. You and Eddie go on out to the plantation. Take Hector and Eli with you. Eli is big enough this year to be of great help. The four of you can take care of the cotton crop. You will be busy all day, anyway, just as you were last year, and I'll have enough household staff here to manage on my own."

"You're splitting up two families, then. What will Sarah have to say about sending her husband and oldest son off?"

"Slaves don't get a vote! They'll do as we say."

"Yes, they will, but it seems rather cruel."

"Sarah will understand. She loves Charlotte, and she's a good midwife. She'll see that it is necessary for her to stay."

"I still don't like it, but I suppose we'll have to make it work. Do you realize that we've never been apart for more than several days at a time?"

"I realize it, probably more than you can imagine. And it scares me to death. But we have a family crisis, it's wartime, and we'll have to do it."

"I'll worry about you. Perhaps we can put off going out to Harbor View for two or three more weeks, which should ease your swamp fever fears, too. And we can come home for Thanksgiving. I suppose we can survive for a few weeks."

106

"Thank you, Jonathan. And remember, as soon as the babies are safely here, we can move everyone to Harbor View until spring."

Young Eddie met the news with ill-concealed delight—not at the news of twins but at the prospect of the freedom that would come with his mother's absence. "It'll work out great, Father," he said. "We'll be able to work longer hours without Mother calling us to quit and come in for a family dinner or to help entertain the neighbors. And we can keep the slaves hard at work as long as there is enough light to see by. We're going to get much more done!"

"Not so fast, son. You have a point about the social interruptions, but we don't want to work the slaves that hard."

"Why not? They're slaves. That's what they're supposed to do."

"Work hard, yes. But no good slave owner overworks his people."

"They're slaves, not people. Remember? There's a law that counts a slave as only three-fifths of a person." He chuckled at the thought.

"Not so, Edward. You need to understand this right now, or you won't go to Harbor View with me." Jonathan's voice was cold.

Eddie stared at his father, suddenly frightened at the anger he saw in his face. "I didn't mean anything by all that," he said.

"Yes, you did. Listen well, now. You know Thomas, our slave driver at Harbor View?"

"Of course."

"What color is he?"

"He's a slave. He's black."

"Is he? Have you never noticed that his skin is actually only a light brown and that he has blue eyes?"

"He's still black, even if he does have blue eyes. That only means that his mother slept with . . ."

"Slept with whom? Remember, he has lived on the Harbor View Plantation all his life."

"Then it must have been with . . ." Eddie's eyes grew round with the realization of what he was about to say.

"That's right. Thomas is possibly your mother's brother, or perhaps her uncle. He's family, and as much a person as you or I."

"But then why is he a slave?"

"Because his mother was a slave. And that's only one of the things that are wrong with this whole system of slavery. Slavery involves one person treating another person as if he or she is nothing but an object. I refuse to do that, even if the current economic system does require me to hold slaves. I will employ them on my land, but I will always recognize and respect their full humanity. You will do the same, or you won't have a role on my land."

"I guess that's why people call you a Damned Yankee."

Jonathan's hand shot out of its own accord and stopped just short of Eddie's cheek. He gasped as he tried to control the rising anger in his chest. "Go to your room for the night. When you can speak civilly to me, we'll continue this conversation, but, for right now, I don't trust myself to refrain from beating you to a bloody pulp."

14

Preparing for Invasion
Fall 1861

Tempers cooled in the next few days, even as the effects of the war heated up. The major topic of conversation in Charleston was the blockade. In the beginning, both sides had thought to interfere with the other's shipping. The Confederates, however, had no naval power to rely upon, and they soon discovered that piracy was outdated. The little boats belonging to pirates were no match for Northern ships, and even the few who managed to escape being blown out of the water learned that European ports did not allow pirates to sail in. They might capture a little loot but would find no market for it.

The North, for its part, faced its own troubles when the Navy attempted to blockade the Southern coast. The situation was simple: British manufacturers depended on Southern cotton, and while they might be willing—albeit grudgingly—to respect an effective wartime blockade of shipping from the South, they found convenient loopholes in international law. If a blockading force withdrew and allowed a Southern ship to get through, the British claimed, England was in no way bound to observe a blockade that existed in theory only. So every time a blockading vessel had to sail away to refuel or restock its supplies, Confederate shippers slipped through the gaps and headed straight for their English markets.

As early as August, the Union was making plans to find a permanent southern base from which to support the blockade. Three areas offered potential harbors—Beaufort, South Carolina; Brunswick, Georgia; and Pensacola, Florida. As the Navy began to assemble a huge fleet to invade one of these areas, rumors swirled in Southern newspapers, for there was no way to hide an expedition that would finally amass over 80 ships and 16,000 men. Everyone along the Southern coastline worried about an attack, but no one was more concerned than the cotton growers whose crops were just ripening. If they were to make any profit, the harvest had to take place as quickly as possible. The race was on.

By October 15, Jonathan knew he could wait no longer. He called his son Eddie into his makeshift office and closed the door. "You've had several days to think about your position, Edward. Are you willing to go back to Edisto Island with me—on my terms—or would you prefer to remain here with your mother?"

"Oh, Father, I apologize for the things I said. I spoke in anger and under the influence of some of my school chums who had been making fun of your kindness to slaves."

"And you agreed with them?"

"No, not really. I may not fully understand why you have taken the stand you have, but I know you're a good man, and I'd rather be like you than like the fathers of those who made fun of you."

"Can you treat our extended family of slaves with the same dignity you proffer to members of our immediate family?"

"Yes, sir."

"Will you attempt to learn and adopt humane policies toward their working conditions?"

"Yes, sir."

"Well, we'll see how well you keep those promises in action. Go pack up your working clothes. We leave for Harbor View tomorrow."

Susan straightened her back and took a deep breath when Jonathan made the same announcement to her. "So soon? Oh, I'm not questioning your decision, but is there something happening that I don't know about?"

"There's a Northern expeditionary force on its way in this direction. No one seems to know where the ships are headed, but their purpose is clear: They need a vast, safe harbor from which to supply their fleet. They intend to enforce the blockade and keep us from selling this year's cotton crop to English mills."

"There will be fighting?"

"Somewhere, yes, but not on Edisto Island."

"But we have a huge harbor right off our beach. Wouldn't St. Helena Sound be an inviting spot for them to land?"

"Actually, no. The mouth of the sound is too wide. It's big enough, certainly, but it can't be defended. I worry about Port Royal Sound, however. Its entrance is narrow and its waters are smooth and well-sheltered. Wherever the Union fleet goes, it is imperative that we get our cotton crop shipped out through Charleston as soon as possible, if we are to avoid bankruptcy by spring."

"But, Jonathan, if they try to take Port Royal Sound, they'll have to attack the fortifications at Hilton Head, and . . ."

"And that's where Peter is. I know." Both parents looked at the ceiling, imagining their lonely and very pregnant daughter on the floor above them. "Try not to say anything to Charlotte. The fleet may go elsewhere, so we needn't alarm her yet. And even if they attack Fort Walker, that doesn't mean that Peter will . . . I mean, he's not a primary gunner or spotter."

"This is all so awful!"

"One thing at a time, my love. Just get through each day. What was that thing my mother used to say? 'Sufficient unto the day are the evils therein'."

"I'll try. And you'll let me know how everything is going, won't you?"

"I can't promise to write you letters. I'm not very good at that. But as we harvest the cotton, we'll be moving it to Charleston as rapidly as possible, so either Hector or I will be coming through often. I won't forget about you. And you will send word if there is any change in Charlotte's condition?"

"Of course."

The plantation work went well, but, everywhere on Edisto Island, the planters were working frantically while keeping an eye on the coastline. On November 1, the ocean waves grew high, and the sky darkened with heavy clouds.

"There's a storm out there, isn't there, Father?" Eddie commented. "Maybe it will be a hurricane and sink all those invading ships."

"An ungenerous thought, my son. The men on board those ships are human beings, too. We cannot wish for their deaths."

"Oh, I'll never be as noble and generous as you are!" Eddie exclaimed. "How can you be concerned about the welfare of people who are headed our way, determined to destroy us?"

"We are all God's children, Eddie. They have chosen one path and we another, but I cannot wish them dead. Soaked to the skin, maybe, and seasick beyond belief. Hungry and homesick and miserable—that won't bother me." Jonathan smiled at his younger son and was relieved to see that the boy was sharing his humor.

Plant by plant, boll by boll, the slaves plucked the cotton fibers and passed them on to the cleaners, who picked away the stems and leaves still clinging to the cotton. Other slaves waited with shakers to remove the last bits of dirt before the packers laced the fibers into their bales and piled them on the wagons for transport. Then the process began all over again. Nearly every day a planter took a wagonload of cotton back up the road to Charleston, hoping to sell the bales to a blockade-runner who could get them through the blockade and on their way to England. Then the rains settled in, and for several days the workers fell idle as they waited for the plants to dry out.

Jonathan took advantage of the lull to consult with Roger Withers, the white overseer, and with Thomas, the family slave driver. "I'm hopeful that we are going to be able to harvest the rest of this crop, if we can get just a couple more weeks of sunshine, but I'm afraid this may be the last cotton crop for a while."

"Are you thinking of shutting down the plantation?" asked Mr. Withers, looking somewhat alarmed.

"Oh, Massa Grenville, you not gwine do dat! Massa Dubois be rolling ober in he grave ifn he knowed . . ."

"No, no, I'm thinking of repurposing."

"I don eben knows what dat mean," said Thomas.

"It means we're going to forget about growing a crop we can't sell and start producing crops we can use. Food—corn, potatoes, beans, turnips, collards, onions—whatever you can put into the ground this winter and harvest within a few months. We're going to take the early profits from this crop and invest in seeds. Root crops will withstand the occasional frost. And no matter what happens with the war, there are always going to be hungry people. Our goal will be to feed ourselves first and then to sell the surplus to the army or to our foolish neighbors who still try to raise cotton."

"Dat good!"

"It's a practical idea. Mr. Dubois might still turn over in his grave to see his cotton fields sprouting turnip greens, but I promised him I would take care of his family—all of his extended family—and I intend to keep them alive and healthy. Wealthy may have to wait a while."

Later that evening, Eddie approached his father, looking serious and carrying a packet of notes. "I have an idea, Father. May I discuss it with you?"

"Certainly, son."

"Remember last year when I was working in the cattle barn and learning about the milch cows? I did some talking to the slave women who make our butter, and they told me that they use the extra milk to make farm cheese for their families. I even took notes on how they did it."

"I had forgotten about the cheese idea, Eddie. Why didn't you remind me?"

"Because I was pretty sure someone would make fun of me for collecting recipes. Admit it—that's really absurd. But I know how the slave women make cheese, and, when I looked up cheese-making in the library last summer, I found recipes for cheeses that will last for a long time if you have some sort of underground cellar to store them in—which we have, by the way. There's a root cellar below the parlor that stays cool and damp even in summer, the slave women tell me."

"Are you suggesting that you want to go into the cheese-making business?"

"It's a ridiculous idea, isn't it?" Eddie looked crestfallen.

"No! It's an idea of pure genius! If we can produce cheese along with our vegetable crops, we should be able to weather this war in fine style. I'm proud of you, son."

15

The Battle of Port Royal
November 1861

As the storm lifted, sails began to appear on the horizon. None of the ships headed straight for Edisto Island, but it soon became apparent that they were dropping anchor just outside the entrance to Port Royal Sound. As they lowered their sails, their masts stood like bristles against the sky. Eddie and Jonathan watched with the kind of fascination that keeps people looking at scenes of terror even as they wish they could look away.

"Port Royal Sound. That's where Hilton Head is, isn't it? And where Peter . . ."

"Yes, but if you breathe a word of this to your mother or sister, I will tear out your tongue!"

"I won't. I'm scared enough for all of them. It looks like the navies of the world out there. Maybe that will scare the soldiers in Fort Walker, and they'll give up without a fight."

"Don't count on that. Soldiers have this thing called honor . . ."

"Which requires them to shoot back at thousands of cannons?"

"'Fraid so!"

"But that would be suicide."

And so it was. The guns began early the next morning. Although Fort Walker was some twenty-five miles away, the sound carried long across the water. The air shimmered, and the reverberations echoed deep in the breasts of all who listened. The barrage was steady, although most of the fleet that outlined itself against the sky had not moved from the anchorage.

"How many guns do you think there are?" Eddie asked.

"I have no idea. But those big warships carry dozens."

"And how many guns are there at Fort Walker?"

"Uh . . . Several."

Eddie fell silent, his eyes big with fear.

The cannonade continued until well after noon. But if the noise had been terrifying, the silence was worse. The Battle of Port Royal was obviously over, and it was just as obvious that it had been a huge loss for the Confederate forces. Even the slaves moved quietly back to their hoes, realizing that, in the first battle over the South's right to hold slaves, many men had died. There was no rejoicing at a Northern victory, only an empty feeling of remorse at the losses suffered for their sake.

Back in Charleston, a different sort of regret was expressing itself. When word came of the imminent arrival of the Northern fleet, Governor Pickens called for a new round of volunteers to protect his state. The message went out to the College Cadets in Columbia. The governor informed that ill-trained band that all able-bodied students were being called up. He had arranged transport for them and would have weapons waiting when they arrived in Charleston. If they were still minors, the law said they were required to have their parents'

permission, but the governor waived even that requirement. It would be enough, he promised, if they could get the permission of one of the college staff, who stood *in loco parentis*, or if they would sign a paper saying that they believed their parents would give permission.

Of course, Johnny Grenville, Alex Croft, and John Calhoun were among the raw recruits who rode a hastily assembled train back to Charleston. They reported their arrival to the governor, but, by the time they were able to do so, the Battle of Port Royal was over. Once again, as in April, there was no role for them. Slightly embarrassed, Pickens sent them off with tents to camp at the Washington Race Course north of the city. They were to serve as his personal bodyguards, should he feel the need for such a guard.

The cadets complained, as soldiers always do, that their tents were too small and their commissary rations barely edible. But the truth was that they were comfortably situated. They sent out scouting parties each morning to buy food from the markets and spent their days lounging, gambling, and chatting with the young women who were drawn to the camp like flies.

They also took turns visiting their homes in the city. Johnny appeared at the Logan Street house one afternoon wearing his dress cadet uniform and strutting like the soldier he really wanted to be. Susan wept in his arms, and Charlotte eased herself down the stairs to pummel her brother with questions about what he had heard of the battle. Fortunately, he had heard little or nothing.

While the reunited family chatted and filled each other in on the changes in their lives, someone knocked at the front door. Sarah hurried to answer it but first peered out of the sidelight to see who it might be. Instead of opening the door, she turned to the assembled group in the parlor, her eyes wide. "It be sum soljer mens," she said.

"They're probably looking for me. Maybe the general has finally found something for us to do." Johnny jumped to his feet and threw open the door with a smile on his face. His smile faded as he realized he didn't know them. "May I help you?"

"We're looking for a Mrs. Rogers. We have a message for her."

"I'm sorry. There's no Mrs. Rogers here. You must have the wrong—"

"Johnny! That's me!" Charlotte was struggling to get up from the settee. "Maybe Peter sent me a letter." She, too, approached the door with a smile on her face—a smile that faded as she saw the expressions of the messengers.

"Ma'am? Are you Mrs. Peter Rogers?"

"Yes. Yes. Where is his letter? Is that it?"

"Ma'am. We're sorry to inform you that your husband was a brave and dedicated soldier, who died while doing his duty and serving his country. This letter from his commander will tell you the details of his final moments. Our deepest regrets, Ma'am."

The speech was well-rehearsed and delivered with all dignity, but Charlotte did not hear it. She had already slumped toward the floor.

Susan reached for her as she fell, lowering her as gently as possible to protect the babies she carried. "My God! My God!"

Johnny took the letter from the soldiers and waved them away. Then he, too, fell to his knees to place his arms around the two grieving women who meant so much to him. Silent moments passed unnoticed, while Sarah hovered around them, wringing her hands.

Susan was the first to pull herself together. "Sarah, go find a couple of strong young men to help us move Charlotte to the chaise longue. Then bring us some cool water and a small clean cloth to bathe her face. Johnny, go after those soldiers and find out if Peter's parents have been notified. Then dash over to Dr. Eastman's house and ask him to come immediately. Tell him Charlotte has had a shock and a fall. This is news beyond terrible, but we must do what needs to be done."

It was a miserable night. Charlotte alternated between weeping inconsolably and raging against anyone who came close to her. Dr. Eastman hovered, checking the babies during those moments when their mother was quiet. "No damage has been done, so far as I can tell, but this upset will do neither babies nor mother any good. I'll leave some powdered valerian root. Put a teaspoon in some hot water and encourage her to drink it. It's a gentle sedative that will let her sleep through the worst of the next few days."

Johnny had reported that the soldiers were on their way to notify Peter's parents. "You don't have to be the one to tell them, Mother. They will be getting their own letter. But what about Father? Surely he needs to know."

"I'll send a slave in the morning. It's too late for anyone to make the trip now. And speaking of late, Johnny, you'd better get back to camp before someone thinks you've deserted the Army. Come back when you can get free. And thank you for being here when we needed you."

Susan sat with her daughter until grief wore her down and sleep took over. Then she went to her own bed, but tossed and worried her way far into the night. She was dozing fitfully when noise in the backyard woke her again. Through the drapes, she could see the flare of torches and hear horses whinnying. Burrowing under her pillow did not help. Then Sarah was at the side of the bed, shaking her and saying, "Wake up, Miss Susan. Massa Grenville be home."

"What! How on earth did he know?"

"Ah don tinks he know bout Massa Peter. He be talkin bout how he be run off de island, an all Massa Eddie kin say be bout sumbody eatin he cows. Ah don know what be gwine on, but ah sho don want fuh be de one what tell he mo badness."

"No, you shouldn't. That's my job. Hand me my dressing gown. I need my husband as desperately as he needs me."

By the time she reached the bottom of the stairs, Susan was crying openly. She ran into the yard and threw herself into Jonathan's arms.

"Steady, my love. I'm so sorry. I never meant to lose your plantation for you. I would have done anything if it would have changed their minds, but talk was useless. We ended up fleeing at gunpoint, bringing only what we could carry with us. Can you ever forgive me?"

"What are you talking about? Did you not come home because of Peter?"

"Peter? What about Peter?" Jonathan held his wife out at arm's length and stared at her swollen and tear-stained face. "No! Tell me it's not so."

"He's gone, Jonathan. Blown to smithereens by a Yankee cannon ball, according to his commander's letter."

"At Fort Walker?"

Susan nodded. "The letter says he and his mates were called forward in the last minutes of the battle to relieve the gunners.

Peter ran to the front, volunteering to man the cannon, but he never got the chance to get off a shot."

Jonathan looked at the house apprehensively. "Is he . . . did they bring his body home?"

"No, they buried him on the battlefield."

"And Charlotte?"

"Asleep. Exhausted. Half out of her mind. Unable to accept that she is a widow. Angry with anyone who tries to talk to her or comfort her. The babies seem to be all right, though. I sent for Dr. Eastman immediately, and he has given her a sedative."

"She's so young to have to deal with all of this."

"I can't imagine how she will cope. I don't know that I could, if it were you."

"You would manage, my darling, and so will she. And we'll be there for her and for the babies as well. It'll take a long time, and it will be hard, but we'll manage."

Susan sniffled and nodded, but tried to straighten her spine. It was then she caught her first glimpse of her second son. He stood, pale and skinny, silhouetted against the light coming from the stable as the slaves unharnessed the horses and unloaded the wagon Jonathan had been driving.

"Eddie. You must be so tired." Susan reached out for him and realized he was trembling.

"Peter's . . . really dead? Dead, as in never coming back?"

"I'm afraid so."

"But he was just a little older than me. I thought old men like Grandfather were the ones who died—not boys."

Susan looked at her son and felt her heart break anew. "You mustn't be afraid. We can't always understand why things like this happen, but we can be strong together to get through them. I'm glad you're home with us."

16

Facing the Unthinkable
November 1861

The days of deep mourning passed in a haze. Mirrors were covered with black crepe. The tall clock in the hallway was stopped, its hands showing 1:00, the approximate time of Peter's death. Close family members wore black. Even the youngest children wore black armbands. Family and friends paid formal visits bearing flowers or food; most left calling cards and departed without seeing any one.

In the absence of a body or a local grave, the Rogers family held a memorial service at the Circular Congregational Church on Meeting Street. Afterward, the congregation witnessed the placing of a small metal marker in honor of Private Peter Rogers, Company B, First Battalion, South Carolina Artillery, Hampton's Legion. The two families did not know each other well, so they lingered awkwardly, united and yet separated by their mourning status. The Rogers relatives encircled the grieving parents and spoke now and then to the distantly related Middletons.

The Grenville and Dubois family members remained acutely aware of the widow missing from their number. As Susan had carefully explained to Charlotte, widows were expected to cry and wail over their bereavement, but not in public. And her advanced pregnancy complicated the issue even further. Propriety insisted that a pregnant widow be secluded from all curious gazes.

Charlotte was slowly moving from the first stages of shock and denial into pure anger. "I'm to be a pariah, then? None of this is my fault. I asked Peter not to go to war. He went anyway, leaving me to this! I may not be able to forgive him for doing that," she said.

"Charlotte, darling, these social norms are designed to protect you. I promise you that you would not want to be at the memorial service with everyone staring at you and waiting for you to have hysterics."

"Am I not to be allowed to mourn him then?"

"A widow's mourning is private. She is not expected to leave her house or receive visitors for months. It will be up to you to decide when you will invite your closest friends to call, but that will certainly not come until the twins have been born and you have fully recovered your strength. You will be expected to wear black for a year or more, however."

"And none of it is my choice! What if I want to go out into the streets and stage a protest against this terrible war? That's what I should be doing. How many other young women are going to have to go through this awful experience? I want to scream at someone. Why can't I scream?"

"You may certainly scream, but only in private, I'm afraid."

"Then get out and leave me to it!" Charlotte struggled to her feet and held the door open, glaring until her mother stepped into the hall. Then she gave it a great push and slammed it shut.

Susan's worry about her daughter mingled with the anger and fear she still saw on Eddie's face, the crushing depression that seemed to engulf Jonathan, and the equally frightening eagerness of young Johnny to go off to war. What's happened to my happy family? she wondered. How did we lose it all in such a short time? And what is to become of us now?

Johnny and the College Cadets remained at the Washington Race Course, waiting for the governor to face a crisis so that they could spring into action. In the meantime, they practiced their close-order drills, cleaned their rifles, and continued to flirt with the steady stream of female visitors who brought them home-baked goodies to supplement their army rations. Johnny tried not to discuss the future with his parents, but he had made it clear that, from this point on, his education would take a back seat to military necessity.

The younger children returned to classes in the lower-level classroom of the house, happy to see their old teacher and to be free from the gloom that permeated the upstairs levels. They had been allowed to put away their black armbands, and, as children do, had quickly forgotten about Peter's death. Eddie simply made himself scarce, avoiding his father's gloom and his mother's smothering affection by hiding out in the stables. If asked, he would have said that he was putting his time to good use, learning as much as possible about how the slaves kept a household running when the masters collapsed.

The Grenvilles had not had time to discuss the events on Edisto Island until after the memorial service. But at last they ran out of polite conversation and social duties. They settled before the fire in the parlor, and Susan met her husband's eyes straight on, ready to probe and deal with whatever it was that kept such a haunted look on his face. "Tell me, now. What happened on Edisto Island?"

"Well, as you know, the battle at Port Royal did not affect us directly. We could see the ships and eventually hear the firing, but we were never in any danger. No one was trying to land a ship on our coastline or pointing a cannon in our direction. Our way to the mainland was still clear, and we continued to ship wagonloads of cotton to Charleston. Work continued without interruption, and I was beginning to feel quite hopeful about our survival. As the slaves finished picking a field clean of cotton, others were turning the plants into the soil and getting ready to plant new winter crops.

"Eddie and I had made elaborate plans to produce mostly food at Harbor View this next year, figuring that both the civilian population and the Confederate Army would pay premium prices to keep eating well. We invested much of the early cotton money in seed. Beyond that, Eddie was setting up a cheese-making process in the dairy barn. Oh, Susan, you would have been so proud of him! You know, he's not the bookish sort, but he has a quick and penetrating mind when it comes to business. He was buying milch cows with the allowance I gave him, and he had organized several slave women to make the cheese for him.

"Then, one morning shortly after the Battle of Port Royal, a band of Confederate troops landed on the island—not the enemy Yankees, mind you, but good Southern boys. They were led by a Colonel Drummond—no idea who he is, by the way—bearing orders from General Robert E. Lee himself, who had just been put in charge here in Charleston. The message was brief but terrifying. I can still hear the words:

> *War has come to Edisto Island, and the Confederate Army cannot defend these Sea Islands. All white citizens are ordered to evacuate immediately. Take your family members, what possessions you can carry, and any slaves you are willing to keep in your employ. Leave all other slaves here. Burn any cotton you have harvested and set fire to your fields. Turn your cattle loose—we will round them up once you are gone and use them to feed the Army. You must be gone before sunset.*

"How awful! But why burn the cotton?"

"To keep it from falling into the hands of the Yankees, although most of us doubted that the Union Army would come looking for our cotton crops. That's why almost no one set fire to anything. A soldier was stationed on each plantation to see to it that the order was carried out, and he had his gun to enforce it. But we told our guard that we had ordered the slaves to do the burning after we were gone. That seemed to satisfy him."

"Is General Lee permanently abandoning the Sea Islands?"

"Apparently so. The Battle of Port Royal sent a clear message about the impossibility of defending a swampy coastline of pluff mud and tiny islands. As I understand it, the plan now is to withdraw all Confederate troops behind a line marked by the Charleston and Savannah Railroad. That transportation link is a vital lifeline, so it must be protected at all costs. But our plantations? They are to be sacrificed."

"So you just packed up and left?"

"We had no choice. I brought our household servants with me, using them to drive the wagons loaded with our possessions and a few foodstuffs. Then I called Thomas into the house and explained the situation to him. Thomas is taking over the management of the plantation and its people. He knows it better than anyone, and he said to tell you that he wouldn't let the family down."

Susan glanced up at her husband from under lowered eyelids. "You know he's really my uncle, don't you? Thomas, that is. He's my father's brother . . . half-brother, of course, but still really family."

"Yes, I'd figured that out."

"But you left him there, at the mercy of the Yankees?"

"He's not in any danger from the Yankees, Susan. They want to free the Negro, not re-enslave him. Besides, Thomas would not hear of leaving Harbor View."

"I suppose not, but I'll worry about him."

"We'll worry about all our slaves, but I'm sure they will be fine. They have good housing. Your father saw to that. And they are well-supplied with food crops already planted and seed to plant more in the spring."

"But will they get the planting and harvesting done without supervision?"

"You wouldn't even ask that if you had seen them on the day of the evacuation. They snapped into action like a well-oiled machine. Did you know there are hidden storerooms under the main plantation house?"

"No!"

"Well, there are, left over, apparently, from the Revolutionary War. I hadn't seen them either until Thomas showed me. They have concealed doors, and the slave women rapidly moved all their foodstuffs into those rooms so that any Yankees passing through would not be able to find them. Then the men did the same with our baled cotton. We'll be able to go back some day and retrieve it, I hope." He paused for a moment, lost in thought about how impossible that sounded at the moment. Then he roused himself from his reverie and gave Susan a shaky grin.

"You would also have enjoyed watching the women move their chickens, goats, and piglets into their cabins so nobody would steal them. Cabin living is going to be crowded for a while, I fear."

"What about the other livestock? Did you turn it loose as they told you to do?"

"No. We brought the horses with us, of course, but the cattle, mules, and sheep were left in their barns. It's a slim hope, but maybe the Yankees will settle for the loose stock they can find and not do a house-to-house search. Whatever happens later, I couldn't let Eddie see me drive his cows away."

"He must have been so upset!"

Jonathan's eyes glistened with tears as he remembered the scene. "I went out to find him when we were ready to leave. He was in the cattle barn, his arms around the neck of one of his cows, and he was crying his eyes out. I had to pry him loose, and all the time he was talking to that cow, apologizing for leaving her and telling her to run fast if anybody tried to catch her."

"Oh, Jonathan! What is this war doing to us . . . and to our children?"

17

Flickers of Hope
November 24, 1861

The Grenvilles gathered for Sunday dinner after attending services at the French Huguenot church. Mrs. Dubois loved taking her grandchildren there to see if they could follow the French liturgy. "That church was your grandfather's favorite building in Charleston," she told them. "He loved the pinnacles on the roof because they drew every eye upward. And after the past few weeks, we need to be keeping our eyes focused on God's plan for our lives."

Susan and Jonathan exchanged one of those looks that said, "Here she goes again," and young Johnny smiled at them in agreement. Charlotte, who had not attended church but joined them for dinner, stared at her lap, wishing herself far away from everyone she knew. Eddie rolled his eyes a bit, but the younger children nodded earnestly in response. Little Jamey munched on a crust of bread, oblivious to the family drama playing out before him.

Susan reached over to pat her mother's hand and said, "Yes, Mother, but we need to do so with hope in our hearts. We've come through a storm, but we're still here, all together as a family, and with hope for wonderful additions to come. Let's think about the promise of the future."

"Well, then, speaking of the future, I was reading my latest copy of *Godey's Lady's Book* and discovered an editorial written by Sarah Josepha Hale. You know I've always admired her for her campaigns to create a national holiday for giving thanks. This year, Abe Lincoln has proclaimed next Thursday, November 28, as Thanksgiving Day, although I know he no longer speaks for us—or to us, for that matter. But since this may be the last Thanksgiving I will be able to celebrate with you, I was hoping we could follow Lincoln's suggestion. And Miss Hale thinks we should take that occasion to share a day dedicated to peace. She asks that we lay aside our enmities and strife and join together in giving thanks for all our blessings."

Charlotte slapped her napkin on the table and rose heavily to her feet. "May I be excused from laying aside my enmity and hatred of the Yankees for just a while longer, at least until I am out of mourning for my poor slaughtered husband?"

Susan half rose to comfort her daughter, but Charlotte shook her off and stormed out of the dining room, letting the door slam behind her.

"Oh, dear, I didn't mean to set her off," Mrs. Dubois said.

"Everything sets her off, Mother. Don't fret about it. She needs to be angry at somebody but can't figure out who is to blame. So she's angry at everyone."

"I just hope the doors of this house can stand up to a few more weeks of being slammed," Jonathan quipped. "And I do understand her feelings. I don't mean to be unsympathetic. It's hard, though, to absorb the brunt of her anger every day."

Susan cocked a sympathetic eyebrow at her husband. Then she stopped, startled, to stare at her mother. "What on earth did you mean about this being the last Thanksgiving you would be able to celebrate? You're not ill?"

"No, my dear. I didn't mean to frighten you. But I do have some plans you are not aware of. I have two lovely first cousins who have joined together in their widowhood to form a household in Flat Rock, North Carolina. They've invited me to join them, and I'm seriously considering doing so."

"Flat Rock? I don't even know where that is."

"It's a resort area in the hills of western North Carolina. The climate is moderate because of the altitude, and it is rather off the beaten track. Lots of Charleston families spend their holidays in the hills during our hot summers. The Middletons, I understand, spend a great deal of time there."

"But you have your wonderful house here . . . and all your family . . . and . . ."

"And a very lonely life. Oh, having Charlotte staying with me last fall helped some, but I miss your father, and I miss spending time with people my own age who share my interests."

"If you're lonely, you could always move in here." Susan felt Jonathan kick at her under the table, but she ignored him.

"You're not hearing what I'm trying to say, Susan. I love your family, of course, but with all seven of my grandchildren in and out, and two more babies on the way, your house would wear me out! I love you, but I don't want to live with you. I want to spend my last years being me, doing as I like. What I want to do is sell that old house with all its furnishings in it, pack a few clothes, and go off on a new, grand adventure. And that's exactly what I intend to do."

"Mother, could we have a regular Thanksgiving, like Grandmother is suggesting?" Mary Sue spoke up in the ensuing silence. "It would be fun to decorate the house with fall leaves and to tell the Pilgrim stories the way we used to. Could we, please?"

Susan cocked her head and looked at her Yankee husband for a few seconds. She could tell that he still felt the conflict between his Northern upbringing and his Southern family ties. "I don't see why not!"

"Our neighbors will not be amused, Susan. Abe Lincoln's Thanksgiving will not be popular in Charleston." Jonathan sighed and then pinched his lips together in a gesture that had come to mean that he couldn't face talking further about the issue.

"Our neighbors don't need to know what we do in the privacy of our own family, and they certainly don't have any business asking what we're having for dinner. Let's do it. Mary Sue, you are in charge of gathering some pretty fall foliage for a table centerpiece. Just be sure you pick good Southern plants!"

"Goody! I'll go out first thing in the morning!"

"Jonathan, do you think Hector can shoot us a turkey before Thursday, or should we just go with one of the hams you brought home from the plantation?"

"If we're going to do this thing, we might as well try to do it right," Jonathan said. "I'll send Hector out in the morning. And Eddie, maybe you and Eli can be allowed to go out hunting with him. It's about time you boys learned how to handle a rifle, and if anyone asks why you're looking for a turkey, we can explain it as a teaching exercise for you."

Johnny had been watching the exchange with some detachment, but he couldn't help snatching a chance to tease his younger brother. "Yes, Eddie, it's about time you learned to shoot. We're in a war, after all. And if things keep going badly, we may even have to make soldiers out of children like you."

"I'm not all that much younger than you, Johnny," Eddie said, "and if I have to go to war, I'll not spend my service prancing around in my dress uniform in the heart of Charleston. I know more about the countryside than you do, I'll bet, college boy."

"That's enough out of both of you. There will be no more family fighting this week, understand? And this will be a complete family affair. Mother, we'll expect you to be here, and, Johnny, you need to ask for a day's leave. Tell them it has to do with your widowed sister, if you have to explain why."

"Yes, Ma'am."

Susan looked around the table with a smile of satisfaction. For the first time in days, she felt a sliver of hope.

Later that afternoon, Susan was walking her mother to the door when a scream from upstairs startled everyone in the parlor.

"Momma!"

Susan sprinted for the stairs, followed closely by Sarah and Mrs. Dubois. The smaller children looked puzzled when Jonathan held up his hands to stop any further movement. "This is women's work," he said. "Johnny, see if your mother wants you to go for Dr. Eastman. Eddie, would you take the children down to the schoolroom and read to them or play a game or something?"

Johnny met his mother as she started to come down the stairs. "There you are. Thank goodness! Please go for the doctor, Johnny. Tell him Charlotte's time has come."

"Yes, Ma'am. I'm on my way!"

Upstairs, Charlotte lay on her bed, eyes wide with fright, hands clutching her belly. "Please, please, I'm not ready for this. Please stop hurting," she begged.

"You must try to relax between spasms," Susan urged. "The doctor will need to know how frequently they are coming."

"I can't. I can't do this. Please, Momma, make it stop."

"When the doctor gets here, he will be able to give you something to deaden the pain. Until then, you must hang on. Take deep breaths when you can. Holding your breath is not the best way to handle the pain. Breathe, darling girl."

"I'll try, but, oh . . ."

"Susan!" Mrs. Dubois stood in the doorway. "I want to speak to you in the hall!"

"Not now, Mother."

"Yes, now!" Mrs. Dubois stamped her foot.

Sarah was edging toward the door. "I be gittin tings ready, Miss . . . sum hot water, an de towel. Good ting I ax Hector fuh bring dat basinette down fro de attic."

"Yes, Sarah, but there will be time for that. First, come here and hold Charlotte's hand while I deal with my mother."

"Please don't let my grandmother stay up here," Charlotte begged. "Please."

Susan fairly shoved her mother into the hall and pulled the door shut. "What is it, Mother?"

"Did I understand you to say, just now, that you would have the doctor give her something for the pain? You're not going to allow him to use ether or chloroform, are you?"

"Actually, it's a mixture of the two, and, yes, I fully intend to have him put her to sleep. She's already faced enough pain."

"I won't allow it. Drugging a woman during childbirth is a sin and a sacrilege. Birthing pains are the will of God—our inherited punishment for the sins of Eve. John Calvin taught us that—"

"Stop it! Stop it right now. This is my house and my daughter, and you do not give the orders here. And I don't care what John Calvin said or what your church teaches."

"I suffered the pains of childbirth for you and your brother and sister, and you endured them for each of your seven children. We love our children all the more when we fight through the pain to give them life. You must not deprive Charlotte of that experience."

"I have news for you, Mother. I took the gas when I gave birth to both Robbie and Jamey. It made no difference in my love for them. It was just a blessed relief. Now go downstairs and wait with Jonathan. Or go home, if you prefer. But I will not allow you to interfere with Charlotte's labor."

Elizabeth Dubois sat in the parlor, her back straight as a ramrod. She refused to go home because she wanted to be present to see the newborn children, but she also refused to talk to anyone. When Dr. Eastman arrived, she glared at his black bag and pointedly turned her back. Each time Jonathan made his way upstairs and returned, she refused to ask the normal questions. Inwardly she struggled with the realization that she would now become a great-grandmother . . . an old woman whose opinions were no longer of importance.

Time crawled. Eddie came upstairs with four very sleepy children and helped them get ready for bed. "There may be a surprise in the morning if you sleep really well tonight," he promised them.

Around midnight came the first faint squall from behind the closed bedroom door. Then a louder cry, and then two indignant little voices raised their first protests at the sudden coldness of their world. Susan came to the top of the stairs, tears streaming down her face to drench a radiant smile. "We have grandchildren," she announced. "A boy and a girl, and they are both perfect. Charlotte is awake and resting."

Jonathan stood and pointed across the room to where Mrs. Dubois sat slumped over against the chair's wing back, mouth open, sleeping noisily.

"Don't wake her," Susan said. "She can wait to meet her great-grandchildren in the morning, but Charlotte wants to see you."

Jonathan dashed upstairs and stood in wonder as he looked at his eldest daughter, a small bundle safe in each arm and her face beaming for the first time in weeks. "Hello, Grandfather," Charlotte greeted him as one of the babies hiccupped in accompaniment.

For the second time that day, Susan looked around her daughter's room and gave silent thanks for the blessings of a closed family circle.

18

A Day of Thanksgiving
November 1861

Thanksgiving Day dawned crisp and clear. The sunshine alone would have been reason enough for most people to be grateful for their lives in South Carolina. The sky had that deep blue color that only comes in the late fall, and, all around, gardens and foliage were showing signs of the new season. In the Grenville house, all was well. The babies were thriving, Charlotte was eager to be allowed out of bed, the younger children were excited, and Susan was smiling as she supervised the laying of the table. Jonathan was in his study working diligently on a project he had not explained. Young Johnny came bouncing in early, waving his day pass and running upstairs to don civilian clothes for the occasion. Mrs. Dubois arrived early, too, flanked by two black serving girls who were loaded down with baskets of pies and breads.

"Where's Eddie?" Johnny asked when he came back downstairs.

"He's in the backyard, carefully plucking his turkey," Susan explained.

"His turkey? You mean he actually shot one?"

"He did, indeed."

"Well, good for him. He's finally growing up, isn't he?"

"More than you realize, Johnny. It would be nice if you could spend a bit more time with him. He could use the support of a big brother now and then, instead of teasing."

"You're right as usual, Mother. I'll go congratulate him on his turkey, for starters."

Dinner, too, went off without a hitch. Charlotte could not yet come downstairs, so Susan carried a plate up to her. "Surprise, Charlotte! Your brothers and sisters took a vote and awarded you the first turkey leg!"

"Yum!" she grinned. Her mood had undergone a major shift since the birth of the twins. Most of the time she sported a silly grin whenever she looked at her son and daughter. "What miracles they are! Won't it be fun when they are old enough to join the family on these occasions?"

"It will, indeed. In the meantime, enjoy your dinner. The boys will be up to visit later, bearing pie. Any preference? Your grandmother has provided mince, sweet potato, and apple."

"A sliver of each, please. When the babies nurse, I want them to get all the flavors of Thanksgiving."

Susan was still laughing as she rejoined the dinner table. "Talk about transformations! All the anger we saw in Charlotte has disappeared under a fat layer of mother love. She's positively giddy over those babies. As she should be, of course. They're so beautiful!"

"Do they have names yet?"

"They will be formally introduced at their baptism as George Grenville Rogers and Anne Elizabeth Rogers. Charlotte thought you would be pleased."

"Of course I am. Pleased and honored to have our family names carry on," Mrs. Dubois said. "We have much to be grateful for today." She mentioned not a word about the dangers and deprivations of drugged childbirth, Susan noticed, a fact she added to her own "I'm thankful for . . ." list.

Once everyone had taken a second helping, Jonathan put down his fork, patted his stomach, and announced, "I have a little more good news. It's not as cute as those babies, but it might give some of you something else to grin about."

"What is it, Jonathan? I know you were gone most of yesterday, and you never mentioned where you had been."

"I went to see Headmaster Adamson at the Apprentices' Library Society—at his request, I might add. He sent a note by on Tuesday, asking me to stop in."

"Oh!" Susan had stopped breathing for a moment. "That's good, isn't it?"

"It's very good, my dear. He actually apologized for dismissing me over that 'Damned Yankee' accusation. Seems that Mr. McDermitt has become known all around town as a troublemaker, so his complaints took on a different character. Then, too, Dr. Adamson had heard about Peter's death—called him a Confederate hero. And to top it off, he had run into our son on the street and learned that he is part of Governor Pickens's bodyguard. Suddenly he is very impressed with the Grenville family."

"And?"

"And . . . he said he'd like to have me back on the faculty as soon as possible. Now wait," he warned as Susan started clapping her hands. "There's nothing definite yet. All the schools in town face an uncertain future because of the war. The younger children still attend classes, of course, but college students and apprentices tend to wander off and join the army every time they hear of a skirmish—as we well know."

Johnny made a small face and then grinned. "Well, somebody has to do it!"

"If there are enough students enrolled after Christmas, I'll have a job for sure. If not, Dr. Adamson said he would be happy to put in a good word for me with the dean at the College of Charleston. I'll be putting up some private tutoring notices, too, in hopes of picking up some high-school-level students, but it looks like I will be back in the teaching business in the New Year."

"Oh, Jonathan, how wonderful! I know how you have missed teaching."

"Does this mean you're giving up your aspirations to be a plantation owner?" Mrs. Dubois's voice had turned colder.

"I'm not giving up anything, but there's no hope of being able to work the land on Edisto until after the war is over. And, in the meantime, my growing family needs to eat."

"Harbor View is not my only plantation," Mrs. Dubois continued. "I had hoped that since growing cotton is problematic at the moment, I would be able to ask you to concentrate on our rice plantation."

"Rice? I . . . I didn't realize that Mr. Dubois had a separate rice plantation apart from the minor crop on Edisto Island. No one has ever mentioned it."

"The center of our rice production is Meadow View, out on the Ashley River, past Drayton Hall and Middleton Place. It's a good-sized operation managed by an experienced overseer, so George did not have to visit it often. We didn't take the children out there to live during the growing season because rice cultivation requires tons of water and mud. The plantation house is rather small, too, just a single story with dormers above. Still, you've talked about wanting to concentrate more on food production, and I don't know anything more important than rice. Of course, if you'd rather teach . . ."

Susan and Jonathan exchanged a volume of conversation without speaking a word. Their eyes showed their agreement and their frustration.

"Mrs. Dubois, I will certainly look into what's happening at Meadow View. But if, as you say, your husband did not have to visit very often, I'm sure I can trust the same overseer to keep things running smoothly."

"The difference is, Harry Philips knew my husband. He doesn't know you."

"True enough, but that is something I can remedy this coming week. Thank you for alerting me, Mrs. Dubois. Eddie, how would you like to go for a ride on Monday?"

"I'm ready to go. I'd love to learn more about how people grow rice."

"That's settled then. Now, when are we going to cut that pie?"

Jonathan and Eddie both enjoyed the ride to Meadow View. "With all these trees meeting above our heads, I feel like I'm riding through one of those Gothic cathedrals you used to teach us about," Eddie said.

"So you were listening!" Jonathan's joking tone concealed the enormous pride he was feeling toward his second son. "You're absolutely right, of course. If you ever get to see the European cathedrals, you'll recognize the same kind of silence created by having a roof so high above your head. Now look.

We're coming up on Drayton Hall. That's a name you'll be hearing a lot more about during the course of this war."

"Why's that?"

"If you remember, Thomas Drayton was the general in command of the Confederate forces at the Battle of Port Royal. And his brother Percival Drayton was commander of one of the Union ships in the invasion fleet. Your mother and I may sometimes face difficulties because we come from different parts of America, but imagine what it must be like for Mrs. Drayton to have two sons on opposite sides of the battlefield."

"I can't imagine. Aren't families supposed to stick together?"

"That's the ideal, son, but the rule that one must stand up for one's beliefs takes precedence, I believe."

Eddie shook his head. "I don't understand war at all," he said. "This one doesn't seem to be doing anything but making everyone miserable."

"Again, you're correct. But throughout the course of history there has seldom been a period without a war. Each generation has to learn the lessons of war for itself. I wish I had better answers for you, but since I don't, let's talk of something more pleasant. The next plantation on the right will be Middleton Place. You won't be able to see much from the road, but try to look through the trees for glimpses of their gardens. The Middletons have imported hundreds of species of flowering plants from Europe and Asia to see which ones grow best here. Their camellia collection is said to be spectacular about this time of year. Your mother might like a bush or two for our front yard."

A few miles further down the road, which seemed to be getting narrower all the time, Eddie spotted a small hand-lettered sign: "Meadow View: A George Dubois Plantation."

"That must be the turn, Father."

But at the side of the road, two scruffy-looking soldiers stood with rifles at the ready.

"Lookin' for sumpthin?" asked one of them.

"Yes. I'm Jonathan Grenville, new estate manager for the George Dubois holdings. This is my son. We are here to talk with Harry Philips, the overseer."

The other soldier snickered. "How you gonna do that, old man?"

"I beg your pardon?"

"I said, how you think you gonna talk with a dead man?"

"Harry Philips is dead? I had no idea. When? What happened?"

The soldiers shrugged. "Don't know, but he be deader'n a doornail."

"Ah kin tells you," said a black man that neither of the Grenvilles had noticed. He had been crouching over a small fire at the side of the road, battered coffee pot in hand. Now he stood and doffed his hat at this new white man.

"Massa Phips, he be out inna barn one day, workin inna loft. Slave fella go out dere lookin fuh he, an dere he be, all sprawl out onna floor uh de barn. Musta fall truh de trap door, we figures. He dun break he neck, sho nuf."

Eddie's eyes were huge and black with fright. "Papa? Should we turn around?"

Jonathan recognized the fear that made his son revert to that childhood name, but he could not let this matter rest. "Then who's in charge here?"

"De captain uh de compny libbing heah now."

Jonathan sat up as straight as possible and stared at the two soldiers. "Take me to your commander," he ordered.

"Don't know where he might be."

"Then we'll find him. Come along, Edward." As the horses moved forward directly at the soldiers, the soldiers jumped back, belying the bravado with which they had made their initial stop. Jonathan kicked his horse into a gallop, all the time holding his breath for fear of hearing a whistling bullet.

As they approached the one-story plantation house, a more presentable soldier stepped out onto the porch. "Who goes there?"

Jonathan repeated his introductions and swung down from his mount. "Act like you belong here, Eddie," he whispered as he tethered the two horses.

"I am Captain Jeremiah Hockingsworth, First South Carolina Cavalry Regiment, Hampton's Legion. You are now trespassing on property in possession of the Confederate Army. I suggest you retrace your route."

"But this land has belonged to my family for generations," Jonathan said. "By what right do you—"

"By right of martial law, declared by General Robert E. Lee. This land has been confiscated because it lies on a direct road to the Charleston and Savannah Railroad. Your family may reclaim the land at the end of the war, if you have the proper deeds. But for the time being, the Confederate States of America has a greater need for it than you do."

"What about the crops being raised here? Surely our produce—"

"Will serve nicely to feed the Confederate Army. Now I suggest you move out before you anger someone. Our recruits are dedicated to the cause, but they tend to be a little trigger-happy."

19

The Fate of Meadow View
December 1861

The trip back to Charleston seemed much longer than its morning counterpart. Instead of curiosity and anticipation leading them on, dejection and embarrassment now accompanied the Grenvilles. Jonathan rode with his head down, almost oblivious to the road, lost in thought. Eddie was more agitated, occasionally glaring at his father and then fighting back tears of humiliation.

As they neared Middleton Place, Eddie could keep still no longer. He kicked his horse to catch up to his father. "Why don't we stop and ask the Middletons if there is anything we can do?" he asked. "They don't seem to be having any trouble with soldiers."

Jolted from his reverie, Jonathan shook his head. "No. We cannot do that. The Middletons don't know us, and you don't just ride up to someone's house without an invitation. You should know better than that."

"But, Father, they might . . ."

"I said no, Eddie. I'll be consulting my own solicitor once we are back in Charleston, but I have not yet sunk so low as to become a beggar at a neighbor's door."

As it happened, however, it was a Middleton who accosted them. As Jonathan and Eddie neared the main entrance road to Middleton Place, a horseman coming from the other direction approached the gateway into the gardens. Noticing Jonathan and Eddie, he drew up his horse and waited for them.

"Hallo!" he shouted. "Looking for the Middletons, are you?"

"No, actually, we are just passing on our way back to Charleston. I'm Jonathan Grenville, heir apparent to Mrs. Dubois's lands back up the road at Meadow View. This is my son, Edward."

"Grenville. I seem to remember that name. Oh, I know! Didn't we meet at that sad memorial service for young Peter Rogers? I'm Arthur Middleton, by the way."

"Yes, of course. Peter was my son-in-law, married to my daughter Charlotte."

"Such a sad, early death. And, if I remember correctly, his wife was expecting a child?"

"Twins, a boy and a girl, who were born just a week ago."

"All is well, I hope?"

"Yes, mother and children are all thriving, or at least insofar as that is possible given the circumstances."

"Well, give them our best wishes. How did you find things at Meadow View? Some strange goings-on around there lately, I hear. I don't get out here much from town, but my brother tells me that there appears to be an Army encampment just off the road."

"The whole plantation has been confiscated. We were invited to turn around, not quite at gunpoint but with a pretty firm display of military authority. A company of South Carolina volunteers are stationed there to guard against any attempt by the Yankees to reach the railroad line."

"And your Boston accent scared them into alertness?"

Jonathan could feel himself flushing. "I suppose it did. I've lived in Charleston for over twenty years, but there's no way to disguise my speech patterns."

"I didn't mean to embarrass you or question your loyalties, not after losing a son-in-law to this war. It must be difficult for you, though . . . being a Yankee and all."

"Well, at the moment I find myself quite angry with the Confederate Army, but that will pass. I have been wondering, however, if there is anything we could do to reclaim the lands."

"This is not the first case that I've encountered. My law firm has several clients facing the same dilemma. I can tell you that, in times of war, military necessity trumps all other rights, and it is only the military that determines those rights. The best you can do for now is to make sure you keep all the records of your property ownership. You should also document the length of their occupation of your land. Once the war is over, no matter who wins, the government will move to restore property to its rightful owners. Until then, I can only counsel patience. And if, later, there is anything the Middletons can do to help, I can assure you of our support as neighbors."

"Thank you, sir."

"No thanks necessary. Enjoy the rest of your travels."

As they continued toward Charleston, Eddie raised another question. "What do you think Grandmother Dubois will say? Will she be very angry with you?"

"Angry with me? Why would she be? I have had nothing to do with the Confederate takeover of her land."

"But you could have . . ."

"Could have—what? Challenged the soldiers? Demanded that they leave? Walked into rifle range and dared them to shoot me? What would that have accomplished? Would you rather have me dead in a desperate attempt to save a plantation I had never seen before? Are you that ashamed of me?"

"Ashamed? No, of course not. But we were so helpless, and I hate that feeling. I hate this war!"

Jonathan finally realized the depth of his son's agitation and guided both horses to the side of the road, where he could face Eddie as they talked.

"No one likes war, son. War removes social barriers and turns men into brutes. Soldiers have to believe that they hate their enemies so that they can justify killing them. Hatred is an ugly emotion, and it clouds our judgment. And if we decide we hate soldiers who are doing what they believe is their duty, we become no better than they are. Once we start hating one another, all is lost. Can you understand that?"

"I guess . . . I know I don't like how I'm feeling right now. What will happen to us if we are surrounded by haters—people who are coming after us, determined to take away what we have?"

"Now you're allowing fear to take over your judgment. Those soldiers are not coming after us. They are Southerners, just as you are. They have no way of knowing that I've been called a Damned Yankee, if that's what you are worried about. They don't want to take away everything we have."

"They stole our plantation."

"Correction, Eddie. They occupied a plantation that appeared to have no owner. The slaves were probably milling around helplessly, not knowing what to do once Harry Philips was found dead. The land appeared to be abandoned, and it lay in a strategic location. It is the last outpost before an invading army could approach the railroad. It's an ideal spot to defend that line, and they took it. I really don't blame them."

"But this is the second time that . . ."

"Yes, I know, and it seems really unfair. But we still have our home in Charleston and all of our family and—"

"Except Peter!"

"True enough. I understand all that. We can choose to rage against our losses or to count our blessings. I prefer to look on the brighter side for as long as we can. This war is going to be terrible, Eddie, and it's going to last for a long time, I'm afraid. We can't allow hate and fear to destroy us at the beginning of a long road."

Eddie nodded, trying to let his emotions drain away. His tears left traces down his cheeks, but he thrust his shoulders back and stuck out his chin. "I'll try to be as brave and patient as you are, Father, but you may have to help me along the way, because inside I'm really scared."

Jonathan placed a comforting hand on his son's arm. "Being scared is nothing to be ashamed of, so long as you don't let fear keep you from doing what needs to be done. And right now, we need to gallop back to Charleston to tell your Dragon-Lady grandmother that her Confederate Army has just taken another of her plantations. That's something to fear, but we're going to do it anyhow."

Eddie grinned—a good sign—and nudged his horse into a steady gait.

Elizabeth Dubois was surprisingly calm when she heard the news. "That's one less property to worry about, then," she said. "I can go ahead with my plans to move to Flat Rock after Christmas without wondering what's going on back here."

"But the income, Mother," Susan said. "Aren't you worried about that?"

"Not really, dear. Your father left me well provided for. Besides, there's still a large tract of land that the Army has not confiscated—at least so far as I know."

"Where is that? I don't recall another plantation."

"It's not a plantation. Oak View is a real working farm outside of Aiken, which will be quite close to where I'll be staying. You probably don't remember it because we found it was too much trouble to move all you children that far for a few weeks every year. Its main house has been closed up for many years, but the overseer keeps it in good repair, and the fields are maintained by sharecroppers."

"Sharecroppers?" Jonathan could not hide his surprise.

"Yes, sharecroppers. They are mostly white families, although there are a couple of free black ones as well. They live in separate houses on the land, and each family works a section of the farm. They pay a yearly rent to use the land, and then, when their crops come in, we receive a small percentage of their profits." She looked at Jonathan with an ironic smile. "Believe it or not, we have such civilized arrangements even here in the deep South. Not all labor is performed by slaves."

Properly chagrined at his own shocked reaction, Jonathan could only nod his head in agreement and give silent thanks that Mrs. Dubois was in a good mood.

20

Conflagration
December 11, 1861

For the first time in days, the house was quiet. Dinner had been cleared, the children had gone to bed without too many complaints, the babies were asleep, and Charlotte had taken herself off to read a book. Jonathan smiled at Susan as she moved about the parlor straightening items here and there. "I hardly know what to do with an evening of peace," he commented. "How would you like to sit on the piazza for a bit? This unseasonably warm weather can't last for much longer."

"What a lovely idea, dear. We probably need to talk about Christmas while the children aren't about."

"Christmas! Ugh! It's been so warm I'd almost forgotten."

"It's only two weeks away," she reminded him. "Last year was so strange, what with secession being declared and the first rumblings of war. I really don't know how to approach it this year. We're still at war, and officially the household is still in mourning for Peter, so we can't do anything ostentatious, but, on the other hand, the children and slaves need not be deprived by conditions over which they have no control."

"You're right, but that's not exactly what I had in mind for this evening. Could we just go outside, watch the stars appear, and smell the night-blooming flowers that are still thriving? I'm badly in need of some relaxation."

"Oh, of course. I know you've been working over your lectures, as well as the plantation account books. Let's stroll around the yard. Have you seen the blossoms on the camellia bushes next door? They keep poking through the iron fence, and I don't have the heart to push them back into their own yard."

"Eddie and I talked about those camellias on our ride out to Meadow View. I thought you might like to have a few plants for our side garden."

"I'd love that! Do you think any of the Middletons would be willing to share? They are the ones who imported them, after all."

"Well, I know whom to approach. We met Arthur Middleton on that same ride out the Ashley River Road, and I've seen him on the street here in Charleston several times since. I'll ask him."

"You're so thoughtful, Jonathan. I don't tell you enough how lucky I feel to be married to you. Come. Let's check the yard." Susan laughed and led him down the stairs onto the grassy pathway to the side garden. As the first breezes stirred, she shook her head hard enough to dislodge some tendrils of her unruly hair. "That wind feels good!"

"Hmmm. Wind's coming up, for sure, and it's out of the northeast. Could be a sign of bad weather ahead. This time of year, a nor'easter off the coast could spell the end of our pleasant autumn."

"And about time, too! Maybe a storm will cool us off and put us in the mood for pine bough decorations and crackling fires."

"Susan, come on! No Christmas tonight, please."

"All right, but it's coming, whether you are ready or not."

Just then, the evening silence was broken by the clang of fire bells, and soon they could hear others ringing from all over town.

"Oh, dear! Speaking of crackling fires! Sounds like someone's in real trouble," Susan said. "They must be calling out several fire companies. Come, let's go back to the street and see if we can spot where the smoke is coming from."

"A big blaze could be disastrous. Most of the fire companies have been decimated by militia members going off to war."

From the front gate, they looked off to their left and saw an orange glow lighting the horizon. "What lies off in that direction?" Susan asked.

"The docks, I suppose, and there are some foundries—"

Jonathan's words were interrupted by a series of faint explosions echoing over the city. Susan clutched his arm. "Are those cannons? Are we being fired upon?"

"No. The enemy wouldn't have been able to gain access to those docks without someone seeing them pass through the harbor. But there are some munitions works over there around Hassell Street. Perhaps that's where the fire is centered. Dangerous, though—fire with all that gunpowder!"

The bells continued to ring, and more and more people were coming out onto the street to see what was happening. Smoke was now clearly visible, rising over the dock area and floating south toward them. The wind really began to rise, and before long it could be seen carrying scraps of ash. Clouds, sailing ashore, neared the area of the fire and reflected a rosy hue contrasted against the navy blue of the evening sky. "It's beautiful and terrifying all at once," Susan remarked. "Why don't they get it extinguished?"

"It looks like it's already out of control!" someone shouted, and Susan clutched her husband's arm more tightly.

"Perhaps I should take a horse and ride uptown to see what's going on," Jonathan said.

"And leave us here? No! Oh, Jonathan, I'm terrified. Please don't leave me."

"Let's get you back into the house. There's nothing to be learned from staring at the sky."

"Wait!" She pointed up the street. "Someone's riding this way."

"Good heavens! That looks like Johnny!" And so it was.

The young soldier leaped from his horse, draped the reins over the hitching post at the street, and bounded up the steps to confront his parents. "What are you doing, just standing here watching the show? Don't you know you're in danger?"

"Calm down, Johnny. We're glad you're here. Do you happen to know what's going on?"

"Father, listen to me! I'm on official duty. General Lee called out our College Cadets because so many of us know the city well. We've been sent to warn people in the path of the fire that they need to evacuate."

"Where is the fire, Johnny? We can't tell from here."

Realizing that he was not going to get his parents' attention until he had satisfied their curiosity, he paused to catch his breath. "It's a huge fire. It started at Russell's Sash and Door Shop and spread across the street to Cameron's Foundry and the munitions dump. That's where the explosions came from. Then it moved up Hassell Street, as well as down East Bay and those side streets. One fire unit seems to have prevented it from destroying the Charleston Hotel, but now it's consuming everything on the south side of Market, and it's moving toward

Meeting. There's not enough water for the pumpers to attack the whole leading edge of the blaze. And with the wind continuing to rise, there seems to be no way to stop it traveling clear across the peninsula."

"Ah, but surely those stone buildings along Meeting Street will stop it."

"Not from what I've seen of it, Father. General Lee has made the Mills House Hotel his base of operations, but even he is worried that the fire will drive him out. As I left, he had the slaves draping wet blankets all over the roof and sides of the building. The wind keeps picking up sparks and burning scraps and dropping them on rooftops. Before you know it, whole buildings have been engulfed. Father, you need to understand that you are in the direct path of the firestorm. You must evacuate now!"

"What do we do? Where do we go?" Susan's voice carried a sharp edge of hysteria.

"That's what I'm trying to tell you." Johnny pushed his parents back through the front door and shut it firmly against the noise from the street. "You have to listen to me. The fire is out of control and moving this way. This house is in its direct path, and there will be no stopping it before it gets here."

Susan stared at her son in horror and stumbled backward as if she had been attacked by his words. Jonathan caught her by her forearms and lowered her onto a chair. Then he regarded young Johnny with a newly attentive respect for his son's authority. "Where do we start?" he asked.

"Get the children out first. I've been assured that the fire will not be allowed to pass beyond Broad Street, so Grandmother Dubois's house should be safe. The engineers are headed out to blow up the buildings along Queen to create a firebreak and protect the northwest part of the city. Then they will do the same on Broad to save the tip of the peninsula. But General Lee has already given up all hope of salvaging this area between Queen and Broad. You'll be hearing the first explosions soon, so brace yourselves for that and know that it's a good thing."

Jonathan nodded and looked anxiously at the stairs. "Susan, don't think. Just go upstairs, rouse and dress the children, and herd them down here to the parlor. Tell Charlotte to bundle up the twins and prepare to go with them. Eddie can stay here for the moment to help. We'll have Hector hitch up the large wagon to carry them all, along with the slave children and a couple of the housemaids."

"Good!" Johnny looked relieved that his father's control had taken over. "If you'll handle that, I'll ride ahead to Grandmother's house and let her know what's happening, so she can get her household staff organized. Then I'll come right back to help you pack up a load of valuables. Let's move quickly!"

Once the wagon was on its way, albeit filled with wailing children and panicked slaves, Jonathan took another deep breath and turned to his wife. "Don't fall apart on me now, Susan. Think! What's most important in this house?"

Susan shook her head in despair. "How can we choose? Condense a lifetime of memories—twenty years of marriage—into a single wagonload of priceless possessions?"

"Do it now, or we lose everything! I'll collect what money we have in the house, along with all our important papers—deeds, the children's baptismal records, the insurance papers on the house, and the plantation books I borrowed from your mother. You start in the dining room. Get one of the slave girls to pack up all the silver. Don't bother with the dishes. Pottery can be replaced easily, but we may need to melt down the silver for money. Then gather family portraits and just enough clothes to allow us each a change or two."

"Don't forget your books, Jonathan. They represent your life's work."

"Eddie, can you do that for me, please? Some of the boxes I brought home from the Apprentices' Library Society are still unpacked. Drag them out here and we'll see how much room we have. And, Susan, perhaps you can find an old quilt to wrap around your melodeon."

For the first time, Susan's eyes seemed to light up. "Really, Jonathan? I can take it?"

"Of course. It doesn't weigh much in comparison to how important your music is to your well-being."

Somehow, bundles of possessions accumulated near the rear door. By the time Johnny and Hector arrived home from their first trip across town with an empty wagon ready to be reloaded, the Grenvilles were ready to leave.

"Oh, what about all the slaves?" Susan asked.

"One more detail," Jonathan said, stepping into the back-yard where the slaves had assembled out of fear and curiosity. Jonathan stood on the back stoop and banged on a metal pail to get their attention. "I'm sure you have figured out by now that this house is in danger from the fire," he said, pointing up to clouds of smoke, ash, and sparks swirling above their heads.

"I am moving the family to Mrs. Dubois's house. Any of you who wish to do so may come with us. But, as of this moment, I am unofficially freeing each one of you."

Gasps and murmurs arose from the gathered crowd.

"The most important thing is that you save your lives and the lives of your families. If you want to make a break for freedom, now is the moment to do it. By morning, this house and all your cabins will lie in ashes. No one will know who you are or where you have gone, and I will not pursue you. Head south across James Island to the Yankee lines. They will welcome you and protect you. If you choose to come with us, we will talk later about the possibility of your formal emancipation. But I repeat: As of this moment, you have a chance to be free, and I thank you for all the service you have done me and my family. Now, take yourselves off, and may God protect us all!"

21

An Aftermath of Ashes
December 12, 1861

N o one slept much in Charleston that night, except for the very young and those who were too old or deaf to understand what was happening. Everyone else was waiting for the next ember to ignite a place they loved. Along the streets, clusters of people huddled with small bundles of their possessions. Others milled about on the sidewalks, trying to decide which direction promised the greatest safety. Mothers called for their children, and husbands for their wives. Some voices carried a note of hysteria. Some sobbed quietly; others wailed with grief. Those lucky enough to have some form of transport filled the streets with their wagons and carriages as their horses pranced nervously and shied away from every floating piece of ash. The animals' whinnying and nickering added another layer to the cacophony of voices.

Above all the sounds of human dismay came the noise of the fire itself. The flames crackled when they touched dry wood and sizzled when they encountered something damp. Roofs burned first and then crashed down upon the floors beneath. Houses collapsing in on themselves made a strange sighing sound as the air inside was driven outward. Window glass shattered, sounding as if someone had fired a shot. And, periodically, a loud explosion would ricochet off the walls that were still standing to echo across the town. All through the night, the Army engineers continued to blow up houses along the perimeter of the fire, hoping to choke it off by removing its fuel source. With each explosion, people startled as if it were the first one they had heard.

The large stone buildings that Jonathan had thought could be trusted to stand made a groaning sound all their own as their mortar softened and the stones began to pull apart. Sometimes the groaning reached the level of a screech before the first stones suddenly parted and came crashing down upon whatever lay below. Then, like a set of Chinese dominoes, the massive buildings came apart, risers of stonework falling one after another with a crash and clatter that seemed to go on forever.

Around 1:00 AM, a light rain started to fall, and every face turned upward, hoping that the drops were only precursors to a downpour that would put out the fire. Instead, the heat of the fire seemed to dry up the raindrops before they hit the ground. The rain had no effect at all on a firestorm that was already sucking the air around it into the center of the blaze. Institute Hall, where the Democratic Convention of 1860 and the vote for secession had taken place, disappeared as if some great vengeful furnace had chosen to consume every trace of the building.

Soon, the Circular Church began its own slow fall. Not until 3:00 AM did the bell tower give way, allowing its huge brass bell to crash down and shatter on the pavement with a clanging that seemed to ring on and on. And at 4:00 AM, the roof and interior walls of the Catholic Cathedral of St. John and St. Finbar burned, destroying the possessions of dozens of parishioners who had brought their valuables there for safekeeping because they believed the church to be fireproof. Perhaps it might have been under normal circumstances, but this was no ordinary fire. The steeple of St. John and St. Finbar fell at 5:30 AM with a great rumbling that seemed to mark the finale of the fire's run.

The blasts continued until the fire reached from the Cooper River to the Ashley River and burned itself out. When it was over, some 540 acres had burned, 600 buildings—most of them private residences—had been destroyed, and five churches had collapsed. Hundreds, perhaps thousands, of people were homeless and destitute. The local papers estimated that the losses would exceed eight million dollars in the currency of that time.

All during that terrible night at the Dubois house on Legare Street, the family had struggled to make sense of what was happening. Susan took the children upstairs to settle them into a semblance of sleep. Charlotte and the twins moved into a small back bedroom, where crying babies would be less likely to disturb the rest of the family. Susan passed out blankets and pillows to the other children and helped them curl into tiny exhausted balls on the floor of her childhood room.

"Eddie, you take the cot in here. You've worked hard tonight."

"I'm not going to sleep, Mother. I need to know what's going on. Don't treat me like one of the children."

"I need you to stay up here with your brothers and sisters. They are likely to wake from the noise outside and be frightened. Stay awake if you like, and watch what's happening from the window. But you need to accept the role of big brother for a while. Be here to soothe and reassure them if they need you. Can you do that?"

"Of course I can. Don't worry about them." Eddie was not smiling as he spoke, but his eyes shifted to the bed with evident longing.

Susan brushed his unruly hair from his forehead, hugged him quickly, and murmured a "thank you" as she slipped out of the room. She tapped on Charlotte's door as she passed and then opened it a crack, not wanting to waken the sleeping babies. "Once the twins are settled, dear, come down to the parlor. We need to talk about what we do next."

Charlotte turned from where she had been huddled over the makeshift cribs. Tears were streaming down her face, her cheeks were blotched with red, and her mouth was twisted into a grimace. "I'm not coming down. I'm not leaving them ever again—not for a single moment! If the world is coming to an end, I'm ready to let it. Just get out and leave us alone!"

"Charlotte, I—"

"Get out! Come back in the morning—if there is a morning."

Susan was still shaking her head as she entered the parlor. "I swear I don't know how to handle that girl," she said to Jonathan. "She's in one of her despairing moods again. I understood her reaction to Peter's death, but she was so happy and excited after the birth of the twins. I thought she was over the worst of her grieving. Now she's sobbing again and threatening never to let the children out of her sight."

"That girl always was the moody one," Mrs. Dubois remarked almost to herself. "Needs someone to slap her smartly into the real world, if you ask me."

Susan glared at her mother but refused to be goaded into an argument. She was simply too tired. "Should we all try to get some sleep?" she asked, turning again to her husband.

"No sleep for me," he answered. "We can't be sure that the firebreaks will hold. This house could still be in danger. We're less than two blocks south of Broad. I intend to keep watch until I see for myself that the fire is out."

"Then I'd better stay with you," Susan said. "Could we see more from the piazza?"

"Best view's from the sleeping porch," Mrs. Dubois suggested, "but don't go opening the doors or windows. I don't want my house filled with all that smoke."

That brewing discussion was interrupted by Hector coming in from the slave yard. "Massa Jonathan? What we gwine do bout all de slave dat come wit we fro Logan Street?"

"How many followed us?"

"Ebry one uh dem. Nobody gwine run off an leave you ifn dis fambly be in trubble."

Jonathan's eyes brimmed with tears at the loyalty of people he had been holding in bondage. "For tonight, Hector, see if they can bed down in the wagons or with friends in the yard. We'll talk about their future once we know exactly what we're all facing. And tell them I said 'thank you' for their faithful service."

"Tell them not to get too comfortable!" Mrs. Dubois shouted after him. "I can't believe you brought all those people with you, Jonathan. You certainly can't expect me to make room for them and support them here."

"Actually, I tried to free them," he answered.

"You did what?"

"I told them they were free to go wherever they liked. But they chose to stay with us to try to help."

"So what do you intend to do with them now?" Mrs. Dubois glared at him in her best Dragon-Lady fashion, and a bit of foam spittle began to collect at the corner of her mouth. "You don't know the first thing about how to treat slaves!"

"What would you have had me do? Chain them to their cabins and leave them there to fry?"

"Oh, of course not, but . . ."

"There is no 'but'—and I don't intend to discuss this with you further. Obviously, we are imposing on you by bringing everyone here, and I'll try to remedy that as soon as possible. In the meantime, there's no point in arguing about what's been done."

Some time after 5:00 AM, young Johnny arrived to check on his displaced family. But this time he trudged up the steps instead of bounding. His feet dragged, as if he were too tired to lift them. His face was smeared with soot and sweat, his uniform tattered, and his left arm sported a rather grimy bandage. "Is everyone all right?" he asked from the doorway.

"We're fine, Johnny, but you look terrible."

"Just exhausted, Father. We've finally been dismissed and sent back to camp. Only right now it seems like a long way to go to find a bed."

"What happened to your arm?" Susan was immediately the concerned mother. "Take that filthy rag off and let me see."

"Don't worry about it, Mother. It's just a burn."

"A burn! That could be serious. How did you get burned?"

"I've been fighting a fire." Johnny's voice was utterly weary.

"I know that. I meant . . ."

"Was I in danger? Not really. Alex almost was, though. He went inside St. Peter's Church to check to see if anyone was in here. It was empty, and he didn't realize it was already on fire above his head. He was so tired that he curled up in a pew to take a quick nap. Then the roof caved in, and a burning beam pinned him to the pew. A couple of other fellows and I had to lift that beam so he could wiggle out from under. I happened to get hold of a hot spot, but I couldn't let go without killing Alex. So I burned my arm. It'll heal." He grinned at last. "And he'll owe me for the rest of his life!"

Even Jonathan shared a quick smile before his face turned serious again. "What are conditions like out in the streets, son? Have you seen our house? And what about the downtown area?"

"Meeting Street, Market, Queen, King, and Broad are all passable but lined with destruction. Not much of anything left. As for Logan Street, I heard someone say that they had managed to save one house, but it turned out not to be ours. And, for now, you can't get down the street at all because some of the debris from collapsing houses ended up in the middle of the street. In general, the fire is out, although there are hot spots here and there. The neighborhood between Broad and Tradd and west of St. Peter's Cemetery is still burning at a pretty good clip. The Cathedral of St. John and St. Finbar is still ablaze, too, but it's just a matter of time before the steeple collapses, and that should be the end of it. For now, would Grandmother mind if I stretched out here on the piazza for a nap before I continue to make my way across the fire zone?"

"Don't be silly. Come in and get some proper rest." Susan glanced over her shoulder at her mother, now snoozing herself in her wingback chair. "Grandmother will never know."

"No, I'm too dirty. And I need to sleep—right now." With that statement, he abruptly sat down on the porch floor, rolled to his good shoulder, and began to snore.

22

The Persecutions of Job
December 1861

Other family members were as exhausted as young Johnny, and one by one they succumbed to an uneasy slumber, their dreams pierced by the sounds of fire bells and explosions. In the late afternoon, Jonathan roused himself and began to make his way to the front door. At once Susan was at his side.

"Where are you going, Jonathan?"

"I have to go out. I have to see the destruction for myself. I have to find our house. Otherwise my imagination and my dreams will drive me mad."

"Then I'm coming with you."

"We can't take the horses back out into the chaos, Susan. I'm going on foot."

"Well, I can walk as well as you. I'm wearing sturdy shoes, and I lost my hoop skirt much earlier last night. Our lives have been nearly destroyed. We need to see what remains together. Go ahead, but I'll be walking right behind you."

They made their way up Legare Street toward Broad without speaking further, but at the corner of Broad they hesitated, and their hands clasped in desperation. Nothing lay before them or on either side in any direction but piles of blackened rubble, the jutting fingers of chimneys, and charred tree trunks stripped of their foliage and small limbs.

"I can't even recognize this street. Are you sure it's Broad?" Then Susan turned to her right and gasped as she faced the skeletal walls of the Cathedral of St. John and St. Finbar. "Where's the steeple? The cathedral is just six years old, and it was supposed to be fireproof, just like the District Records Office. How could it burn?"

Her thoughts were addressed to Jonathan but answered by an elderly priest who had been shuffling past them. "I ask myself the same thing, but in reality I know the answer. We cannot subvert the laws of nature and expect God to intervene to save our foolish lives. Our souls, perhaps—yes—but not our pride-stiff necks."

"But how . . .?"

"Our parishioners knew the cathedral was made of stone and glass and iron and copper roofing. And so they brought us their loads of valuables—their silver and gold, their portraits and their books, their rich fabrics. They even propped the great west doors open so they could carry their treasures into safety. And the winds out of the east blew straight in through those open doors, carrying the sparks and burning ashes with them. They set fire to all those treasures, as well as to the wooden pews with their padded seats and cushioned kneelers—luxuries our congregants were sure they needed and deserved. The heat and the flames went straight up, as nature decrees, and the mortar softened, the glass broke, and the iron and copper melted. All was lost."

"Were they able to save the bishop's library?" Jonathan asked.

"Those 17,000 books, in which he took such pride? All ashes now, along with our Bibles and our missals."

"What about the residence of the Sisters of Charity?" Susan asked. "Are the nuns safe?"

"Safe? I suppose so, but homeless, nevertheless. The convent, the girls' school—all gone." Tucking his hands into the sleeves of his cassock, he shuffled away, still muttering, "All gone . . . everything lost . . . everything."

Susan stood in shock, slowly shaking her head, until Jonathan pulled at her hand. "Look beyond these ruins, Susan. Look eastward along Broad Street. See those pinnacles, more visible now against the blue sky? That's the Huguenot Church. It still stands. We can reassure your mother on that count, at least."

"She'll be pleased for Father's sake. But . . . oh, Jonathan, I'm afraid to turn around. Our house should be just a short block behind us. I keep thinking that as long as I don't look, it will still be there."

"It's gone, Susan. I can't even tell which of those burned and crumbling chimneys belonged to us. But don't look, if it helps you. Remember the house on Logan Street as it was yesterday and all the days before—filled with children's laughter, the busy clatter of household chores, your music . . ."

"We were happy there. That's what I will remember most."

"Then cling to that, as a reminder that we can be happy again. We saved all that really mattered—not material possessions, like those that helped cause the destruction of the cathedral, but our lives and the lives of our children."

"Are you ready to go back to Mother's house?"

"No, not quite yet, if you're up to another walk. I need to see Meeting Street. Johnny said they were able to save the Mills House, but north of there . . ."

Trying to avoid as much of the damaged area as possible, they walked up Broad and then turned onto Meeting. The whole first block had survived—the Charleston Courthouse, housing the city's library and museum; the District Records office, fondly called "The Fireproof Building"; Hibernian Hall, home of the Irish Benevolent Society; and the iconic Mills House Hotel. But on the other side of Queen, the entire aspect of the city changed.

"Jonathan! Our church! Our beautiful Circular Church!"

The Circular Church had been a massive domed structure, built in the style of the Pantheon, with seven doors and twenty-six windows. Its central sanctuary had held 2,000 congregants. Now only curved sections of the outer walls remained, along with the base of the bell tower and the shattered fragments of its brass bell. Even the tombstones in the churchyard, some of them dating back to the seventeenth century, lay shattered and scorched by the fire. Susan and Jonathan stared at the remains from across the street, trying to absorb the enormity of the damage, until a somewhat familiar voice interrupted their thoughts.

"Grenville? Jonathan Grenville? Have you survived, then?"

"Oh, Dr. Adamson. Sorry. I wasn't expecting to see anyone I knew. How . . .?" It was a question Jonathan was reluctant to ask. "How is the Apprentices' Library Society?"

"Gone, I'm afraid. Our new building burned to the ground, taking the entire Apprentices' Library with it." The headmaster's face was gray.

"What will you do?"

"I don't know. No one knows anything at this point. I'm sure that we will not be able to do any rebuilding so long as this war wages on. Neither laborers nor materials can be had. And many of our wealthiest benefactors have lost everything, as well. No money for rebuilding from those sources, either."

"Could you . . .? Is there anywhere . . .?"

"To carry on with classes? No. The heart of this city has been wiped out. And the war is doing a similar job of killing off our students. Our school was a noble venture, but its time has passed." Eyes brimming, Dr. Adamson gave a curt nod in Susan's direction and strode off through the ruins of Horlbeck Alley.

Jonathan watched him go, lips pressed tight as if to contain his own emotions. At last, he sighed. "There goes the last possibility for my teaching career."

Susan was watching him anxiously. "You could always—"

"Don't! Don't offer me any faint hopes. Look around. Look down this street. Institute Hall has disappeared—that great bastion of South Carolina's independence. The Theatre, the Art Gallery with its historic collections of fine paintings—melted into colorful puddles now, I'd guess. The Southern Express Office, the Savings Institution." Without realizing it, Jonathan had allowed his voice to boom out his anguish, and other passersby joined his recounting.

"I hear they managed to save all the records from the savings bank, though. Nice of them. Our culture's gone, but the record of my loan is safe," someone commented with a note of irony in his voice.

"They saved the jail and the workhouse, too, while decent people lost everything."

"At least they also saved Roper Hospital and the Medical College."

Jonathan didn't want to hear any more. "Words cannot do justice to our losses, and seeing it first hand is not helping. Let's go home, Susan."

"Home?" She sounded bitter.

"Back to our family. That's all we have left of home."

By Sunday, most people were desperately seeking ways to restore a touch of normalcy to their shattered lives. Mrs. Dubois announced that she had every intention of attending Sunday services at the Huguenot Church, and she offered to take the grandchildren with her.

"But what are your plans?" she asked, turning to Susan. "Your Congregational Church is rubble, I understand."

"A church is more than a building, of course. The *Charleston Courier* says that we will be holding meetings on the second floor of Hibernian Hall, while the Catholics use the first floor."

Jonathan was reluctant to agree. "If it weren't so far, I'd suggest going out to the Second Presbyterian Church instead. I haven't had a chance to talk to Reverend Croft since the fire. I'd like to hear his words of comfort, but I don't think it would help to trudge through the worst of the destruction to get there."

"I think you're right, Jonathan. For that matter, I really don't need any form of Calvinist interpretation right now. What about visiting St. Philips? That beautiful building escaped the flames, and I would appreciate being in sacred surroundings rather than a borrowed meeting room. The traditional Episcopal liturgy might be just what our troubled spirits are longing for."

The organ music and candlelight did help, and the droned prayers and responses were comforting. But then came the reading of Scripture—an all-too-familiar description of grief from the book of Job—and the Grenvilles cringed when the homily, too, turned out to be based on passages from the same book:

"In Chapter One, Job lost all his worldly possessions—7,000 sheep, 3,000 camels, 500 yoke of oxen, 500 she-asses, seven sons and three daughters and all their great houses," Reverend Howe reminded them. "And how did he react? Here's what the Bible tells us:

> *Then Job arose, and rent his mantle, and shaved his head, and fell down upon the ground, and . . . worshipped,*
>
> *And said, Naked came I out of my mother's womb, and naked shall I return thither; The Lord gave, and the Lord hath taken way; blessed be the name of the Lord.*
>
> *In all this Job sinned not, nor charged God foolishly.*

"See how Job grieved, as was his right and duty, but he did not falter in his faith. And in Chapter Two, Satan again attacked this good and upright man:

> *So went Satan forth from the presence of the Lord, and smote Job with sore boils from the sole of his foot unto his crown,*
>
> *And he took him a potsherd to scrape himself withal; and he sat down among the ashes.*
>
> *Then said his wife unto him, Dost thou still retain thy integrity? Curse God and die.*
>
> *But he said unto her, Thou speakest as one of the foolish women speaketh. What? Shall we receive good at the hand of God, and shall we not receive evil? In all this did not Job sin with his lips.*

"Job saw that all his suffering was neither punishment nor betrayal from God, but rather a test of his faith. And he trusted in his Lord. Can we do any less?"

As they left the church, Jonathan wore that tight-lipped expression that Susan had come to associate with his anger. In an attempt to lighten his mood, she nudged his arm and said, "See, it's not so bad. You haven't lost all your camels and she-asses."

"It's not funny, Susan. Reverend Howe's point, I take it, was that none of this is our fault, so we just have to trust and wait for God to make it all better. I don't agree."

"But . . ."

"It is our fault. It's my fault, and all those who have let the cancer of slavery distort their view of humanity. It's the fault of everyone who voted for secession and everyone who cheered the idea of war. Job may have been an innocent man, but none of us are that pure. We have been bringing the wrath of God down upon ourselves. And I am, perhaps, the most guilty of all."

"How can you say that? You've done nothing to deserve having your house burn down."

"Ah, but I have. Even the fire can be traced back to the war, which caused the shortage of firefighters. And I, as a citizen of Charleston, am also responsible for the war because I did not speak out. I, of all people, should have understood the dangers of a society based on slavery. I am a historian, but I have failed to learn the lessons of history. I am a New Englander, but I have turned my back on the ideals of my forefathers. I—"

"Stop it!" Susan whirled around and confronted him. "I won't listen to another 'woe-is-me' word from you! You're being ridiculous. There's nothing you could have done to stop anything that has happened to you—your lost job, the confiscated plantations, the fire. You're just not that important, my love."

Jonathan glared at his wife as she shook her finger under his nose. "Enough. We won't talk of it again, since we obviously do not agree. I shouldn't expect you to understand how I feel."

"That's not fair. I'm trying to . . ."

But Jonathan was already striding ahead toward home.

23

Reminders of Christmas Past
December 1861

The Grenvilles finished their walk in silence. As they entered the house, Jonathan spoke without looking at Susan. "I'll be in the library. Please don't interrupt me for dinner. I'll find something to eat later if I get hungry."

Susan stared helplessly at the closing door. The scenario was familiar. This was how Jonathan avoided argument and confrontation. In the Logan Street house, she had been able to gloss over his absences, but here, in her mother's home, it would be more difficult. Taking a deep breath, she walked into the parlor to find Mrs. Dubois and the children waiting.

"How was the service at St. Philips?"

"Depressing. I have never liked the Book of Job, and that was the whole focus of the service."

"You would have heard the same scripture among the Huguenots," Mrs. Dubois said. "And I would be willing to guess that it played out in every church across the city this morning. Everyone is feeling persecuted and betrayed, apparently. I just hope that attitude will not continue much longer. We need to move forward and forget our suffering."

"That may be easier for you to say, Mother, since your house was not affected!" Susan surprised herself with the vehemence of her reaction and sought to smooth it over. "Still, I agree that donning sackcloth and ashes has never fixed any problem."

"Particularly at Christmastime," Mrs. Dubois added. The children looked up with smiles and sparkling eyes, hoping they would learn more about what lay in store.

No matching smile touched Susan's expression. "I agree, Mother, but can we wait a couple of days to discuss that further? Jonathan is particularly upset at the moment, and he dislikes Christmas displays even in the best of times."

"Men can be such sourpusses! Where is your long-suffering husband? You didn't abandon him at the church, did you?"

"He went straight to the library when we came in. He really doesn't want to be disturbed, even for dinner."

"How inconsiderate! Well, you'll just have to cajole him out of his black mood. I haven't time to pamper a grown man. With eleven unexpected houseguests and a dozen or so extra slaves in the yard, I have my hands full enough already."

By Wednesday, Mrs. Dubois had had enough of closed doors and irregular comings and goings. Knocking sharply at the library door, she announced, "Mr. Grenville, I need to see you in the parlor at once."

Even Jonathan recognized the tone of the Dragon Lady's voice—the equivalent of a mother addressing her children by their full names to let them know when they had crossed the borders of impropriety. His face was still grim as he emerged and followed her obediently down the hall. Susan and the two oldest children had already assembled.

Without preamble, Mrs. Dubois launched into her agenda. "Christmas is one week from today. The rituals and holidays of our world arrive on their own schedule without regard for our troubles or anger or inconveniences. Your small children have a right to believe that Christmas will come without fail on its appointed day and that Saint Nicholas will arrive with his rewards for good behavior. Our slaves also have a right to expect that they will be given a few days of relief from their duties and that they will receive their semiannual provisions of clothing and food stores. We are not going to disappoint them."

Taking the silence for agreement, she went on, ticking off the items for consideration. "First, we must let the slaves know when they can celebrate their Slave Yule. I propose that their holiday start after lunch on Saturday and continue through Monday. That will put them back to work by Christmas Eve. That will also give the cooks time to prepare some cold meals that will carry us through the weekend. But, more important, we must be sure that they receive their due allotments. I have already laid aside two sets of winter clothing for each of my slaves, plus provisions of sugar, salt, flour, salt pork, molasses, and cornmeal for each family. But what about our newcomers?"

"You taught me well, Mother. I had our provisions and clothing set aside long before the fire. I brought with me the bundle of clothes, and their foodstuffs went into your own larder when we arrived. All our slaves will have something to celebrate."

"And celebrate they will. We have always allowed them to build a large bonfire in the slave yard in the evenings and to hold a ritual Stomp, even if it goes on far into the night. They are also accustomed to holding wreath-making parties in the yard and decorating both their own cabins and the main house, so be prepared for pine boughs and winter flowers everywhere, starting almost immediately. The children will have their Christmas tree, too."

"They always love the tree, but there won't be much under it, I'm afraid." Susan's smile faded. "Saint Nicholas is on short rations, and there's almost nowhere left to shop."

"Leave that to me," Mrs. Dubois said. "You haven't been up in our attic for years, but you would find that it is stuffed with the remnants of your childhood. When you and Robert and Annaliese tired of your toys, I stashed them away in hopes of someday having grandchildren who would love them again. It's time to drag out those reminders of Christmases past."

At that reassurance even Jonathan began to look pleased. "Thank you, Mother Dubois. It may be hard to ignore the circumstances all around us, but we will make the effort for the children's sake."

"There's one other matter on which we need to clear the air. My plans have not changed because of your altered circumstances. I am still leaving Charleston on January second. I will be sending a wagon on ahead with my trunks, while I board the train for Flat Rock. The slaves I am not taking with me have already been assigned to other families in the neighborhood."

"Sold, you mean?" Jonathan's voice carried a sharp edge.

"No, not sold. No money has changed hands, and it never will. I have simply arranged for the slaves who are staying here to do whatever needs to be done to close up the house. Then they will move elsewhere to be taken care of. I don't consider them possessions, Jonathan, no matter what you may think. They are, however, my responsibility, and I have provided new accommodations for them."

"So if you decide to come home, they will be able to come back," Charlotte suggested.

"No, make no mistake. This is not a test run or brief visit. I do not intend to return to Charleston, and I am glad to put it and its memories behind me."

"Perhaps when the war is over, you'll—"

"What? Feel nostalgic? Change my mind? No, I fear Charleston has been ruined for me forever by the events of the past year. If I could, I would sell the house, but, as my solicitor informs me, I only hold it in trust for Susan, who inherits it on my death."

"Mother! Don't even think about that."

"I'm simply outlining my circumstances as I understand them. This house is my own personal albatross hanging from my neck for as long as I live. Susan, you, too, have a responsibility to it. You are at the moment homeless, so, if you like, you may take over the upkeep of the house now and live in it. It would seem a viable solution to your problems, although personally I do not want to see you remain in Charleston throughout the coming years of the war. I fear that we are just seeing the beginnings of Charleston's suffering. I would prefer that you help close it up and move elsewhere until such time as it is safe and appealing to move back here."

Susan and Jonathan were staring at each other, trying to gauge each other's thoughts. "May we think about it, Mother? Right now there is so much going on. May we wait until after Christmas to decide? That needn't affect your plans in any way. No matter what we choose, I will accept the responsibility of taking care of the house."

"I think that's a very wise decision. For now, let's let the slaves know about their holiday schedule, inform the children that they need to prepare for a visit from Saint Nicholas, and then . . . Can we have dinner together tonight, please?"

Despite the desolation that enveloped Charleston on December 25, the Dubois Christmas was a day to remember. The family started the day with a reading of the Christmas story in the parlor. Then they moved to the slave yard to distribute their largesse. Besides the sets of new clothing and food supplies, every man received a small penknife and every woman a comb and bandanna. The children happily clutched sacks containing an orange, some pieces of rock candy, and a small toy.

"Why do we give the slaves gifts?" little Robbie asked. "Doesn't Saint Nicholas visit their houses? Does he just come for white children?"

"No!" Jonathan jumped in to answer the question. "Saint Nicholas just needs help now and then, so we pass out the gifts for him. It doesn't matter to him whether children are black or white."

Susan smiled, amused to see that Jonathan had accepted his role in the celebration while not sacrificing his principles.

Christmas dinner, too, exceeded everyone's expectations. The tablecloth was nearly hidden by platters of ham and roast turkey, fried fish, oysters, corn pudding, sweet potatoes, green beans, field peas, and rice with gravy. Wine for everyone over the age of sixteen and sweet tea for the children helped wash down second helpings. The sideboard featured blackberry pie, a tall coconut cake, a trifle, gingerbread men, and fruitcake.

"Mother, this was truly a feast."

"This is perhaps the last we shall have together, so I wanted Cook to make it special. But I don't want to think of that now. I peeked into the parlor a short time ago, and there were several mysterious boxes under the tree. Shall we adjourn there and see what Saint Nicholas may have left?"

The children, well-schooled in containing their excitement, sat cross-legged around the tree, with the adults taking chairs behind them. Mrs. Dubois suggested they begin with the youngest and move upward. Little Jamey beamed and then squealed as he pulled wrappings off a set of wooden blocks, a top, and a hobbyhorse. "Your mother played with those when she was your age," Mrs. Dubois told him. "She kept them in very good condition, so you will have to do the same."

Next came Robbie, who sat puzzling over a tube-shaped package, trying to guess the contents before opening it. Mrs. Dubois squirmed with impatience. "Please be careful with it, Robbie, and open it before you drop it and break it."

"I . . . I don't know what this is," he stammered.

"It's a spyglass, dear, one that belonged to your Uncle Robert. Here, let me show you. You look through this end and it brings distant objects much closer. You can use it to look out over the harbor and watch passing ships, or point it at the night sky to study the stars, or look into the trees and watch birds up close."

"Just don't point it at the neighbor's windows," young Johnny laughed.

"And don't you go giving him ideas!"

Next it was Becca's turn. "Your present comes in two packages," her grandmother told her. "Open the smaller one first." Becca looked into the box and carefully lifted out a small doll

187

and dozens of pieces of furniture. Her brow furrowed as she looked at them.

"What . . .?"

"Now just lift up that huge box. You'll have to stand to do it." As the top came off, the little girl gasped and fell to her knees. "It's a house! It—it looks just like this house!"

"Yes, it does. Your grandfather built that dollhouse for your mother. He carved the furniture, too, while I sewed tiny curtains and rag rugs and bedspreads."

"Oh, I adored that house," Susan said. "Becca, you may have to let me help you play with it."

"That would be fun!"

"Now, Mary Sue. You have only one package to open."

"It feels like a book," she said, trying to hide her disappointment.

"So it is. Open it."

"*The Care and Feeding of Horses*," she read. "Why . . .?"

"You're going to need all that information as you raise your new foal."

"My foal? You mean . . .? Oh, Grandmother! I'm getting a baby horse?"

"Mother!" Susan looked horrified.

"Now don't fuss at me, Susan. This young lady has been asking for a pony for years. She didn't get one, and now she's getting too big for one. She needs her own horse, but I wanted her to have the experience of raising the animal. So Mr. Dickenson down at the livery stable has a brand new foal. She's too young to leave her mother just yet, but as soon as she is weaned— and as soon as you are settled somewhere—he has promised to deliver her. In the meantime, Mary Sue can visit her every day, and they can get to know each other. In fact, we may be able to walk down there tomorrow morning."

"Oh, I can't wait! But I'll start reading right away."

Eddie's gift came in an even smaller box. He jiggled it carefully and then opened it to reveal a key. Holding it up, he turned to his grandmother. "What does it open?"

"The rest of your present. In the library, there is a glass cabinet. Behind that locked door is your grandfather's huge collection of agricultural books, explaining everything from raising cotton to fighting rice weevils and setting chickens to hatch. He valued that collection more than almost anything else in his possession—said it had made him a successful planter. I thought you might feel the same way."

"Can I go and look now?"

"Not quite yet. We have a few gifts left. Young John, so dapper today in your cadet uniform, you are missing one important item—your ceremonial sword." From behind the sofa, Mrs. Dubois pulled a carved leather scabbard holding a shining steel sword. "This blade was first used in the Revolutionary War by your great-grandfather. I trust you will use it sparingly but well."

Johnnie was speechless as he strapped it to his belt.

"And Charlotte. You have a special position in our family, since you have been the first to give us another generation. And so I am entrusting you with the family Bible. It carries the birth, marriage, and death dates of your Dubois ancestors, going back to Martinique and before that to France. I have entered the names of Georgie and Annie for you, but, from here on, I entrust you with keeping the family history. And to go along with it, this box contains two hand-embroidered baptismal gowns, one worn by your mother and one by her brother

Robert. I would be pleased if Georgie and Annie could wear them when they are christened."

Charlotte clasped the Bible to her chest. "I am honored that you would trust me with these. Thank you."

"Now can we . . .?" Eddie was still poised to flee to the library.

"No. You may think of your parents as old, but to me, they are still my children, and I have an envelope for each of them. Susan, this contains the deed to this house. It is now yours to do with as you will. And, Jonathan, this is the deed to Oak View Farm outside of Aiken, South Carolina. If the two of you choose to stay in Charleston, the farm will provide you with a steady outside source of income. My attorney there will continue to administer the land and its sharecroppers. But, if you decide to leave Charleston, I hope you will at least visit the farm and consider the opportunities it may offer you to start over."

24

And a Happy Christmas to You, Too
December 1861

At nightfall, as the rest of the household settled around the fire to doze or relive the charms of the day, Jonathan found Susan on the piazza. "It's cold out here, my love. Why don't you . . .?"

"I have my shawl. And I feel no colder out here than I would in my mother's parlor."

"What's going on? It's Christmas, and you've been so looking forward to having a family holiday."

"That was before my mother blindsided me."

"What? I don't understand. What's wrong?"

"Everything! Don't you realize what the Dragon Lady has done?"

"Dragon Lady? I thought you hated that term."

"That was before. Now I see how fitting a description it is."

"She's been wonderful to us. Our children have had the best Christmas of their lives—something we could not possibly have given them this year."

"And you're just like them—enjoying the idea of your gift without noticing what her generosity does to your manhood."

191

"Now wait a minute. You'll have to explain that remark." Jonathan was growing more agitated as he absorbed Susan's mood. Not wanting to disturb the family inside, he lowered his voice even further, but the scowl on his face left little doubt about his anger. "What is your problem?"

"My mother is my problem! She has given each of us wonderfully expensive presents. They come wrapped in silk and velvet, but not even the softness of velvet can disguise the harshness of the chains with which she has bound them. Oh, the three youngest children received toys, and there's not too much to worry about there, although that dollhouse of Becca's will some day represent to her what it has meant to me. It's an exact model of this monstrosity of a house, and she'll come to see that she can never escape it. The dollhouse will always remind her of her familial duties."

"I think you're exaggerating!"

"No, I'm not! Look at the older children and their gifts. What is their grandmother saying to them? Mary Sue gets a horse. A horse, Jonathan! Horses live for twenty or thirty years, and this one belongs to a child. She'll be responsible for it for much of her adult life."

"She can always sell it."

"Sell it? Her grandmother's gift? Not likely! She'd feel horribly guilty if she did. And it will tie her to this community and its high-class society, in which horsemanship is a mark of gentility. Whether you see it or not, that horse is a symbol of what her grandmother expects her to become. And she'll do as she's told, because she won't see that she has any other choice. And Eddie? The same is true of him. That valuable agricultural library he now owns marks him as a planter for the rest of his life, following in his grandfather's footsteps. He doesn't get a choice, either."

"And you see this as some sort of diabolical plot on your mother's part?"

"Yes. That's exactly what it is. Johnny gets his ancestral sword. She knows I never wanted him to have a military career, and she well remembers that I refused to send him off to a military boarding school several years ago. Now he wants to join the Confederate Army, and she has just given him the ultimate badge of her approval. If he is hurt in this war, I shall hold her personally responsible."

"That's a bit unreasonable, my dear."

But Susan was not to be put off. "And poor Charlotte! Now saddled with the responsibility of carrying forward the family saga. She thinks she is 'honored.' She's barely twenty and already expected to assume the role of matriarch, passing the lineage on to her children and grandchildren. Oh, maybe she'll be strong enough, someday, to toss the family Bible away and live her own life, but that won't happen if her grandmother keeps the pressure on—which I'm sure she will."

"They are our children, not hers. You're behaving as if you have no further influence over them."

"I won't have!" Susan stomped her foot to emphasize her point. "That's what I'm trying to make you see. My mother holds all the cards at the moment. We're homeless and destitute. She has wealth, property, power, and influence. And she'll use them all—she has used them all—to get her way."

"She's given her property away, Susan."

"Hah! And you think she did that out of the pure generosity of her parental heart? Do you really believe that she has not taken over your future, just as she has chained your children?"

"She has given us a choice."

"A choice? Did you hear her say that you might want to take us all back to Boston? Did you hear her suggest that we might want to wait and see if our house insurance will allow us to replace what we have lost? Did she even mention that you might be able to get a teaching job here or elsewhere? No! She has given me a house—one that has been my destiny ever since I received that same dollhouse as a little girl. And she has given you a sharecropper's farm, in a godforsaken corner of this state, in a place you have never even visited. That's our choice— between her house in Charleston or her farm in Aiken. Either way, we are bound to her forever because we will be expected to be eternally grateful."

"She's leaving South Carolina."

"Yes, but she'll be just across the border and within easy striking distance. Do you remember her conditions when she agreed to let us move to the Edisto Island plantation? I can quote her verbatim:

> *I will visit whenever I please, and I will always have access to the planta-tion accounts. All profits beyond your actual family expenses will accrue to me for my lifetime. In other words, you will manage Harbor View for me, Jonathan, but it will not be yours until your wife legally inherits it.*

You watch: She'll impose the same restrictions this time, and she'll mean them."

By now Susan was crying softly, and she turned away from her husband to look out over the darkening neighborhood. "How is it possible that such a familiar view can suddenly appear to be a huge trap? I have always loved it here, but I also hate it."

Sometimes, Jonathan knew, silence was the only possible answer. He stood beside her at the piazza railing, pulling her close with one arm around her shoulders. For several minutes, that was enough, and Susan gradually brought her tears under control.

"Sorry," she whispered.

"Me, too. I'm trying to understand."

"I know. This is coming from a lot of old scars that reopened in the middle of all that Dragon-Lady-Bountiful demonstration this afternoon."

"What would you have me do, Susan? In the past you have advised me to let your mother think she was winning every argument. Have you now changed your mind? Do you want me to defy her?"

"No, of course not. That would gain us nothing. I think . . . I think we had best just try to avoid all discussions of what we're going to do until she leaves. Once she's safely out of the way in Flat Rock, we can discuss our options rationally." She laughed softly. "And yes, I think we do have options. I've just been too angry about her manipulations to consider them. Sometimes, you know, a dose of righteous anger can be healthy. I had to let it out for a few minutes."

"We can do that, I think. But I do have one suggestion— something I've been thinking about, if you're ready to hear me out."

"Surely."

"Well, this Aiken farm she has seen fit to hang around my neck: I don't have a very clear picture of what it's all about, and, from what you've said, you don't know much about it, either. I'd rather not make any decisions about it until I know more about its condition. Your mother said it would provide a source of income, but that could mean anything from a few pennies for luxuries to enough to support the whole family. We need to know."

"But if you ask her, she'll think you're stepping right into her trap."

"I have no intention of asking her, my dear. I want to see it for myself. What I'm thinking is this: She leaves for Flat Rock the day after New Year's. Why don't I volunteer to accompany her, at least part of the way? I'll pass it off as being a dutiful son-in-law who's making sure she is safe and on her way. Then I'll veer off at the Columbia junction and catch the next train to Aiken. I can spend a couple of days nosing around, talking to the fellow who is overseeing the sharecroppers and finding out for myself if the house is habitable."

Susan nodded. "I think it's a good idea. Mother is so self-absorbed that she will only pay attention to the fact that you will be helping her onto the train. I'll bet she'll never think about where you are going when you leave her."

"And can you please be pleasant and sociable and grateful for a week or so, even if you resent the hell out of her?"

"Jonathan!" She swatted at him and then smiled. "Of course I can. I've been doing it my entire life."

25

The Great Migration
January 1862

Getting Mrs. Dubois off to Flat Rock was a complicated project with scattered periods of controlled chaos. She changed her mind several times about what furniture and household items she wanted to take with her to her new home, and each change necessitated the repacking of the wagon. Susan watched without comment. If she was silently cataloguing the value of the items her mother was taking, she gave no obvious sign of it. Jonathan was more vocal in his complaints as he traipsed up and down the long staircase carrying armloads of quilts and heavy winter draperies. "You'd think she was headed to Canada!" he grumbled.

"Let's see now," Mrs. Dubois said. "You rescued all the Grenville silverware, so you won't need mine. I'll just drop it into a box and take it along in case the girls don't have enough. And we might as well add the good china while we're at it. It goes so well with my silver pattern. Oh, and I don't want to forget that little velvet rocker in my bedroom. It holds so many memories of happier days. What do you think, Susan? Will the girls have enough books, or should I take my own reading material?"

As her mother's attention flitted from one room to another, Susan kept taking deep breaths and trying to smile to hide her impatience. "You won't be all that far away, Mother. If you discover that you and the girls need something once you're in Flat Rock, we can always ship it to you or bring it when we come for a visit."

"I know, dear, but the slaves are making the trip with the wagon anyway. We might as well load it up."

"You don't want to overdo it, Mother Dubois," Jonathan said. "The horses will have some rather steep hills to negotiate between here and there. You don't want them to have to unload and leave some of your possessions by the side of the road."

"I suppose you're right, but I didn't expect retiring in my old age and leaving my previous life behind to be so difficult."

"It looks to me as if you're taking most of that old life with you." Susan spoke under her breath and then gave her mother another artificial smile.

At last, Mrs. Dubois's most trusted slave set off with a team of her best horses. Several other slaves perched amid the trunks at the back of the wagon, waving good-bye to Elsie, who would be traveling with her mistress on the train.

"I thought you had arranged for new homes for your slaves," Jonathan said. "It looks like you are taking most of them with you."

"Well, I have to have my own cook and personal maid. And our horses are used to Michael being their driver. So those three have to go along, and that means taking their families with them. As I keep telling you, Jonathan, I am a benevolent slave owner. I wouldn't think of breaking up families just to satisfy my own whims."

"Of course not."

At the train station, Mrs. Dubois kept a hand firmly on Jonathan's arm. She had, at first, protested that he need not accompany her, but, now that the day of departure had arrived, she was grateful for his presence. With her free hand she reached out to touch Susan's cheek. "Take care of my house, darling girl."

The strain of the last few days was beginning to wear on Susan, but she smiled gamely. "Of course I will, Mother. I know you have loved it, and it will always be ready if you want to return."

For a brief moment, Susan felt a flush of anger at Jonathan. *He's leaving, too. So who's going to listen to my gripes, once Mother's safely out of the way? I can't share my resentment with the children. Oh, but she makes me so angry! She's leaving her family as well as her beloved house, but all she can think of is the house. I'm tempted to paint the whole thing in garish primary colors just to spite her.*

At that moment, Jonathan caught her eye, and his lips formed the words, "Good girl." Despite herself, she smiled, and her spirits lifted as she made her way home.

Unfortunately, Jonathan's mood took a downward turn as the train chugged out of the station. Mrs. Dubois fussed as she settled into her seat. With a gloved finger, she checked for soot on the window ledge and made a little clucking noise when she found plenty of it. She twisted her shoulders in an expression of general discomfort and seemed reluctant to let her feet touch the floor. "It's sticky," she explained as she stiffened her ankles. With a critical sneer, she examined their fellow passengers and dismissed them as not important enough to be bothered with. "Would you check with the porter and find out if they have any clean drinking water?" she asked Jonathan, and he was only too happy to have an excuse to leave the compartment.

Swaying with the rhythm of the train, he slowly made his way from carriage to carriage, noticing how many native Charlestonians were among the passengers. The trip might have been a festive municipal outing at some other time, but, on this day, these people looked more like refugees, their faces displaying expressions of sadness and loss. In the third carriage, he was startled to see Arthur Middleton. That normally self-possessed gentleman was looking as discomfited as Jonathan felt. When their eyes met, Middleton jumped up and stepped into the corridor.

"Grenville, isn't it?"

"Yes, sir. I wasn't expecting to see anyone I knew on the train. Are you traveling far?"

"My uncle, Oliver Middleton, is moving to Flat Rock," Middleton explained. "His whole family was burned out of their New Street home, as I suppose you have heard—lost everything, every stick of furniture, family portraits, cotton rescued from his Edisto plantation—everything. My wife and I are going along to help them get resettled. What about you, my friend? Did your house survive?"

"No, burned to the ground, I'm afraid. We were lucky, though. We were able to pack up most of our valuables and take refuge in my wife's family home. That's the reason for my own trip today. Mrs. Grenville's mother has turned over her house to us and is moving to Flat Rock to combine households with two beloved cousins. I'm accompanying Mrs. Dubois on the first leg of her journey to make sure she gets there safely."

"A fine gesture on your part. Few sons-in-law would be so considerate. But she's going to Flat Rock, too, did I understand you to say?"

"That's right. Actually, I have some business to take care of in Aiken, so it was convenient for me to travel with her, partway at least."

"Well, you needn't worry about escorting Mrs. Dubois any farther than the Columbia and Aiken junction. She is more than welcome to join our party. In fact, we have an entire compartment to ourselves with several empty seats. There are just my aunt and uncle and the Countess Bentivoglio, as my wife prefers to be called. Why don't you go get Mrs. Dubois, and we can all become acquainted to pass the time."

Mrs. Dubois was impressed. "Oliver Hering Middleton? The one who married Susan Chisholm? And Arthur's wife— a real countess? How delightful of them to invite me to join them!"

Jonathan didn't correct her. He could have pointed out that the invitation came from Arthur Middleton—his acquaintance, not hers—but he was too relieved that he would soon be freed from responsibility for her. And luckily, Elizabeth Dubois and Susan Chisholm Middleton were soon chattering away as if they had indeed known each other all their lives.

When the train reached the Columbia junction, Jonathan stood to take his leave. He had the distinct impression that Mrs. Dubois did not even register the fact of his departure. He took formal leave of Oliver Middleton and shook hands with Arthur. "I'm grateful to you and your family for helping out in this way," he said.

"Think nothing of it! I had been struggling to carry on a conversation with Aunt Susan, who could not talk of anything but how she escaped from the fire with her spectacles but left their case to burn. As if that were the most important of their losses! Now she has a whole new audience and a new kindred spirit. There's nothing quite like old ladies who have lived their whole lives as privileged Charlestonian mavens, is there?"

"I know what you mean. They are totally oblivious to anything except their own small circle of friends. But we can be grateful that these two have found each other to talk to about their mutual inconveniences. Thank you again."

"You're welcome. And good luck in your business venture in Aiken!"

It was long past nightfall when Jonathan alit from the railway carriage and peered through the mist at the darkened Aiken station. The train had paused only briefly to let him off, and, as it chugged away, Jonathan felt a moment of unreasoning panic. What would he find in this place? Did it hold an answer to his family's problems, or was it merely another way station on the downward-spiraling path he seemed to be following?

A small hand-lettered sign in the window of the station door directed him toward Schwartz's Hotel across the street. There he at least found a desk clerk, who roused himself sufficiently to welcome the traveler to Aiken and hand him a key to a private room. The brief encounter did nothing to alleviate Jonathan's loneliness. The lantern burning on the single table in his room only accentuated the gloom of this night. Without even thinking about unpacking his valise, he slipped off his jacket, loosened his suspenders, and kicked his shoes aside. Then, cringing slightly at the thought of all the stragglers and wanderers who had passed through this room, he slid under the ragged quilt and pillowed his head on his arm. He squeezed his eyes closed and drifted off to sleep, his dreams populated with strangers all pushing and shouldering their way past him, seeking goals he could not even understand.

A watery but welcome sun awakened him and sent him off in search of breakfast in a more optimistic mood. Just off the side of the hotel's grimy desk, a cavernous dining room was filled with other travelers—noisy families and hungry-looking salesmen, little old ladies and squalling children, several soldiers, and lots of self-important businessmen. A cadre of bustling waitresses moved efficiently among the long trestle tables, carrying steaming platters of biscuits, sausages, fried potatoes, and country ham. Pitchers of gravy and pots of coffee passed from hand to hand. A harried gentleman at the doorway greeted him. "Morning, sir. New, are you? Must have checked in last night. Well, don't hesitate. Just grab any seat you see empty, and somebody will bring you a plate."

Jonathan's tablemates were much too busy shoveling food to do more than nod in his direction, but he did not feel unwelcome. We're all in the same boat, he realized, just doing what necessity demands. He was surprised, however, at the number of people on the move. This war has upended our world, he thought, and dumped us all into unfamiliar territory. Can we all be lost together, or is perpetual movement the new real world in which we live?

26

Aiken Explorations
January 1862

L ater that morning, Jonathan set out to explore this new town. He was surprised by several aspects that caught his attention. From the corner of Union and Park Avenue, he could spot the courthouse, city hall, and post office, all constructed of the same red brick, all reflecting the same federalist style of architecture—symmetrical and gabled, and decorated with fanlights and cornices above the central entrances. The streets were 150 feet wide, many of them boulevards with trees down the middle islands. Tall church spires pierced the sky in several neighborhoods. Storefronts were open, and customers hurried in and out, arms full of parcels. People smiled and greeted one another. Carriages moved through the town at a leisurely pace.

The law offices of Anderson, Kittridge, and Winchester occupied an impressive two-story red-brick building that reflected the style of the courthouse across the street. A young clerk in formal dress met him at the door, nodding at his greeting and waving him into the front hallway. "How may I help you, my good sir?"

"Uh, I'm Jonathan Grenville. I believe Mr. Jamison Winchester is expecting me."

"Very good, sir. This way, if you please."

Jonathan stood a little straighter and tugged at his coat and tie as they made their way to a room at the end of the hall. This was a much more formal atmosphere than he had expected, he realized. Not that I thought they'd be country bumpkins, but these quarters would fit right in with the stuffiest offices in Charleston.

Winchester himself proved to be friendly and welcoming. "Grenville! At last! Mrs. Dubois has written me so much about you that I feel as if we are old acquaintances. How was your trip? Comfortable, I hope? Where are you lodging?"

"The train was convenient, but I got in so late last night that I just checked into the railroad hotel. It's fine."

"Schwartz's? That fleabag? No, no, that won't do. I'll have my man go by there and pick up your things. We'll get you settled at the Magnolia Inn later this afternoon. Can't have one of our largest property owners rubbing elbows with the *hoi polloi.*"

Jonathan caught his breath, and his eyes widened in surprise. "Uh, I'm not a wealthy man, Mr. Winchester—far from it. I'm an unemployed teacher, and all my worldly possessions went up in flames three weeks ago. The railroad hotel is as much as I can . . ."

"Nonsense! Didn't Mrs. Dubois tell you what the annual income of the Oak View estate is?"

"She called it a farm. I didn't think to inquire beyond that. I'm just looking for a place to bring my family as a refuge until we can get back on our feet."

"Well, consider yourself as having found a pretty solid foothold."

"I don't understand. Mrs. Dubois told me it was a small farm with four sharecroppers. How valuable can that be?"

"You now hold the deed to half a square mile of some of the most valuable agricultural land in this area. That's 320 acres. Part of the land has been subdivided into four 50-acre farms, each one rented out to a long-term tenant, not a sharecropper. Each of your tenants pays you a yearly rent, which yields enough cash to support your family."

"I had no idea!"

"Wait. That's just the beginning. The tenants also pay you a small percentage of any profit they make from their land, and, in all but the worst drought years, they make a tidy sum above and beyond their own living expenses. So there's another variable, but comfortable, cushion for you. That leaves you with a so-called farm of 120 acres.

"On your own land, there is a roomy and completely furnished manor house with a yard, a big barn, and other outbuildings, including two small cabins for slaves or paid employees. You have a few acres for a kitchen garden, as well as 20 acres of pasturage for some 40 animals—yours or those of your tenants. The rest of your acreage is divided into two parts: One contains 40 acres of valuable hardwood trees—hickory, ash, sweetgum, and oak—all of which can be selectively cut to provide a constant supply of timber to the local lumber yard."

"And the rest of the acreage? Will I be expected to raise crops on that? I don't own slaves, I'm not much of a vegetable farmer, and I know the market for cotton has been cut off."

"Hardly! No, you have a very large orchard—some 1,200 trees, mostly peach trees, but small stands of figs and apples as well—and 10 acres of grape vines, mostly muscadines, which produce grapes for our local winemaker."

Jonathan could tell that his mouth was hanging open, but he was too shocked to pull his chin up. "Has anyone been taking care of all those trees?"

"Of course. That's been part of my agreement with the Dubois family. Trees pretty well take care of themselves during the year, you know. No plowing and such. At harvest time, I hire workers to go out and pick the crop, and we join together with several other fruit growers in town to sell our fruit all over South Carolina. Mr. Henry William Ravenel, warder of the local Episcopal church, has a huge orchard, and we are able to work with him to get cheap shipping in the railway freight cars. You'll do well, my friend. Very well, even in wartime."

"I'm beginning to understand, now, why the Dubois family had to hire a lawyer to manage the land. It sounds like a major corporation."

"Well, not quite that. But, yes, it is a money-maker, and it requires some understanding of land management, which happens to be my specialty. I'll be happy to continue to manage the property for you, if you wish, but now that you are the official owner, you may want to make other arrangements or handle it yourself."

"No. I have no idea how to manage property. As I told you, I'm not much of a farmer. I'm a teacher by education and experience. All I'm really hoping for is a place to bring my family, a place we can live in safety, away from the constant bombardment of this horrible war. If we can use the house and immediate grounds, I'll be happy to leave the agricultural property in your capable hands."

"Well, then, let's make sure that the house will meet your needs. It's nearly dinnertime, so perhaps we should stop by the railroad hotel, pick up your luggage, and then drop by the Magnolia Inn. They do the best midday meal in town, and that will give you a chance to look over their accommodations before we check you in. Then we'll drive out to Oak View Farm. It's about three miles outside of town—far enough away to maintain your peace and quiet but easily accessible to all of our urban refinements."

Jonathan was seldom at a loss for words, but now it seemed that all he could do was nod mutely and follow Winchester to the stable yard. The Magnolia Inn turned out to be a stately plantation-style house, one that would have fit comfortably in the finest neighborhoods of Charleston. A semi-circular drive led to the portico, where liveried slaves took charge of the horse and carriage. The two men entered the wide doors off the portico.

Winchester, still very much in charge, spoke to the receptionist outside the dining room. "Tell Mrs. Bennett that we'll be just two for dinner, and bring us whatever is the special of the day."

The *maître d'hotel* led them to a corner table, fawning and fussing over the proper drapery of their napkins. Jonathan looked around curiously, wondering if he could fit into this elegant world. At last, he spoke. "I am overwhelmed, sir. I came here expecting a farm and a small country town. Instead, I see an elegant, upper-crust society, rich in history and culture. How does it come to be located out here, so far from the normal centers of population?"

"Thank the climate for much of that atmosphere." Winchester smiled. "After the War of Independence, many of our forebears discovered that their constitutions were not geared to the cold winters and damp shorelines of the east coast. In the hills of South Carolina, they found brisk and dry air, warmish winters, pure spring water, rich soil, pristine scenery, and freedom from insects. Almost overnight, this area became a resort for those whose health was suffering in New York or Boston, and we've flourished ever since. I promise you, Grenville, you and your family are going to be content here."

After a sumptuous dinner of roast beef and vegetables, they drove to Jonathan's new land. The fields and small houses at the edge of the property were neat, well-kept, and as prosperous as fallow fields can look in January. Here and there, Jonathan noticed that, despite the season, some fields were sporting fresh growth. "Do crops grow here all year long?" he asked.

"Yes, of course. With proper planning and a good dose of manure, it's possible to grow three crops on the same piece of land, which is what most of your tenants do. What you're seeing now is rye grass, which stays green and grows rapidly all winter. The farmers get two or three cuttings in three months, and that provides enough hay to feed their cattle all year. They plant beans and cowpeas on the same land starting in February and harvest them in early summer. Then they plant their root crops to be ready in the fall, and, as soon as they have dug those, the rye grass goes in again. Their animals thrive on the rye and pea vines, and produce enough manure to keep the fields rich. It's quite a system, as you'll discover."

Winchester clucked at the horse to slow him into a wide turn. The tree-lined road led toward a white clapboard house that loomed up in front of them. Jonathan caught his breath in surprise. "It's a New England farmhouse!"

"I thought you'd recognize it. Mrs. Dubois mentioned that you had family in New England. The original owner came here from Boston with a lung ailment and stayed for the rest of his life. He wanted his wife to feel at home, so he duplicated their New England farm. I'm not sure how your own wife will feel about it, but I was pretty sure you'd like it." Winchester pulled up at the side entrance. "The front steps had a branch crash down on them last week and will need to be rebuilt—a small job, but I didn't see any sense in scheduling it until I knew someone would be living here. For now, we'll just use the side entrance."

He led the way up several steps to a small porch and unlocked the door. It opened onto a central hallway that ran across the width of the house rather than in the plantation style of front to back. A dark room on the right had clearly been used as an office. On the left, a steep stairway led to the second floor. The hall then opened onto the parlor, which appeared well furnished, although everything was draped in sheeting. "We can have this cleaned out in no time," the attorney said. "That fireplace works well, by the way. And beyond the parlor lies a dining room that the family never used much. You'll see why as we go through here." He stepped aside and motioned Jonathan to precede him through the doorway on the left.

"A kitchen? A real farmhouse kitchen! I've been in the South so long, I had almost forgotten that New England kitchens are a part of the house, not a separate building out back." Jonathan looked around in amazement, his mind cataloging the features he would describe to Susan when he got home. A woodburning stove stood opposite the doorway. To its right, a cluster of chairs and a small occasional table stood by a window and offered a place to get warm, read a book, or have a cup of coffee. To the left of the stove, a metal countertop surrounded two deep sinks, one of which featured its own hand pump. "Water?" he asked.

"Yes, there's a deep well under the house, and this pump provides all the fresh water you'll ever need, without having to haul it in from outside. And with the window above the sink, you can still look outside while you pump."

The interior wall nearest the door featured a bank of inset shelves for dishes, pans, or pantry items. The focal point of the kitchen, however, was a huge oak slab table surrounded by benches and armless wooden chairs. "I see now why the dining room would not get much use. You could fit a family of ten around that table, with room to spare."

"Yes, the rest of the house is just window dressing. This is where the family centers itself."

"I love it! It'll scare Susan to death at first, but she'll see the wisdom of the arrangement soon enough. And upstairs?"

"Four bedrooms, with a center hall. The two front rooms have a connecting door so that the smaller one can serve as a nursery. The two back rooms are separate. I believe the original owners called them the girls' room and the boys' room. And there's a full below-ground basement as well, accessible both through that small doorway there and through an outside entrance, so that it can be used for crop storage. The privies— two of them—are just beyond the porch over there in that stand of trees. And then, of course, in the yard you have the barn, the stables, the chicken house, and a small kitchen garden plot. I think you'll find you have everything you need."

"I'm sure of it. How soon can you arrange to have it ready for us?"

"I'll hire some cleaning people to come in, and a crew of carpenters to fix the front porch and a couple of shaky shutters. It should be ready by the first of February."

Jonathan held out his hand. "Thank you, sir. You have given me and my family a new start in life."

"Think nothing of it, my boy. I'm happy to think of the place being occupied again. And, by the way, did you say you were a teacher by trade?"

"Yes, I was, before the war drew away all our students and the Charleston fire burned down our school." Jonathan shrugged.

"Well, come see me when you bring the family back and get yourselves settled. We have a new school in town. We've always had a military academy, but last year two distinguished gentlemen, Professors Sams and Anderson, opened the Female Seminary, and it is already drawing girls from as far away as Virginia and Florida. They may be interested in talking to you."

27

Conflicting Priorities
January 1862

Jonathan rushed from the train station to the Dubois house, anxious to share his news with Susan. As he knew she would, she met him at the door, flying into his arms and clinging to him until he dropped his valise and held her close.

"I haven't been gone all that long, my love."

"Maybe not, but it has seemed like forever. Things are so awful here."

Immediately concerned, he pushed her shoulders back so that he could see her face. "What has happened? Tell me."

"Johnny's gone!"

"Gone? I thought the College Cadets were still in camp at the Race Track."

"They are, but he isn't!" She was wailing through her tears.

"What? Slow down, Susan, and start from the beginning. Where is Johnny, and when did he leave here?"

"It was the same day you left. If I didn't love him so much, I'd say it was a calculated move to avoid your wrath and drop one of his bombshells on me when I was already vulnerable."

"What bombshell this time?"

"He and Alex Croft—curses on his evil influence!—have quit school and gone off to enlist officially in the same regiment as Alex's brother, Harris. The others had mounts of their own, so Johnny took one of our horses—that big roan you call Major—and the three of them left to meet Harris's regiment somewhere near Edisto Island."

"Three? Who were the other two?" Jonathan was still shaking his head as he tried to piece the story together.

"Alex and his slave, Monday. That was another thing—Johnny wanted to take Eli with him. Said every soldier needed a slave to take care of him." She was sobbing and gulping as she tried to explain. "I drew the line there. Told him he could take a horse into war with him but not another human being. So he left in a huff, and I haven't heard from him since."

"We'll hear from him, Susan. He'll settle down and realize that you were only concerned for his safety. And I'm sure he'll be all right."

"You said the same thing when Peter left for Hilton Head. Look how that turned out!"

"You must not think in those terms. There's no fighting going on south of here now, as far as I know. For that matter, the next Union attack is much more likely to come against Charleston than against an island inhabited only by harmless slaves who have been left on their own. He'll be perfectly safe—perhaps safer than he would be here. Which leads me to my own news—"

"That's not all!" Susan was sobbing again. "Charlotte is gone, too, and the babies."

"Don't tell me she has joined the Army!"

"No, of course not, but we had one of our epic arguments. I mentioned that we were trying to decide whether to remain in

Charleston or find somewhere more peaceful to live, and she flew into a rage. Said she would never leave the city where Peter had lived. She as much as told me she would not allow us to move out of this house. When I pointed out that she had no right to dictate such a decision, she started slamming doors in my face again. She packed her things, called Rosie to help her carry the twins, and stomped off down the street. She called back over her shoulder that when I changed my mind, she would be at the Rogers's house. I haven't heard from her, either."

"Poor darling. You have had a time of it, haven't you?" Jonathan pulled her back into his embrace and gently rocked her to and fro until her sobs quieted. "You can look at this in two ways: Either we've produced two childish but headstrong ingrates, or we have raised two independent and capable adults who are ready to fly the nest and make their own lives. I prefer to believe the latter."

Around the dinner table that evening, Jonathan tried again to broach his own news. "I'm officially calling a family meeting. We are about to embark on a grand adventure."

Susan flashed him a warning look, her small chin jutting out in determination and her eyes squinting in defiance. "Embark? Oh, no. I've had a rough enough week. I'm not sure I'm ready to hear this."

The children were looking at one another, trying to gauge what their own reactions should be. Eddie, by now a gangly fifteen-year-old whose hands and feet were still too big for his body, was trying his best to look like a serious and attentive grown-up. Mary Sue, barely twelve but trying to be equally sophisticated, raised an impertinent eyebrow and waited to hear the rest of the story. Becca and Robbie had been subjected to a great deal of emotional turmoil in the last few weeks and had come to fear that their world would never be stable again. They clutched each other's hands under the table and held their breath. And Jamey pounded his small fist on the table, pleading, "I want to get down. Now!"

"Jamey, be still and eat your peas." Susan, too, hoped to deflect the coming pronouncement, but Jonathan was not willing to wait any longer.

"We are moving to a wonderful farm in Aiken," he said. In his enthusiasm, he hardly noticed the fear and anxiety building around him. "I didn't know what to expect when I arrived in Aiken, but I found it a lovely and cultured little city, prosperous, well-kept, and free from any taint of the war that haunts us here. The climate is healthy and the soil is fertile. It's peaceful there, and the farm that we have inherited is a rich piece of land that promises to make us wealthy. The house is comfortable and in great shape. It's being cleaned and opened up for us as we speak. And the portion of the land on which we will live will allow us to learn valuable new lessons in self-sufficiency."

"What does that mean, exactly: 'self-sufficiency'?" Susan's face was beginning to flush—whether from incipient tears or anger, Jonathan was not quite sure—but he plunged ahead, directing his next descriptions at the children.

"There's a huge barn, big enough to hold a small herd of cattle, Eddie. And acres and acres of pasture. With a little hard work, you should be able to indulge every one of your dreams of producing dairy products and cheese. The stable is roomy enough for your colt, Mary Sue, and there are pigpens and chicken coops enough to surround yourself with your beloved animals. As for you youngsters, there's room—room for you to grow and explore and discover your own interests."

"And you plan to become a farmer? You can't hope to sell either rice or cotton. What will be your crop of choice? Turnips?" Susan's words fairly dripped with sarcasm.

"No, as a matter of fact, our portion of the land is woodland and orchard. We're going to be growing peaches."

"Peaches? Surely that's a joke. What would we do with peaches? Do you envision putting me to work making jam?"

"I'm serious. The land has been producing peaches successfully for years, and the shipping arrangements are already in place. We'll be supplying all of Charleston with fruit by the end of the summer."

For the first time, Becca showed a bit of a smile. "Ooh, think how lovely it will be when all those trees are in blossom! Will we be there in time to see that, Father?"

"Of course," Jonathan replied, but, at the same moment, Susan said, "We'll have to see about that."

Their eyes locked in a struggle of wills while the children watched apprehensively. In the silence, Eddie spoke. "I don't know if I'm ready for another round of cow-raising. After all the disappointment of the last time and the fear that all my pets were going to become soldiers' dinners, I think I'd rather raise turnips."

And now that the first opposition had been raised, Mary Sue joined in. "And how will we ever get Sable Girl all the way to Aiken? She's still a foal. She can't walk that far."

Jonathan looked from one to another, shaking his head. "What's wrong with all of you? I thought this would be good news."

"It's too much, Jonathan," Susan said. "So much has been happening that we're all just trying to sort out our reactions. We need a period of peace and quiet, not another move."

"Peace and quiet? That would be nice, wouldn't it? But you seem to forget that there's a war going on, and—"

"I never forget that—not for one single moment!"

"Of course not. But we don't have the luxury of waiting for a more convenient time. I was worried about our safety even before the fire. This city is a natural target for a Union attack, and I don't want my family in the middle of it. In case you missed the news, the Navy sank a whole fleet of ships loaded with stones to the bottom of Charleston Harbor to block the shipping channels. It happened on December 20, because it was the first anniversary of the vote to secede. We were still so shocked by the fire that we took little notice of it, but it was a sure sign that Charleston is in the Union crosshairs. They are determined to block our harbor so that no ships can get in or out. Whether they now attack or let us just starve doesn't matter all that much. This is a dangerous place to be, and droves of people are fleeing the city. We are fortunate to have a wonderful refuge waiting for us, and that's where we are going."

"But . . ."

"No! I don't want to hear any more protests. Eddie, if you don't want cows, we'll buy you some goats. They smell terrible, but their milk produces good cheese. Mary Sue, trains transport horses as well as people. Quit creating problems where there are none, both of you. And Susan, we'll discuss your hesitation later." He slammed his napkin onto the table and stomped out of the room.

"Don't you dare slam the door!" Susan shouted after him. "And, you children, finish your dinners. Sarah is waiting to clear the table."

28

Insurmountable Differences
January 1862

S usan followed Jonathan down the hall and found him standing on the back porch overlooking the slave yard. "You
know I don't like to leave arguments half-finished or hard feelings unresolved. You can't run away from the fact that the rest
of the family is not as excited about this proposed move as you
seem to be."

"That's understating the problem. When did everyone in
this family get the idea that they can protest all decisions at will?
I didn't ask for a vote. I've made up my mind, and it's my decision to make. Even if there are aspects of life on the Aiken farm
that you will hate, you're going to have to accept my judgment
that the move is for the best."

"Aha! I don't have all the story yet, do I? What is it that I am
going to hate?"

"Well, for one thing, the house is a replica of a New England
farmhouse, which means the kitchen is in the house itself. In
fact, it is the main living area of the home, the one place where
the family congregates, as much to keep warm in the winter as
anything else."

"There's not a separate cookhouse? Isn't that incredibly dangerous?"

"No, not really. I grew up in a house like that. It's quite pleasant, actually. A big iron woodburning stove heats the whole downstairs in cold weather. There's a pump in the washing-up area, so you don't have to go outside for water. A huge slab of a table serves for informal meals as well as a workspace for any number of projects, like canning vegetables or making cookies. And there's enough room for all the members of the family to help with the chores."

"Chores! Canning vegetables! Oh, that's right. You don't believe in having slaves anymore, either, do you? So who does all this cooking and baking and canning and washing up? Those are going to be my jobs, aren't they?"

"Susan . . ."

"And in that kind of kitchen the whole family can sit around and watch me burn the dinner. How wonderful! I've never cooked anything in my life, Jonathan. You can't just tell me to go do something and expect . . ." Tears were flowing again.

Jonathan stretched out his hand as a peace offering, but Susan took a step backward, emphasizing the chasm that had opened between them.

"Give it a chance, Susan. I wasn't expecting much when I got off the train in Aiken. I was pretty sure I was going to be disappointed. But, by the time I left, I had fallen in love with the place. I started seeing its possibilities instead of its drawbacks. The same thing just might happen to you."

Susan shook her head. She moved to the end of the porch, rested her elbows on the railing, and stared out over the slave quarters. "Do you see those people out there? Our slaves? Do you understand what I see when I look at them?"

"Tell me."

"I see people who make my life possible: The ones who cook my food and make my clothes. The ones who do the laundry and sweep the floors. The ones who hitch the horses to my carriage and shovel the manure from the barn. The ones who chop the wood for our fireplaces and tote the ashes away. I see the hands that cared for me whenever I was ill and cradled my children when they had colic. They polished the silver, changed the rugs, hung the curtains, and made the beds. I am here, and I am who I am, because of all the things they have done for me."

"Of course you are grateful to them, but . . ."

"And do you know what I see when I look in a mirror? I see an ornament, a caricature of a woman, a helpless creature who has never learned to take care of herself because there was always a faithful slave to do it for her. And now, in a single swipe of your hand, you propose to take all those people away, leaving me to do a thousand things I've never learned to do. And I'm frightened. Afraid that I cannot survive without the support of slavery. And if I can't survive, what happens to my children? How do I keep from destroying them as well as myself?"

"Perhaps that's part of the curse of slavery, Susan. We Northerners tend to worry about the people who are enslaved, but all too often we forget that the enslavers are also chained to a system that deprives them of developing their own capabilities. Does that make sense to you?"

"I suppose it does, but it doesn't do anything to change the situation."

"It's a first step." He joined her at the railing, mimicking her pose. "Would you like to know what I see when I look out at the slave yard? I see people who have not only lost all their God-given freedoms as human beings but have also been reduced to the status of children. They, too, are incapable of many things. They cannot read or do arithmetic. They have no concept of geography or their place in the world. I made a terrible mistake the night of the fire when I told our slaves they were free to go wherever they wanted to go. What did they do? They followed us because they had no choice. They didn't know where else to go.

"And think of your discussion with your mother about Christmas. If the slaves need clothing, it comes from us. If they need rations from which to prepare their meals, those rations must come from us. They live in cabins we have built for them and do the work we give them to do. They even celebrate their holidays whenever we give them permission. They are as incapable of taking care of themselves as you think you are. And slavery has made them that way."

"So, in your eyes, we are all incompetent. It must be wonderful to be you—so strong, so smart, such a Yankee!"

"Sarcasm does not become you."

"And I liked you better as a brow-beaten Job than I do now, when you're acting like a holier-than-thou abolitionist."

Hurtful words hung between them, reducing them both to silence. A few birds singing their night songs chirped in the trees, seeming to mock their voices. At last Susan spoke. "I'll end up doing as you ask. I'll go. But don't expect me to be happy about it."

"You'll have help, I promise. I intend to ask Hector, Sarah, and their children to go with us as our paid employees. I'll formally free them, and they will have salaries and their own house on the property, but they will continue to help with the housework and planting and other jobs that need doing."

"And that will be a salve to your Puritan conscience? They will do the same work, but it won't be the same because money

224

passes between you? I don't understand that way of thinking. Why can't we just go on the way we always have? The Southern way of life has worked for you for twenty years. Why do you have to change everything?"

"Yes, I've lived with slavery for twenty years for your sake, but it weighs heavily on my conscience. Why can't you grant me the same favor and try my way of life for a while? You might even like being a real housewife."

"I'll hate it. You can't do this to me."

"Do you realize how much you sound like your own daughter? Isn't that exactly what Charlotte said to you?"

"That was different. Besides, she'll come home again. She will have to change her mind about the move, just as I will have to."

"But how is her opposition to our plans any different from your own endless argument?"

"Well, because . . . because I'm your wife, not a child."

"My wife . . . my helpmate . . . but not a very helpful one at the moment."

"I didn't know you needed any help. I thought you had the answers to everything."

This time Jonathan refused to acknowledge her attack. "I don't know what to do about all our slaves. I admit that. It's one thing for me to say the system is wrong but quite another to know how to make it better."

"You're still intent on freeing them?"

"Absolutely. I'll be meeting with Judge Oglethorpe next week to get the paperwork straightened out. Each one will get a notarized certificate of emancipation. But then, what do they do? Where do they go? I can't simply turn them out onto the streets."

"I can think of a couple of things. You could load them up on the big wagon and drive them to the Union lines—letting the Union Army solve the problem. You're a Yankee. The soldiers would probably see you as a heroic rescuer. Or you could talk to Reverend Croft. Doesn't he work with a colony of free blacks somewhere in the interior?"

"Yes, he does. He even helped organize their own Zion Presbyterian Church. But I don't know that they would be willing to take in indigent strangers."

"Then don't leave them indigent. Stake each one to a set amount of money so that they can support themselves for a little while. You say you believe in emancipation. Are you willing to pay for it?"

"All right. I can do that. But what if they don't want to leave Charleston?"

"Then they take their chances. A few minutes ago you were fussing because they relied on their owners for everything. Now you want to offer them guarantees? You need to think this through. Please talk to Reverend Croft and see what he recommends."

"I'll think about that, but I'm not sure I want to bother him further. And, to be honest, the advice he's given me so far hasn't worked out terribly well."

"In what way?"

"Well, he advised me to send Johnny off to Columbia to keep him out of the war, and that certainly didn't work. He also preaches compromise, and it is precisely the compromises I've made so far that most trouble my conscience. No, I think this is my problem to solve."

29

Provisional Solutions
January 1862

The next day, Jonathan decided to ask Hector for his opinion about the move. He walked out to the slave yard after dinner, hoping to have a quiet conversation at the end of the workday. But he did not expect it to be this quiet. He hesitated on the back porch, straining to look through the twilight for signs of activity. The yard was ominously deserted. After a few moments, he went back inside to find Sarah, who was still clearing the dinner table.

"Where can I find Hector?" he asked. "He doesn't seem to be in the yard."

"He prob'ly be down hind da stable smokin he Christmas pipe," she said, refusing to meet his eyes.

"Sarah? Is something wrong? Where is everyone?"

"Don know." She scooped up a pile of plates and pushed past him to head for the pantry.

More and more puzzled, he ventured out into the yard, peering into the stables where the horses were placidly waiting for their oats, and the cookhouse where children normally assembled seeking scraps of leftovers. Not a slave in sight. Then he noticed a slight movement in the shadows and strode toward the chicken coop, where he found Hector at last.

"Why on earth are you feeding the chickens?" he asked. "Isn't that someone else's job?"

"Ah be da onlies one lef fuh do it. Nobody be sloppin da pigs, neider," Hector replied.

"Why? Where is everyone? What's going on?"

Hector put the bucket on the ground and turned to face him. "Dey be gone. Dat what be happnin. You tol dem dey be free, an dey near all takes off whiles you be gone. We be tryin fuh hol tings togedduh, Sarah an me an de udduh, but dere be lot uh work fuh do."

"How many are still here?"

"Don know bout Missus Lizbet slave. I tink dey all gone. Out uh de Logan Street slave, we only gots me an Sarah an de chillun . . . an Gemma de cook an Samuel de hostler an dey gal Rosie an . . ." He was counting on his fingers. "Oh, Moses, he still be heppin fuh take care uh de anmal, but he not be much good fuh ennyting else. He jis hang roun cause he old."

At a complete loss for words, Jonathan picked up the feed bucket. "Here, I'll finish the chickens. You check on the pigs. But our conversation is not over. I'm going to want to know more."

"What else you wants fuh know?" Hector seemed reluctant to abandon the conversation now that a touchy subject had opened between them.

"Where did they go?"

"Don know."

"You don't know, or you're afraid to tell me?"

Hector's jaw muscles tightened as he simply shrugged his shoulders.

"Look, Hector. I'm not going to go after them. I'm hoping they all got away safely. I was the one who freed them, after all. I told them they could go. But I've been worrying about what will happen to them once they no longer have our protection. Will they be safe, wherever they have gone?"

"Ah tink dey be headin sout fuh de Yankee soljer. You say dey gwine save dem."

"If they can get that far, yes. Do you think we'll ever hear if they make it to safety?"

"Probly not. Dey nun uh dem kin write, an ah don tink dey gwine come back fuh tell you." Hector picked up a bucket of slops he had left at the entrance to the chicken coop and stomped off, shaking his head. "White folk!"

Later that night, as Jonathan filled Susan in on the great slave exodus, he worried aloud. "What have I done? They've gone ahead, trusting in my words, but they don't have any official papers. What if some small-town constable catches them and tries to find their owner by beating the truth out of them?"

"I don't know, my dear. Surely they have their own ways of escaping to freedom. We hear about things like the Underground Railroad and abolitionist missionaries who guide runaways to safety. You'll just have to have faith that they will make it. The very idea of them running off bothers me, though. It seems rather ungrateful of them, after all we've done for them."

"After all we've done? By keeping them enslaved for generations? How can you be so callous?"

Susan shrugged. "They didn't leave until after Christmas, I noticed. They got their new clothes and their winter rations before they took off."

"I see that as a smart move on their part. What else would you have had them do?"

"I don't know, really. It all just seems so . . . so unnecessary. I can't believe the life they are running to will be as good as the life they were living with us. And look at Hector and Sarah, and Gemma. If escaping was such a good idea, why didn't they all go?"

"I honestly don't know, Susan, but I'm grateful for their loyalty. And I think we owe it to those who stayed to have a long talk with them about the future and what we can offer them to make their lives better."

"Is that really our job?"

"Of course it is. We are responsible for these people, and I for one want to do right by them."

"And just what would you have us do?"

"We can start by taking them to Aiken with us."

"All of them?"

"All of them, provided they are willing to go. I intend to call them all together in the morning, and I want you and Eddie to be there as well. Everyone needs to understand what is going to happen."

"Of course." Susan looked properly solemn and did not let a triumphant little smile touch her face until Jonathan left the room.

Calling a group of slaves together in the dining room with their owners and asking them to talk to one another was a challenge in itself. The slaves knew they were not allowed to sit down in the house, so they shied away from the offered seats and hung back at the doorway with lowered eyes. Family members, however, glared at the slaves with growing impatience.

Jonathan slapped his hand on the table, making everyone jump. "Pay attention to me," he demanded. "You are free, remember. I've promised you your freedom, and I intend to follow through on that. So quit behaving like slaves and do as you're told. Sit down!"

Susan couldn't help herself—she snickered at the incongruity of that last statement and then tried unsuccessfully to turn the snicker into a cough. "Sorry," she mumbled.

Jonathan then launched into a description of his plan to move the entire household to the Aiken farm. The former slaves listened with puzzled expressions or widened eyes. At last Sarah spoke up.

"Massa Grenville, ah always bin a part uh dis fambly. You knows dat. An ah wants fuh go wit Miss Susan, sho nuf. Bu dat farm be a fur piece way. How we gwine git dere wit all we stuff?"

"You are right, Sarah. It is pretty far away, but we'll all be going by train."

"Not we black folk. Dey don lets black folk onna train."

"This time they will." Jonathan was wound up now and pleased with his own plan. "I'm arranging for a freight car that has horse stalls in one end, people benches in the other, and a place in the middle to drive our wagons right onto the car. All we have to do is take all of us and all our baggage to the station, and then you'll all ride to Aiken."

Susan gritted her teeth to keep from speaking up. How little he understands himself, she thought. He is in love with the idea of freeing these slaves, so much so that he doesn't even seem to realize that he still thinks of them—and treats them—as slaves.

The slaves get to ride in a boxcar with the horses and the rest of the baggage. How lovely for them.

"An we gits money fuh workin now?" Hector asked. "Do dat mean you won gib we enny mo clothes an food? We gots fuh buy we own?"

"No, no, I'll be making sure that you are taken care of, same as always. There are cabins on the property, and we'll have regular clothing and food distributions for all workers. But you'll also get a salary every week, which you can spend in town or save up to buy a farm of your own some day. And you'll be able to work for me as long as you like."

"Dat still soun like uh slave tuh me," Moses said.

"But you'll be free."

"Free fuh do what? Kin ah tells you ah not gwine work sum days?"

"Certainly. But you won't get paid for those days."

"Den ah not free. Cause ifn ah don work, ah don get fuh eat."

"Well, yes, Moses. In one sense, that's true. But it is true for every man, white or black. If we want to eat, we have to earn our living. I need to work, too. That's why we're moving to Aiken. Here in Charleston, I don't have any work, so I'm going to start working on my own farm. That way I can make sure that all of you who depend on me will eat. Does that make sense to you?"

"Ah hears you, ah spose, but ah not sho ah blieves you."

"All right, then. I'll just have to ask you to trust me. If you can't do that, you are, of course, free to leave now. But I really hope you won't do that. I need your help. The whole family needs you. In fact, we all need each other."

Moses was still not buying the argument. "You jis needs we sos you don need fuh work."

Jonathan sighed with frustration and looked at Susan, hoping she would jump in. She looked away, preferring to let him stew a bit longer.

"No. I admit that I don't know much about the kind of work you do, but I should. I want to learn from you, and in return I intend to help you learn the things you need to know if you are going to enjoy your freedom."

"Lak what?"

"Here's my plan. I, with the help of the rest of our family, will teach all of you what you need to know in order to run your own lives as free citizens—the basics of reading, writing, and figuring. In return, we need you to teach us the everyday skills we lack. In your case, Moses, I want Eddie here to learn all he can from you about caring for animals. He wants to run a dairy farm some day, so you and Samuel need to show him how to fatten a calf, how to treat a sick cow, how to groom a horse, and how to calm a frightened animal. In between chores, he can show you how he plans to keep records of milk production."

"Eddie be a good boy. Ah kin do dat."

"Thank you. Hector, I need you to teach me how to manage a farm, how to know what to plant and when, how to prepare soil, and all the other things you have been doing for us. From now on, I'll be working right alongside you. And, at the same time, you're going to learn how to manage money and set up a savings account to buy your own plot of land.

"The women will be busy, too. Gemma and Sarah are going to be teaching Mrs. Grenville and the girls to cook, clean, sew, and help with the kitchen garden. Rosie will be helping with the housework and with the twins, if Miss Charlotte decides to join us. And everyone—men and women, grown-ups and children—will have regular lessons. If we do this right, by the end of the war, we'll all be able to live and enjoy our lives independently. Will you help me?"

30

Challenges
February 1862

The moving process turned out to be less complicated than Jonathan had feared. Everyone pitched in, seemingly willing now to cooperate in this new venture. Within a few weeks, the trunks had been packed, the supplies loaded on the wagon, and the house closed up for an indefinite period. Even loading everything—wagons, horses, and people—onto the train went smoothly.

Susan still worried about how Sarah and the others would fare in the boxcar. When they reached Branchville, where their train needed to take on coal and water for the remaining four-hour ascent into the foothills, passengers got off and stretched their legs. Jonathan hustled the children from the train to get them some much-needed exercise in the park across the street from the depot.

Susan alighted from the passenger carriage gratefully and hurried back to the rented boxcar. To her surprise, she found the newly freed slaves sitting on the platform, happily munching on bandanna-wrapped packets of cornbread and sausage. "Is everyone all right?" she asked.

"Course we be. Ah jis finish waterin de horse, an dey now be eatin dere oat whiles we hab we lunch," Hector answered.

"Were you terribly uncomfortable?" Susan persisted.

"Miss Susan, you stop worryin bout we. We be doin jis fine," Sarah said. "When dey shut de door, eberting be dark, so we does what we does all de time when it git dark. We curls up on de bench an take a sleep. De train rock we so gentlelike. An when we stops and sumbody open de door, we in a bran new place. It be lak magic."

"Magic?" Susan laughed. "I guess it is magic, at that. We have about another four hours to go when we leave here, so I hope you enjoy your afternoon naps as well."

The afternoon went smoothly, too, up until the last few miles. Outside of town, the train jerked to a stop. Outside the carriage windows, men were rushing back and forth doing something mysterious to the cars with cables.

"What's happening, Jonathan? Is this normal?" Susan was suddenly nervous as she realized they were sitting between what appeared to be rocky outcroppings.

"This is a unique feature of Aiken, my dear. Part of what makes the climate here so lovely is the city's location at the top of a mountain ridge, where it catches every breeze. The problem is that the ascent into town is so steep that a train engine cannot make the climb. The engineers' solution was to make a railroad cut straight through the town and run the tracks some 40 feet below ground level. Even so, they've had to mount a stationary engine on the west side of town to hoist the train up and down the slope with cables."

"Is it safe?"

"Of course it is! Jerky, but safe. The tracks and cables will hold, I promise."

Jamison Winchester was on hand to greet the Grenvilles when they finally arrived at the depot. After introductions, he led them off to a waiting multi-seat carriage. "The station hands will see to your baggage," he explained, "and they know where to deliver it. But it's too late to take you out to the farm this afternoon. Besides, we've been having a lot of rain. Ever heard the expression 'God willin' the creek don't rise'? Well, evidently God wasn't willing enough and the creek did rise. It's over the bridge between here and the farm, so I've taken the liberty of booking you a group of rooms at the Magnolia Inn. The water will go down overnight, and we can go out in the morning."

Susan was relieved at the thought of a comfortable place to recover from the trip, but Jonathan hesitated. "There's one problem with that, Mr. Winchester. Back in the baggage car, I have a cadre of eight workers with me. They are newly freed slaves, and I assume the Magnolia Inn might raise objections to them staying there."

"Oh dear, that is a problem. But never fear. Schwartz's Railroad Hotel has a barracks for slaves. They can stay there overnight. Why don't you take Mrs. Grenville and the children on out to the Magnolia Inn and have some dinner? I'll take care of your slaves."

"Free farm workers," Jonathan corrected.

"Of course."

Susan woke the next morning feeling unusually optimistic. The beds had been comfortable, the food delicious, and the layout and furnishings of the inn resembled those of any Charleston mansion. Maybe this isn't the end of the world after all, she reassured herself. But the feeling did not last long.

Mr. Winchester met them at the inn around 10:00 AM. "Hope everyone slept well," he greeted them. "The creek's all settled down, so we can head out to the farm if you're ready. My foreman had your slaves—uh, workers—up at the crack of dawn so that they could get your things unloaded and the house warmed up. I've also taken the liberty of purchasing some fresh groceries for you—eggs, vegetables, and the like. Are you ready to see your new home?"

"Yes!" the children shouted. Jonathan grinned in anticipation. Susan looked apprehensive.

As the carriage made its way out of town, Winchester kept up a steady monologue on the buildings they were passing. Susan soon gave up trying to retain all the bits of information and just allowed herself to take in the scenery.

After a few minutes, Jonathan touched her arm. "See this road on the left? It marks the edge of our property. If we were to turn here we'd come to four small houses, each rented to one of our tenants. Their holdings spread out behind the houses, but their families can live in some proximity to one another."

And then the carriage was turning into the next road. "And this is all ours," Jonathan said.

Susan smiled gamely, but all she could see were fields and small stands of trees. "I assume there's a house in there somewhere."

"Right around the next bend." As he spoke, the house came into view. "See that grove of oaks?"

"That's it?" Susan wanted to bite her tongue the minute she spoke, but it was too late. Her tone had made her feelings all too clear. "It's . . . uh, it's a box. Freshly whitewashed, I see, and decorated with a couple of shutters, but . . ."

"I warned you that it was a New England farmhouse, my dear. In Boston, one does not need wide piazzas and lots of airy openings. Nor is that style of construction necessary here."

"But the Magnolia Inn last night looked just like a Charleston residence. I assumed . . ."

"Sorry." Jonathan's voice was clipped, and the children stared at their parents fearfully. Even Mr. Winchester had run out of things to say.

The adults made their way to the front door, while the children looked curiously around what passed for a front yard. "I had the steps fixed," Winchester said.

"Yes, I see. Thank you."

Then Jonathan had his key in the lock. As the door swung open, curls of smoke greeted them.

"What the . . .?"

"The house is on fire!" Susan didn't know whether to laugh or cry.

"Lawdy, lawdy, Massa Grenville! Ah don know what fuh do." Gemma the cook rushed out the door, flapping her ample apron. "Ah jis light de stove, an soon as de wood ketch on fire, de smoke come out de door."

"Here, let me handle this." Winchester pushed his way through the crowd at the door and ran to the back of the house. Within seconds, the smoke began to lift, and Winchester reappeared. "No problem, really. The cook failed to open the damper and close the ash pan before she lit her kindling, so the flue couldn't draw the smoke upward. Nothing's on fire, Mrs. Grenville. We'll get a few windows open, and that will take care of the problem. But Miss Gemma, I need to give you a lesson on using that stove."

"Ah be sorry, Massa. Ah aint neber seen one uh dem iron stove befo. We alltimes hab a fireplace an a chimbly."

And that was the family's first introduction to their new home.

As they were sorting themselves out, picking bedrooms and finding boxes of belongings, a new crisis arose. Young Robert was the first of the Grenville children to ask where the toilet facilities were. Because he had his hands full at that moment, Jonathan simply nodded over his shoulder and said, "Out back. You'll see a grove of trees with two small outhouses. Take your pick." He thought no more about it until a piercing scream tore through the air. "Papa! Help! There's a monster in the privy!"

Everyone hurried outside, just in time to see Robbie running headlong from the woods, his trousers down around his knees and hands outstretched, until he tripped over a root and fell, his face in a mudhole.

Susan was the first to reach him. "My God! What have you done to your hand?" She stared in horror at the tiny palm now studded with what looked like three-inch needles.

"I don't know," Robbie sobbed. "I opened the door to the privy and there was this . . . this horrible monster inside chewing on the seat."

"What?"

"He was! I promise. He was big, about the size of a pig, and he had soft-looking fur on his face. But then he turned around and lifted his tail, kind of like a skunk does, and all these horrible things stuck straight out all over his body. I was just reaching out to move him and my hand barely brushed him. Then all these things stuck in my hand. They sting and burn, and they smell bad, too."

By now Jonathan had reached them and knelt beside the hysterical boy. One look was all it took. "You've met your first porcupine!"

"My first one? You mean there are more of them?" Robbie's eyes were wide with terror.

"Probably, but from now on you'll know not to get close to one."

Susan, too, was staring at Jonathan. "What's a porcupine? I didn't know we had an animal like that in South Carolina."

"Well, we didn't, not on the coast at any rate. They live in the woods where they can find hardwood trees to chew on. They love eating wood, especially when someone has been kind enough to cut it up for them—into boards, I mean. So you can often find them in outbuildings."

"No more lectures, please. Help me pull these nasty things out of his hand." With that she grabbed one and cried "ouch" just as Robbie screamed.

"No, Susan, don't. You can't get them out that way. Here, let me carry him into the kitchen." Without a thought that the table was also used to eat on, Jonathan laid the boy down in the center of it, mud and all. "Gemma, get me some vinegar," he ordered. "And a pair of scissors and some tongs."

"What are you going to do?" Robbie asked, shrinking away from his father's touch.

"I'm going to get rid of those quills. It's going to hurt, and it will take some time, but I know you can be brave."

Systematically Jonathan set to work, the knowledge of how to deal with a porcupine attack rising from one of his own childhood memories. "Trust me, Robbie. This happened to me when I was about your age, so I know how much it hurts. But I'll take care of it if you'll lie still and let me work." He poured the vinegar over the boy's hand, cringing himself as his son cried out in pain.

"This makes your skin pucker a little bit so that it draws away from the quill. Next we cut the tops of the quills off. Each one is a hollow tube, with air trapped inside to make them stiff. When the air can get out, the whole quill starts to get soft. See?"

Robbie sniffled and nodded, not trusting himself to speak.

Next, Jonathan took the tongs Gemma had found for him, grasped one of the quills, and gave it a quick jerk. It came loose, leaving behind a small bleeding hole. One by one, the others followed until they were all removed, leaving only a very frightened young boy whose hand still shook with the pain.

"Now I need two more things," he said, turning to Susan. "Some honey and a clean piece of cotton cloth."

Eventually Sarah found the cloth while Gemma produced the honey. "What de honey fuh?" she asked. "He gots fuh eat it?"

"No. I can't tell you how I know, or why it works, but a thin spread of honey will keep these wounds from getting nasty until they heal. So don't put the honey away. We'll need it for several days."

"I know I'm never going near that privy," Mary Sue declared, and her sister nodded in agreement. Even Eddie was looking apprehensive. "Can we get rid of the porcupines, Father?"

"There are probably more of them around than there are of us. But I think we can outsmart them. They chew on wood to get salt. So we're going to go into town and buy a salt-lick."

"What's that?"

"A very hard block of salt. We'll stake it out in the woods away from the outhouses, and the wild animals will go and lick that rather than eating our toilet seats."

"Gosh. There's a whole lot to learn about living here, isn't there?"

"And we've barely begun. Tomorrow's Sunday. We're going to church to meet our new neighbors. But lessons start Monday morning."

31

Settling In
February 1862

"Come on, slugabeds! The sun's up, and farmers should be, too. Breakfast in twenty minutes, and I want everyone dressed and ready for work." Jonathan pounded on doors on his way downstairs, trying to sound more cheerful than he felt. Would the family be ready for their new life, or would some of them find it intolerable? Would his wife be supportive, or was she already longing for home? He just didn't know.

After a pick-up meal of toasted bread and coffee, he led the children on a tour of the farm. "I intend to assign each of you some chores, but I would prefer you to be sure you will enjoy them. I want you to look around at the buildings we have in place and start thinking about what you want to do.

"This first building is the stable." He swung open the heavy doors, startling Moses, who was still asleep upstairs in the bunkhouse room. "Rise and shine, Moses. These horses did some heavy work yesterday, and they're hungry!" he shouted.

"Ah'se comin, Massa."

"Now, Mary Sue, you see that stall against the far wall? That's where we will house Sable Girl when she arrives. It has a window for fresh air, room for her to move around a bit, and next to it is a cupboard where you can keep all her tack and feed."

"When is she coming, Father?"

"By the end of the month, I've been told. I'll want you to be completely responsible for her care, so that she learns to trust you and need you. That will ease the task of turning her into a horse you can ride."

"If I'm to work in the stable, will I be responsible for all our horses?"

"No, certainly not, although I'll be grateful if you keep a casual eye on all of them to make sure they remain healthy. You're going on thirteen, Mary Sue. While you'll be spending a good deal of your time with Sable Girl, you also need to start learning some wifely duties. When you're not needed out here, I expect you to be at your mother's side, learning to cook and manage a household."

"Ugh! I'm not interested in becoming a wife anytime soon. Besides, all the boys my age will probably get themselves killed off in the war. I'll settle for life in a stable, thank you."

"No, you won't." Jonathan was laughing at her. "You'll change your mind soon enough once you've shoveled some manure."

"Can't be worse than changing dirty nappies," she quipped.

"Oh, yes. Think amounts! Now let's move on. Next comes the cattle barn—your territory, I believe, Eddie."

"You were right when you said it was big, Father. We could stall a dozen or more cows in here, but can we afford to fill it up?"

"Not at first, but I'm counting on you to keep expanding our herd. In the next day or two, you and I will need to go into town and visit the feedlot. We'll look for a milch cow and her calf and maybe two other producing dairy cows. That should give us enough milk for the family's needs and leave some extra for you to practice your butter- and cheese-making skills."

"But we'll also need a bull, won't we? To keep the calves and milk coming, I mean." Eddie blushed a little as he noticed his sisters looking at him curiously. "A milch cow needs to calve regularly."

"I doubt that either one of us is prepared yet to handle a bull, Eddie. But I already inquired among our tenants. There are two other bulls on our land. If we need to, we can borrow one. For the most part, I'm counting on letting nature take its course when all the farm cattle are loose in the pasture."

"It might be wise to look for a cow with a bull-calf. That way we could raise him to be gentle."

"Maybe. And if he turned out to be mean, we could always eat him."

"Father!"

"I'm joking, son. The cattle-raising business is all yours. I will leave those decisions up to you. And if you need more advice along those lines, our tenant farmers will be happy to help."

Next, he led the group to the other side of the yard. "Becca, Robbie—you're next." The two younger children looked at each other in anticipation. "Here's a well-built chicken coop—"

"Me!" Becca, normally so quiet and retiring, was hopping up and down. "I want the chickens!"

"Really? They're a lot of work, you know. There are eggs to be gathered each morning, and you have to put the chickens to bed every night, locking them into their coop so predators don't carry them off."

"Predators? Like . . . what?"

"Chickens have lots of enemies—snakes, rats, weasels, coyotes, raccoons."

"Porcupines?"

"Well, no, probably not porcupines, but occasionally a hawk."

"Will I have to fight all those things?" Becca's eyes were wide with concern.

"I'll tell you what. We'll get you a dog or two to help, and possibly a small flock of guinea fowl. They can be loud and annoying, but they defend property from all comers. Predators will tangle with a guinea hen just once before choosing to hunt elsewhere. And we can let the guineas produce chicks, too, if you'd like that."

"Oh, yes, they're so cute and fuzzy when they're little."

"And, just like chickens, they grow up to be dirty and smelly with a vicious side when someone tries to steal their eggs," Robbie reminded her.

"Chickens don't do that—not if they know you. And I'll be like their mother."

Robbie was laughing. "What do you have in mind? Sitting on their eggs? That should be fun to watch."

"Stop teasing me. I know they take work, but I like them. And you'll be grateful when you have eggs for breakfast instead of dried bread."

"And in case you'd like some bacon with those eggs, Robbie, our next stop is the pigpen."

"I can have the pigs?" Robbie's eyes brightened as he considered the possibilities. "No one will be able to yell at me if I get all muddy. That's part of the deal, isn't it?"

"Yes, you lucky boy. But you have to promise not to get too attached. We need to raise a couple of pigs each year, but only for their meat. From what I understand, breeding them is really difficult, so we'll be purchasing piglets in the spring and fattening them for slaughter before winter. You'll also become our garbage man, since they need to be fed kitchen scraps as well as grain. Deal?"

"Deal! That means I get the winters off!"

"Not so fast there, son. You'll spend your winters doing school work."

"What about Jamey?" Robbie looked back at his younger brother, who had been trailing the group and trying to look like he belonged. "Jamey's almost six. Doesn't he get any chores?"

If he were honest, Jonathan would have to admit that he still thought of Jamey as the baby. Now, looking at the little boy's sturdy legs and earnest expression, he knew Robbie was right. "Come here, Jamey. What animals do you like?"

Jamey bit his lower lip with concentration. "Cats. I love cats."

"Well, we certainly need cats on a farm. Without them, we'll have mice in every bucket of feed. If we find a mother cat and her kittens, do you think you could take care of feeding them, Jamey?"

"Yes, sir." Jamey nodded vigorously.

"Well then, I think we're done out here." On the way back to the house, the group made one more stop next to an overgrown patch of weeds. "I've made arrangements for someone to stop by this week and plow up this field. It is destined to be our kitchen garden, where we'll grow food crops for the family. All of us will be eating, so all of us will have to pitch in and help with the garden. You may choose what vegetables we plant. Your mother and I will choose last, however, to make sure we don't end up with all peas and carrots. Now, run on and finish your explorations of the farm."

Later that afternoon, Jonathan drew up his shopping list for the feedlot: at least one milch cow and calf, a dozen chicks and a couple of laying hens, a pair of guinea fowl, two piglets, a dog, and a cat with kittens. *What have I gotten myself into?* he wondered briefly. Then he smiled. He hadn't felt this contented in a very long time.

While Jonathan and the children were thus occupied, Susan was having a learning session of her own with Gemma. The cook had confronted her that morning. "Massa Grenville, he say you gwine larn fuh cook, so you gits fuh make dinner."

"Gemma, I don't know a thing about cooking."

"Den you kin larn, an ah kin hep. We gwine make soup fuh dinner."

"Why soup? That sounds complicated."

"Cause you caint burn soup."

Even Susan had to laugh as she recognized the truth of that statement. "All right. How do we start?"

"Wit dese bone an stuff." Gemma held up a cheesecloth bag of chicken bones from the previous night's dinner, along with potato and carrot peelings, some onion skins, and a few celery leaves.

"That's garbage!"

"Not til we boils de goodness outta it. Here, you takes dis big soup pot an fills it wit water."

"Water?"

"Yes'm. Fro de pump dere." Gemma was enjoying herself. "Aint you neber pump water?"

After a few tries, Susan managed to get the water flowing and found the feeling exhilarating. "It is handy to have a pump right here," she admitted.

"Yes'm. Now you dumps dis bag uh garbage inna water an add sum salt—bout wha you kin cup inna hand."

"The whole thing—bag and all?"

"Yes'm, lessn you wants fuh fish all dem bones outta de soup one by one. Dey makes hard chewin."

While the soup boiled, Gemma taught Susan how to chop vegetables—more potatoes, carrots, and onions. "See what you be missin when de cookin git dun out inna cookhouse?"

"I never knew onions made people cry," Susan said, wiping her cheeks.

"Dat be jis one uh de ting you don know. Now, lift dat bag outta de soup. Here, use dese tong. Dat be a bag uh garbage, sho nuf. But don de water smell good now? You kin add dese chopt tings, wiles I gits sum udduh stuff fro de cellar."

When Gemma returned, Susan was surprised to see that she was carrying jars of canned green beans, tomatoes, and corn. "Where did those come from?"

"We'uns can dem las summer. Ah pack dem up when we lef de house on Logan Street. Ah figures we needs fuh eat, no matter where we be. We gwine put up mo dis year, cause Massa Grenville say we gwine hab we own garden. You gwine larn how fuh do it, too. Nuttin mo portant dan habin nuf food."

Later that afternoon, Gemma came looking for Susan again. "Time fuh make de biskit."

"Biscuits." Susan looked skeptical.

"Yes'm. An you gwine git you fingah dirty. Biskit need fuh be rub wit de fingah."

"What is this greasy white stuff?"

"Dat be lard."

"Pig fat? In biscuits?"

"Sho nuf. Dat what make dem flaky. Now, start rubbin dat flour inna it an don squish it. Dat make de dough tough."

By the time Gemma declared the biscuits ready for baking, most of the kitchen table wore a white coating of flour, but Susan was enormously proud of herself.

Jonathan wandered into the kitchen just as they were cleaning up the mess. He took Susan by the shoulders and planted a kiss squarely on her flour-covered nose. "Domestic arts suit you, my love. You look good in flour."

"Why, thank you."

"Yes. You remind me of my mother."

Susan stared at him, half amused and half horrified. Gemma grinned and busied herself with the biscuits.

32

Letters from Missing Children
March/April 1862

Jonathan was smiling as he arrived home from his trip to town. "Susan! Where are you? We have a letter from Johnny." She came running, as he knew she would. "What does he say? Is he all right? Where is he?"

"Slow down, and quit acting like a worried mother. I haven't read it—I saved it to share with you. But of course he's all right. The letter is in his own handwriting—not the kind Charlotte received from a commanding officer."

"But it's been so long since we've heard anything . . ."

"Don't wait any longer. Open it and read it to me."

Her hands shaking noticeably, she sank into her favorite rocker in the kitchen and tore the envelope open. For a moment, tears blurred her vision; then she read aloud:

> *Dear Parents and Brothers and Sisters, one and all,*
>
> *I take my pen in hand to let you know that I am on the land, living and actually thriving in this man's army. I have not written before because we were always on the move through the Sea Islands, trying to avoid Ol' Abe's troops,*

who seem to be nosing about everywhere. Now we have set up a permanent camp on Goat's Island, and conditions are more peaceful.

"Where on earth is Goat's Island, Jonathan?"

"It's in the middle of the Folly River. But, my God, it's nothing more than a sliver of land, full of pluff mud and sea grass and . . ."

". . . and snakes and alligators, according to this! He says they traveled by boat to Cole's Island and then had to carry all their gear on foot through the swamp."

"That's a good long distance, too. Cole's Island guards the Stono Inlet, if you know where that is."

"Yes, of course I do. It's on the way to Edisto."

"Well, Goat's Island is about a mile upriver from there."

"But what would the Army be doing there?"

"Guarding the approach to Cole's Island, I would surmise. The Confederate Army has several batteries of guns protecting the entrance to the Stono River to prevent the Yankees from reaching the interior of James Island."

"There's nothing much on James Island, either, from what I remember. What makes it so important?"

"Just swamp and a few plantations. But from James Island, an enemy would have a clear shot to Charleston, so . . ."

". . . so it's a dangerous place to be!"

"Don't worry until you know there's something to worry about. He says things are peaceful. What does the rest of the letter say?"

There are too many sand fleas and ticks here for comfort. The water is green and slimy, promising malaria, and the confounded sand gets into everything, including our food. As far as our food goes, it's pretty short rations. I share a mess tent with Alex, his brother Harris, their Uncle Joe, Alex's slave Monday, and one other soldier. Our rations for a three-day period include all the hard tack we can gnaw on, plus an ounce and a half of sugar, 6 gills of rice, some hominy and salt, and a fair amount of tough beef. Monday does a pretty good job of cooking the mess into something of a stew, but we are all starved for sweets, fruits, and even vegetables. Alex has been pleading with his mother to try to send us some candy or fruit, along with some fishhooks, but I don't expect we'll ever get some.

"Oh, Jonathan. I wish there were some way we could . . ."

"You know we're too far away."

"So maybe we shouldn't have come here. If we were still in Charleston, we . . ."

"We still wouldn't be able to get him everything he needs. But maybe, when our peaches ripen, we could ship a big box of them to Mrs. Croft, and she could send them on to the boys. Does he say anything else?"

I must close for now, as it is almost time for close-order drill. Such is the life of a soldier. Give my love to the children and tell them I would like to hear from them, one and all.

Your loving son, Johnny Grenville

P.S. You can send letters to me addressed to Company A, 24th South Carolina Volunteer Regiment, Hagood's Brigade.

"How strange it feels to be getting a letter from our son! I know that a proper upbringing always includes the art of letter writing, but I've only had to do so when writing thank-you notes to distant relatives. And I've almost never received a letter—certainly not one from a beloved family member. We've always kept family close. It feels lonely and foreign to be so separated that the only skein holding us together is a piece of paper."

"Wartime changes everything, I fear. It forces us apart in ways we never anticipated. I'm grateful, though, that even in wartime, mail delivery continues to function, even if it's a little slow now and then."

"It's certainly been slow, and this is not a very long letter after all the time Johnny's been gone."

"It's a letter, and he misses us. Be thankful for what you have, Susan."

"I am. Of course I am. But oh, Jonathan, I miss our two oldest children. How did they both get away from us?"

"Children grow up, and we have to let them go."

"No one said we had to like it. And I intend to worry about Johnny every minute until this horrid war is over. As for Charlotte, I'm not sure what to think. She knows where we are, and yet not a word from her."

"Have you written to her?"

"Well, no, but I think she owes us an apology."

"The two of you are too much alike. At this very moment, if I could ask her why she hasn't written, she would say, 'Because Momma owes me an apology,' and her lower lip would stick out just as yours is doing now. Write to her. Tell her you miss her. Tell her how nice it is here. Tell her we are saving the other front bedroom for her because it is already decked out as a nursery. And then, you watch—she'll come around."

Their discussion was interrupted as Mary Sue and Becca burst into the kitchen, shouting for them to "come quick!"

"What's wrong?" Susan was instantly on her feet.

"Nothing's wrong. It's beautiful. Come on. You have to see!" The girls dashed back out the door and down the steps, their parents following.

"Slow down, girls. We're coming, but I'm not young enough to run as you do," Susan said. "Where are you taking us?"

"The orchard!"

Jonathan grinned as he realized what was happening. "Welcome to life in a peach orchard, Mrs. Grenville," he whispered. "Haven't you always wanted to live in a spot where delicate pink flowers burst out in every direction you look?"

"It is gorgeous," Susan sighed, "and Charlotte would love it. I'll write her and tell her about it. Maybe I could enclose a blossom or two."

"I think we have enough to spare a small branch." Jonathan laughed and broke off a twig, shoving it into her hair. "Here, take that back to the house and press it into your letter."

Two weeks later, a letter from Charlotte arrived. Susan opened it shakily, wondering what her difficult daughter had in store for her.

Dear Mother and Father,

I seat myself to send you a line and tell you how happy I was to hear that you are well-settled. The flowers were still fragrant, Mother, and I thank you for them. Perhaps next year I can see them for myself, but I am afraid I'll miss this year's blooming. The twins are thriving, but, at just four months, they are still too young to make that kind of trip. You must also remember that I am still in mourning, and it would be improper for me to be traveling across the state by myself.

"Just listen to her, Jonathan! She must know we wouldn't demand that she travel all this way alone. And if she had just come with us in the first place . . ."

"Susan, you're doing it again. You'd even argue with her when she is a hundred miles away."

Susan wasn't listening. "And she makes it sound as if I don't know the first thing about babies. I, who have raised seven of them! They're going on five months, and they should be holding their heads up by now. If she waits much longer, they'll be able to crawl and she'll really have problems traveling with them."

"I'm sure you're right, but she's their mother, and it's her job to make those decisions. How many times did I hear you tell your mother to keep her nose out of your child rearing?"

"This is different. Charlotte's my daughter."

Jonathan held up his hands to signal defeat. "What else does she say?"

> *Mr. and Mrs. Rogers are very nice to me, and we are well taken care of. You needn't worry about us. Only one thing bothers me some, but it's minor and only happens infrequently. Mr. Rogers has befriended a young man who comes to Charleston periodically, conveying herds of cattle from Tennessee to Army Headquarters here and elsewhere. When he is in town, Mr. Rogers invites him to dinner and encourages me to spend time talking to him. He says the young man is homesick for his family and I should be friendly. But I am afraid the young man himself is not looking at me purely as a fill-in for his younger sister.*

"Jonathan! Would Mr. Rogers be trying to marry his son's widow off to some strange young man?"

"Surely he wouldn't do that. Charlotte is probably being dramatic, as usual. Or perhaps she finds herself attracted to him, too, and wants her mother to tell her to stop it."

"You always think the worst of her, Jonathan." Unable to come up with a better retort, she continued reading.

> *Charleston is a lonely place these days. More and more people are doing as you did—packing up and leaving. There's apparently little possibility of rebuilding the city until the war is over, so most businesses have closed up shop even if they were not burned out. Finding the necessities of life gets more and more difficult.*
>
> *I am happy that you are well-situated and have the opportunity to raise your own food. Before the summer is over, you may have to start sending us packages of vegetables, and peaches, of course.*
>
> *Your loving daughter, Charlotte Rogers*

"She's still trying to make us feel guilty."

"Perhaps she is, Susan, but I'll remind you once more that she is an adult—a mother with two children—and you have to let her make her own decisions and her own mistakes. We can keep checking on her, and we can now and then repeat our offer to have her come to live with us, but we can't make her do what she does not want to do. Those days are over."

"They were over a long time ago, I'm afraid. My mother always called her a willful child, and so she is still."

33

More Damned Yankees
Late May 1862

Jonathan had gone to town on Wednesday for a chat with Jamison Winchester. He was hoping for news about teaching positions in Aiken, but he also planned to pick up the mail and do some shopping for another cow. The cow search was futile; the only one he found was priced at $55. "Ridiculous," he mumbled. "We paid less than half that for our last one. Eddie will just have to make do with the ones he has."

At the post office counter, he was pleased to find another letter from Johnny. As had become his habit, he stuffed it in his pocket to take home to Susan so they could read it together. Next, he stopped by Mr. Winchester's office for a brief visit. Winchester welcomed him warmly. "Sit down, Grenville. I'm glad to have a distraction from all this horrible news from Charleston." He gestured at the pile of *Charleston Mercury* newspapers littering his desk.

"I haven't seen the news recently," Jonathan admitted. "The farm has been keeping me occupied from sunup to sundown. What's going on in Charleston now? Or don't I want to know?"

"The trouble is not in Charleston itself but in the surrounding countryside. General Lee appointed John Pemberton to take

261

over the Army in the Low Country, and Pemberton seems to be systematically destroying his own defenses. He's pulling the batteries from all along the coastline, leaving it vulnerable to invasion."

"I've not even heard of the man. Why would he do that?"

"Because he's a damned Yankee, that's why!"

A cold fist of fear slammed directly into Jonathan's gut. He flashed back to the first time that term had been applied to him, kicking off the whole series of disasters that had befallen him. He had hoped that he had left that kind of thinking behind, but here it was again—that partisan hatred for the enemy, expressed in a label without regard for the individual behind it.

Trying desperately to keep his face neutral, he asked, "As I said, I haven't heard of him. Why do you call a Confederate general a Yankee?"

"Because he was born and bred in Philadelphia and raised as a Quaker, that's why. Then he fell in love with a Virginia heiress and threw it all over—his family, his own inheritance, even his religion. You can't trust a man like that. He tries his best to make himself out to be a Virginian now, which is why Lee likes him. Their wives are friends, I believe, which probably explains how he got his military appointment."

"But just because he was born in the North, that doesn't mean he isn't loyal . . ."

"Of course it does. Here, just listen to this letter that appears in last weekend's *Mercury*." He shuffled through the pile on his desk and extracted one sheet that had been folded back. "These words were written by a prominent Charleston woman, Mary Boykin Chestnut, whose husband was our U.S. senator and is now an aide to President Davis."

Men born Yankees are an unlucky selection as commanders for the Confederacy. They believe in the North in a way no true Southerner ever will, and they see no shame in surrendering to Yankees. They are half-hearted clear through: Stephens as Vice President, Lovell, Pemberton, Ripley. A general must command the faith of his soldiers. These never will, be they ever so good and true.

"She has the truth of it. Yankees can never be Southerners, no matter how hard they try. You have to be born on this land to be a part of it."

Unable to trust himself any longer, Jonathan stood. "I'm sure you are right, sir, but I'm afraid I must take my leave. I only stopped by to ask you to keep an eye out for someone who has a cow for sale. That's where my only concern lies these days."

As soon as he left the office, he hurried to a newsstand to get a copy of the latest paper. Settling on a park bench, he scanned the pages to glean any tidbits about the Sea Island defenses. Winchester's facts had been correct, he discovered. Pemberton had ordered the dismantling of the batteries on Cole's Island, and the editor of the paper raged over the new dangers of that move. Now frantic with worry about Johnny, he tore open the letter he had been saving. Johnny's words confirmed his fears.

We've been moving around a great deal, which is why I haven't been able to write to you. General Pemberton ordered us to help evacuate Cole's Island, because he needed those cannons to defend Charleston. Our job was to disguise what was happening so that the enemy would not know the batteries had been removed. We had a great deal of amusement from our efforts—cutting down trees and propping up their trunks to look like cannon barrels from a distance. We scurried around in circles, so as to look like a great parade of men, when really there were only a few of us. I must admit we made a pretty good job of it.

Leave it to Johnny to find fun in whatever he is asked to do, Jonathan thought. Despite his fear, he smiled briefly at the imagery. Then he returned to the letter.

Unfortunately, an ungrateful slave gave the whole game away. You may have heard about Robert Smalls, who worked on a gunboat loaded with some of the cannons we were removing. He managed to steal the boat right out of Charleston Harbor and sail it to the enemy lines. So now the game is up, and the Yankees are on the move toward the Stono River because they know it is undefended. Reports say there are several Northern regiments now on Edisto Island and another group sailing toward us out of Hilton Head.

Our whole 24th South Carolina Regiment has been assigned to fortify James Island against their incursions. We are encamped near a small summer resort town called Secessionville. Apparently, several years ago, some younger planters built themselves an alternative refuge so they could secede from the stuffiness of their parents' Charleston society. Well, the little town is seeing a different kind of secession now. We are building an earthworks in the center of the island. It stands on a narrow spit of high ground between two swamps and will block the only path from the Stono River to Fort Johnson overlooking Charleston Harbor. Our fake cannons may not have stopped the Yankees, but our guns surely will.

How easily he speaks of guns, Jonathan thought. He felt sick inside, both from the shock of hearing "Damned Yankee" again and now from the image of his son firing a gun into a troop of his countrymen. I thought I could escape from the war by coming here, he realized, but it has followed me as surely as night follows day. The dark clouds of war roll over us, and there is nothing we can do to stop them.

Intent now only on regaining the peace he had begun to find as a man working his own land, he headed home. Instead, he arrived in the midst of a scene of sheer chaos. As he rode down the long driveway, he heard a child scream. Kicking his horse into a gallop, he dashed for the yard. Becca stood in front of the chicken coop, looking fearfully upward, her arms held out at her sides, fingers splayed. Her mouth was wide open as if to scream again, but no sound was coming out. From the kitchen doorway, Susan came running. Eddie and Mary Sue dashed out of the barn to see what was wrong, and Hector crouched nervously at the edge of the yard, clutching his hoe as he looked around, surveying the yard for danger.

At first, Jonathan saw only the people, each caught in a tableau of terror. Then his eye fell on the chicken coop itself, and he instantly understood what had happened. Two partially dismembered hens lay in the dirt, their blood splattered over the ground and wooden fence posts. Several small piles of yellow feathers were all that remained of yesterday's flock of newly hatched chicks. And when he looked above, in the direction his daughter was staring, he could see them—two large red-tailed hawks making lazy circles overhead.

He slid from the saddle and took his small daughter in his arms, lifting her up and pushing her head into the comfort of his shoulder. "Don't look anymore, baby. The hawks are flying away now, and we'll make sure they never come back. I promise you it won't happen again. And we'll get you a new clutch of chicks."

"I never want to see another chicken," she said between sobs and hiccups. "I hate chickens."

"No, you don't. If you must hate something, hate chicken hawks. You must never blame the victims instead of the ones who are guilty."

"How can you keep them from coming again? I always lock the chickens into the coop for the night, but as soon as I let them out this morning, the hawks just dived down from the sky, and I couldn't stop them."

"We're going to put chicken screening across the top of the pen. It's my fault. I should have done that from the beginning. I'm sorry, Becca. So sorry." When she quieted, he handed her off to her mother and strode off to clean up the mess, hoping to work off his anger.

From the kitchen, Gemma emerged with a dishpan in her hands. "Put dem chicken parts in here," she said. "Dey kin still be good fuh eatin."

"No, Gemma. We can't ask Becca to eat them. Not after what she has just seen."

"We caint ford fuh waste good food," she argued.

"This time we can. We're going to bury them. Becca will want to do that."

34

Ultimatum
Late May 1862

Later that night, once the children were abed, Jonathan pulled Johnny's letter out of his pocket. "You'll want to see this, Susan. It's not good news, but it's not the worst, either. Johnny may soon be in the thick of a battle, but he's not afraid, and I don't want us to be, either."

Susan read the letter quietly, her jaw tightening visibly as she reached the end. "It's bad, isn't it?"

"We don't know that. Johnny seems pretty confident of their ability to hold that swamp. And you know, from what I've seen, those damned Yankees will get themselves so bogged down in the pluff mud, they won't be able to lift their feet."

Susan stared at him, a half-smile competing with utter surprise. "Did you just use the term 'Damned Yankee'?"

"Yep. I guess I did. And you know what? It felt pretty good."

"But the whole family has been careful never to let those words be spoken because . . ."

"I know. But I learned some important lessons today."

"Today? What else happened?"

Briefly he told her about the scene in Winchester's office, his automatic reaction of fear mixed with anger, and the way that fear had affected his reaction to Johnny's letter. "I was still raging as I headed home. Then our little girl's scream changed everything."

"How?"

"I saw Becca's reaction when I took her in my arms. She clung to me as if I were life itself, and, as her scream turned to sobs, then whimpers, and finally deep, peaceful breaths, I could feel my own anger ebbing away. She taught me an important lesson—a lesson about the unimportance of fear and the power of love. The scare she had experienced didn't seem to matter any more. What did matter was the comfort she found in my embrace."

"But there's still hatred in the world and prejudice and violence. We can't hug everything we fear and drive it out of existence."

"No, of course not. And there may be worse to come. But we'll have an important defense against the things that terrify us if we can keep our family ties strong."

Jonathan was quite proud of himself for that insightful pronouncement, so he was more than a little surprised when it was met with silence. Susan was staring at him with an odd expression on her face. If I didn't know better, he thought, I'd say she was sneering at me.

"Susan?"

"You're hopeless, you know that? Completely clueless about the world and how it operates."

He stared back, stunned at the vitriol he heard in her voice. "What . . . what did I do?"

"It's what you didn't do. I gather you didn't even mention the possibility of Winchester helping you get a teaching job."

"No, I didn't. I was too upset. But I doubt that anything will come of that idea anyway. Most of the young men in town have gone to war, and parents are unwilling to send their nubile daughters off to school in such turbulent times as these. They're probably going to be closing schools, not expanding them."

"Do you know that?"

"No, but it's pretty obvious. If there were a job available, I'm sure Winchester would have mentioned it. It's just my luck to be unemployed at the wrong time."

"So we're back to your persecuted Job phase again, I see. You're the innocent victim of circumstance, helpless to react or take action to better your situation." She was shaking her head in disgust.

"Susan? What's going on?"

"Nothing's going on. That's the problem. You dragged us all out here, promising that it would mean a better life, that you could return to teaching, that we could escape from the hazards of war. None of that has happened, and you seem to want nothing more than to sit among the ashes of our former lives and trust that some day your tormenters will lift the plagues that have fallen upon you and we can live happily ever after. Rubbish!"

"I don't believe that everything is my fault. The war . . ."

"Ah, but that's exactly what you believe. You try to control everything that happens to this family. You become despondent when something bad happens because you take it personally."

"No, I don't. I—"

But Susan was not to be stopped. "You saw Mr. McDermitt's charge against you as personal name-calling instead of what it really was—a symptom of the deep split between North and

South. You grew angry when the Army took over our plantations because you saw those moves as personal attacks on you.
I suspect you even saw the fire as a deliberate insult on the part
of the wind that blew the flames in our direction."

"That's ridiculous!"

"Yes it is, but not for the reasons you think. You believe
you ought to be able to control everything. But I have news for
you. You are just another insignificant speck on this planet. You
control nothing. You are helpless and hopeless, but you strut
around pontificating to the rest of us as if you were master of
the world. And you expect me to listen to you with awe and
wonder. I think I'm through doing that. And there goes your
whole theory about our strong and invincible family."

"You don't mean that. You're just afraid for Johnny and taking it out on me, which is completely unreasonable."

"Of course I'm afraid! I'm living in the middle of nowhere,
working like a common scullery maid. We have no friends or
family here. Our children are shoveling manure instead of
attending classes. I've just learned that our son and his friends
are going to be facing thousands of Union troops with nothing
but a few guns and a pile of earth to defend them. And you?
You tell me everything will be all right because you want it to
be so."

"I don't want to fight with you, Susan."

"No, you don't. You never do. You don't want to hear an
opinion that contradicts your own. I'm supposed to be the perfect Southern wife, submissive to your authority and grateful for
your superior knowledge. Well, no more."

"What is it you would have me do?"

"I'm angry. I want you to be angry at the world right along
with me and for the same reasons. I want you to understand why

I'm afraid about Johnny being a soldier. I want you to order him to come home. I want you to order Charlotte to come home, too, instead of telling me that I must just accept their decisions. I don't want your logic. I want you to be a parent."

"Their parent? Or yours?"

Now it was her turn to stare at him. "Is that what you think? That I see you as a father figure to me as well as to the children?"

"The Romans had a name for the head of a household, you know. *Paterfamilias* was the father of the family to both wife and children. It's a traditional role in Western society, and I try to live up to it."

"And now you are patronizing me—telling me something I know as well as you, lecturing me as if I were a student in your classroom."

"You asked what I thought. I just told you."

"So you did." She turned away, moving to the window to stare up at a moon waxing full, as the silence in the room grew heavier.

At last she turned and faced him one more time. She was dry-eyed. The angry flush had faded from her cheeks. She smiled gently. "I'm over my anger, Jonathan. I'm a little sad. But mostly, I'm empty and lonely. And we're not going to argue any longer. We can work out the details of this new empty life without shouting at one another. This is my ancestral home, although by law you hold the title to it. We will continue to share it, so that our children will at least have the benefit of both parents being available to them. It's fortunate that Charlotte has not come with us. I can move into the connecting nursery, and the children need not know that we no longer share a bed. We'll continue with our usual sharing of responsibilities."

"That's not what I want, Susan."

"No, it probably isn't. But it's all you're going to get."

Throughout that long night, Jonathan tossed and turned, nursing the idea that, by morning, Susan would have calmed down. He headed downstairs as soon as it was light, cheered to hear the usual sounds of pots being moved around the stove. "Morning!" he greeted everyone from the doorway.

"Good morning, Papa," Jamey answered, but the other children glanced at him furtively without responding. Susan, her back to him, seemed to stiffen a bit but did not turn from the stove.

"Coffee smells good." He tried again.

Susan pushed the pot toward the edge of the stove but did not offer to pour it. He helped himself to a mug, using the movement to peer over her shoulder and ask, "What's a fellow have to do to get a plate of that fried mush?"

"Wait your turn," she snapped, handing plates to Eddie and Becca instead. The children bent over their breakfasts, refusing all eye contact.

Jonathan sighed and carried his coffee to the window where he could look out over the sprouting garden. "Crops are doing well."

No one answered. As they finished eating, the children meekly carried their plates to the sink and then scurried off as if each one had a terribly pressing obligation to fulfill. When they were alone in the kitchen, Jonathan broke the silence again. "So much for hiding our argument from the children. They are keenly aware that something is wrong. It's not fair to use them as pawns in this dispute, you know."

"I'm doing no such thing. I simply want to be left alone for a while. Is that too much to ask?"

"Of course not. You have certainly earned the right to take a break, but don't make the children feel as if they have somehow made you angry."

"If you tell me one more thing that I ought to do, Jonathan, I will not be responsible for my behavior." She slammed the spatula onto the table. "Fry your own mush if you're hungry." But he no longer wanted any breakfast.

Routines develop only because they consist of actions that are repeated every day. Within a few days, the family routines adjusted so that husband and wife did not have to cross paths too often. The new atmosphere of formality and veiled hostility began to feel normal. Susan continued to prepare meals on time but seldom ate with the family. Conversations, when they occurred at all, centered on chores to be completed or supplies to be ordered. Jonathan threw himself into renewed efforts to offer reading lessons to all the former slaves in their employ. Sarah and Hector agreed to allow their small cabin to be used in the evenings as a schoolroom, so Jonathan visited there regularly as soon as he finished supper. The reading and writing exercises continued until bedtime.

Susan asked Eddie and Eli to rearrange some furniture for her. In the largely unused dining room, they shoved the table to the far wall, arranging the chairs around only three sides. Then they carried in Susan's melodeon and set it up in the cleared space.

"Are you planning to play a concert in here?" Eddie asked. He had meant it only to tease her, but she answered as if she had taken him seriously.

"No, I'm not nearly concert-ready. I need a private practice room—some place where I can close the door and keep everyone out while I work."

"Work? I thought you played because you enjoyed it."

"I want to be good at what I do. That takes practice and hard work."

"All right, but we like hearing your music. Are we allowed to listen through the door?"

"You can find better things to do with your time," she snapped.

He didn't broach the subject again, nor did anyone else. Susan shut herself away in her music room every afternoon, and Jonathan disappeared to his makeshift classroom every evening. The children turned to one another for comfort and support when things went wrong or to share their pride when their efforts were successful. Sarah talked to Susan, and Hector talked to Jonathan, and, if the two former slaves discussed the Grenvilles as a couple, they did so only in complete privacy. No one was willing to risk breaking the fragile truce that had replaced the family bonds of love and affection.

35

The Battle of Secessionville
June 1862

"Mother, why aren't you and Father speaking to each other?" Mary Sue kept her head down, concentrating on peeling potatoes as she asked the question.

Susan looked up, startled. "We're not . . . uh, not speaking. What gave you that idea?"

"But you don't talk to each other anymore. Not the way you used to. Even at dinner, you both talk to us but not to each other. I never see the two of you together. And the other night, when I came to wake you because Jamey was sick, you weren't even sleeping in the same room."

"That's really none of your business, Mary Sue."

"Maybe not, but I know the younger children are scared, and I am, too. It feels like our family is coming apart. We've lost our house. We've left all our friends behind. Johnny and Charlotte are gone, and now you two are fighting. There's nothing I can trust anymore—nothing that I'm sure will still be there tomorrow." Tears blurred her vision as she risked a quick glance at her mother.

Susan looked at her daughter and felt a rush of guilt. "I'm sorry, Mary Sue. I know this move has been hard on all of us. Your father and I are feeling overwhelmed, too, which may be why we don't seem to be getting along. But things will get better, I promise. There's nothing for you to be afraid of." It wasn't a real answer, and she was fully aware of that, even as she tried to change the subject. "If you're finished with those potatoes, could you run out and see if you can find some spring onions in the garden to season them with?"

Mary Sue used the chance to escape, but her steps dragged as she headed for the back door. Susan watched her sadly and resolved to make more of an effort to be pleasant to Jonathan. Not that her anger had softened, she realized, but because she needed to put the welfare of her children first.

Later that morning, Jonathan came in to announce that he was headed for town. "Have some seeds to pick up," he said. "Do you need anything?"

"Not from the general store, no," Susan said. "But I hope you're planning to go by the post office. We haven't heard from Johnny in a long time."

"I'll do that and try to pick up a Charleston paper, too. I've been wondering whatever happened to the fort they were building on James Island." Cheered by her willingness to ask him to do something for her, he patted her arm. "Remember, though, they say that no news is good news. The boys are probably too busy to write letters."

"Busy fighting, you mean?" Then, realizing that she was still being argumentative, she smiled back at him. "I guess mothers will always worry, no matter what. Be patient with me?"

"I'm worried, too, if that's any comfort," he said. "Let's hope for a letter."

There was, indeed, a letter waiting for the Grenvilles, but not the one they were hoping for. This one came from Mrs. Croft, Alex's mother. For a few moments, Jonathan felt sheer panic wash over him. Then he shook his head and gave himself a stern lecture. You know better than that, he thought. If something had happened to Johnny, the word would come from an official source, not a neighbor lady. He contemplated opening the letter immediately but decided to wait until he and Susan could read it together. And by the time he reached home, he was able to walk into the kitchen with a little bounce to his step.

"News from the home front," he announced. "It looks rather like a gossipy chat from Alex's mother. It's addressed to both of us, so I waited to open it."

Susan whirled, her eyes big with anxiety. "Johnny?"

"Let me get it open and we'll see."

My dear Mr. and Mrs. Grenville,

I hope this letter finds you in good health and spirits in your new home. I had the pleasure of talking with your son Johnny last night, and he asked me to write to you and let you know that he is safe and healthy. By now you may certainly have heard about the Battle of Secessionville, which was a glorious victory for our Confederate forces. Our sons were both at the battle, although they seem not to have taken a direct part in the fighting.

Susan felt her knees go weak with relief, and she pulled up the nearest chair. "Thank the Lord for His favors! Go on, Jonathan."

Alex said he was stationed off to one side on picket duty to make sure the attacking Federals did not try to go around the fortification and gain access from the rear. When the fighting was over, the boys' unit was designated to battlefield reconnaissance, looking for wounded men and recovering lost weapons.

And now Alex and your Johnny are both on ambulance duty, which is how it came about that I saw them last night. There were a great many wounded on both sides, and the little fort at Secessionville had no hospital facilities, so they are transporting both patients and prisoners to Charleston. By last night, Roper Hospital was turning them away for lack of beds, so Alex and Johnny brought several of their wounded comrades to our house.

We are still in the city because the Reverend Croft has suffered a small attack of apoplexy and now is experiencing some difficulty with his right leg and arm. Since he is currently unable to travel, we have postponed our own plans to move up to North Carolina. While we are closeted here for the duration, I felt it only right that we do our part for the war effort by turning our parlor into a convalescent ward for our wounded.

I must admit that one of our patients, a young man by the name of Tavernor, appears unlikely to recover from his wounds, but we will do our best to make him comfortable.

You must not worry about your son. He appears well and strong, although understandably tired from their continuing duties. I have told both boys that they are welcome to come here for sleep and food anytime they can get away. We will continue to monitor their fortunes as the war continues.

Sincerely, your humble servant,
Margaret Harris Croft

Susan sat quietly, eyes closed, trying to take it all in. Jonathan leaned toward her, folding her hands within his own. "Everything's going to be all right, Susan. He's safe, and I'm sure he'll write when he is able."

She nodded, still not trusting her voice. Then she offered a watery smile before pulling her hands away. "I'm fine now, but the fear never entirely goes away, does it?"

"Of course not. But I remain convinced that we can handle any fear if we lean on one another when we are most afraid. Can we try to do more of that?"

"For the sake of our other children, I suppose we must."

Tensions eased in the ensuing days. With the arrival of summer weather, the garden was flourishing. Mary Sue pointed with pride to her row of tomato plants, where the first green globes were starting to show tinges of orange and red. "All it took was a couple of warm nights. I knew they'd be fine," she said.

The other children had their favorite crops as well. Even little Jamey had a row of ruby radishes, while Robert happily plucked peas and shelled them without complaint. Becca had a longer wait for her sweet corn, but she measured the stalks every day. "They're going to do much better than 'knee high by the Fourth of July'," she announced, only to have Eddie tease her by telling her that was because her knees weren't very high to begin with.

Even the animals seemed to be joining in the general mood of good will. A cow was getting ready to calve, and the hens and ducks were sitting on clutches of eggs. Kittens romped in the hayloft, and this year's piglets were enjoying every chance they got to roll in the mud. Best of all, the orchard was bursting with the new crop, peaches so heavy the branches bowed under their weight.

In early July the long-awaited letter from Johnny arrived. This time, Susan was the one to read it out loud.

> *Dear Parents and Brothers and Sisters All,*
> *I take my pen in hand to assure you that I am still on the land, living and without a single blemish. By now you have surely heard the story of*

the Battle of Secessionville that took place here on June 16. It was my first experience of real combat, and the memories remain fresh in my mind. We were wakened from sleep after a hard day's work with the warning that the Yankees were approaching our earthworks. Quietly and with purpose, we took our places and prepared to defend our land. Our own unit was posted off to the side of the earthworks to keep anyone from trying to circle around it. The position meant that we were left out of the fight while having a front-row view of all that was happening.

Once the firing began, things seemed to happen almost in slow motion, and, after a while, the noise of the guns faded away as well. Line after line of Yankees attempted to climb our parapet. They weren't firing their rifles, because they had their bayonets attached. The closer they got, the more tightly packed they became, for the land narrowed to a tiny spit surrounded by swamps. And against those serried lines were our own brave soldiers, firing their cannons directly down into the masses of invaders. When we ran out of cannon balls and grape shot, we began packing the barrels with anything that would fit—bricks, rocks, pieces of old chain, broken pottery. Every loose item became a projectile. And when even that ammunition was used up, the cannoneers began rolling down upon the Yankees the logs that we had used to move our cannons into place. The bodies of their men piled up at the foot of the fort. Just as it seemed that we had no further way to hold off the attack, the Federal commander gave them the order to retreat, and we watched them march away, leaving their casualties behind. Later reports tell us that their officers, as well as many of their men, were drunk on whiskey by the time they got to our fortifications.

Whatever the case, it was a glorious victory, and I found my spirits soaring. Alex seems fairly shaken by the experience. He is now talking about applying for the Signal Corps so that he can avoid further combat. But as for me, I have never felt so alive. I am hungry to experience the full nature of combat. I keep picturing the men on both sides—their eyes wide open, their mouths stretched into wide grins, their lungs gasping for air, their limbs *churning—all appearing to be caught up in some great ecstasy. It must be an experience like no other.*

"Oh, dear Lord," Susan whispered. "Can this be my son, the gentle boy I raised to nurture all life? What has this war done to him?" She let the thin blue paper slide from her fingers, unwilling to read further.

Jonathan came to her at once, letting his hand rest on her shoulder as he bent to retrieve the letter. "War changes boys into men, Susan. We have to expect Johnny to be different now, but that doesn't necessarily mean that he will be a worse man. He's simply maturing more rapidly than you expected. Let's see what else he has to say."

The word here is that we will be moving out soon. The 24th South Carolina is being sent to the Mississippi theater to help defend river traffic and the port of New Orleans. I'm looking forward to seeing what for me will be a new and exciting part of the South. I wish I could come home—or rather, come to Aiken—to see everyone and learn about your new farm, but that will have to wait until we deal with these troublesome Yankees.

Your loving son,
Johnny Grenville

"He sounds more like himself in this final paragraph. And at least he didn't refer to them as 'Damned Yankees'. Maybe the rest is just bluster, trying to convince himself that the war is a good thing."

"War is never a good thing, Jonathan, and he knows that as well as anyone. I fear he will come out of this permanently changed, and not for the better."

"We simply have to trust that eighteen years of good training cannot be undone by one experience of battle. Believe in our son, Susan. It's all we can do for now."

36

Pickles, Pigs, and Peaches
Summer 1862

As summer heated up, so did the work of keeping the farm productive. Dawn came too early. Daylight lasted until mid-evening, and so did the chores. Meals were fresh and plentiful, but there was little time to dawdle at the table. Quarrels subsided, and complaints had no time to fester. Work appeared to be the best cure for all the fear and anger that had plagued the family in their first few months in Aiken.

Susan and Jonathan came downstairs one morning to find Sarah already bustling about the kitchen, while Hector and Eli struggled to push small barrels and crocks up the steep stairs from the basement storerooms. The kitchen table, now pushed to one wall, was still wet from having been freshly scoured. A pile of cabbages, both green and red, threatened to topple across the tabletop. On the floor stood boxes of empty jars, and the sink was full of cucumbers.

"What's all this?" Jonathan asked. "Did we oversleep and miss breakfast?"

"No room fuh brekfas in here," Sarah said. "Ifn you hungry, use de table in de dinin room."

"Can I get to the stove to cook some eggs?" Susan asked.

"Only ifn you does it quick. Ah be busy."

Susan and Jonathan exchanged one of those looks that warned each other to be patient. "What are you up to, Sarah?"

"You aint be noticin, but de garden be ripe. Dose crops aint gwine set out dere an wait fuh you fuh get hungry. We gots fuh put dem up fuh winter, or de bug an varmit gwine eat dem all up. Oh, an Massa Jonathan, you needs fuh git me sum splies fro de store in town."

"Supplies? What do you need?"

"Ah gwine needs mo vinegar an salt an sugah fuh start wit. Ah gots muh own dill an musturt fuh de pickles, but ah needs sum alum, too."

"Can it wait until Saturday? I plan to go in then anyway to see about pickers for our peaches."

"Nah, sir, Ah needs em today. Ah kin walk to town, ah spose, but den ah not be dun fore dinnertime."

The blackmail worked, and Jonathan held up his hands in mock surrender. "Fine. Can you give me a list of how much you need?"

"Massa Jonathan, you knows ah caint writes dat good yet, but you kin take Hector long. He know what ah needs."

"And I suppose you need everything this morning?"

"Well, de cukes gots fuh soak fuh a while, an de cabbage need choppin, but ah needs em purty quicklike."

"Susan, what about you? Do you have a shopping list for me?"

"I have no idea!" Susan was laughing in spite of herself. "When it comes to laying up for winter, I just do what I'm told. But be sure to bring lots of sugar. I noticed blackberries getting ripe at the edge of the orchard, and I'm hoping for some jam."

By the end of that day, vinegar fumes permeated the kitchen. Sarah had put both girls to work sorting the young cucumbers into piles according to size. The smallest ones went into a crock, where they were covered with hot water and salt and then weighed down with a plate and a rock to keep them submerged. "Dose gwine be 14-day pickle," Sarah explained. "Dey gots fuh soak fuh a whole two week fore dey be reddy fuh dey spices."

"Are they going to sit right there in the middle of the room for fourteen days?" Mary Sue asked...

"Dat right. We gots fuh keep an eye on em."

"Why?" Becca was wide-eyed with wonder at this new activity. "What are they going to do?"

"We don wants dem fuh do nuttin. But dey cud git dried out or start growin slime or mold, ifn we not be careful. So you lets em be an start cuttin dose bigger cukes intuh spears lak dis. Measure dem wit de jar. Caint use spears dat be taller dan de jar." She demonstrated with a couple of deft moves and then turned over the knife to Mary Sue.

While the girls worked, Sarah boiled a pan of vinegar, salt, sugar, and water on the stove. Becca sneezed as she sniffed the vinegar, but she gamely kept working on her task of stuffing the cut spears into waiting jars. Mary Sue trailed behind, adding heads of dill, a scattering of mustard seed and peppercorns, and a couple of peeled garlic cloves to each jar. Sarah saved for herself the ticklish job of ladling the boiling vinegar over the pickles without splashing.

Mary Sue sniffed. "They do smell wonderful," she said.

"Dat dey do. But don you start plannin fuh eat dem ennytime soon. Dey gots fuh rest fuh long time fore dey be reddy."

By afternoon the new cooks had moved on to chopping cabbage, and the girls were finding it great fun to pretend they were really chopping heads. The first time Susan heard her sweet daughters say, "Here's what I'd do to a Yankee," she shuddered. But then it occurred to her that there were a few heads she'd like to take a chop at, too.

"Do de green cabbage fust, cause it go intuh de sauerkraut crock," Sarah explained. "De red cabbage need to set out obernight. An be sure dos slices be really tin." As the girls piled up their shreds, Sarah sprinkled salt over them and then packed them into layers in the waiting crock. With each small batch, she pressed the cabbage down until juice came to the top. When the crock was full, she covered it with a clean muslin cloth and then weighted it down with another plate and rock.

"No vinegar?" Susan asked.

"Don need nun. De cabbage make it own sourness. It be needin fuh work fuh five or six week, an we has fuh spoon de scum off it ebry day."

"Does it spoil?"

"Course it do. Dat what make it sauerkraut." Susan did not inquire further. Some things were just better not to know.

Sarah had been deliberately saving the red cabbage for last because she wanted the boys to watch the process when they came in from the barn. Eddie protested. "What do I want to look at cabbage for?" he asked.

"You gwine see." Sarah carefully spread the red cabbage shreds out on pans and then sprinkled them with salt.

"Wow!"

"Ugh! It's turning blue!"

"We're not gonna eat that, are we?" Robbie asked, backing away from the table.

"Sho you is, but it not be finish yet. Come back morrow an see what happen."

"What's going to happen?" Susan asked after the boys went back to their chores.

Sarah grinned. "You gwine wait, too."

The next day, heavy foot traffic filled the kitchen as everyone traipsed past the table, sneaking glances to see what was happening to the cabbage. As far as anyone could tell, it appeared simply to be getting bluer. But at last it was time for the next step, and Sarah let all the children gather around. Even Eddie and Mary Sue were staring intently at the cabbage, their curiosity overcoming their usual teenage boredom. Sarah deftly stuffed the blue shreds into glass jars, and then, with a flourish, poured boiling vinegar over it. And once again the gasps went up.

"It's red!"

"It's gorgeous!"

"How did that happen?"

Sarah shrugged. "Tol you dat would be good nuf fuh eat!"

"Tired?" Jonathan and Susan were finally settled into comfortable chairs near the window, relishing the cool night breeze.

"Exhausted, but exhilarated, too. I don't think any of us minds working hard when the results are so tangible and piled up for all to see. The glass jars lined up in rows, the crocks of pickles, the promise of good things to eat during the coming winter months—everything we did today seemed important. And the children enjoyed themselves, too. I loved watching their earnest little faces as they learned new grown-up skills."

"I agree. This is exactly what I was hoping for when we moved here. The idea of a family working together for the common good is something we were missing in the old Charleston days."

"Those days when we relied on slave labor, you mean?"

"Well, I wasn't going to put it quite so bluntly, but yes."

"Just remember, today's whole exercise happened only because we had our former slaves to teach us."

"But the key in that statement is the word 'former.' The teaching takes place now because we are on a more equal footing with Sarah and Hector. They feel free to boss us around when we demonstrate how totally inept we are."

Susan smiled at the truth behind that statement. "But then, they always did that. What else have you learned today? I know you were meeting again with Mr. Winchester."

"I did, and he invited me to accompany him to the semi-monthly meeting of the Aiken Vine Growing and Horticultural Association. It is quite a vibrant group, with elaborate plans for improving crops and awarding annual prizes for the best locally grown specimens. And some of the most prominent members of the community were there, including Reverend John Cornish, pastor of St. Thaddeus Episcopal Church, and Henry Ravenel, who owns many shares of the local railroad—all good men to know."

"Did you find out anything about how we handle the peach harvest?"

"That, and a whole lot more. The peach crop is nearly ready to be picked. Winchester has already hired our picking crew, although I intend to have the children out there working alongside them. They can handle the lower branches while the experienced pickers deal with the treetops. Harvest should start next week. We've also ordered the shallow cases that are used to store and ship the fruit so that it does not get terribly bruised."

"Shipped? Where does it go?"

"Almost all the surplus crop—what farmers do not use for themselves—goes to Charleston and the markets there, or at least what's left of them. There seems to be some worry that too many people have left the city and that the fruit will not sell, but the other growers even have hope of mitigating that loss. Mr. George Balkin, another of the biggest peach growers in the area, has taken it upon himself to write a letter to the editor of the *Charleston Mercury* about arranging to have our peaches shipped on to the Army units in the vicinity. And of course, Mr. Ravenel is instrumental in handling the shipping in his railcars."

"So there's some hope of making a profit?"

"They say that in a good year we could expect anywhere from $4,000 to $6,000. The war has weakened the market, of course, but I am still optimistic."

"Just listen to us!" Susan was laughing like her old self. "A year ago we were talking about the Apprentices' Library Society and fancy dress balls. Now we're concerned about pickles and peaches."

"I can make even more of a contrast. Add pigs to your list."

"Pigs! What on earth . . .?"

"Well, Winchester also reminded me that we did not purchase those piglets last spring just to listen to them squeal and root around in the mud. It seems that the local slaughterhouse is already taking appointments for turning Pinky and Porky into hams and sausages. So I went ahead and put our names—or rather, our pigs' names—on the schedule. I'll be delivering them on October 1, and we'll be able to pick up our winter meat supply the following week. Of course that means I'll have to get our smokehouse back in working order by then, so that we can hang our hams and flitches of bacon, and also preserve the chops and salt pork."

"So that's how it works. In the back of my mind I've been nursing a niggling little worry about how we could slaughter Robbie's pigs without causing permanent trauma. I'm glad he won't have to witness it."

"I'd been worried, too. I was afraid I might have to do it myself, and I was pretty sure I'd make a mess of it—literally. Now I think we'd better get some rest while we can. The fruit crops are still to come in."

37

What Do We Do about Charlotte?
Fall 1862

The peach season stretched itself out through September, and the Grenvilles remained too busy with farm chores to indulge in petty arguments. The crop was plentiful, and Jonathan watched with pride as he sent cartload after cartload of large, blushing fruit trundling off to the train station and far-off markets. Susan, for her part, was determined to use as many of the peaches as possible to feed her family. They started with whole fruit, or sliced some for a quick pie or cobbler. Sarah spent several afternoons cooking jam for winter, and when those jars threatened to take over the fruit cellar, she switched to more creative recipes for things like peach butter and peach leather.

The younger children were especially fascinated by the fruit leather, which required nothing more than a hard-boil to thicken the fruit and a bit of sugar or cinnamon for flavor. It then became their job to pour the mixture out onto waxed paper in thin layers, tent it with cheesecloth to discourage the flies, and let it dry out for a day or two in the hot sun. When it was smooth and stiff to the touch, they rolled it up in its paper and stored it away, ready to have a strip pulled off and chewed between meals as a quick snack. Susan also experimented with drying peach halves, hoping to use them for peach pie in the dead of winter.

It was Jonathan, however, who topped everyone by producing a recipe for peach brandy. He started with a syrup of two parts water to one part sugar, and, when it was boiling freely, stirred into it the peels and pits from a large bowl of peaches. "No sense letting any part go to waste," he explained. The mixture was then poured into glass jars, sealed as tightly as possible, and buried about a foot deep in the yard. "No one disturbs it for six months," he ordered. "People who taste it before its time is up will regret it—if they live long enough. Until it has aged, it's pure poison."

When it came time to settle up with the other peach growers, however, the income was disappointing. The Charleston markets were, for the most part, not open, and whole shipments of peaches had rotted while they sat on loading platforms waiting for nonexistent purchasers. The growers' representatives had had better luck selling to the Confederate Army, but those bills had been paid for with nearly worthless scrip. Once shipping costs were taken out of the proceeds, Jonathan cleared about $200—nowhere close to the thousands that had been predicted. Still, he put the best face possible on the situation. "It's $200 we didn't have before. It didn't cost us anything to grow the peaches, and they did make money for us. Next year will be better."

Susan bit her tongue and withheld comment. Besides, there were other matters to worry about. She followed the war effort as best she could, devouring the newspapers that Jonathan brought home in hopes of finding some mention of the 24th South Carolina Regiment. She was alternately frustrated and relieved to realize that the papers were concentrating on activities in the North rather than in the Deep South. She and Jonathan did not discuss the battles often. Susan wanted to crow over Confederate successes at Second Bull Run and Harper's Ferry, but she knew he would point out the terrible Union losses and suggest that such rejoicing was inappropriate in the face of all those lost lives. She was sickened by the huge Confederate losses at Antietam, but secretly proud of the Rebel stance at Fredericksburg. Each victory carried with it a promise that Johnny might some day come home; every loss, a tremor of fear that he would not.

As for Charlotte, her letters were arriving with greater frequency, but Susan fretted over a trend she sensed in them. In nearly every letter, Charlotte now mentioned Henry Pickford, the young man taken up by Mr. and Mrs. Rogers as a sad substitute for their own lost boy. Charlotte had, at first, referred to him as Mr. Pickford but now addressed him as Henry, a familiarity that Susan felt was out of place.

"Just listen to this, Jonathan!" Susan waved the letter in front of him in pure exasperation.

We would be quite lost here in Charleston if it were not for Henry. With so many of the markets closed and shuttered, it becomes increasingly difficult to find the bare necessities of life. Flour and sugar are prohibitively expensive, and butter rancid or nonexistent. But Henry always arrives on the weekends bearing gifts, usually meat and dairy products from his own cattle, so we eat quite well while he is here.

"What's wrong with that? I should think you'd be grateful that they have that kind of help," Jonathan answered with a shrug.

"I worry that Charlotte is being unduly swayed by his generosity."

"Perhaps he is just a lonely young man who appreciates having a second family to turn to when he is far from home. Must you always think the worst?"

"In this case—when it involves our flighty and impressionable daughter—I must certainly question his motives. There are two young children to worry about as well, and I fear that Mr. and Mrs. Rogers are too wrapped up in their own sorrow to see what may be going on."

A few weeks later, Susan became even more concerned. "Read this week's letter, Jonathan, and tell me that I am imagining Charlotte's infatuation with this young man."

Sometimes I don't know what any of us would do without Henry. He accompanied us to church this past Sunday, although he sat in the back, not in our family pew. Just as Rev. Abernathy began his homily, the twins became obstreperous. Georgie pulled Annie's hair, she kicked him back, and in no time they were both howling. At such times, the grandparents are no help at all. They love the twins, but, when the babies make a fuss, they simply look on in disapproval of my failure to better manage my children. I had no choice but to put one child under each arm and lug them outside. They were still wailing when I put them down amid the gravestones, and I was ready to cry right along with them. At that moment, Henry appeared, tickling first one young hellion and then another, until their angry shrieks turned to giggles. He had followed us outside, understanding that I badly needed help. Once the twins had been jollied out of their tantrums, he put them to work building piles of acorns and thus kept them occupied until the service was over. He is just incredibly good with children, and I am ever so grateful for his help. They need the firm hand of a male figure in their lives, and the dour Mr. Rogers will never be able to fill that need.

"Now tell me that I am imagining things! She sounds positively love-struck to me."

"Be that as it may, there is probably little you can do to change her mind."

"Perhaps not, but there's little you can say to keep me from worrying about it, either."

Realizing that she was getting little sympathy from Jonathan, she quit mentioning the subject and tried her best to distract herself with the other news from the war front. But one day in mid-November, as she browsed the *Charleston Mercury*, a small notice caught her eye and sent her off to find her husband.

"Look at this, Jonathan. How did you miss it?"

"I don't usually read the small police notices, my dear," he answered. "What's so important?" Then he glanced at the article she was handing to him.

Prominent Local Solicitor Found Dead

Congregants at yesterday's morning prayer services at the Circular Church were shocked to find the body of attorney Hiram Henry Rogers slumped over the commemorative stone placed as a memorial to his son, Peter Middleton Rogers, who was killed one year ago on this date at the Battle of Port Royal Sound. Police quickly determined that Mr. Rogers had died of a self-inflicted gunshot wound. Thus does the price of war expand its cruel grip over our citizenry. Mr. Rogers is survived by his wife, Mrs. Prudence Middleton Rogers, and two grandchildren, Master George Grenville Rogers and Miss Anne Elizabeth Rogers.

Jonathan squeezed his eyes closed and covered his mouth for a long moment. "How utterly sad," he said finally. "I have often tried to analyze the impulse to suicide, but it's hard to imagine. His grief must have been overwhelming. Peter was his only son, after all. Undoubtedly, the anniversary of the battle brought all those emotions surging back in a flood he could not control."

"How could he do that to the rest of his family? Grief I can understand, but it doesn't help to compound it for those who are left behind."

"I'm sure he wasn't thinking rationally at the moment he pulled that trigger."

"But it was a well-thought-out act. People don't usually visit graveyards carrying a loaded pistol!"

"We can't know what was in his mind, Susan."

"Perhaps not, but it still makes me angry. And what are we going to do about Charlotte?"

"I don't know what we can do about her, my dear. She is there and, no doubt, in the middle of a storm of emotions. But she chose to stay with the Rogers family, and surely she understands more about Mr. Rogers than we can from such a distance."

"It will have been so hard on her, coming as it did on the very date of Peter's death. Don't you think we should go there?"

"To Charleston, you mean? No, I don't think so."

"But she will need . . ."

"She will need to concentrate all her attention on dealing with those details that Mrs. Rogers cannot handle and on caring for the children in the middle of a house in turmoil."

"As if I didn't already have enough to worry about! If I were there, I would at least know how she is. And I could . . ."

"I said no. We would have nowhere to stay because your mother's house has been confiscated by the Federals for back taxes. We would have so few resources to help and so little comfort to offer that we would only make things worse. When Charlotte needs us, she will let us know. You will want to write to her, of course, telling her that we saw the article in the paper, extending our condolences to the family, and assuring her that we stand ready to help."

"Small comfort that will be." Susan was still grumbling as she left the room, the newspaper drooping from her fingers.

38

Christmas in the Country
December 1862

The next letter from Charlotte, when it came, proved to be everything Susan feared. The death of Mr. Rogers had shattered the carefully controlled atmosphere of the Rogers home in Charleston. For almost a year, the family had kept up the pretense that everything was fine. Emotions were hidden beneath forced smiles and strict routines. Charlotte had welcomed the quiet regularity of her life there, even though she recognized the turmoil beneath the surface. Now Mrs. Rogers was a hysterical wreck, wandering through the house, wringing her hands, wailing, and periodically erupting into fits of violent anger. Charlotte described the situation without her usual flair for the dramatic.

> *I understand how she feels, as perhaps no one else can, but I'm also help-*
> *less to relieve her grief. All I can do is keep the children out of her way and*
> *wait for the storms of anger to subside. I'm glad I'm available, however. She*
> *seems to pull herself together when I am around, so I am serving the purpose*
> *for which I was sent here, I think. I know, as only another widow can know,*
> *that in time the good memories will replace the nightmares, and I seem to help*

*her brace against the worst. I do not want to think what might become of her
if she were left alone, especially as Christmas approaches.*

"We have raised a very compassionate daughter," Susan
remarked to Jonathan. "I was hoping she could come here for
the holidays, but I understand why she doesn't think that possible. Poor girl, it will be a desolate season for her, but luckily
the twins are still too young to be affected by the absence of
Christmas merriment."

"I suppose it's time for us to be thinking of how we are
going to spend the holidays, too. You know I have always hated
the party season, but at least here we don't have the pressure of
social obligations. I rather fancy the idea of an old-fashioned,
home-centered Christmas, one that keeps fresh the true meaning of the season rather than indulging in expensive gifts and
alcoholic excess."

"Little chance of overindulgence here!" Susan remarked.
Then, recognizing the tinge of discontent in her voice, she has-
tened to soften her words. "Of course, there's always that peach
brandy you buried in the yard. But you're right. This new house
offers us the chance to start building a whole new tradition of
how we celebrate Christmas. The children will have to receive
gifts, of course, but we can make sure they are necessary items,
not frivolities. We can decorate with materials we find in our
own yard and put our emphasis on attending church services
and retelling the Christmas story. And instead of surrounding
ourselves with important guests, we can enjoy the time we spend
together."

"That sounds delightful to me. I'm happy to know that we
are anticipating the same sorts of activities. Personally, I'm hoping for a Christmas snow that . . ."

"Oh, Jonathan, now you're really dreaming! This is still South Carolina, remember?"

"Yes, but we're much higher than we were in Charleston, which means the temperatures drop more precipitously. We've already seen one frost. It could snow. Miracles do happen on Christmas Eve. I'd love the chance to teach the children to build a snowman and have hot chocolate ready when they come in."

"Well, if it doesn't, we can always let the fires die down so that we shiver a bit."

"There is one other thing I'd like to do, Susan. In the spirit of making room at the inn, I'd like to invite Hector, Sarah, and their children to be a part of our holiday. They are rather isolated here, and we really are their only family. Can we invite them to share our Christmas dinner, not as servants but as our honored guests?"

Susan stared at her husband for a moment. He really does have some of the most extraordinary ideas, she thought. Then she smiled. "Why not? It's a lovely and generous idea."

"I'm not trying to be generous, Susan. It just feels right."

"Of course it does. Why don't you broach the idea to Hector? Just to be sure they don't have plans of their own."

If Jonathan was anticipating surprise and gratitude for such an invitation, he was quickly disabused of the idea. Hector dropped the pitchfork he had been using to clean the stable and took a step backward. "Ah don tinks so, Massa Jonathan," he said.

"Oh dear, do you already have plans for Christmas Day?"

"Uh, yassuh, we does, but ifn you wants we fuh work dat day, we kin do dat."

"No, I didn't mean that I wanted you to work. We wanted you to join us as honored guests. Without you, we probably would not have survived this past year, and this is just a way for us to show you how much you mean to us. Perhaps we can have a family dinner on another evening?"

Hector was still shaking his head. "Ah tinks we needs fuh talk. Ah bin puttin dis off, but ah tinks now be de time."

Jonathan wrinkled his brow as he stared at his former slave in puzzlement. "Is something wrong?"

"Not zactly, but dis winter be a portant time fuh slaves."

"You're not a slave anymore, Hector. How many times do I have to tell you that?"

"Ah knows you gib we de pieces uh paper dat say we be free, but dat don change who we be or how udduh folk sees us. Sarah an me an de chillun, we be born black, an as long as enny black men be slave, we all be slave. You may say we free, but udduh folk don see nuttin but de color uh we skin."

"So other people are wrong. What does that have to do with your willingness to share our table?"

"Dat be muh point. You be like udduh people, Massa Jonathan, eben ifn you don know it."

"I'm not! I see you as my equal," Jonathan argued.

"No. Look round. You an yo fambly live in dat big house. We lives in dat lil cabin ober dere. We comes here cause you brung we here. It not be we choice. You pays we fuh work, dat true, but it be de work you wants dun. You makes de rule an tells we how much you gwine pay. We works when you wants we fuh work an go home only when de work be dun. Jis like when we be slave, you gibs we de cabin we lives in, de clothes we wears, an de food we eats."

Jonathan opened his mouth in protest and then found he didn't know what to say.

"Ah calls you 'Massa Jonathan,' but you neber calls me 'Massa Hector.' Ah still be yo slave, eben ifn ah hab a paper dat say ah be free."

"Oh, Hector, I don't want to argue about this with you. Mrs. Grenville and I were only concerned that, since you don't have any friends here, you might have to spend Christmas alone. We didn't want that, so we thought it would be nice if we all spent it together."

"An what make you so sho dat we don hab no friens?"

"Well, because there aren't many other free blacks around, and we never see you socializing with anyone."

"Course you don see we. We socialize wit udduh black folk, wheder dey be free or not. We goes tuh a black chuch an we knows lots uh slaves. We don hab much time fuh gitten togedduh, an when we does we goes tuh de chuch."

"I didn't even know there was a black church in Aiken."

"De black chuch aint gots no building, cept sum Praise Houses on de various plantations round town. We moves round so as fuh keep trubblemakers fro bodderin we. But dat where we gwine be on Christmas, an ebryday uh de holiday. We be gittin reddy fuh de Day uh Jubilee."

"Day of Jubilee? What's that?"

"Aint you read de Bible, neider? De Day uh Jubilee come fro de Bible, sho nuf. It say . . ." Hector stopped and pulled from his pocket a ragged piece of paper. "De preacher man write dis down fuh dos uh we who kin read—an now dat be me:

> *Proclaim liberty truh out all de land unto all de habitant dereof: it shall be a jubilee unto you; an ye shall return ebry man unto he possession, an ye shall return ebry man unto he fambly.*

"Dat what de Bible say, an dat what be comin on New Year Day, when Uncle Sam make de mancipation clamation, fuh sho."

"The Emancipation Proclamation! Of course, I had forgotten that was coming."

"Dat cause it aint portant fuh you. But fuh we black, dis be de good news. It say we all gwine be free all ober de lan, an we gwine get we own tings an we gwine go home tuh we famblies—ifn it really gwine happen. Dat why we all gwine be in chuch ebry night, prayin fuh de Day uh Jubilee."

"All right. I understand. Whether you believe me or not, I want to see slavery end in this country as much as you do."

"Ah doubts dat, Massa Jonathan. An what all uh de white folk gwine do when de black folk be free at last? Who gwine work fuh you?"

"We'll do our own work. That's why Mrs. Grenville and I have been trying to learn from you and Sarah."

"'Mrs. Grenville an Sarah.' Do dat soun equal fuh you?"

Again, Jonathan could do little more than stare at this black man, who seemed to be standing up straighter than he ever had before.

"If you and Sarah are unhappy here, I . . ."

"We not be unhappy. Sarah love Miss Susan, an you knows dey be cuzzins. But we does long fuh we own land. Dat what else ah be wantin fuh talk bout."

"Your own land?"

"Yassuh. We bin savin all de pay you gib we eber since we comes here. An now we gots ober hundert dollar in a jar. Ah wants fuh buy a lil corner uh yo lan, on de udduh side uh de creek. You knows where ah mean?"

"That little side pasture that we seldom use because the cows don't like to cross over there?"

"Yassuh. Dat de one. Ifn you sells dat tuh me, ah kin build a lil house fuh we, an we kin start growin we own crop. Maybe gits we a goat or two an a couple uh chikkun."

"Hector, if you want it, I will be happy to let you use that piece of unused land."

"No, Massa Jonathan. Ah wants fuh buy it, sos it really be muh land."

"I understand. But it's only about ten acres and not worth more than forty dollars. That will leave you enough money to stock it and build your house. Fair enough?"

"Yassuh. Tankee."

"No need to thank me. This is a business deal. We need to shake hands on it, and then I will have Mr. Winchester draw up the deed. And Hector? When the New Year has come and gone—and you feel like a free man indeed, with your own land for your own family—can we have a friendly dinner sometime? One that Susan cooks for you?"

"We be likin dat jis fine."

For Susan Grenville, this decision simply meant another Christmas disappointment and another reason to raise arguments with her husband. The winter months dragged along—gray, chilly, and monotonous. The atmosphere seemed to promote more family quarrels. The children were itchy with their constant confinement to the kitchen and the heat radiating from the woodburning stove. At the same time, they grumbled about the need to go outside to tend to ungrateful animals that seemed as miserable as they were. Lessons helped to pass the hours but did little to inspire their curiosity. Even the garden bounty they had

305

helped to put up in the fall failed to taste as good as they had expected.

As for Susan and Jonathan, they tried to control their own irritability, but, beneath the surface of their relationship, the same old disagreements festered. War news was particularly likely to set off hostile exchanges, all the more so when it appeared that neither side was winning. Both sides turned to the question of a draft in early 1863, raising concerns about Eddie's soon-to-be eligibility, and talk of new black regiments being recruited for the Union Army carried with it the threat that needed laborers might be drawn away from their agricultural jobs.

Rather than addressing those issues directly, the Grenvilles found that their disagreements continued to erupt over the wisdom of Jonathan's sale of land to their former slaves. "Hector and Sarah certainly aren't around much anymore," Susan grumbled. "Every time I look for one of them to help with the things that need to be done around the house, they seem to be off working on that grubby little cabin of theirs."

"We agreed that, during the winter, they could have the time off, Susan. If Hector can use these winter months to get that house built—and it's not a grubby little cabin, which you would discover if you ever went over there—he'll have more time to work for us during the growing season."

"Well, it doesn't look much different to me than the cabin they had here. A waste of time, if you ask me, as well as a move that cost us a great deal in terms of land values. If you had held onto that piece of land until the war was over, you could have made a tidy profit on it."

"Maybe not. You can't know what will happen several years from now. And, in the meantime, that sale was worth its weight in goodwill. You don't seem to realize how important it was to

Hector to become a property owner. Emancipation was a promise of freedom, but the possession of land makes that freedom tangible."

"Emancipation doesn't mean anything here in South Carolina, anyway. As far as I can see, it only applies to areas that are part of the United States, and we no longer are. Lincoln can't make laws that affect us because we're a separate country."

"Oh, Susan, come on. That's secessionist folderol. The Confederacy hasn't a chance of surviving this war anymore, and the Emancipation Proclamation made doubly sure of that."

"How?"

"Look: No country survives without a stable economic base, and the South doesn't have one. Our only commodities, even in peacetime, were agricultural products that depended on slave labor. Now that the Federals have made every black man free, there will be a mass migration to the North, and that will cause the Southern economy to collapse. I haven't wanted to mention it until I knew for sure, but Samuel has told me that he and Gemma are thinking about leaving in the spring to try their luck in the North. And, of course, they'll be taking their daughter Rosie with them. So there will go three of our paid employees. And so, too, would we have lost Hector if I hadn't made it possible for him to exercise that freedom here, close to us."

"A lot of good it does to keep him close if he's never available to work."

39

A Wedding Announcement
March 1863

One day in March, the mail train from Charleston brought an unusual letter from Charlotte. Rather than her typical chatty tone, this one was written on a single sheet of hotel paper, folded so that it made its own envelope. The message was curt and uninformative:

> *Bringing the twins for a visit. Arriving Aiken on Friday next via afternoon train.*

"What do you make of this, Jonathan?" Susan asked, frowning as she turned the paper toward the light to catch the Mills House watermark at the top. "Why would she be using hotel stationery?"

"I have never understood anything our wayward daughter has done, so don't ask me. Maybe she couldn't find any other paper and was just in a hurry to be sure we got the message before her arrival."

"But there are no details about how she's going to manage the trip. Surely she can't be planning to juggle the twins and luggage all on her own. They are barely able to walk. And you'd think that if she's bringing a servant or a friend to help she would mention it so that we could be prepared."

"I suppose we'll find out on Friday. In the meantime, don't buy trouble, Susan."

"Well, we're still going to have to make some preparations. I'll have to move back into our bedroom so that she and the babies can have the nursery."

Jonathan tried to keep his expression neutral as he answered, "Ah, yes, I suppose you will."

By Friday, the children were jittery with excitement over the impending visit. "I've really missed having Charlotte at home," Mary Sue commented, "and I'll bet we won't even recognize the babies. They were just squalling and red-faced the last time we saw them. I hope they're more fun now."

"Babies?" asked Jamey. "Will they try to play with my toys?"

"I doubt it," his mother said. "They're still pretty young. But you'll all have to help us keep an eye on them so they don't tumble into the fire or fall down the steps."

"Ugh," he mumbled. "How long are they going to stay?"

"We don't know. A long time, I hope."

"I hope not. They sound like more trouble than they're worth."

"Someone might have said the same thing about you, you little pest," Robbie snorted. "Maybe we'll just stick you with baby-tending duties. It would serve you right for all the trouble you were when you were little."

"Mama!"

"Don't tease your brother, Robbie."

"When do we meet the train? And can I wear my new dress?" Becca asked.

"Wait just a minute, here." Jonathan stepped into the discussion. "We don't know who's coming or how much luggage there will be. We'll take the large carriage, but you children can wait right here at home. We're not filling the train station with a welcoming party."

The train was late, as usual, and by the time the gears of the pulley started to turn to help the engine crawl up that final incline, Susan was pacing and biting her nails.

"Relax, dear. She'll be here any minute, and all your questions will be answered."

"Maybe so, but I'm not sure I'm going to like the answers."

"Look, there she is! She's just stepping off the third car, and it looks like the conductor is carrying the babies for her."

"That's not a conductor. She must have charmed some fellow traveler to help. Charlotte! We're over here!" Susan was waving frantically, and Charlotte waved in response. Then she turned to the gentleman behind her, lifted one of the babies to her hip, and pointed in their direction. The two of them walked together across the platform.

"Mother! Father! It's so good to see you! Look, Annie, it's your grandma and grandpa." The little girl responded by wailing in fright and burrowing into her mother's shoulder. Charlotte looked at the accompanying gentleman with a smile and a shrug. "Georgie's usually the one who pitches a fit, but maybe today we'll be lucky."

Susan's welcoming smile had faded, and she was now staring at this young man with tightly pursed lips. "Are you going to introduce us to your . . . uh . . . friend, Charlotte?"

Charlotte was grinning as if she knew a delightful secret. "I was going to get around to that, but I thought you'd want to see the twins first. Here, Henry, I'll take Georgie for a minute. Now then—Mother, Father, I'd like you to meet Henry Pickford."

She let the moment drag out, as her father's mouth opened and closed without a sound coming forth. Her mother's lips tightened even further. Silence reigned. "Did you hear me? This is Henry Pickford—my husband!"

Henry looked at Charlotte in surprise. "You didn't tell them?" he asked. Susan gasped and covered her face. Jonathan stared at his daughter, shaking his head in disbelief. It was Henry who broke the tableau by stepping forward, hand extended toward his new father-in-law.

"I'm sorry, sir. I thought you knew. I know it's a bit late, but I'd like to request your daughter's hand in marriage. I assure you, my intentions are honorable. I intend to cherish her and the children for the rest of my life."

The porter chose that moment to trundle up to them pushing a cart. "Beggin pardon, Missus Pickford. What you wants dun wit de luggage?"

"Uh . . ." She looked helplessly at her father and husband, who were locked in place as they sized one another up.

"I think that's our carriage right over there . . . if we are welcome to stay, that is . . ."

Susan shook herself into action. "Of course. Let's move this little drama off the center of the train platform, shall we? No need to entertain the entire town. We need to go home. We can discuss this further once you are settled."

The drive back to the farm was the longest and most silent that any one of them could remember. Then, as Jonathan pulled the horses to a stop, the farmhouse door burst open, and five children ran down the steps to surround the carriage. The younger ones were chattering in excitement, but Eddie caught the tension in the air. "What's wrong? Has something happened?"

"No, no," Jonathan said. "Everything is fine, but we need a few more minutes to talk to your sister. Could you round up these noise boxes and see to it that they take care of their barnyard chores before you come back in for the evening?"

"Sure, Father. Come on, troublemakers—let's get the animals fed and watered."

Susan led the way into the front parlor and motioned to the new arrivals to sit on the sofa. "Now, tell us everything. From the beginning, Charlotte, if you please."

"Everything has happened so fast, I hardly know where to begin. But it started when Mrs. Rogers decided one morning last week that she was going to close up the family house immediately and go to Flat Rock to join her Middleton cousins. I tried to suggest to her that she might want to take some more time to consider her options, and she flew into a rage. She demanded that I take my children and get out of her house, right then. The twins were already scared by the tone of her voice, so I took them for a walk in the park, thinking she would calm down. But when I came back, I found my trunks sitting on the front porch. She had had her maid Lulu pack everything that belonged to me, and the front door was locked against me. I didn't have a key—had never needed one—so there was nothing I could do except . . . I put the twins down for their naps on the lounge chair, and then I sat there on the steps and hoped she would change her mind. That's where Henry found me a couple of hours later. He was arriving for the weekend and had no idea what kind of a storm he was about to face."

Henry stepped into the story. "I certainly didn't, but I thought I could handle things. I knocked at the door and called out to Mrs. Rogers, but she only peered out of the side window and motioned me to go away. Well, I couldn't leave Charlotte and the children there in the chilly evening, so, after several attempts, I took them to the Mills House, where I had intended to stay, and signed over my room to them. Once they were warm and had something delivered to the room to eat, I went back to see Mrs. Rogers. That time she let me in, but she was still adamant. She was packing to leave, and she wanted nothing more to do with her daughter-in-law. She seemed to think that Charlotte was trying to take over the house for her own. I couldn't reason with her, so I finally just gave up. I knew she had been under great strain ever since her husband's suicide. It seemed that it might be best to let her go and join her distant family, far from the site of her bereavement."

"I was in shock, too," Charlotte said. "I had been trying my best to support Mrs. Rogers as she grieved, but nothing seemed to help. I don't think I ever gave her cause to feel that I was conspiring against her, but there was no way I could replace her husband and son in her affections. The next morning, Henry came back to the hotel. We had breakfast in the hotel dining room and then talked for hours about what I could do. I thought about trying to get Grandmother Dubois's house back, but it would have been much too big, anyway. So the only logical choice was to come to you, as you had been asking me to do. But, then, Henry offered me another option."

She paused and smiled at him as she remembered the scene. "Right there in the lobby of the Mills House, with Army officers and traveling salesmen bustling all around us, he got down on his knees and proposed. I said no—I said it was impossible—I said we couldn't possibly—and then . . . I asked, why not?"

"I can think of several reasons," her father suggested.

"I'm sure you can. But none of them would change the fact that I needed someone to protect me right then, or that Henry is quite possibly the kindest man I have ever known, or that the children love him as much as I do. Do you want to hear the rest of the story, or have you been shocked enough?"

"Continue, please. Let's hear it all."

"Well, it was Saturday, so we had to wait until Monday to find out how we could get married quickly. We spent Sunday in church, and I did pray that I was doing the right thing. On Monday, we went down to the courthouse and learned that there was a 48-hour waiting period before we could come before a judge. So it was on Wednesday morning that we walked downtown again, dressed in our Sunday best, children in tow. On the way, Henry bought me this plain gold band to serve as a wedding ring and a small bouquet of early japonica blossoms from a street vendor. It was a quick ceremony, but no less meaningful and solemn for all that. And by late afternoon we were back in the dining room of the Mills House, ordering an elegant tea to celebrate. Our maid of honor and best man were so tired by then that they napped in their highchairs." She was smiling at the memory. "And now we are the Pickford family, and I couldn't be happier."

"But what will you do? Surely you're not planning to stay here."

"Of course not, sir." Henry stepped into the discussion even though the question had not been directed toward him. "I am half-owner, with my brother, of a cattle ranch on the Cumberland Plateau north of Chattanooga, Tennessee. We have nearly 500 acres of grazing land, as well as a fairly new farmhouse. The cattle have always afforded us a comfortable living, but until now the house has lacked a woman's touch and the warmth that a family can provide. My parents live in the city now, and I want them to meet Charlotte as soon as possible. We plan to leave here Monday morning on the train to Chattanooga."

"You talk about this all so casually. Have you forgotten that there is a war going on?" Jonathan was still glaring at the happy couple.

"No, sir. I'm all too aware of the war. I've spent the last year driving beef cattle down here to feed the Confederate Army, so I'm familiar with troop movements. Everything I have seen and heard tells me that the focus of the war is moving toward the Mississippi River. In fact, that's another reason why I pressed Charlotte to marry me now. It appears that I will not be doing any more sales in South Carolina because the armies are both headed west."

"The papers write that Nashville is still under the control of the Union Army commanded by General Rosecrans."

"Yes, sir, but Nashville isn't all that close to Chattanooga. I'm not taking Charlotte into a war zone. And our ranch land is not anywhere close to a military target. She and the twins are going to be perfectly safe."

The discussion might have continued much longer, but the twins had had quite enough of being ignored. Their whines and wails soon had their grandparents dancing attendance on them in the kitchen, while Charlotte and Henry wandered out to the barnyard to find Charlotte's brothers and sisters.

"Don't let my parents scare you with their stern questions, darling. They like to make a fuss when they are not in charge, but they'll soon come around. Despite all their bluster, they are only trying to make sure that we are all right."

40

A Weekend in the Country
March 1863

Charlotte had hoped that her parents would graciously accept what had already been done, but her mother was not nearly finished. She continued to question Henry over breakfast the next morning.

"I still don't understand how you hope to continue your business now that the war is shifting to the western theater. You said yourself that you didn't expect to sell any more cattle to the Confederate Army."

"Yes, ma'am, I did, but the Union Army is still a good customer, particularly since they have converted our state capital into a major supply post. They have taken over many of the buildings to serve as hospitals and prisons, and, since Nashville is a railroad hub, provisions can roll in and out of that city easily."

"Union provisions?" Jonathan spoke up for the first time. "I thought you said you sold to the Confederates. Which side are you on?"

"I'm on the side of hungry soldiers, sir, no matter what their politics. I'm not on either side. I'm just a businessman, interested in selling my products to anyone who can afford to buy them."

"That's preposterous! The entire country is at war. How can you think of nothing but making money off the conflict?"

"I don't think that's what he's doing, Father." Charlotte tried to interrupt the discussion, but no one was paying attention to her.

"When a soldier is hungry, I don't believe he stops to ask whether the bit of beef on his plate was raised by a Yankee or a Rebel. He's just grateful that someone has provided the meal. I could not, in good conscience, take a side and say that I refuse to sell my beef to one side or the other. I will not withhold food from anyone who needs it. I'm sorry if you disapprove of that, but I'm rather surprised. I understood that you and Mrs. Grenville had settled your own political differences."

"That's not the point! Our politics are none of your business."

"I might make the same statement." Henry was glaring at his new father-in-law now. He was not used to having his motives questioned so closely. "But let me pose this question to you, sir: If a wounded soldier came to your door right now asking for food, shelter, or medical help, would you help him or would you inquire about his politics?"

"Well, if one came here, he would most likely be a Confederate soldier, but of course I would help him."

"And what about you, Mrs. Grenville? If he were a Union soldier, would you tend his wounds?"

"I would. We are compassionate people, Mr. Pickford. And I would be hesitant to turn him over to the authorities."

"And what would you say to your husband about the Confederate soldier he found on your doorstep? Would you let him turn that man into a prisoner of war?"

"I would argue against it, of course."

"And how is that different from what I do?"

"We are arguing at cross purposes, I'm afraid, and we have strayed far from the question of whether our daughter will be safe with you."

"That's not the issue, Mother." Charlotte was angrier now. "It's too late for you to be raising such questions, anyway. We are married. I am of legal age, and, as a widow, I needed no one's approval of my marriage but my own. I hoped you would be happy for me, but, if you are not, we will need to move on without your blessing."

In a gesture that was becoming more and more common in their family discussions, Jonathan held up both hands, palms out. "The discussion is at an end. We will not bring it up again. We are all adults and entitled to our own opinions."

"Wrong as they may be," Eddie mumbled to his sisters. And then he winced as his older sister kicked him under the table, bringing back memories of a simpler time.

Charlotte smiled at her parents in appeasement. "I have an idea. Eddie, why don't you take Henry out to the barn and introduce him to your cows? Since you are both cattlemen at heart, you are sure to find much in common. And perhaps the girls can show me the animals they are raising. Mary Sue, I never did get to meet your young horse. How is he doing?"

"He's beautiful, Charlie. Come see." She jumped to her feet, hands extended to her sister.

Charlotte held up a cautionary finger. "Just a minute, love. Remember, I have a couple of extra responsibilities now. I need to tend to the twins first, unless . . ."

"Ah be takin care uh dem, Miss Charlotte," Sarah spoke from the doorway. "Ah aint seen dose babies since ah dun birthed dem. An Miss Susan an me gots sum dinner plans we gwine make. You runs long an spend sum time wit de udduh chillun."

Eddie and Henry wasted no time in escaping from the breakfast table, and they were already deep in conversation before they got out the back door.

"What breed are your milch cows, Eddie?"

"Breed? I don't know. They're just cows."

"No, they probably are of one breed or another, and it makes a huge difference in their milk quality, you know. Let's go check on them. And then perhaps I can give you some pointers on how best to feed them to increase their milk production."

And that was how they managed to pass the weekend. Had they still been living in Charleston, the close quarters might have led to further arguments, but here, the acres of farmland offered an escape from difficult confrontations. Eddie and Henry disappeared for hours. When they returned, muddy and disheveled from their walks in the pastures and orchards, Eddie had his ever-present notebook filled with tips and questions to be answered. Charlotte had made time for each of her siblings, even crouching in the barn with Jamey as he showed her the newest litter of kittens.

"They're very important, you know," he told her earnestly. "Robbie and Becca make fun of me all the time because their animals provide food for the family, but Papa says that it's my cats that keep the rats and mice away from the animal food."

"I'm sure they do." Charlotte grinned as she tickled a furry little chin. "They make the barn seem like a friendlier place, too. There's nothing like a purring kitten when you want to cuddle something. And these days, we could all use a little more cuddling."

The train to Chattanooga departed early Monday morning, so only Susan and Jonathan accompanied their daughter and her family to the train station. As they waited in the predawn chill, conversation was strained.

"Be sure to write us as soon as you get there, to let us know you are safe," Susan warned.

"We're going to be safe, Mother. I keep telling you that. The only danger would come if the train ran off the track, and you'd be sure to hear about that if it did."

"Don't even think like that!"

"Oh, Mother, you're too superstitious."

"You're my daughter. I have a right to worry!"

Charlotte sighed. "Well, if we're going to share worries, I wish you'd let me know if you hear from Johnny. He's the one who's being shot at."

"Do you think you need remind me of that? You children who insist on wandering all around the country will be the death of me. And these babies—do you think they are warm enough?"

"Of course they are. They're so bundled up they can barely move."

"Maybe their clothes are too tight. It doesn't do to swaddle them too much as they are growing."

Charlotte sighed. There didn't seem to be any safe topic this morning. The arrival of the train, creaking slowly up the steep incline, simply brought with it another worry.

"Don't be in too much of a hurry to board," Jonathan warned as Henry grabbed the bags. "Be sure they've set all the hand brakes first. We don't want to see it suddenly hurtle back down the hillside with you aboard."

"We'll be careful, Papa." Charlotte stood on tiptoe to press a kiss on his still-bewhiskered cheek. Then she hugged her mother quickly and scooped the twins into her arms. "Thank you for the weekend. We'll write," she called as the conductor lifted the steps and closed the door.

Jonathan and Susan stood side by side but oddly apart as they watched the train pull away from the station. Each of them was caught up in a separate knot of emotions. Jonathan risked a glance at Susan and then caught her hand as he saw the first tears overflow. "She'll be all right," he promised. "Pickford is a good man. He'll take care of her."

"That's not what I'm worried about. I agree that he's a good man. Much as I wanted to hate him, he was charming and so good with the children—all of them. It's Charlotte that I . . . that I'm crying about. She's my firstborn, and by rights I should love her more than any of the others, but . . ."

"But?"

"But while I will always love her, I don't always like her very much, and this is one of those times. She's shallow . . . and self-centered . . . and . . . and supercilious!"

"She's young."

"She doesn't have time to be young any more. She's an adult, the mother of two, a woman living through wartime and already on her second husband. She has responsibilities, and she should have worries. She should be thinking about the future and making practical choices, not following whatever whim suits her fancy at the moment."

"And she wouldn't let you act like a mother hen. She wouldn't listen to your advice—wouldn't even ask for it. She's always been stubborn and headstrong. Why did you expect her to change now? You need to let her go, Susan."

"I just did."

41

Months of Boredom, Moments of Agony
Early Summer 1863

The rest of March and much of April dragged by, most days drenched in spring rains and mired in mud. Jonathan urged the children to get their vegetable gardens started whenever the clouds lifted, but their efforts were futile. Heavy downpours washed the onion sets out of the ground, and the potato buds failed to sprout. Corn blades turned yellow and drooped. Not even Jamey's radish crop survived. In the orchards, the fruit trees struggled to open their blossoms, only to have their petals beaten to a pulp.

Already feeling pessimistic, Susan surveyed the muddy pools of water covering the garden and began cutting back on the family's use of provisions put up from the previous summer. "If this rain does not let up soon, we're not going to have anything left to eat," she fussed. "I've been looking forward to spring vegetables, but, at this rate, we'll be reduced to grits and water in no time. I don't even see any dandelion greens sprouting."

"It's not that bad," Jonathan assured her. "It's almost May. Summer will be here before we know it, and this buildup of the water supply will assure a great late-summer crop."

For once, Eddie sided with his mother. "Have you been out to the orchard, Father? I took a shortcut through there on my way back from the cow pasture, and I didn't like what I saw."

"Such as?"

"Well, the fruit has started to set, particularly on the edges of the peach acres, but it looks weird—almost like walnuts rather than peaches. The knobs are brown and wrinkled. I don't remember that happening last year."

"Peaches don't look like walnuts, Eddie. Are you sure you were looking at the peach grove?" Jonathan sounded exasperated enough to discourage Eddie from arguing further. He simply shrugged and went off to deal with the milking.

The warning rankled, however, and the next day Jonathan rode his horse out to investigate. What he saw terrified him. Where there should have been plump green globes, only brown knots showed on the branches. Many of them were already falling to the ground. The leaves that should have been turning bright green were a sickly yellowish shade. Jonathan cut off an affected branch and rode straight to town.

He burst into the office of Mr. Winchester, still clutching the branch. "What is this? Have you ever seen peach trees that looked like this?" he demanded. "I thought you said peach crops didn't need much special care."

Winchester looked up, faintly annoyed at the interruption. Then, as he realized what he was looking at, he clasped his hand over his mouth. "Oh, my word! Looks like you've got the yellows!"

"I've got what?"

"Don't know what the technical term for it is, but growers around here just refer to it as the yellows. Haven't seen anything of it for the past few years. Must be the rain."

"But what is it? And what do I do about it?"

"It's peach blight, my good man, and I'm afraid there's not a whole lot you can do about it. Once that gets into your trees, your crop's done for—maybe your whole orchard, unless you get rid of it immediately. Stuff spreads like the blazes."

Jonathan felt his knees go weak, and he sat down abruptly. "That can't happen. I can't let it happen. How do I get rid of it?"

"Only way I know is to cut off all the affected branches and burn them. But maybe you'd better consult with George Balkin. He knows more about peaches than anybody around here, but don't go carrying that branch into his groves. Leave it in your saddlebag unless he wants to see it. You don't want to infect anybody else if you can help it."

Jonathan passed by the Episcopal Church on his way and stopped when he saw Reverend Cornish in the churchyard. When he showed him the affected branch, Cornish was shocked. "I've never seen it," he admitted. "Let me get my horse, and I'll ride out to Balkin's orchard with you. I'd like to hear what he has to say so that I can spread the word to the Horticultural Association."

George Balkin easily confirmed Winchester's analysis. "It's definitely the yellows," he said. "Doesn't happen often, but heavy spring rains tend to bring it on. I suggest you round up every hand you can find, Grenville, and do as Winchester said: Cut off every affected branch, burn them down to ash, and then bury the remains. Your trees will look horrible, and they won't produce this year. But, with luck, they'll come back better than ever next year."

"Small encouragement, that."

"Be thankful it's only peach blight. You can still get an apple crop and a good harvest of scuppernongs. Had it been an insect or worm infestation, you might have lost everything."

Jonathan offered a rueful nod. "No matter how bad something gets, it could always be worse, I suppose."

Susan did not find that conclusion particularly soothing when he relayed it to her later that afternoon. "I don't want to think about how much worse it could get. The world is in bad enough shape as it is. Have you had a chance to read last week's *Mercury* yet?"

"No, why? Something new going on in Charleston?"

"Quite a lot, actually. During the first week of April, the Union fleet made an attempt to seize the harbor and put an end, once and for all, to blockade-runners. From what the reporters say, it was a farce from beginning to end. The Confederate defenders decided they didn't have enough ammunition or men to defend the city, so they spread the word that they had mined the harbor. It seems they created some sort of ridiculous hoax—using rope netting suspended from floating empty barrels, as if that would stop even the smallest ship. But they started the rumor that the barrels marked the locations of underwater mines and torpedoes."

"Don't tell me anybody believed that!"

"Apparently so. Admiral DuPont brought seven warships to the mouth of the harbor, but they were scared off by the fear that those barrels were dangerous. Three hours later they sailed away, having done no damage whatsoever."

"Sounds like a good outcome."

"Maybe not. The blockade-runners were still sailing right through the so-called barricade, so now DuPont is reported to be planning direct attacks on Fort Sumter, then Morris Island,

and finally the city of Charleston itself. And this time he'll probably be harder to fool."

"Maybe Charleston's defense arrangements will have time to improve as well. Does the paper say anything about Johnny's unit?"

"Only that they're somewhere in Mississippi, getting ready to help defend the Mississippi River from the Yankees. I do wish we'd hear from him directly instead of having to comb through the fine print of the newspaper."

Jonathan let the remark pass. He preferred to rely on the principle that no news was better than receiving one of those black-edged envelopes.

In due course, the April rains passed, allowing May and June to bring a gradual improvement of sunshine and warmer temperatures. Once the mud had a chance to dry out, the family gardeners hurried to plant a second round of crops, hoping for a late fall to balance their late spring weather. Jonathan could hardly bear to look at his butchered peach orchard, but the apple trees were thriving, and the grape arbors were heavy with ripening fruit.

The long-awaited letter from Johnny arrived in mid-June. In it, he described the Capers' Regiment's preparations to hold the city of Jackson against reinforcements for Grant's drive down the Mississippi. General Grant had been determined to seize the city of Vicksburg because it was the last Confederate fortification blocking the Union's free use of the Mississippi River. Jackson lay some forty miles directly east of Vicksburg, on the only real road giving access to the river port. The 24th

Regiment had been in place in early May, but General Johnson had changed his mind about the Confederates' ability to defend against the powerhouse that was the Union Army. At the first sign of trouble, he ordered the city of Jackson evacuated and sent his troops north to join the Army of Tennessee. Johnny's letter reflected the same pessimism.

> *And so I have missed another chance to experience a real battle. In some ways, I had hoped that we would be sent to Vicksburg, but I'm afraid that city is destined to fall. The Union holds both ends of the river as it passes through Confederate territory—Memphis and New Orleans. We hold only Vicksburg at one relatively small bend in that river. The fortifications there are strong, but clearly the North has more to be gained by winning this confrontation. Only one spot stands in the way of their free use of the river. If General Pemberton manages to hold the fort (which I doubt he will be able to do), he will put a crimp in the Union plans. But what does the South gain from such a victory? Call Vicksburg the Gibraltar of Mississippi if you must, but, if we win at Vicksburg, we still have control of only that one small point, not the whole river. Poor motivation, that.*
>
> *I find I am looking forward to seeing Tennessee. From what we hear, General Rosecrans is nowhere as formidable an enemy as General Grant, and the Confederate forces are under the command of Generals Braxton Bragg and James Longstreet, both superb leaders unafraid of marching into battle. I join them with high hopes.*

"What is it about Tennessee?" Susan wondered out loud. "Both our children headed there—one telling us there is no danger and the other hoping to see real fighting."

"If I get a choice, I vote for Charlotte's view," Jonathan answered, "but since we don't really get a vote, we shall just have to trust that some higher power will keep them both safe."

42

Battle of Chickamauga
Late Summer 1863

In its turn, June gave way to July and a general heating up of the war, with accompanying discouragement for the Confederate States. In Pennsylvania, at the Battle of Gettysburg, General George Meade put an end to Robert E. Lee's plans to carry the war into Northern territory. The toll of deaths and wounded was staggering. Between July 1 and July 3, there were some 50,000 casualties as Lee was forced into ignominious retreat to Virginia. The very next day, General Pemberton was forced by the threat of starvation to surrender to Grant at Vicksburg, thus opening the Mississippi River to Union traffic.

The South's only good news in July came from Charleston, where the Union forces had made a second attempt to take Charleston Harbor. This time, the plan was to attack Morris Island in order to open a land path to the city. Despite hurling all available forces against Fort Wagner, which guarded the beach of Morris Island, the invaders were repelled by a small but entrenched number of defenders. The battle gained much fame, especially when the 54th Massachusetts, one of the first black Union regiments, braved certain death in an attempt to take control of the fort. The siege continued for several weeks, but, in the end, the Union lost some 1,500 men, while the Confederate defenders suffered only 200 casualties.

Susan professed to be confident now that Charleston could stand against all comers. "Our city is the heart of the Confederacy. The war started there, and it will end there. A fire couldn't destroy it, and neither could the Union Army. I wish we were back there to share in the celebration."

Jonathan was less enthusiastic. "It's just one battle, and, while I personally laud the idea of putting free blacks into the service of their country, I suspect that their training was not the best. From my point of view, the Union Army used those ex-slaves as cannon fodder, sending them up the ramparts of Fort Wagner to certain death while the white soldiers waited on the beach. The Union had no hope of winning that battle, but the South has no hope of winning this war, Susan. Please don't get your hopes up that we can ever go back to the same beautiful city we once knew."

Susan refused to accept that conclusion, but Jonathan's words proved to be prophetic. On August 21, Admiral DuPont sent a message to those in charge at Charleston, telling them that he was about to commence shelling of the city. He warned them to evacuate all civilians from the harbor and downtown areas. The message arrived that night, and the Charleston authorities refused to accept it. Instead they sent the letter back, questioning its authenticity. Surely, they said, a fine upstanding general would not consider destroying a city full of sleeping women and children. Besides, they pointed out, the message did not have all the required signatures. If they were smiling at their cleverness in postponing the fight, their smiles must have soon faded.

Shelling began at 1:30 AM, and well-aimed missiles rained down upon the city. Many of the houses along the Battery were by now closed up for the duration of the war, but other intrepid citizens were shaken from their beds and forced to flee for their lives with whatever they could carry. Almost nothing south of Calhoun Street managed to avoid some scar of destruction.

According to the local papers, General Beauregard called the attack "an act of inexcusable barbarity" and predicted that history would confirm that judgment. As for the city itself, later papers reported that it had been deserted by everyone but the rats, while weeds and grass grew in the streets. In Aiken, the Grenvilles read the grim descriptions, and Susan dropped all discussion about their eventual return to Charleston.

Early in September, a brief note from Johnny arrived, telling them of his promotion to the rank of corporal and expressing his usual optimism that, in Tennessee at least, the Rebels had the Yankees on the run. The news was what Susan wanted to hear, so she focused on that, while Jonathan worried privately that Charlotte and Henry might someday find themselves in the center of one of those clashes that Johnny was so eager to see.

There was little to be learned about what was happening in Tennessee, however. The only papers arriving in Aiken with any regularity were those from Charleston, and the *Mercury* concentrated on the continuing struggles for possession of the city. Union forces were now reported to be tunneling their way into Fort Wagner, while Confederate experiments with torpedoes and primitive submarines plagued their own forces as much as they threatened Union ships. Fort Sumter had been damaged but not put out of action during the August bombardment of the city, and the Union Navy saw that small rock island as making a continuing mockery of their power. No one except Jonathan and Susan seemed to care much about what was happening elsewhere.

The Grenvilles received the long-dreaded letter in early October. True, it did not carry a black border, but it arrived with an official army stamp, and the news it carried was no less devastating.

> *Mr. Jonathan Grenville*
>
> *Dear Sir:*
>
> *General Bragg appointed the morning of September 20 as the time for our forces to move against the strongholds of the Union forces being directed by General Rosecrans near Chickamauga Creek in northern Georgia. We arrived at our appointed station in the early morning hours and rested briefly while we waited for daylight. Directly ahead of us was a narrow road through the trees, sloping steadily uphill toward some unseen destination. When we reached the top of the hill and broke out into a clearing, we found ourselves facing a log fortification, behind which Union soldiers were firing at us at will. There also came enfilading fire from our left. In the next thirty minutes, nearly one-third of our regiment fell. As we retreated into the safety of the trees, we tried to identify our dead and carry away our wounded, but some of our men remained unaccounted for. One of those was your son Johnny.*
>
> *A member of his squad reported that he saw Corporal Grenville fall victim to a gunshot to his leg, but that was the last anyone saw of him. I feel certain that he was not too badly wounded and that the Federals have taken him prisoner. Several others of our men are also missing. We have searched and searched for them but in vain.*
>
> *Johnny is a noble young man and a brave soldier who is beloved by all his associates. He is like a brother to me, and I lament his capure. You have my sympathy and prayers in your deep affliction. If it can possibly be done, I will send his knapsack and traps home to you as I have no doubt you would like to possess them. His watch and what money he had were on his person.*

If any further intelligence of his fate can be had, I will inform you in due time.

Yours truly,

Col. Ellison Capers

24th South Carolina Regiment

They sat in stunned silence for a moment before the questions emerged. "What does it mean, Jonathan?" Susan asked at last, her eyes brimming with tears. "What will happen to him?"

"Keep remembering this, my dear. The colonel beliueves he is alive. And he is no longer fighting. No one is shooting at him any more."

"But he's wounded! And he is probably locked up in some little cell somewhere . . . maybe abandoned . . . or starving . . . or being tortured!"

"I doubt that he is locked in a little cell. Prisoner of war camps don't have that sort of facility. He's probably in a tent, just like the one he left behind."

"Jonathan, you are maddening! You're trying to pretend this is nothing to worry about, when we both know . . ."

"That you are overexaggerating. The truth is that neither of us knows anything at the moment, and we shouldn't be trying to imagine something we know nothing about."

"But we have to do something! Maybe we could go visit Charlotte and start looking around there for places they might be holding prisoners. Or we could ask Charlotte and Henry to—"

"No! No one's going anywhere, and I won't have you trying to involve the Pickfords in this, either. You have no idea how dangerous that could be for all concerned."

"So you admit there is grave danger."

"Of course there is danger. It's wartime. You will have to trust the Union Army to be as compassionate to a wounded man as you have said you would be under similar circumstances. He will get medical care if he needs it. And there's also a good chance that he will be released eventually in some sort of prisoner exchange. That happens frequently, particularly in cases where there is no danger that the released prisoner will go right back to the field to fight again. We have to be patient."

"Patient? That's asking a lot." Susan threw up her hands in disgust and stomped her way to the back door. Jonathan watched her go in silence, but his expression drooped as he admitted to himself that he was as restless and frightened as she was.

At the dinner table that night, he broached the news to the children, trying to couch it in mild enough terms that it wouldn't frighten them but would help them understand why their parents were worried about the situation.

"He got shot? How exciting!"

"Hardly that, birdbrain!" Robbie snarled at his little brother. "Don't you understand anything?"

"What's going to happen to him?" Becca asked, her eyes wide.

"He's going to recover from his wound, and then, we hope, he'll be home. We don't know how long that will take, though, so there's nothing for any of us to do right now."

"Maybe if I volunteered to take his place, they'd let him go," Eddie suggested.

"Don't you even consider it! Not for a moment! Do you hear me?" Susan was close to tears again.

"As I said, there's nothing to be done. We wanted you to be aware of what is happening, but nothing around here changes. We go on with our lives, as he would want us to do. We get the crops in, we prepare the ground to winter over, and we care for the animals and for each other. We hold the family together, so that when Johnny can finally come home, he will find us all together, all ready to welcome him back among us."

The whole family tried to pretend that all was well, but tempers were short and conversations faltered. The only thought that held them together was the one no one was willing to say out loud. They went to church together that Sunday, and, if their prayers were all a bit longer and more fervent, they still pretended that nothing was wrong.

Then, on Monday, Susan called Hector into the house as soon as Jonathan and the children had headed for the orchard to check on the apple crop. "I want you to bring the wagon around and load the melodeon onto it. Then I'll need you to drive me to town."

"What you be up to, Miss Susan?"

"I'm delivering the melodeon to the church."

"Massa Jonathan, he don say nuttin bout dat."

"It's not his melodeon, Hector, so what I do with it is none of his business. And don't you go telling him, either. Just do as I ask, please."

"Ah don know," he mumbled, but he did as he was told.

When Jonathan came in from the barn late that afternoon, he found Susan busily scrubbing the dining room floor. "What are you doing down there on your hands and knees?" he asked.

"I'm getting this room fixed up so that we can use it as a bedroom for Johnny when he comes home. He probably won't be able to use the stairs, and I wouldn't want him to have to share a room with the younger boys anyway. He'll need his privacy."

"But, Susan . . . wait! What have you done with your melodeon?" He looked around the room in puzzlement.

"It's gone. I gave it to the church."

"Why? Why would you want to do that? Your music is the one thing that holds your spirit together. That instrument is the most important possession you have."

"No, it's not. My son is my most important possession, and I'll do whatever it takes to get him back."

"I'm sorry, but I'm confused. I don't understand what you're saying."

Susan turned her head away from him and mumbled something.

"What?"

She turned and glared at him. "It's my bargain with God. I promised God that if He gave my son back to me, I would give up my melodeon as a token of my gratitude. So that's what I have done, and you have nothing to say about it."

"God doesn't demand a price for granting a prayer, Susan."

"Maybe not, but it's what I offered to do. I wanted Him to understand how important this is to me. It's a token of my faith and a private sign that I do believe that God answers prayers. I'll thank you not to interfere."

43

Wounded Warriors
December 1863

J onathan had recognized the tone of Susan's voice from long experience. It was a moment when a single wrong word would have unleashed a tirade, and he could not face another quarrel. He shrugged his shoulders and left the room. Sighing, he glanced around the empty kitchen, grateful that none of the children were lingering there. He was tired—tired of suffering, tired of smiling when he wanted to cry, tired of trying to reassure his whole family that everything was going to be all right.

Aimlessly, he wandered toward the comfortable chairs in the corner. There on the table was the family Bible, opened to the seventh chapter of the Book of Job. His eye fell on the now familiar words:

> . . . *my soul chooseth strangling and death rather than my life.*
>
> *I loathe it; I would not live alway; let me alone, for my days are vanity.*
>
> *What is man, that thou shouldest magnify him? And that thou should set thine heart upon him?*
>
> *And that thou shouldest visit him every morning, and try him every moment?*

> *How long wilt thou not depart from me, nor let me alone till I swallow down my spittle?*
>
> *I have sinned; what shall I do unto thee, O thou preserver of men? Why hast thou set me as a mark unto thee, so that I am a burden to myself?*

"I have little of Job's patience," he said out loud. "And I have had more than enough of suffering, both in my own soul and for my children."

His hand lingered over the Bible; then he closed it firmly. Striding to the back door, he took down the shotgun from its pegs high above the doorframe. He didn't bother with his coat, although the grass was still showing tinges of the overnight frost. Looking neither left nor right, he headed toward a distant stand of trees.

In the yard, Hector and Sarah had just finished cutting a crop of winter turnip greens and were headed toward the kitchen. Automatically, Hector raised a hand and called, "Mornin, Massa Jonathan." But Jonathan showed no sign that he had heard.

"Sumptin aint right," Hector said. "Jonathan always be friendly. Here, Sarah, you be takin dese greens tuh da house. Ah gwine check fuh see what be wrong." He followed Jonathan at a distance, watching him carefully. Near the copse of hardwood trees that marked the far edge of Grenville land, he lost sight of Jonathan temporarily. Then a single shot rang out. Hector broke into a run.

Topping the crest of a small hill, he could look down and see Jonathan sitting on the ground under a gnarled live oak, the gun beside him and his head buried in his hands. "Massa Jonathan! Be you hurt?"

Jonathan looked up at last and shook his head. "No. Worst luck. I don't seem to be able to do anything right."

"What you means? What you bin shootin at?"

Now, face-to-face, Hector could see that his former owner's cheeks were flushed and streaked where he had tried to scrub away the evidence of his tears. When Jonathan did not answer the question, Hector understood that what he had feared was true. "Why? What else gwine on wit you? Mo news bout Massa Johnny?"

"No. No. Nothing new."

"What, den? You bes be talkin tuh me, cause you look fuh be in big trubble."

"I'm just tired, Hector, tired of my struggles in this life. I've fallen into a deep, dark pit, and I can't seem to dig my way out. I'm tired of trying and failing. And I'm tired of bringing disaster down upon the heads of everyone I love. My family will be better off without me. And that includes you, so why don't you just go on and leave me to it."

"Ah aint gwine leaves you nowheres, Massa. Lookit. Neber mind what else ah says. Ah's jis a po black man what mind he own bidness. But you be muh fren all dese year, an ah aint gwine let you do nuttin stupid."

"On the contrary. This might be the smartest thing I have ever done. I should have considered it the first time God punched me in the face."

"God not be doin dat!"

"I worked hard to teach my students right from wrong, and He let me be fired. I struggled to learn the cotton business, and He let the war steal my crops and my land right out from under me. I allowed my daughter to get married to the love of her life, and He blew him to smithereens. I took pride in my house, and He burned it to the ground. I moved the family here to protect them, and He's caused them to suffer mightily from the loss of their friends and from actual poverty, which is only going to get worse now that the peach crop has failed. I let my son become a soldier, and now He's allowed him to go missing in action. At every step of my life, I have failed to reach my goals, and God has punished me by allowing those I love to suffer on account of my failings. Have you ever heard of Job, Hector?"

"Job? He dat fella in de Bible dat hab all de bad luck? Preacherman tell we bout he all de time. He say we gots fuh believe, jis like Job do, an sum day we gwine walk de street uh gold."

"Yes. Well, that street paved in gold is in heaven, Hector, not in this life." Jonathan's laugh was bitter.

"Ah still don see what dat got fuh do wit you. What happen tuh Job not be cause uh what he do."

"Job believed his troubles were caused by his own sins, and he wanted to die."

"But he dint! An neider kin you, cause ah be stoppin dat foolishness. You may be hurt by what be happnin, but you aint be daid. Gib me dat rifle." Hector grabbed it before Jonathan could make a move. He looked around with a keen hunter's eye, then sighted the gun and fired. Across the clearing a rabbit flew into the air with the impact of the shell. Hector walked over, picked it up by its ears, and carried it back to Jonathan.

"What's this for?"

"Dat what you gwine tell Miss Susan you be doin out here—gittin sum meat fuh de stew. But whiles you be carryin it home, ah wants you fuh take a good look at what it mean fuh be dead. Dat rabbit be happy, hoppin round in de grass, til trubble hit he fro behind. It not be he fault. He jis happen fuh hop past when ah need a victim. But sumwheres dere's a furry lil lady bunny wondrin what happen to he. Maybe Mister Rabbit fail

340

at sumptin or be a sinful rabbit. But take uh look at dat lifeless body now an ax what good it do dat rabbit fuh be daid."

Jonathan looked at the rabbit and felt his gorge rise. He handed the lifeless body back to Hector, saying, "Here, you take it to Sarah. I couldn't eat it now. I'd feel like a cannibal."

"Lak uh what?"

"I mean, it reminds me too much of myself. But thank you, Hector. You've taught me another valuable lesson. You seem to be doing that a lot lately."

"You bin good tuh me all muh life. Ifn ah kin hep you, dat what ah gwine do."

Susan asked no questions when Jonathan entered the kitchen and replaced his rifle above the back door. Jonathan said nothing more about the melodeon. But when their eyes met, they spoke volumes about their shared suffering and about their mutual understanding. Later that night, as they were getting ready for bed, Jonathan put his arm around Susan and drew her close. "For all our married lives, we've handled troubles best when we stood together, united by our love. We'll survive this as well. Just be here for me, as I will be for you."

She nodded mutely and hugged him back.

Another Christmas was fast approaching, and again the Grenvilles sought ways to make the occasion meaningful and memorable for their children. One night, the girls asked if they could still make presents for Johnny. "I've been knitting socks, and Becca's working on a scarf. We could keep them wrapped for him until he comes home," Mary Sue explained.

"That's a lovely idea, darling. I'm sure he'll be impressed with your efforts." If her heart was breaking, Susan managed to conceal it.

Without the melodeon there would be no parlor music, so Susan suggested that they take the carriage and travel to their neighbors' yards to sing Christmas carols for them. A frosty night and a full moon made the adventure a magical one, and several of their tenants invited them in for a cookie or a warm drink. "You know, I'm beginning to feel at home here in Aiken," Susan said. "It just takes a little effort."

To top off the holiday, Hector and Sarah agreed to bring Eli and Annie and share a Christmas dinner. They were all finding that the longer they lived in proximity on this land, the more comfortable they felt with one another. As they lingered over the last pieces of pie, Susan reached out to take Sarah's hand. "I've always known that we were related by a common grandfather, but now that we have shared so many new experiences, I feel our bonds of cousinhood binding us ever more tightly." And as the two women smiled at each other, Jonathan and Hector, too, shared a nod of recognition.

The season had one more gift in store for the family. Just before the New Year, a letter arrived from Nashville. Susan did not recognize the neat woman's hand, but she did not stop to speculate before she opened the envelope.

> *Dear Mr. and Mrs. Grenville,*
>
> *I take my pen in hand at the request of your son Johnny to tell you that he is doing well. Corporal Grenville arrived here at our hospital as a prisoner of war shortly after the Battle of Chickamauga. He had suffered several gunshot wounds in his left leg, which made it impossible for him to escape capture. Those wounds were swollen and badly infected by the time*

he was transferred from the prison car and came into our care. He was also impossibly thin and emaciated. Despite the welcome presence of laudable pus, the skin around the wounds was turning black, and the doctors here despaired of being able to save his leg. When he was given the alternatives, he told us he would rather live with one leg than die with two. Therefore, the leg was amputated in November.

Susan swayed and almost crumpled to the floor as Jonathan read the words. Then she took a deep breath and urged him to read on. "He's not dead. This is good."

By now the stump has healed well and without incident. It has been important for his general health that we strengthen his body through rest and good nutrition, so we have not rushed his recovery. We shall soon have him up and walking on crutches, however. Perhaps later, he can have an artificial limb fitted to him. When he feels strong enough—and that will depend entirely upon him—the doctors here will try to arrange an exchange of prisoners so that he can return home.

It is not possible at this time to allow our prisoner patients to have visitors, but they may receive letters and small gifts from their families. I hope to keep you informed as to his progress.

Sincerely yours,
Nellie M. Chase, Head Matron
U.S. Military Hospital #3
Nashville, Tennessee

"So letter writing becomes a substitute for taking care of our loved ones, too. I can send him small gifts, but will that make him feel loved the way a mother's hand on his cheek would?"

"Of course not, Susan, but it should lift his spirits, and the Lord knows he will need that in the days and months to come."

44

Mothers and Daughters
March 1864

The winter of 1863-1864 was harsh in South Carolina. Cold rains and strong winds lashed the farmland, turning plowed fields into mud holes and beating down the sprouting winter grass crops. On the Grenville farm, the family was still feeling the effects of peach blight. With the failure of the entire peach crop, there had been no income with which to stock provisions for the winter. Susan and the girls had worked diligently to put up vegetables, jams, and various forms of pickles, but fears for the future threatened their normal sources of protein.

Chickens had to be kept alive to produce eggs, no matter how badly Susan hankered after a good chicken stew. The last pig had been slaughtered, and the smokehouse was stocked, but there would be no money in the spring to purchase new animals. Ham and bacon had to be rationed to last for a two-year period. Eddie had been experimenting with cheese recipes, but the results were still not entirely successful, and, in the meantime, one of the cows had gone dry. That meant that most of the milk supply had to go straight to the family, not to another batch of cheese curds, whey, and rennet. Sugar and flour were in short supply as well.

There was firewood enough to keep the house warm, but clothes for outdoors were another story. The children kept growing out of coats, and shirts were becoming threadbare. Everyone tried to put a good face on the things they did have rather than on those they lacked, but Jonathan suffered each time he saw his family making do with less. The whole family seemed to be sleeping more than usual, perhaps because the beds were still warm with handmade quilts. But no one had much energy, and life dragged on through the months of January and February.

Susan tried to stir up some enthusiasm for the coming of Easter, but March was too cold to allow much appreciation of spring. When the children woke on Easter morning to find a skiff of snow on the ground, their reaction was a groan rather than the delight that snow would have brought in former times.

For Jonathan, the only benefit of the cold months was that the weather had driven both armies into winter quarters and the papers were no longer full of stories of slaughter. True, Charleston had suffered another rude bombardment on Christmas Day, but, since then, all had been quiet. The great war was still waiting, however. Everyone knew that when the weather improved, new battles would break out and more men would die.

Susan had finally given up hoping for letters from her absent children, so she hardly noticed when Jonathan dropped an envelope on the kitchen table. "That came for you this week," he said. "Looks like it's from Flat Rock."

"Flat Rock? Mother? Surely not. She hates writing letters as much as I do." But it was. Susan ripped open the envelope, noticing in passing that the handwriting was rather shaky.

Dear Daughter,

I hope that this small letter finds you and yours in good health. We are all still waking up each morning, which is about all one can expect from three old ladies. I take my unaccustomed pen in hand to let you know about two developments of which you may be unaware.

First, your daughter Charlotte came to visit me recently, bringing her new husband with her. You didn't know she was going to do so? I thought not. From what she said, I gather that the two of you are on the outs again. Never mind. She and I had quite a few talks about family relationships. We two have always gotten along, so she seemed rather surprised to hear that I have fought with you for your entire life, and that my own mother and I seldom spoke to one another. I am convinced that the real punishment God wreaks on women is not childbirth but the bestowing of daughters, who spend their days making our lives miserable. The other side of that coin is that the greatest blessing God bestows is the love for one's granddaughters. I have offered that bit of wisdom to Charlotte, but I don't believe she understands it yet. Perhaps she will when little Annie Rogers turns to you rather than to Charlotte.

In any event, I promised Charlotte that I would offer you my honest assessment of her new husband, who was, and is, all too aware of your disapproval. Truth be told, I find him delightful and charming. He loves your daughter beyond all reason, which is no easy task in itself, and he adores the twins. He is making a wonderful father for them. He has a knack for demanding respect and great love, all at the same time. They may talk back to their mother, but they obey him instantly and then cover him with kisses.

Indeed, I was tempted to do so myself because he made himself so useful while he was here. He added to our wood supply and stacked it closer to the house. Then he fixed the bannister that was coming loose on the front porch and added a handrail to our cellar steps. He cleaned out the ash pits and checked all the flues to be sure we would stay warm and safe all winter. He even caught a wily mouse that had been raiding our pantry. Charlotte has found herself a rare jewel in the ranks of men, and I couldn't be happier for her and the coming baby.

347

Susan sat down abruptly, letting the letter flutter from her fingers.

Jonathan, looking up from his own perusal of the latest newspaper, caught her distress. "What is it? Is she all right?"

"Yes, yes, I assume so. She's up to her old tricks of avoiding important news and then dropping a huge bombshell, however. She was rattling on with details about woodpiles and mice, and then casually mentioned that Charlotte is expecting a baby."

"Another one? Well, indeed! She is legally married, so I suppose that shouldn't be a surprise, but one would think she would tell her own parents rather than letting her grandmother do so."

"Precisely! Here—read it for yourself." Susan squeezed her lips together as if to keep from saying something she would regret. Instead, she walked to the window and stared out over the farmyard.

Jonathan read silently and then joined his wife at the window. Being careful not to touch her, he spoke in a gentle tone. "She's really lecturing you, isn't she? What she has done with this letter is a perfect example of the mother-daughter divide she talks about."

"I suppose it is. She insists on perpetuating our quarrels by doing things like this. If Charlotte asked her to tell us about the baby, she could have done so with a great deal more excitement and joy. This way is just . . ."

"I understand. Really, I do. On the other hand, you must realize that she can't hurt you unless you let her. Can you manage to ignore her barbs and be happy for your own daughter?"

"Of course. I certainly don't want to look in the mirror and see my mother. She is so infuriating. And she's written more, hasn't she?"

"Yes, there's a second page, changing the subject entirely."

I have also been worried about the Legare Street house since you and your family closed it up and abandoned it to its fate. I know I told you that you could do with it as you wished, but when the damned Yankees started lobbing shells at it, I grew concerned. I feel protective toward it although I do not ever expect to see the house again.

Not long ago I ran into the Countess Bentivoglio on the street—your Jonathan will remember her as Mrs. Arthur Middleton, one of the ladies I traveled with on my way to Flat Rock.

"Only because I introduced your mother to her," Jonathan grumbled.

"See? Keep reading, dear. Don't let her get to you, too."

The Arthur Middletons' son, Benti Middleton, stayed on in Charleston when the rest of the family left. He was living in the townhouse that belonged to his uncle, Williams Middleton, right there at the corner of Meeting Street and the Battery, until the shelling became too great. Then he moved in with Alex Croft, who was guarding his family home on Meeting Street.

"Now that we have the whole pedigree . . ."

"Jonathan . . ."

The Countess volunteered to have Benti go over to Legare Street and find out about the condition of my house.

"Her house! She deeded it to me!"

"Yes, dear, she did. But she will always think of it as her house. You knew that and informed me of it on the day she gave it to you. Remember? But listen to this."

> *Benti, that dear boy, says that the house is fine, at least from the outside. It was not hit by any of the bombardments. Now, however, there is a damned Yankee general using it as the headquarters for his staff. I can just imagine what they have done to the inside—cigar smoke, booted feet on the settees, and coffee cups on the mantles, at the very least. The Countess says that Arthur believes you should be able to reclaim the house once the war is over, so be sure to hold onto your deed. You'll need it to press your claim.*

"See, she calls it your house. It sounds to me as if she has no intention of returning to Charleston herself."

"Maybe not, but . . . You know what she's doing, don't you? She's getting ready to force us to go back there as soon as the war is over."

"That almost makes me wish the war wouldn't end. I notice that she's rather overdoing the 'Damned Yankee' references, too," Jonathan grumbled.

"Let's not worry about it for the time being. That's a problem for the future. And maybe by then, she'll be . . ."

"What were you going to say, Susan?"

"No. It would sound terrible."

"What would? Look at me. What were you thinking?"

"Well, her handwriting is very shaky, and that's unusual. She's not young anymore. Maybe by the time the war is over, she won't be able to . . . No, I won't say it. She's my mother, like it or not, and I would never wish her ill. Forget I even thought about it. For that matter, none of us may outlive this war. We won't talk any more about it—or her. One day's troubles are enough."

45

Reunions
Summer 1864

The Grenvilles were busy that spring. The weather turned warm in June, promising good crops for the vegetable garden, and the children had gotten together and decided to expand their special plantings. After the lean winter they had suffered, everyone felt the need to pitch in with the farm work. Mary Sue added several kinds of peppers to her tomato patch, arguing that Sarah's best recipes always called for more spice than her mother had available. Robbie decided that green beans could get a start while his pea crop was ripening, and then the climbing beans could take over the old pea supports. Becca added pumpkins and acorn squash to her corn hills, a lesson she had learned from reading about the Indians. And even Jamey agreed to plant some carrots along with his radishes.

Susan watched with pride, always concealing her laughter at how eagerly the children ate the crops they planted. "Next year, we'll try them on rutabagas and brussels sprouts."

"That's not necessary, my dear. Let's keep limiting them to growing vegetables that taste good," Jonathan suggested. "If you produce another bumper crop of cabbages and cucumbers, and Sarah's potatoes and turnips do well, we'll be feasting next winter without resorting to brussels sprouts." He was laughing as well. Summer seemed to be lifting everyone's spirits.

In the orchard, the peach trees had recovered from having half their branches lopped off. They had burst forth with a blaze of pink blossoms, and now their green leaves were dark and glossy. Early fruit formation promised there would be ample peaches for table and market, provided, of course, that the market improved this year. Because it was still early in the growing season, it was easy to hope for an improvement in the economy by fall.

Even the animals seemed to be cooperating in the general celebration of summer. Much to everyone's surprise, the cow that had gone dry the year before was now obviously expecting a calf. "I don't know how that happened, Father," Eddie claimed, "unless one of the neighbor's bulls got into our pasture, or she jumped the fence into theirs."

"She wouldn't be the first cow to turn into a jumper," Jonathan said. "I wouldn't try to stop her as long as she jumps back to her own pasture when she's done flirting with the bull. Let's hope her calf turns out to be a little heifer, and they both become long-term milk producers."

The chickens, too, were restless. Several chickens had become broody hens, signaling the need for a family rooster to allow them to start hatching their own chicks. "I don't know about that idea. Roosters can be awfully noisy," Susan protested, "and they can be nasty-tempered, too."

"Yes, they can—just the thing to get our family up and going in the mornings. Let's at least give it a try. If the old rooster proves to be a nuisance, we can always stew him."

Counterbalancing the cheerfulness with which the Grenvilles had approached the summer of 1864 were the reports that the Union forces were on the move from Chattanooga toward Atlanta. Week after week, the newspapers followed William T. Sherman's advances through Pickett's Mill, Marietta, Kolb's Farm, and Kennesaw Mountain. The Confederate troops under Joseph E. Johnson seemed unable to resist the stronger force. In July, President Davis appointed General John B. Hood to replace Johnson, but a series of frontal assaults failed to deter the Union advance. The city of Atlanta fell on September 2, 1864.

Jonathan read the accounts with mixed emotions. Much as he wanted to see the war come to an end and the Union preserved, the grim descriptions of the smoldering city of Atlanta chilled him. Journalists referred to the new policies of the federal forces as a "scorched earth" approach. This was no longer a gentleman's fight but total war in which not only armies but civilians suffered. Crops burned, livestock slaughtered, infrastructure destroyed— these images haunted Jonathan as he imagined what such an attack would mean for his own small patch of land.

"Surely they won't come here," Susan said. "We're no threat to anyone."

"Don't count on that, my dear. Sherman's not going to stop with Atlanta. He is determined to destroy the South for all time. If you look at a map, you'll see that Aiken lies almost due east from Atlanta and not far off the direct path from Atlanta to Charleston. I don't mean to alarm you unnecessarily, but we need to face reality. We may need to bury what's left of the silver and cash we have on hand, along with finding places to stash food supplies, just in case."

"Jonathan, you always see the worst in any situation lately," Susan grumbled.

"Perhaps so, but being prepared never hurt."

In early October came the news everyone had been secretly hoping for. Nurse Nellie Chase wrote:

Dear Mr. and Mrs. Grenville,

I am pleased to inform you that your son Johnny is about to become a free man. He is fully recovered from the effects of his amputation, although he has steadfastly refused to accept any sort of wooden appendage. Now that the focus of the war seems to be moving away from the Tennessee area, General Rosecrans has decided to close many of our Union hospitals here in Nashville. Confederate prisoners who are unfit to return to active military service will be released as part of a massive prisoner exchange to relieve the crowding in our remaining institutions. You may expect Johnny to arrive in Aiken by train sometime during the week of October tenth.

I must warn you, however, that the man who will return to your family will little resemble the boy who left there several years ago. We find that our veterans on both sides of this conflict experience some difficulty in resuming their civilian roles. Some are abnormally fearful, experiencing repeated nightmares and reacting to the slightest noise as if it presages an attack. Others become angry—even violent—with little provocation. And of course there are those who simply slip into a prolonged period of great sadness and hopelessness. Alcohol use is common as well. There are no sure methods for dealing with such problems, but it is best that you be prepared for whatever comes. Do not rush your soldier back into his former life. Give him time to adjust, and follow his lead as to what he needs.

It is my sincere hope that in time the deep scars that this war has caused will heal over and allow us all—combatants and civilians alike—to return to normalcy.

Sincerely yours,

Nellie M. Chase

Head Matron, Hospital #3

Nashville, Tennessee

Susan and Jonathan met every arriving train that week, but it was not until Thursday afternoon that they spotted a lanky young soldier hopping down from a car near the back of the train. He wavered a bit on his crutches but shook off a porter who rushed to his assistance. Slowly he made his way toward them. Susan was crying openly, and Jonathan coughed to cover his own emotions, but there was no corresponding reaction from young John. If anything, he looked angry. He looked around the town with a sneer.

"So this is the fabled city of Aiken? Could you have found a more godforsaken spot?"

"It's a lovely little town, Johnny," Susan said. "Give it time before you judge. And wait until you see the farm!"

"Right."

"Where are your things?"

"What things? Prisoners of war don't have anything of their own—only what we wear on our backs. Good thing, too, since I'd be hard-pressed to carry a pack."

Susan and Jonathan glanced at each other in discomfort. This was not the way a homecoming was supposed to go. "Come, then. Let's get you into the carriage." Jonathan reached out a hand to assist his son, but Johnny knocked it away and then staggered against the horse's flank. As the horse shied, Jonathan again tried to help, only to catch a whiff of alcohol on his son's breath. "Have you been drinking?"

"Yep. Fellow on the train and me—we shared a flask. What of it?"

"Uh, only that it's a little early for whiskey, isn't it?"

"Not where I'm coming from. Gets me through the day."

The situation did not improve when they reached the farmhouse. The children came bursting through the door to the front porch, only to stop short as they stared at John's empty pant leg.

"What're you looking at? Ain't you ever seen a one-legged man before?"

Only little Jamey spoke up. "Where is it? What did you do with it?"

"The leg? Somebody cut it off. With a saw. Want to see?"

"Ewww. No!" Becca clasped her hand over her mouth and ran for the woods.

"Wonderful to be home. I even scare little kids."

"Johnny . . ."

"Leave me be! I need a nap."

Day after day, the difficulties multiplied. Johnny had no interest in the farm and refused to venture out to the barns to see what his brothers and sisters were up to. He knew no one in town, of course, so he stayed in the house all day and night, always a presence, although never offering to be of assistance. Family members grew used to shutting doors carefully rather than letting them slam, lest the sudden noise set Johnny off on a fear-filled rage. At night, the children pulled their pillows over their ears to block the sounds of his latest nightmares.

Of all the family, Eddie was the most upset by the changes in his older brother. For all his life, he had looked up to Johnny as a model for his own behavior. While Johnny had been off as a soldier, Eddie had envied him his experiences and looked forward to a time when Johnny could tell him what war was really like. Now, however, there was a cold barrier that Eddie could not break down.

One day, hoping to reclaim some of their former camaraderie, Eddie found Johnny sitting hunched over a newspaper at the kitchen table. Eddie approached him from behind and gave him a playful slap on the shoulder. "What's new in that—"

He didn't get to finish the sentence. Johnny whirled in his seat and slugged Eddie full on the chin. Staggered, Eddie sat down on the floor abruptly, shaking his head to clear it. "What was that for?" he asked.

But now Johnny was looming over him, balanced on one crutch and flashing a lethal-looking knife blade. Johnny's eyes were strangely unfocused. "Where are the rest of your troops, Yankee? What are you doing on our land?"

"Johnny! Stop! It's me—Eddie. I wasn't attacking you. I was just trying to be friendly."

Jonathan and Hector came running through the back door, alerted by the sounds of shouting and chairs falling. Terrified of provoking Johnny further, Jonathan spoke softly to Eddie. "Move backward, son. But do it slowly and carefully. Get yourself out of arm's reach."

"Yes, sir."

"Everything's all right now, Johnny. The men are gone. The danger is over. You can put your weapon away." Gradually the tension eased and the crisis passed. Jonathan sat down at the table and looked at his battle-scarred son. "I didn't know you had a knife," he said. "Do you carry it all the time?"

Johnny looked at his hand, still clutching the handle. He seemed surprised. "Yes. Yes, I guess I do. It's so much a part of me I'd almost forgotten about it. But threaten my safety and I automatically reach for it." He looked disturbed. "That was Eddie, wasn't it? I thought he was the enemy. I wouldn't have really stabbed him . . . At least I don't think I would have."

"Perhaps not, but I'd prefer you not to carry a weapon in the house. Your brothers and sisters are trying very hard to be careful around you, but . . ."

"But I could be a danger to them. I should have gone back to my unit."

"Son, you've done your duty. Time to let others carry the flag."

"No, Father, I'm not saying that out of a sense of duty. I meant that the battlefield is where I belong now. It's all I know. That moment when our line began to advance was when I felt most alive . . . a part of something bigger than myself. Time stopped, danger disappeared, we moved as a single person. It was beautiful. I want to feel that again. I need to feel it again. If I'm not a soldier, I'm nothing."

"You have a whole life ahead of you, Johnny. You need to find a new role to play in it."

Johnny stared at his father, realizing that they could no longer understand each other. "How?" he asked.

46

A Leg Up
September 1864

It was Hector who came up with a solution. He appeared
at the kitchen door one morning, looking for Johnny. "Ah
wants you fuh come wit me, Massa Johnny," he said. "Dere be
sumbody you needs fuh meet."

"I'm not interested in meeting anyone."

"Dat not what ah ax you. Come wit me. De wagon be waitin
outside. You git in!"

Whether it was the long boyhood habit of doing what
Hector told him or just not caring enough to get into an argument, Johnny did as he was told. "Where are we headed?"

"You see, soon nuf." About halfway to town, Hector turned
the horse down a country lane and pulled up in front of a small
shack.

"Jacob! Sumbody here fuh see you!"

An elderly black man emerged from the dark doorway and
walked across the porch. "Dis de boy you be telling me bout? De
one wit de missin leg?"

"Dis be Johnny Grenville. You an him gwine git quainted
while ah goes tuh town. Git down, Massa Johnny."

"You can't just leave me here!"

"Yes, ah kin!"

With a slap of the reins, Hector drove off down the lane. Johnny leaned on his crutches and glared at the old slave. "What do you want with me?"

"Come on up here. You kin do it wit dem crutches."

"How do you know what I can do?"

"Ah bin dere, boy."

"How would you know—you with your two good legs?"

"Dat show what you knows, boy. Git up here."

Jacob led him inside and pointed to a chair. Johnny sat down gratefully but was still suspicious. "What now?" he asked.

"Ah gwine show you." Jacob pulled the suspenders from his shoulders, unbuttoned his pants, and let them fall to the floor.

Johnny stared at the sight in front of him. "What's that contraption?"

"Dat be muh own fake leg," Jacob grinned. "Made it muh-self when de Army docs tried fuh gib me one uh dem dere peg legs."

"Army docs? You were in the Army?"

"Sho nuf. Went wit muh owner at de start uh de war fuh take care uh he in de camp. But a stray shell dun take me out. Ah tought dey gwine shoot me lak a lame hoss, but Massa demand dey treat me lak a soljer. Dey dun it, too! Dey hacks off muh leg an trew it outta de window. Den dey offers me a peg leg an sends me home. Dis be muh own vention."

Johnny stared at the artificial leg, fascinated. At the top, a basket-like holder surrounded the stump of his leg, with straps that fastened it to a belt around Jacob's waist. From the basket curved slats mimicked the shape of a thigh, down to a hinged section that formed the knee. Then another set of slats formed a calf that descended into a regular shoe.

"What's it made of?"

"Odds an ends uh stuff. De slats come fro a whiskey cask. Dey bin aging a long time, so dey strong an springy. De stump holder be a sweetgrass basket a Gullah lady weave fuh me. De back uh de knee be nutting but a door hinge, an dere a pin dat slip in an out fuh let de knee bend or keep straight."

"Can I . . . can I try it?"

"Sho nuf. Dat why you be here. Drop dose drawers."

Johnny shucked out of his trousers and watched as Jacob unstrapped the contraption from his body.

"It doesn't weigh much," he said. "How can it support you?"

"Dat be de secret. A spring don weigh much neider. It jis hafta gib wit you weight."

Johnny fastened the belt around his waist and then sat down to ease his stump into the basket. "Why, it's soft!"

"Course tis. You don want it rubbin. De linin be pack wit duck down an goose fedduh. Here. You needs fuh fix dese straps til de leg long nuf."

Tentatively, Johnny stretched the contraption out in front of him so he could get a better look at it. "Still don't seem strong enough."

"Sho tis. Stan up now."

Johnny pushed himself upright with his good leg, holding the artificial one out at an angle. He couldn't bring himself to let go of the back of his chair.

"You gots fuh trust it. Lessin you be fraid."

"I'm not afraid of anything anymore," Johnny snapped.

"Den let go uh dat chair."

"Uh . . ."

"Scairt?"

Johnny loosened his death grip on the chair, then gasped and grabbed it again. But a slow smile began to spread. "It does feel like a spring."

"Dat what I bin tellin you. Now it gwine bend at de knee, too. When you kick it out an step down, de hinge latch, but when you takes de weight off it, it git loose agin."

"How do you make it do that?"

"Dat be muh secret. But it work!"

"Can you make me one like this? I'd pay you almost any price."

"Sho nuf. I don hab much else fuh do dese days. You pays muh Gullah woman who do de sewin part, an you brings me de whiskey cask, an I gwine fix you up."

"Where do you get the empty whiskey casks? I haven't been to town since I got home, so I don't know what is available."

"Nobody say nutting bout no empty whiskey cask, boy. Full one be jis fine wit me."

Johnny stared at him for a moment, puzzled, and then grinned. "I see. Tell you what—I'll not only buy you the casks, I'll help you empty them."

"Nah, suh, ah don go drinkin wit no white man."

"Well, I don't usually go out drinking with a colored man, either, but I've never refused to have a drink with a fellow soldier."

Now it was Jacob's turn to grin. "Fair nuf. When you gots em, tote em on ober here an we gwine git started."

Johnny spent much of the fall sitting on Jacob's porch, sipping at a tin cup of whiskey and watching as the older man whittled away at the cask staves. Sometimes they talked about the war. More often, they were comfortable just sitting in companionable silence. One evening, a sudden cold snap drove them indoors, where Johnny lay sprawled in front of the fire, tin cup in one hand and stogy in the other.

"Where you find dis rotgut?" Jacob asked. "Taste lak turpentine."

Johnny grinned. "Don't you make fun of this fine concoction! It's the recent product of a certain old South Carolina boy who lives back in the woods above town. He doesn't volunteer about what goes into his whiskey, and I don't ask. All I know is that it doesn't kill you, and it has one hell of a kick. Might be some spruce tips in it, I suppose, or some pine bark to give it some coloring, but he uses only fine oak barrels to give it that characteristic oaky flavor. The barrel staves are top-notch. If you don't like the whiskey, I'll take care of that part for you."

"Dint say ah dint want fuh drink it. Jist taste diffrunt, dat all."

"It does have a smoky taste to it, or maybe that comes from your leaky fireplace smoke."

"You kin open de window a crack ifn it be gittin too tick in here."

"Nah, I like the smell of the fire. Reminds me of better days, when we were sitting round a campfire at night after a hard day's march. I always found comfort in that particular combination of smells—wood smoke, cheap cigars, whiskey fumes, and . . ."

". . . An dirty socks?"

"Yes, that, too, and wet leather. But they were familiar smells. Let you know you were among friends and safe, at least for the moment."

Jacob had quit sanding one of the staves and was watching Johnny curiously. "You miss de war?"

Johnny cocked his head and narrowed his eyes against the smoky air. "Yes, guess I do. It was terrible at times—scary and deafening and exhausting. But at night, when everything stopped with the coming of dark, there was such a peace that descended over a camping army. You'd hear strains of music as somebody blew on his harmonica, or somebody chuckling over a passing joke. And you knew that the man crouching there beside you around the fire was just like you—with the same experiences and the same feelings. You could trust him and rely on him and love him like a brother, even if you didn't know his name. For those hours of darkness, there was no fear or worry about the next day. We just let everything go and absorbed the smells and sounds of the camp. They were our only reality."

"Really? You dint worry bout who be gwine take a bullet de nex day?"

"No. It's curious, now that I think about it, but I don't ever remember feeling fear during those evenings. Not like the fear that runs through me now when I wonder how I can ever find my way back into a world that seems forever changed. Maybe it was because we weren't responsible for anything. We were just cogs on a wheel, doing what we were told, not thinking about the past or the future, not trying to understand what it all meant. We didn't make decisions or plans. We just put one foot in front of the other until somebody told us to halt. And that love we felt for the guy sitting next to us around the campfire? If he bought the farm the next day, we just loved the fellow who took his place. Things were so simple then."

"An life aint simple now?"

"No. Now it's hard, because everyone expects me to settle back into our old family life, and I don't know how!"

That thought seemed to settle over Johnny like a pall. He closed his eyes and sighed—then took another slug of whiskey and hoped it would drown the fears that now haunted him day and night.

Jacob worried over the same thoughts as he tried to understand what Johnny was describing. After a long pause, he grimaced and shook his head. "So what you gwine do when ah finishes dis here leg an you don hab no mo reason fuh hide behind dat war wound?"

Johnny stared back at him. "I don't know, Jacob. I don't know that, either."

"Well, you bes be tinking bout it, cause dese staves be bout ready. You member de fust day you come here? You look at me an sneer at muh two good legs. Dat how people gwine see you once you wearin dis new-fangle leg. Dey aint gwine know dere be ennyting wrong wit you."

"What I wish . . ." Johnny shook his head and stopped. "Never mind."

"What you wish? Go on an say. Nobody here fuh care. Jis me, an ah don count."

"Well, I wish I knew some other soldiers around here who have come back from the war. You and I can't be the only ones. But I've never met another Rebel, wounded or otherwise. Where are they all? Where do they go? Or are they all huddled off in their own little holes somewhere, each one believing that he is the only one left?"

"Dat be sad, but it probly be de trut. None uh dem gots nowhere fuh go."

"That's what I wish, Jacob. I wish there was a place for us—somewhere we could meet once in a while to chew the fat and tell war stories, to remember the good times. And somewhere where we could get help for whatever ails us. Like you, Jacob. If it hadn't been for Hector, I'd have never known you were living out here in the woods with the greatest invention an amputee ever saw!"

"An ah wudn be wasting muh time makin a leg fuh sumbody who don know what he gwine do wit it."

"One might say the same about you, Jacob. You have a real talent and an idea that deserves recognition. You should be making money from it. If returning soldiers knew about you, they would probably keep you busy making artificial limbs full time. You could . . ."

"You white folk. You tinks money be de answer fuh eberting. It not!"

"All I'm saying is that there ought to be a place for old soldiers—white and black—to get together and help each other find ways to move forward. A place where we could get medical help, or legal advice, or financial assistance—or an artificial limb, if that's what's needed. Whatever it takes. What's wrong with that?"

"Well, fust, black soljer an white—we be diffrunt. We aint gwine work togedduh. An dis notion you gots—dat sumbody need fuh take care uh we—dat already be happnin, but only fuh de Fedrals. We Rebels be losin dis war, an aint nobody gwine take care uh we."

"Why can't we do it for ourselves?"

"Cause it be nuttin but a pipe dream, boy. You be breathin in too much smoke. Best you be tinkin bout tryin on dis leg an larnin fuh walk normal. Dreamin be fuh dose who gots both time an money fuh lose."

"Maybe so, but if I'm going to have a new leg, I intend to use it to some good purpose."

47

Johnny's March
November 1864

For the next two weeks, Johnny spent every afternoon with Jacob, learning how to walk again. "I can't believe how difficult this is," he complained.

"Sho tis. You aint walk since dat leg got shot."

"But I managed on crutches."

"Dat right, but when you on crutches, you be hoppin, not steppin. Now, git bot feet on de groun. Dat new foot aint nail tuh de flo. You kin lift it up an kick it forward. Put de heel down fust, den rock ahead onna yo toes."

Over and over they practiced. Jacob proved to be a tough taskmaster, and Johnny was frequently near tears as he fought to make old muscles move in new ways. But, bit by bit, the movements became more familiar. Still relying on the crutches to keep himself from crashing to the floor, Johnny worked at taking a step based on a natural stride. "Look, Jacob. Am I finally walking like a real person?"

"Nah sir. Real fellow don hab dos wood props in he armpit."

"But . . ."

"Time fuh drop de crutches."

"Both of them?"

"Well, git ridda de one on de good side fust. Dere aint be nuttin wrong wit yo raht leg. Trust it." And so the drill began again, over and over, until the steps began to feel normal.

One afternoon, Jacob led Johnny out to a rail fence and positioned him with the rail to his left. Then he pulled the remaining crutch away and tossed it aside. Johnny staggered and clasped the rail to keep from falling. "Hold on ifn you has tuh, but you gwine walk de length uh dis fence, down tuh de gate."

"That's too far."

"Dat be where you kin git de crutch back ifn you needs it by den. Now, git walkin."

Again.

"Let go uh dat rail now an den. You not made uh taffy. You not gwine collapse."

And again.

"You fuhgittin bout dat nachral stride. You looks lak uh baby, barely liftin dat foot off de groun."

"I can't!"

"Yeah, you kin. Ah promise. The bigger de step—de faster de step—de easier it git."

And again, until one day when Jacob started shouting out a cadence: "For'd march. Hup, two, tree, fo."

Johnny automatically responded to the familiar order, stepping out in a firm and steady stride.

"Swing dos arms!" And he was walking without support. The two former soldiers met at the gate, and neither would ever admit that he saw tears in the other's eyes. Johnny saluted, and Jacob saluted back.

Johnny grinned. "Feels great, but I'm exhausted."

"Sho you is. Dis be hard work. You not gwine wear dat leg all de time. Do lil bit atta time. Walk a while, crutch-hop a while. Anudduh mont or so, you be losing dos crutches fuh good. But ah aint got nutting mo fuh teach you. We dun now. Wear dat leg home an let de fambly see what you kin do."

Johnny had his own plan for revealing his new leg to the family. He slipped it into his room one day when everyone else was out of the house. At night he practiced walking. Then, one quiet morning, he strapped on the leg and walked out to the kitchen.

Mary Sue was always the sharp-eyed one. "Johnny! What are you doing? You're walking! Is that an artificial leg?"

The others looked up with varying expressions. "Hey, neat!" Eddie said. "Where'd you get it?" The other children gathered around, each trying to figure out how the leg attached to Johnny's thigh.

Jonathan smiled quietly, fully understanding why his son had tried to downplay the drama of this moment. But Susan turned from the stove at the sudden commotion, gasped, and threw her hands in the air. A spatula clattered to the floor and only Jonathan's shout kept her from tipping over a whole skillet of eggs. "Johnny! Oh, praise the Lord! I've been praying for this moment. Just look at you, all straight and proud again. That's the best melodeon I ever spent!" She had spoken without thinking, but the words did not escape notice.

"Huh?"

"What?"

"Mother?"

Susan cringed as she realized what she had said. "I mean, uh, it's the best . . . gift . . . we could ask for."

The children looked back at her with puzzled expressions. "But you said . . ."

"Never mind. We all say silly things when we're excited," Jonathan said, trying to cover her mistake. "I want to hear from Johnny. Where did you get the leg, and how does it work?"

Over a late and cold breakfast, Johnny described the days he had spent with Jacob, watching as the ex-slave pieced the leg together and fitted it to his needs. "It's an amazing invention," he told them. "He could probably be making a fortune for himself if he wanted to. But he's a former slave. He doesn't think like that. The creation of an artificial leg is a gift he makes to those he likes. He doesn't see it as a source of income at all."

"Well, it's a miraculous gift," Jonathan agreed. "Perhaps we can repay him somehow."

"I think that might insult him, Father. From the beginning, he asked only for payment for the sewing and the sweetgrass basket an old woman made for him. I'd like to find other amputees who could be helped, though. I could tell that Jacob really enjoyed seeing the improvement in my attitude as I learned to walk with the leg. That's what gives him pleasure, not the accumulation of money."

"Are there other amputees in Aiken?" Susan asked. "I've never noticed one."

"Well, when you find yourself chopped into parts, Mother, it's hard to go out in public and display your missing limbs for all to see."

"Oh, Johnny. I'm sorry. I didn't mean to . . ."

"It's all right, Mother. But that's why I've stayed so close to the house since I came here. I didn't want people to feel sorry for me—or ask painful questions. I think there are probably others just like me, and I'm going to try to find them. In fact, I've been thinking about devoting myself to some kind of service to other returning soldiers. I may look like I have two legs, but I'll never be able to fight again. I'd like to think that's another way I can help the war effort."

Later that day, Jonathan joined his son on the front porch. "Just relaxing?" he asked. "Or making plans?"

"I was thinking about people who could help me find those who have been damaged by the war—somebody at the church, maybe?"

"Good idea! Reverend Cornish may have some suggestions."

"Of course. I'll go and see him. But first, what did Mother mean this morning when she mentioned the melodeon? I've noticed that it's not around, but since no one else said anything about it, I didn't ask. But this morning . . . It was such a strange comment that it's been bothering me. Is she all right?"

"Mothers are strange and wonderful creatures, John, as you should know by now. When their children are in danger, they turn into wild beasts . . . or master criminals . . . or whatever else it may take. And when a mother prays, not even God can resist. Your mother risked her most prized possession for your safety, and she considers it a good bargain. I can't always explain her logic or her methods, but I can't deny her results."

"Did she sell her melodeon? For me?"

"Sell it? No. She gave it to God, and He was evidently well-pleased. Now, if I were you, I would never mention it again. Some truths we need to keep silently in our hearts."

The next few months passed in a blur, shadowed under a national cloud of fear and despair. Almost no one denied that the Confederate cause was doomed to failure. Both men and supplies were woefully lacking, and pundits had quit asking if the war would be lost. Now the question was only when would it end. In the Grenville household, the grown-ups read the newspaper accounts of what General Sherman was up to, now that his Union troops had seized Atlanta. Each new prediction caused more trepidation.

"This columnist says that Sherman is about to start out on a march to the sea," Susan said. "Does that mean he will be coming here? Are we in his pathway?"

"Well, that depends on whether he aims for Charleston or Savannah, I suppose. Most folks think he's talking about Georgia at the moment, but it's hard to believe that he will not attack South Carolina at some point. This state is such a symbol of the Confederacy that he can hardly ignore it. We're going to need to be prepared for that eventuality."

"He's a horrible, vicious brute," Susan grumbled. "I read a report that said his goal is nothing short of the total destruction of the South. What does that gain him, pray tell?"

"He seems to think it's the quickest way of ending the war. And I'm not sure I'd argue against that view."

"The phrase I keep hearing is 'total warfare'," Johnny added. "By that I take it he means warfare against civilians, against women and children, against private property. How can you justify that, Father?"

"If it means a quick end to hostilities, an end to battles that kill thousands of our young men, I think I can. At least I can understand the argument. On the other hand, I worry about the long-term effects. His policy seems destined to guarantee that Southerners will hate the North for as long as they live. Battles may cease, but hatred is much harder to root out."

And so the citizens of Georgia and South Carolina watched and waited. Sherman's troops—some 60,000 of them—left

Atlanta on November 16. They immediately fanned out across Georgia in three different directions so that it was impossible to say whether their path would take them to Macon or Augusta or straight to Savannah. The uncertainty served to increase the fear. Most small towns had no protection except for a local militia of a hundred or so men. Against those numbers, the sheer magnitude of the troop movement reduced the local population's will to resist.

Soon, the Union marching orders became public knowledge. Because they were moving away from their established supply depot in Chattanooga, the men were instructed to forage at will from the countryside. They were to try to keep a ten-day supply of food for men and horses, even if that meant seizing the local civilians' crops, food stores, and fodder. Violence without mercy was permissible, especially if the civilians spouted resistance or expressions of hostility. Any mills or cotton gins along the way were to be burned. Rail lines, bridges, and telegraph wires were to be ripped out and destroyed.

In Aiken, even the younger children were now reading the newspaper reports, all too aware that there was a threat against them.

"What's a Sherman's necktie, Father?" Becca asked one afternoon.

"Ah, that's a trick the Union soldiers use to frighten the locals into submission. They rip out a section of rail along the railroad line and wrap it around a tree, crossing the ends to be sure it cannot be removed."

"They bend a steel rail? How can they do that?"

"By heating the center of the rail over a terribly hot fire until it softens and glows red. With several men holding onto the ends of the rail, they run the softened center up against a tree and pull it around until the ends cross. As soon as the steel cools, it hardens again and can't be removed."

"So they just destroy the rail."

"Yes. It's a warning that men who can bend steel can destroy anything else they choose."

"But that's wasteful . . . and mean . . . and . . ."

"And it's an example of the viciousness of warfare." Jonathan bent to hug his youngest daughter. "Don't try to understand men in war, Becca. There's no logic to their behavior."

"But they're coming here! What will they do to us?"

"We don't know that they are coming here, honey. Don't imagine trouble before it arrives."

48

Standoff
February 9, 1865

I t was a cold morning, and several of the Grenville children were still dawdling over breakfast in the warm kitchen, reluctant to start their chores. Susan was reheating the acorn coffee in the forlorn hope that it would taste better if it also burned their taste buds. Jonathan, as he often did after reading more disheartening news from the war, was staring off into space, lost in his own haunted world of failed opportunities and disappointed expectations. Without warning, the back door crashed open, and Eddie burst into the kitchen, shouting, "Papa!"

At the unusual epithet, Jonathan shook himself from his reverie and stared at his son. "What now, Eddie? Has something happened to your beloved cows?"

"No! The cows are fine." Eddie shook his head impatiently. "But when I finished milking and came out of the barn, I saw a line of soldiers marching through the lower pasture. There are hundreds of them. Their uniforms are dirty and ragged, but they sure look like they were once blue. I think the Yankees are coming."

At the word "Yankee," young Johnny lifted his head from his bowl of mush as well. He usually ignored his younger brother, but if the Yankees were out there . . . "Sherman! At church yesterday, there was a lot of talk that Sherman's march toward Columbia might pass through Aiken as well."

"Sherman?" Susan shuddered. "It might be a good idea for you to put your leg on, son."

"Why? So they won't know I'm weak? I'd rather let them see what they've done."

"Pastor Phillips said that the rumors were nothing more than idle gossip," Susan said. "We shouldn't jump to conclusions."

"Maybe so, Mother, but Pastor Phillips hadn't seen the line of soldiers headed for our yard. What should we do? Do we run or attack?" Eddie's eyes were wide with excitement.

"Attack? With what?" John's words were scornful. "With a one-legged cripple, a despondent old man, a couple of green youngsters who can't shoot straight, and a bunch of girls?"

"Maybe they won't even stop here. The place certainly doesn't look prosperous enough to bother with. We won't even have to hide the silver, since we sold it a long time ago. Just ignore them and hope they pass by."

"That approach didn't work in Georgia, Mother, and it won't work now. These fellows are vicious and relentless. They burn everything they see, whether it's valuable or not, just for the sheer meanness of it. We need to hide in the woods until they pass. Get the children out first." Johnny was already struggling to stand and get his crutches tucked into his armpits.

"No!" Jonathan slammed his palm onto the table. "No! I've run too often. I've hidden long enough. I'm through being bullied. I'll take care of this, once and for all."

"Jonathan! Where do you think you're going? You can't go out there all alone." Susan tried to grasp his arm but he shook her off.

"I can and I will."

His entire family was staring at him. It had been months since they had seen their father acting so decisively, and the children found his anger as terrifying as the prospect of a Yankee attack.

Susan looked desperately at her older sons. "John, take the younger children into the woods, please. And Eddie, can you get to Hector's house without being seen? Perhaps he can round up some help."

"No! Keep out of this, Susan. Everyone stays here." He strode toward the door.

"Jonathan, at least take a shotgun."

"No. I go unarmed, as a man of reason, not as another creature of violence. Somewhere out there, there must be a reasonable man, someone I can talk to."

"But . . ."

Unwilling to waste another moment, Jonathan left the house, stomped across the yard, and assumed a spraddle-legged pose, hands on hips and belligerent chin held high. He waited, staring across the field at the dark line of men moving ever closer to his last bit of property.

At the front of that line, an indistinct figure detached itself and resolved into a man on horseback. Accompanied by two other riders, one holding an American flag aloft, he galloped toward the farmhouse. Jonathan simply waited until the horseman pulled up in front of him.

"Union Major General Hugh Judson Kilpatrick, at your service, sir. Whose property is this?"

"Mine, General. I am Jonathan Edwards Grenville, and you are trespassing on my land."

"Your land? It is Rebel land, as far as I can see, and that makes it the property of the United States Government."

"No, sir, it doesn't! There is nothing about this land that is rebellious."

"Who lives here with you? Who's in that house?"

"Only my family."

"A family of Rebels?"

"No, sir, an American family, going about their daily business."

The general stared at him in frustration. His brow wrinkled and his eyes narrowed. Then he tossed his reins to the soldier at his side and dismounted. "Now, see here, my good man, you—"

"I am not your man, General Kilpatrick. But I am a citizen of the United States, and I demand to exercise my right of freedom from unreasonable search and seizure."

Perhaps unconsciously, the general mimicked Jonathan's stance, spraddle-legged and hands on hips. "This is South Carolina—Rebel territory."

"Yes, sir, it is, but that says nothing about who I am."

"Well, then, suppose you tell me."

"As I said, I am Jonathan Edwards Grenville, born and raised in Massachusetts. I graduated from Harvard College in 1838 and came to South Carolina to take a proffered job as a teacher in what was then an innovative educational experiment, the Charleston Apprentices' Library Society, the first free public institution of education in the country. We offered a free classical education to ordinary men—skilled workmen, artisans, and laborers—who wanted to follow the American dream of bettering themselves. I taught American history and took great pride in fostering in my young scholars the values of our country's forefathers, including the rights to life, liberty, and the pursuit of happiness."

The general cocked his head and let slip a small half-smile as he noticed that a woman had come out of the farmhouse and was walking across the yard toward them. "You found other attractions in South Carolina, I presume?"

"Sir?"

"Of the female persuasion. You found a wife, I meant."

"He did, General," Susan said as she moved to Jonathan's side and took his hand.

Jonathan glanced down at his wife and squeezed her hand in gratitude. It was the first time in a long while that they had held hands, and he held on tightly. "Yes, this is my wife, Susan Dubois Grenville . . . and, before you ask, she was born and raised in Charleston, the daughter of a wealthy and prominent cotton planter. We married in 1840 and, as best we can, we are raising a family of seven children, despite the disparities of our backgrounds."

"What are you doing on a run-down farm in Aiken, if I may ask?"

"The fortunes of war, sir. I was fired from my teaching position in 1860—yes, after over twenty years of service—for being what one parent called a 'Damned Yankee.' I hoped to be able to support our family by taking over one of the Dubois cotton plantations. The invasion of Port Royal Sound put an end to those plans, when the Union Army claimed the Sea Islands and the Confederate commander ordered the evacuation of our plantations. We thought of moving to an inland property held by the family, only to discover that it had been appropriated by the Confederate Army. I considered doing some private tutoring in my home, only to have the house burned to the ground in the Charleston Fire of 1861. You will forgive me for feeling a bit snake-bitten by circumstances."

"Indeed. However, it still doesn't explain how you came to be living here."

"This is the last remaining piece of land owned by Mrs. Grenville's late father, George Dubois. His wife—Mrs. Grenville's mother—gave it to us as a Christmas present when she decided to leave Charleston. And we came here hoping it would be a refuge from the turmoil of a war we wanted no part of."

Once again, the general was watching something behind Jonathan. "Do I see a couple of black faces emerging from the so-called refuge behind you?" he asked with a skeptical sneer. "You are a slave owner, I see."

"No, sir. I freed all our slaves in 1861, long before President Lincoln's Emancipation Proclamation." Jonathan half-turned and motioned for Sarah and Hector to join them. "Let me introduce you to Hector and Sarah Gresham. They are freedmen who now work as paid employees on our farm. They have both learned to read and write, and they have purchased their own land not far from here. Their children have grown up with ours, and we are proud to call them friends and neighbors."

As the Greshams came to stand next to the Grenvilles, Susan reached her other hand out to Sarah. "We are also cousins," Susan added. "Sarah and I have the same grandfather. They are more than friends—they are family."

The general opened his mouth and then closed it again, confounded, as he saw another line of people coming from behind the house. The Gresham children, Eli and Annie, walked hand in hand with Eddie, Mary Sue, Becca, Robbie, and Jamey, all led by Johnny on his crutches. They lined up behind their parents, each one of them staring defiantly at the general.

"These are our children, General Kilpatrick—we're only missing one of them. Our daughter Charlotte is a war widow, now living in Tennessee. As you can see, the war has not left my family untouched. Charlotte's husband was killed at the Battle of Port Royal, and my son Johnny lost a leg at Chickamauga. We have lost almost everything we ever owned, but we have retained what is most important—our independence, our freedom, and our love for one another.

"Our Founding Fathers established a nation of people who followed their consciences. That is what we are still trying to do. We live here peacefully, united as equals—male and female, young and old, black and white, Northerner and Southerner. And we ask nothing more than the right to continue leading our lives here.

"Our goal is, and has always been, self-sufficiency. We have no desire to grow rich—we only hope to support ourselves and protect our family. And we have done so through our own hard labor. My wife has become an excellent cook, and I am a passable farmer. Our children learn their lessons at their own kitchen table, side by side with our employees and their children. We have little of value beyond those things that satisfy our bodily needs for clothing, shelter, and nourishment, but what we have we will gladly share with those who come in peace.

"This land may be one of the last bastions of harmony and safety in this entire state. I will not—we will not—give you permission to destroy it. I ask only that you move on to whatever your purpose and destination. And I hope that when you reach your goal, whatever it may be, you will remember that where a person lives has little or nothing to do with what he believes or what he deserves.

"If you cannot do that . . . if you must slash and burn your way through our land only because it lies in your path . . . then we cannot stop you. But I will not be moved. This is the end of my journey. I take my stand here for justice and liberty."

General Kilpatrick threw up his hands in a helpless gesture. Once again he started to speak and could find no words. Then he turned on his heel, drew his sword, and raised it above his head. The line of soldiers behind him had come to a halt, watching his every move. For a long moment that stretched out forever, no one spoke or breathed.

"Stand down! Holster your weapons. Reverse your march. Withdraw to the road. We move on to the next town."

The Grenvilles stood motionless and watched them depart. Tears were streaming down Susan's face, while the older children stared at their father in amazement. At last Hector broke the spell. "Sumbody need fuh do dat a long time ago!" he said, slapping Jonathan on the back. "Now we be gittin back fuh work. Dis be we land, fuh sho."

Late that night, when the children had all settled down, Susan nestled close to Jonathan and rubbed the back of his neck. "Did you mean it? What you said about wanting to continue to live our lives here? Has this farm become enough for you?"

"I believed every word I spoke this morning. I didn't even have to think about what I was saying. So I suppose the easy answer to your question is 'yes.' I could be satisfied to live out my days here, in this place, surrounded by my family and friends. But that doesn't mean that I would not be open to other possibilities if they presented themselves. I've learned not to try to outguess the future."

"And our long-range plan to return to Charleston? What has become of that?"

"I don't know. When we left the city, I was an outcast. The Damned Yankee label told me that I didn't belong there, and I kept hearing it in my head—like an accusation that I could not escape. I don't hear it anymore. The people of Aiken do not see me as an enemy, so I'm more comfortable here—at least for the time being. What will happen when the war is over? I just don't know. The hatred of all Yankees may be stronger than ever, now that Sherman has decided to teach the South a lesson it will not forget. That worries me—the possibility that people will never forget—nor forgive someone like me for having been born in the North."

"Do you really think the bitterness will continue once the fighting stops?"

"I think it will linger, at least for a while. How long? I don't know. I would gladly return to Charleston—and teaching—if I thought people would accept me for who I am. But I will no longer tolerate being treated as an outcast simply because I happen to have been born in Massachusetts instead of South Carolina. That's why I'm willing to take some time before I make any decisions about change."

"How long?"

"I don't know, Susan. A year? Maybe two? Please don't pressure me into a quick decision."

"I wasn't trying to pressure you. But I am uncomfortable with uncertainty. If there's no hope that we will ever go home again, I'd rather know now than later."

"This war has been hopelessly destructive of both property and human lives. Recovery will not come quickly, if ever. I'm willing to wait and see what happens. I continue to hope that everything will work out for the best. That's all I can promise you. Will you wait with me?"

"Oh, Jonathan! I've put up with you so far! I'm not about to give up now."

49

Going Home Again
April 1867

Susan sat by the train window, peering through the raindrops as she tried to recognize some familiar landmark. "I can't tell where we are," she grumbled. "In this weather, everything just looks gray and fuzzy. Whatever happened to the glorious sunlit days of April Charleston used to have before the war?"

"Come, now, my dear. Surely you can't be blaming the weather on a war that's been over for two years."

"Well, something's different! I thought I'd be excited to be coming home after all this time. Instead, I can't even tell where home is."

"That's because we're not there yet. Have you really forgotten how much of South Carolina is blanketed with piney woods? We won't break out of this landscape until we are practically on the coast. Give it time. Now, what's really worrying you? I doubt that your mood is entirely the result of the rain."

Susan sighed and looked at her husband fondly. "You're reacting like an optimist, aren't you? How I envy that attitude sometimes! It would be wonderful to start each day with the certainty that everything will work out for the best."

"I haven't usually felt that way, as you very well know. But you're right that I'm expecting good things to come out of this trip."

"Do you really believe now that we'll be doing the wise thing by coming back to Charleston?"

"Susan, this isn't a final step. It's a reconnaissance, if you'll forgive the military metaphor. Arthur Middleton has been handling our business affairs here ever since we moved up to Aiken. Now he says we have important decisions to make, and I trust his judgment. We're going to listen to what he has to say, and then we'll consider all our options. I don't have any idea what our final decision will be. Maybe we'll come back. Maybe we won't. But I have faith in his advice and in our own ability to choose what's best for our family. That's the good thing I expect to come out of this trip—a firm understanding of our affairs instead of a bunch of unanswered questions hanging over our heads."

"You make it sound so simple. Why, then, am I so afraid of what we're going to find?"

"The unknown is always frightening, my dear, but the only way to deal with it is to face it and turn your doubts into known facts. Now look!" He reached over to the window and wiped away the steam. "What do you see out there?"

Susan caught her breath. "It's pluff mud! Oh, I wish I could smell it!"

"I'll remind you of that wish sometime when the swampy, rotten-egg odor threatens to choke us."

"I don't care! Pluff mud smells like home."

"And it looks like we have arrived."

They stepped from the train onto the platform of the Camden Train Depot on Ann Street just as the rain and the cloud bank that had followed them all the way south started to lift. "Take a deep breath," Jonathan laughed, "and absorb some of that homey smell."

Jonathan collected their valises and hailed a waiting carriage-for-hire. "We're headed for the Mills House," he informed the driver, "but we're also in town for the first time in several years. Could you take us on a quick detour?"

"What you want fuh see?"

"How about taking Meeting Street all the way to the Battery, and then back up Legare Street to Queen?"

"Yassuh. We kin do dat."

Susan looked at Jonathan doubtfully. "Are you sure you want to see all that fire damage?"

"I'm not looking for the damage. I'm looking for signs of recovery. Drive on, my good man!"

Susan could scarcely bear to look at the empty swath of Meeting Street, where whole blocks of buildings had burned to the ground. Jonathan, however, pointed to the remains of the Circular Church. "Look there, Susan. All that scaffolding could mean the rebuilding process has begun. If that landmark can be restored, others will follow its example. I suspect the city is chock-full of optimists, just like me, who think this city can recapture its former beauty and charm."

A bit further down Meeting Street, Jonathan started pointing out other familiar buildings. "Look at the Croft house, still standing in all its glory. Johnny told me that Alex had continued to live in it all through the Yankee bombardment, but I didn't expect it to look so prosperous. And even the houses along the waterfront appear to have withstood the missiles lofted at them. This city is still beautiful, Susan."

As their carriage turned up Legare Street, Susan grasped his hand. "I'm not sure I want to see Mother's house. What if it's the one that has suffered all the damage?"

"That's fear talking again, Susan. Remember what Benti told your mother? It's going to look great."

"Even if it does, I'm not ready to see it inside."

"We won't stop. And you can close your eyes as we pass if that's what you want. But I want to see how it looks, so that I'm better prepared for what Arthur Middleton has to tell us about its status."

"I just may close my eyes, but . . . oh, there it is . . . and it looks . . . normal."

"Just as you remember it. Feel better now?"

"I'll withhold judgment until I see inside, but for the moment I am relieved."

Susan's good mood lasted only until their carriage turned onto Queen Street where, once again, the landscape was one of utter devastation. She turned her head to look up at the side of the Mills House Hotel, only to cringe at the way the outer wall had been blackened by the fire. The carriage turned the corner and pulled to a stop in front of the arcaded entry to the hotel. There was little sign of the fire here on the Meeting Street facade, but the wrought iron balcony seemed oddly festive in contrast to the blackened ruins of the buildings just around the corner.

Jonathan helped Susan down from the carriage while the bellman carried their luggage in to the registration lobby. Jonathan wisely refrained from commenting until they were in their room. Susan looked around and visibly relaxed. "It's still lovely, isn't it?" she said. "I've always heard about the canopied beds here, the chandeliers, the gas lights, the marble mantels above the fireplace. And look, Jonathan, in the alcove there's a basin with running water."

A knock at the door interrupted her continuing inventory of the luxurious surroundings. John Purcell, the owner and manager, had arrived to make sure their accommodations were satisfactory.

"We're quite comfortable, thank you," Jonathan assured him. "I wonder, though—we're a bit soot-stained after the train ride. Are there bathing facilities?"

"Certainly, sir. The lady will find eight private baths with attendants just down the hall, and similar gentlemen's facilities are on the first floor. If there's anything else you need, please use the bell pull, and someone will respond immediately."

"Oh, I could become used to this!" Susan said.

"I'm sure you could, but don't get comfortable yet. We need to make our way to Arthur Middleton's office in a few minutes and find out if we have enough money left to afford this room. It's only a block or so down the street, so I thought we would walk."

"I'm ready. Let's see what he has to offer."

The law firm offices, like the hotel, belied the devastation that lined the streets outside. Middleton offered the Grenvilles leather armchairs around a polished mahogany table and poured chilled water into crystal goblets. "How are things in Aiken? Peach trees starting to blossom? I was happy to hear that there was not much damage from Sherman's March in your area."

Susan glanced at Jonathan with a slight grin but simply nodded at Mr. Middleton in response.

"Well, then, let's get down to it, shall we?" Middleton continued. "You are extremely lucky, Mr. Grenville. Your insurance underwriter has managed to come through the war without going bankrupt—an anomaly, I assure you. In fact, I have been holding a check for you in our vault, and I understand that it is payable in U.S. dollars. You have been compensated for the loss of your Logan Street house."

Jonathan took the proffered envelope and opened it carefully, his eyes widening in surprise and disappointment. "One thousand dollars for the entire house?"

"Not full value, of course, but generous. You were one of the lucky ones to get your claim considered early. Later war damages have not been compensated at all. Now, however, we need to think about the Dubois house."

"We saw it earlier. It appears to have been undamaged. We could probably move right back in if we decided to do so."

"Except that it is no longer yours. The Federals took advantage of an act of confiscation passed in June 1861. It said that all states under Union control could be taxed to support the war effort, and if property owners refused to pay that tax, their land could be confiscated by the government. It was easy for the tax commissioners to concentrate their efforts on houses that had been left unoccupied. A bill for taxes owed pushed under the door of an empty house was unlikely to be paid, and the whole property could then be seized. That's what happened to the Dubois property.

"Again, however, you were lucky. The house did fall into Federal hands but became the headquarters of a fairly civilized Union general. He used it as accommodations for his staff, but from what I have been able to determine, they treated the house and its furnishings with care and respect."

Susan gave a sigh of relief. "Thank goodness. Mother has been so worried about careless damage."

"But do we want to reclaim it?" Jonathan asked. "I still have some doubts about the wisdom of returning to Charleston. Is there real hope for the city's recovery, or would we be pursuing a pipe dream?"

Arthur Middleton looked slightly wistful as he answered. "You probably are unaware that the plantation house at

Middleton Place was burned by the Yankees when Sherman's troops came through. All that's left is the guest wing off to one side. The family is still living there, however, and they have found that they rather enjoy their smaller quarters. The grounds are still beautiful. The camellias and azaleas have burst into frantic bloom as if to make up for that one scar on the landscape. And I see that as a metaphor for this city."

"In what way?" Jonathan's face revealed his skepticism.

"Charleston has suffered grievous damage. You saw the marks of destruction as you came in from the train depot. But I believe that the real qualities that made the city great still exist. We lost five churches in the Great Fire, but we didn't lose the faith that built those spires. We lost buildings, but we haven't forgotten the architectural designs that made them beautiful. We have lost the political battle, but we have retained the cultural heritage that characterized this city. We can still take pride in our educational institutions, our music and art, our shared history, our love of beautiful gardens, our hospitality, our pride in family, our warmth and gentility. And I firmly believe that Charleston can bloom again more beautifully than before, provided that good people—like yourselves—are willing to invest their time and energy to restoring what was best about this city."

"That's a powerful argument. I hope you are correct."

"There is one thing you need to know about the Dubois property," Mr. Middleton said, grimacing before he delivered the bad news. "The general took a strong antislavery stance and had the slave buildings in the backyard demolished. Everything's gone out there—even the cookhouse. They did put in a new privy, but otherwise the yard has been scraped bare."

"But how did they get by—do laundry, cook their meals?" Susan was shaking her head. "Surely they needed those facilities. They can't have just done away with them."

"I'm afraid they did exactly that. Without slave labor, one's needs shrink. They cooked in the warming kitchen on the lower level, and as for laundry . . . Well, I never knew soldiers to be overly concerned with cleanliness."

Jonathan interrupted the discussion of housekeeping matters. "Be that as it may," he said, "how could we regain possession of the property?"

"The law says you can do so if you can produce papers showing ownership prior to the war, and if you can pay the back taxes."

"Which will be how much?"

"I have no idea, although I'm fairly sure that you'll have no trouble paying it out of your insurance award. You'll have to submit your claim before they'll give you a quote. I would suggest that you do so immediately. I have already had my clerk draw up a formal request for restoration. If you have your deed, you can turn the paperwork in to the tax office this afternoon, and we should have an answer by tomorrow. I think you'll find it fair. General Rufus Saxton is in charge of all reparations, and he's an honest man. He's been in South Carolina since 1862, so he understands what all has happened here."

"We shall see. In the meantime, there's one other matter I would like to look into. You mentioned the current state of the educational institutions in Charleston. We have four children still in school, and I was a teacher before the war. I want to be sure that the children's education will not suffer if we should move back here. And I'm also interested in reclaiming my role as an educator."

"I think you'll find the answers to those questions satisfactory as well, but let me do some checking on the details. If you like, I can also ask for permission from the tax office to let you see the inside of the Dubois property before you make a final determination. Shall we agree to meet again at ten in the morning?"

The Grenvilles met Arthur Middleton at the Legare Street property the next day. Susan realized that she was holding her breath in fear as he opened the door and ushered them inside. It took some effort for her to lift her eyes and look around. And then, suddenly, the years seemed to fade away, and she was looking at her childhood home—slightly dusty, but warm and comfortable. She wrinkled her nose as she sniffed at the air. "There's a whiff of tobacco smoke, but it's no worse than when Uncle Grover used to come for a visit. A good airing will take care of it. What about the fittings—are the dishes and linens still here?"

"As I told you, Mrs. Grenville, the Yankees treated your belongings with respect."

"Then I see no reason why we wouldn't want to take possession of the house."

"Just a minute, Susan. There are still questions to be answered. Do we have a bill for the back taxes, Arthur?"

"Yes, and it's reasonable enough—six hundred and fifty dollars will release all Federal claims on the property."

Susan stared at Jonathan, the longing so apparent in her expression that she didn't need to say a word.

"The insurance payment will more than cover that and some necessary additions as well. We'll need to open a bank account and make the necessary transfers of funds. Can we take care of that now?"

"Yes, of course," Middleton said, "but you also had questions about education. We probably should clear that up before you make a final decision."

"I'd almost forgotten. What did you learn?"

"Well, the news is good there, too. You should be well aware that Charleston has always had a reputation for free public education, and that tradition continues. A few grade and secondary schools resumed classes last year, and several more private schools are scheduled to open this fall. There will be ample opportunities for your children. But even better, you should have no problem finding employment, if that is what you desire.

"The College of Charleston is still hiring faculty, and there are two other new schools that may interest you. The Avery Institute is designed to be the first free secondary school for blacks in South Carolina. It is being managed by the American Missionary Association of New York City, and they are particularly interested in hiring Harvard-trained educators. The other institution is the Holy Communion Church Institute, a school designated for former soldiers and those orphaned or left destitute after the war. Its founder is Dr. Anthony Toomer Porter, whose own son was killed in the war. They have a building next door to the U.S. Arsenal, and I understand that General Sherman is strongly in favor of letting them take over the Arsenal itself to expand the school. In both cases, the fact that you have a Boston education, along with close ties to Charleston, will stand you in high favor."

Jonathan was listening, but his eyes were locked on a vision of the future. "The gods seem to be favoring us. Let's get the details taken care of. I want to be settled in Charleston by mid-summer."

50

Restoration
June 1867

It may have taken Jonathan two years to make a decision about returning to Charleston, but once he had made up his mind, matters moved quickly. Before he and Susan returned to Aiken, they had opened a new bank account, deposited their insurance payoff, paid the taxes on the Legare Street house, and hired a cleaning crew to come in and give the house a complete scrubbing. At the same time, a team of groundskeepers did what they could to spruce up the backyard by turning it into a grassy garden.

Jonathan wasted no time in contacting those who might offer him a teaching position. He admired what the Avery Institute was attempting to do for newly freed slaves but found them somewhat restrictive in their Missionary Society-driven curriculum. He was much more comfortable discussing educational goals with Dr. Porter. Within days, he had signed an agreement to conduct classes at the Holy Communion Church Institute. He would be lecturing on American history and politics for Confederate veterans who had finished most of their secondary education but had not yet matriculated at a college. His classes would start in September.

The next step, of course, was to go home and announce the decision to the rest of the family, and, as had always been their custom, Jonathan did so over a family dinner to which Sarah and Hector Gresham and their children had also been invited. As he looked around the table, he was acutely aware that eleven other lives would be impacted by his actions—eleven people whom he loved and for whom he was responsible. But there was no way to soften the announcement.

"Susan and I are going back to Charleston," he said. "We've regained possession of the Dubois House on Legare Street, and I have signed a new teaching contract with a school whose purposes excite me. We plan to keep the property here in Aiken as a summer home—after this summer, of course—but we'll be living in Charleston from September through April. Your thoughts? Questions?"

For a moment everyone sat in stunned silence. Then the table erupted in questions: "How?" "When?" "Why?" and "What about me?"

Susan grinned and cocked an eyebrow at her husband. "You asked for this," she reminded him.

"All right. Let's deal with our family first. Johnny and Eddie, both of you are really adults. You have begun to carve out careers for yourselves here. I would not blame you for rejecting the idea of returning to Charleston. The house is here and available for your use. If you choose to stay here, we'll do everything we can to help you, so long as you accept the fact that the rest of us will be descending upon you every summer."

"Mary Sue and Becca, you are well into your teen years, and it is time for you to receive a little spit and polish. Debut years will be coming up, and you have much to learn before then. Your mother has been talking about such things as dancing and voice lessons, French elocution, and classes in deportment and fashion—all of which can only happen in Charleston. And Robbie and Jamey, you need to get used to being in a regular classroom rather than doing sums at the kitchen table. So the four of you will naturally be coming with us and continuing your education in a city that can once again offer you high-quality schools and teachers."

Throughout that summer, the Greshams had been sitting with downcast eyes. Although Susan called them family, it was at times like this that they felt most sharply their slave origins. Hector let out a small sigh, which Jonathan immediately heard.

"What this all means for Hector and Sarah is less clear," Jonathan said. "I don't really know. Have you wanted to be back in Charleston? Would you prefer to be there with your friends, or have you thought about moving even further south to Edisto and the black communities that are growing up there? Or do you want to stay here on the land you have claimed as your own?" He shook his head as he pondered the answers to his own questions. "That's one of the prices of freedom, I suppose—that you have the freedom, as well as the burden, of making those decisions."

"Ah sho don know, Massa Jonathan. It still be hard fuh me fuh tink bout muh life as sepret fro yours. Ah be proud uh dat house ah be buildin, but would ah still lak it ifn all uh you not be here? Sound lonely tuh me. But dat house do belong tuh me. Ah kin sell it ifn ah wants, caint ah?"

"Of course."

"Sarah?" Susan asked. "How do you feel?"

Sarah shrugged. "Ah don know, neider. Ah miss Chastun, an ah really wishes ah could see muh fadduh down on Edisto, but ifn de boys gwine stay here, dey gwine need sum hep fro sumbody. Gemma mebbe could come back an cook fuh you, an Moses hep wit de barn, mebbe, but . . . But mebbe dat mean we needs tuh stay here." She looked at her children, Eli and Annie, but they were sitting with eyes on their laps, refusing to be drawn into the debate.

At last, Eddie spoke up. "What I'm going to say is going to sound awfully selfish, but I have no doubts about what I want to do. For years I've been trying to set myself up in the dairy business. It's what I love and what I'm good at. Right now, my herd is developing nicely, and I've been corresponding with Charlotte's husband about doing some swapping of bloodlines between his herd of beef cattle and my dairy cows. I'm not ready to give that up. I lost my first cows when we were driven off Edisto, and I can still remember the pain of knowing that soldiers were going to . . . to eat my pet cows for lunch. I won't go through that again. I'm staying here, one way or the other, whether or not any of you stay with me."

"Are you saying you'd like to stay here alone, Eddie, or will you welcome company? Because I'd rather stay in Aiken, too." Jonathan questioned his brother but his eyes never left his parents' faces.

"What about college, Johnny?" Susan asked. "Don't you want to finish your studies?"

"College life is a long way behind me, Mother. I lived that life for a year and a half, and I enjoyed it. But it wasn't offering me anything in the way of practical training for a career. Now I think I've found a calling of my own. Reverend Cornish and I have been doing a lot of talking about what returning soldiers need in the way of counseling, retraining, and resocializing. He seems to think I'll be good at helping them find access to those things. We've been planning a Veteran's Center there at the church, where they could meet with each other or find advice and a sympathetic ear from one of us. I'd be a kind of spiritual advisor, and Reverend Cornish is willing to take me on as an acolyte minister. I'm not going to bypass that chance. I'm staying here, too, and I'm willing to go it alone if I have to, although I suspect I'll be awfully glad to see all of you when you come to visit."

Johnny paused for a few moments and then turned to his brother. "What do you think, Eddie? Can the two of us manage a bachelor household here? Or shall we invite Eli to make it a threesome? I know you'd like to have his help with the cattle."

"Oh!" Eli's eyes were wide with excitement as he looked from one brother to the other. "You mean I cud. . . I cud stay here, too, an hep wit eberting? Dat would be good fun!"

"See dere now, what you dun!" Sarah glared first at her son and then at Jonathan. "Nobody gwine let dese tree boys on dere own up here witout nobody fuh take care uh dem when dey gits intuh trubble. But den who gwine take care uh de Grenvilles when dey all de way down in Chastun?" Her voice rose higher and higher until she was nearly wailing. She looked back and forth between her son and Susan, torn by her conflicting loyalties.

"Stop worrying about the boys for a minute, Sarah." Susan slapped her hands down on the table as she frequently did when she had made up her mind. "I think we all need to stop and think. For the past five years, we've been driven by outside influences, knuckling under to the exigencies of war, making huge personal sacrifices in order to assure our survival, being afraid to look toward the future for fear we weren't going to have a future. Now, for the first time, we have free choices, and I think we need to take full advantage of them. We need to stand up like Jonathan did to Sherman's Army and like Eddie just did. We need to say, 'This is what I want!' I don't want to hear any more about what someone else expects us to do or what we should do. This is our chance to take control of our lives, and I, for one, do not intend to miss that chance."

"What you sayin, Miss Susan?"

"I'm saying, Sarah, that I am going back to Charleston with my husband, and I am taking my minor children with me. My adult sons can do as they like—because they are adults, and adults get to make their own decisions. You, Sarah, also have an adult son, and he can do as he likes. You are not responsible for him or for my sons. Neither are you responsible for me or for my family. It's time you and Hector do exactly what you want for yourselves. That's what freedom is all about. Maybe we've forgotten to teach you that, but I want you to learn it now."

Sarah stared at her cousin for a moment, and then she slapped her hands on the table in deliberate imitation. "Den ah wants fuh go tuh St. Helena Island an Edisto an see what be goin on in dose black communities. Ah wants fuh see muh fadduh an fuh be wit muh own people. Hector, be you goin wit me or no?"

"Ah not gwine miss dat! Ah kin always build anudduh house."

The grown-ups were smiling at each other now, but it still came as a surprise to hear a giggle from the far end of the table. The younger children were laughing, too, enjoying the rare moment when their parents were happy at last.

The train trip back to Charleston was easier than their first venture to Aiken, perhaps simply because everyone better understood the routine. Again they crammed luggage onto a wagon and then loaded the wagon, horses and all, onto a rented transport car. The entire family had chosen to make the trip. Even Eddie had agreed to leave his beloved cows in the care of Moses and another trusted neighbor for a few days so that he and Eli could help with the heavy lifting involved in the move. Johnny took over as group tour guide, making sure that everyone was comfortable and that all their belongings made it safely onto the train. Sarah and Hector, with Annie in tow, had volunteered to come along to Charleston just long enough to help the family get settled. Then they planned to move on to Edisto and points south. All of them felt an undercurrent of excitement—a realization that this trip marked a momentous change in all their lives.

At the Legare Street house, the Grenvilles found that Arthur Middleton had arranged for a cook to come in and prepare a cold supper of roasted meats and salads, so that the exhausted travelers could relax after their day on the rails. The young people carried in the luggage from the wagon, piling it rather unceremoniously in the back hall until morning. Susan watched them work, proud that her children were growing into responsible human beings. "Don't worry about which valises go where," she told them. "We can sort all that out tomorrow."

"Except for this crate, Mother," Johnny said. "It came with us, but it doesn't seem to be luggage. Do you want it in a special place?"

"No. What is that? I've never seen it. Do you suppose we've carried off someone else's belongings by accident?"

Johnny made a show of turning the crate and examining all its labels. "It's not a mistake. It says right here that it belongs to Mrs. Jonathan Grenville at this address."

"Maybe your father sent something I don't know about. Jonathan!" she called over her shoulder. "Could you come here and tell your son where to put this box?"

"It's not my box," Jonathan said. "What's in it?"

"Well, obviously we won't know until we open it."

"Then let's open it. There's a pry bar on the wagon."

Johnny pried up the lid, letting the box sides fall away. Inside, a shapeless mass wrapped in crumpled paper did little to solve the puzzle. Casting a sidelong glance at his mother, Johnny began to rip away the wrappings. He freed a small bench from the main object and set it aside. Then the last of the wrappings, a soft cloth, came away to reveal the object.

"It's . . . it's a . . . melodeon!" Susan gasped. "Where did it come from? Who?"

Johnny could not hide his expression any longer. Grinning at his mother, he took her hand and led her to her new instrument. "It's a small thank-you gift from some of your grateful children."

"A thank-you gift? For what?"

"For doing your part to hold this family together even in the worst of times. For leading us on this adventure. For helping us grow into strong, independent adults. For bringing music into our lives. Is that enough reason?" Johnny pulled her into a tight embrace and then stepped back. "Come on. Show us where you want to put it, and Eddie and Eli will set it up."

While the entire family assembled to watch, the boys carried the new instrument to a place of honor in the ladies' parlor.

Johnny put the bench in place and gently pushed his mother to a seat. "Let's try it out," he encouraged.

"I'm not sure I remember how," she protested.

With tears in her eyes, Susan began to pump the pedals, slowly filling the bellows with air. Then, cautiously, she let her fingers touch the keys at random until the sounds rang out. Then, with growing confidence, her hands dropped onto the keyboard, and the strains of "Jesu, Joy of Man's Desiring" filled the room and their hearts.

Jonathan's hand came to rest lightly on her shoulder. "Take a bow, Mrs. Grenville. We've survived, and we're stronger than ever. Welcome home."

###

Thank you for reading!

Dear Reader,

I hope you enjoyed *Damned Yankee*. This book was my first attempt at writing pure ficion, and I have to confess, I really enjoyed creating Jonathan and Susan. Although the setting and the events are based on historical fact, most of the characters are creatures of my own imagination. What fun it has been to take them through a series of absolute disasters and bring them safely out of harm's way.

As an author, I love feedback. You, the reader, are the reason I keep writing. So, tell me what you liked, what you loved, even what you hated. I'll enjoy hearing from you. You can write me at schribercat4@yahoo.com and visit me on the web at katzenhausbooks.com.

Finally, I need to ask a favor. If anything in this story has touched you, or inspired you, or brightened your day in some way, I'd appreciate a review of *Damned Yankee*. As you may know, reviews from readers like you are the life blood of an author. Your comments have the power to make or break a book. If you have the time, please return to the website where you found the book, and leaave your comment, so that others can share the same experience.

Here's a link to Carolyn P. Schriber's Author Page on Amazon. You'll find all of my books here: http://www.amazon.com/-/e/B003ZM9GVE.

Thanks again for spending some time with me, and with Jonathan and Susan.

Gratefully,

Carolyn P. Schriber

10851650R00232

Made in the USA
San Bernardino, CA
29 April 2014